**"Let me help you write the truth about them,"
she said.**

Far gone as he was, Kilpatrick knew that was a bad idea. He knew, for instance, that Allyn's version of Randy Stapleton's business career was ominously distant from reality. But balance, judgment, faltered in his alcohol-sodden brain. Maybe she was right. Maybe nothing in the Stapleton world was what it seemed. Maybe even Randy wore a mask that concealed the hatred and rage that was destroying his daughter.

"All right," he said. "But we need proof."

"I'll get you proof," she said.

THEY HAD PROMISES TO KEEP—
AND ILLUSIONS TO MAINTAIN . . .

Fiction by Thomas Fleming

Liberty Tavern
Rulers of The City
Promises To Keep

Published by
WARNER BOOKS

PROMISES TO KEEP

Thomas Fleming

WARNER BOOKS

A Warner Communications Company

WARNER BOOKS EDITION

This Warner Books Edition is published by arrangement with
Doubleday & Co., Inc., 245 Park Avenue, New York, N.Y. 10017

Cover art by Jim Dietz

Warner Books, Inc., 75 Rockefeller Plaza, New York, N.Y. 10019

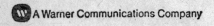 A Warner Communications Company

Printed in the United States of America

First Printing: October, 1980

10 9 8 7 6 5 4 3 2 1

To be an American is of itself almost a moral condition, an education, and a career.
—George Santayana

No defeat is made up entirely of defeat—since the world it opens is always a place
formerly
unsuspected.
—William Carlos Williams

What is history? What you cannot touch.
—Robert Lowell

PROMISES
TO KEEP

I

Agatha Stapleton Slocum descended the red-carpeted stairs from the second floor of her Victorian house in the center of New Grange Township. She loved the house, with its ambience of another time. Outside, it was painted a glistening white. Festoons of gingerbread on the gables and dormers added elegance to its lofty dignity. Inside, it was an antique collector's dream, with graceful spreadbacked tub chairs and short-legged vesper chairs, beaded, multicolored lamps and corner whatnots, framed samplers on the walls, shelves crowded with tiny bone china replicas of cottages and castles. The house was listed as a landmark by the Hamilton County Historical Society. Once a year, to raise funds for the local United Hospital Fund, Agatha permitted several hundred paying visitors to troop through it, ogling its treasures.

In the dining room, Agatha found her cousin Peregrine Stapleton already at the table sipping his aromatic Turkish coffee. Propped against a Sardinian green china pitcher by W. T. Copeland, the famed English successor of Spode, was Peregrine's copy of the local paper, *The Garden Square Journal*. Patches of September sunshine

9

splashed across the massive circular table, an orginal by John Henry Belter, the most gifted nineteenth-century American furniture maker.

"Good morning, Agatha dear," Peregrine said, a polite smile passing across his Dorian Gray face. "Did you sleep well?"

"Until about six," Agatha said, pouring American coffee from a modern percolator on the marble-topped sideboard. "Then I had a strange dream. Paul and I seemed to be at a hunt. But we'd gotten separated from the other riders. It was years ago. Paul was looking quite young. I took a bad fall going over a fence. Paul jumped down to see if I was all right. Then we saw the dogs. They were coming after *us*. They were huge, twice, three times the size of our hounds. Paul told me to run for some trees. He turned to face them."

"How prescient," Peregrine said. "You must be growing psychic in your old age."

"What do you mean?"

"Take a look at the second section of the paper."

Agatha looked. "Oh dear," she said.

The Garden Square Journal had once been the best paper in New Jersey. It had been owned and run by the Darling brothers, two bright, lively Princetonians whose family had rented the pew behind the Stapletons at the First Presbyterian Church. Agatha had chosen the younger brother, Eugene, as one of her escorts at her coming-out party in 1919. Eugene had died of heart disease ten years ago. His older brother, Edgar, was senile. Their children had no interest in the paper. Last spring, the *Journal* had been sold to one of those faceless New York syndicates, who let the editorial staff do what they pleased, as long as the advertising revenues came in.

In the center of the opening page of the second section was a column written by someone named Dennis Mulligan. It was a regular feature, entitled "Cityscope," which Agatha never read. It was usually devoted to the trivialities of local politics, a subject Agatha no longer found interesting, although her niece Paula was married to the mayor, a favorite Mulligan target. Today he had a different victim.

THE ARROGANCE OF THE ARISTOCRAT

Tomorrow, in obedience to the latest decree of Judge Paul R. Stapleton, the city will bus another 20,000 children in the meaningless shuffle known as "court-ordered integration." Who is Paul Rawdon Stapleton? He is a man whose family has ruled this city and state for the 80 years of his life and for 100 years before that. When he was born, the Stapletons were the richest family in the state. They are still worth countless millions. How did they get it? By stealing it, dear readers, first from the pockets of railroad passengers, for the 50 years that they owned every mile of track in this state, and then from the sweat of immigrants in their famous Principia textile mills, down on the city's waterfront. No one enjoyed working at Principia Mills. If you got caught looking out a window, you were fined 50¢. If you did not come to work for two days in a row, you were fired no matter what your doctor's certificate said. If you were Irish, you were the last to be hired, the first to be fired. When the mills started to falter, Paul Stapleton turned to law. He used his money to buy up the best legal talent in sight and organized Stapleton, Talbot, a law firm dedicated to making rich corporations even richer. Their tentacles soon reached into every courthouse in the state. Stapleton, Talbot opinions were commands in the legislature in Trenton. Thanks to them, the reforms Woodrow Wilson had enacted against corporations were abandoned, and New Jersey went back to being the traitor state, where a corporation could get away with anything, if it had Stapleton, Talbot representing them. Meanwhile, the Stapletons decided to get out of the textile business and sold Principia Mills for a reported $100 million to a big corporation that moved the company South, leaving 8,000 people in this city without jobs. This is the man who is telling us how to educate our children.

Surrounding this diatribe was a series of pictures and texts, describing the Stapletons past and present. In keeping with the hostile tone of the column, the emphasis was on wealth and power. Agatha's mother alighted from one of those expensive cars she loved. It looked like a Stoddard-Dayton Knight. Agatha stood beside her while she waved goodbye from the A deck of the *Berengaria,* on her annual trip to Europe. There was Agatha's father at the helm of his racing sloop, *Principia.* There was her grandfather in 1912, at the gate of Principia Mills, backed by a dozen soldiers with fixed bayonets, warning a line of pickets. Another picture, taken fifteen years later, showed her brother Malcolm doing the same thing. There were several pictures of Agatha's coming-out party, asserting it had cost an incredible $500,000. These led to a half dozen pictures of Bowood, the Stapleton city mansion, with ridiculously high estimates of what the house and furniture were worth.

Next came pictures of Paul's New Grange Farm, taken for the local weekly paper years ago when he gave his annual party for the Hamilton County Hunt. The pictures made the house and barns look gigantic. More outrageous were distant pictures of the houses of Paul's youngest sons, George and Ned, taken by some photographer who had sneaked as close as he dared. Ned's house was a replica of Bowood, George's was a small Mexican hacienda. Agatha thought both were somewhat tasteless, but that did not give a newspaper the right to speculate on their cost. The sons were also pictured at play, Ned on his sloop, *Principia II,* when he won last year's Bermuda race, George at the small press he financed so they would publish his obscure poetry. George had been foolish enough—or drunk enough—to give an interview about his poetry to one reporter, who made it sound ridiculous. As in all George's poems, the poignancy of the sample the reporter published was apparent only to the initiated.

Mockery

    is a boy's voice asking
    why is a girl's voice asking
    where is a woman's voice asking
    how is a man's voice asking
    when is a god's voice asking
    now is a lost voice asking
    who is a hoarse voice asking

Last but by no means least painful were several pictures of Paul's oldest granddaughter, Allyn, daughter of his dead son, Randy, dancing at a city disco with that muscular young Italian politician with whom she had reportedly had an affair last winter, posing in a bikini on the dock at the Paradise Beach Yacht Club, clowning with her business partner, a Jewish girl named Chasen, in front of the women's art gallery they had opened in the newly designated "Historic Town" section of the city.

"What disgusting, vicious journalism," Agatha said. "Not a single word in our favor. Not so much as a mention of the settlement houses we financed—the city symphony—Father endowed it in his will—Washington Park, which we *gave* to the city—the fact that Bowood is now the mayor's residence, another gift—"

"Or your hospice," Peregrine added, "which certainly deserves some praise, no matter what I think of it."

Agatha had founded the Anne Randolph Stapleton Hospice for the dying fifteen years ago. The idea of the place appalled Peregrine, who considered even the mention of death déclassé.

"I would not want or expect any credit for that—especially from these people," Agatha said, giving the second section of *The Garden Square Journal* a brisk shake. She winced at Allyn in her bikini. God knows, she had been no angel when she was Allyn's age. But she had not worn anything like that in public. Agatha tried to accept the mores of the young but something about bikinis brought her goodwill to a dead stop.

"Perhaps we could sue them," Peregrine said. "It would be entertaining."

"Paul wouldn't even consider it," Agatha said. "But I will say this. It makes me think Ned is right, we ought to have that book about the family written."

"*How* it should be written, that is the more important question," Peregrine said. "Are we going to get down off our pedestals? Or jack them up a little higher, with the help of some willing hack?"

"I've told you already, Peregrine. I suspect your motives."

"And I've told you that I don't hate Paul any more. I would just like to see the truth—or a semblance of it—told. I think it would be the best thing we could do for the younger generation."

13

Agatha wrestled with several clashing emotions. She wanted to believe Peregrine when he said he no longer hated her brother Paul. She wanted to believe the truth would help the younger generation. Opposing these wishes was a surge of distaste for the idea of telling anyone the truth about the Stapletons. Even more inconceivable was the idea of her brother Paul revealing his private self, which was where so much of the truth lay. But the wish to reply to these slanders momentarily engulfed everything.

"Perhaps we should just try it," she said, "and see what happens."

II

Ned Stapleton slapped his wife, Tracy, on the rump as he passed her on the way to the bathroom. She smiled at him. They had had a good time last night. Too often lately Tracy was either reluctant or tired, which made her about as responsive as Nefertiti's mummy. But last night had been a throwback to honeymoon days. After fifteen years of marriage, Ned knew that meant she wanted something. As he shaved, he wondered what it would be: A new car? A trip to Europe? He hoped it was not another African safari. That one had cost $10,000 and they were still paying it off, two years later.

Oh well, Ned sighed, lathering his angular Stapleton face before the mirror, there was always good old Pete Ackroyd at First National. He liked to loan money to Stapletons. He knew that someday it would come back and meanwhile there was all that 12 percent interest accumulating. Pete had been Ned Stapleton's roommate at the Pennsgrove School and at Kenyon College. They used to call themselves the Straight-C Twins and do a skit at the fraternity house annual show.

15

We're the boys who could
Not get into Harvard so
We're here to play.
If you're good
You go to Harvard
Where you work all day.

Pete Ackroyd had written to his sister about the show and she had been idiot enough to show the letter to his father, who icily informed Pete that failing to get into Harvard was no laughing matter. Ned had been in a sweat lest Walter Ackroyd, who was a partner at Stapleton, Talbot, might tell Paul Stapleton about it. Ned would have gotten more than an angry letter. It would have meant a two-hour talk about his irresponsible attitude toward life.

Until recently, Ned had given life about as much responsibility as he thought it deserved. Somehow, above, beneath or around responsibility, he also wanted to enjoy himself. Best of all was combining responsibility and enjoyment. He had managed this in the city's Bicentennial parade last July 4, presiding over a Sons of the American Revolution float of a log cabin while Tracy and two of their sons cooked an imaginary meal over a pile of red light bulbs. Ned was a firm believer in the importance of history, even though he rarely read a history book.

Downstairs at the breakfast table, Tracy was wearing a formidable frown. Ned instantly wondered what he had done wrong. But he quickly discovered that others had committed the misdeed that had destroyed Tracy's smile. He read the story in the second section of *The Garden Square Journal* with mounting rage. "The sons of bitches," he said. "They hinted they'd get even when I refused to be interviewed."

"I wish I could hide it from the kids," Tracy said. "But there's no point. Everybody at school will tease them about it. I hate to think of how Paul will react."

Ned and Tracy took parenthood seriously. Part of the reason was the awareness that they were under the stern eye of Ned's father, now that it was clear that their sons would be the bearers of the Stapleton name in the next generation. Two of Ned's older brothers were childless

16

and the third had had only the one daughter, Allyn, who was so well displayed in the paper.

Paul, their oldest son, was a fourth-former at the Pennsgrove School. Last year he had been suspended for three months for smoking marijuana. The headmaster said that he had gotten involved with a group of young cynics called "the swingers." It had caused Ned to have some unsettling second thoughts about his own life style. He had struggled through several talks with Paul that left him more uneasy than when they had started. Ned found it hard to reach the cool, oblique teen-ager that his son had suddenly become. Paul seemed totally unimpressed by Ned's apostrophes to responsibility and the Stapleton tradition. Paul seemed to think such attitudes were passé. In desperation Ned had sent him to a Maine summer camp run by Pennsgrove, hoping he would make some new friends.

The two younger boys, Rawdon and Kemble, came clattering downstairs. Rawdon was twelve, Kemble ten. Both were Stapletons, especially Kemble, with his piercing gray eyes and precise mouth. While they gulped down their orange juice and Wheat Chex, Tracy tried to explain the story in the paper. Her inability to conceal her own embarrassment irritated Ned. "If anyone asks you about it," he said, "tell them it's a pack of lies."

"Let's see it," demanded Rawdon, who resembled Ned in build and temperament. His eyes roved the page while Kemble peered perfunctorily over his shoulder. "Look at Cousin Allyn. She's some dish," Rawdon said.

"That is not a polite way to talk about your cousin," Tracy said.

"Sorreee," Rawdon said, making a face at Kemble, who struggled to suppress a giggle.

"That's right," Ned said. "She's part of the family. We've got to stick together."

"Why? Are the natives restless?" Rawdon said.

"It's because we're rich," Kemble said. "Nobody likes rich people."

"That's not true," Ned said.

"We're not rich, we're just well-off," Tracy said.

"They don't like us because of what your grandfather is doing," Ned said. "Trying to make sure everyone gets a

17

good education, whether they're white or colored. I explained it all to you last year, remember?"

"Yeah," Kemble said automatically. There were no blacks in his private country day school, so the whole uproar in the city was unreal to him and his brother.

The school bus honked at the head of the lane. Rawdon and Kemble seized their book bags and hurtled out the front door. Tracy sighed and shook her head. She picked up the paper and glared at it. "What in God's name did your brother George think he was doing, giving these creeps an interview?"

"He'll do almost anything to get some attention for his lousy poems," Ned said.

He took the paper and scanned the obnoxious page again. Rawdon was right, Cousin Allyn was some dish. Ned wished she would get married. It upset him to think of her running wild. It shook his confidence in the family's stability. Allyn had been more like his baby sister than his niece, during the years she had lived at New Grange Farm. Ned had nicknamed her Babe, and everyone in the family had called her that, until she announced that she did not like it. The few times he had seen her lately, she had treated him with mocking condescension, as if he was a 1910 fuddy-duddy on a cane and she was someone from the twenty-first century. It was unpleasantly similar to the superior tone his son Paul had tried to take with him, until Ned modified it by threatening to beat hell out of him.

Tracy stirred her coffee angrily. "I can practically hear the remarks I'll get at the country club. Maybe it's my southern blood, but I'll never understand what possessed your father to take that judgeship. Especially when he knew this thing was coming. What does it matter how many colored—"

Their plump black maid, Nancy, emerged from the kitchen with Ned's scrambled eggs. Nancy groaned when she saw what Ned was reading. She always read the paper on the bus and gave them her personal news commentary with breakfast. "Oh-oh-oh, I see you readin' it, Mr. Stapleton. I almost made a fire with that paper this mornin'. I wish I coulda made a big bonfire of the whole ee-dition. Smearin' yo fatha because he's tryin' to help

18

black people. Tellin' lies about you and him and your aunt and your grandmother. Don't you worry about one thing. It ain't gonna change the minds of any black people. They praise God for yo fatha every mornin'. They pray for him every Sunday."

"That's nice to know, Nancy," Ned said. "Could I have some marmalade?"

He went back to reading the paper. His temperature rose again. "Two hundred thousand dollars—that's what they say *Principia II* is worth. I wish I could get it. I'd sell it tomorrow."

Tracy patted her frosted hair in place beside her small exquisite ears. "That reminds me," she said. "I put a down payment on a marvelous piece of furniture at Brundisi's yesterday. A Philadelphia lowboy from Benjamin Randolph's workshop."

"How much?" Ned asked.

"Eighteen thousand."

"Jesus, Tracy."

"But it will complete the bedroom set. Every piece will be authentic. We can display it at the museum and get a tax deduction."

"For the moving costs."

"It's an investment. We can get it back anytime."

"Can we get it up, that's the question."

"Why don't you ask your father, for once."

"Absolutely not. He considered this whole house an extravagance. You know that. If he found out we're trying to fill it up with antiques—at eighteen thousand a throw—"

"Go see Pete Ackroyd."

Ned sighed. "Okay. But we owe him almost thirty thousand now. I promised him we'd get it down to twenty-five by the end of the year."

"Use your charm, Neddy dear."

For a lively moment, Ned hated his smiling wife. Maybe he would use his charm to find himself someone who gave him a good time in bed on a more consistent basis. But now was not the moment to make those kinds of waves. Not that his father would ever write him out of the will. Ned was fairly certain that he could prevent that. It was not mercenary fear, it was the simple wish to avoid displeasing him, disappointing him any more. He did not want to see that sour, downcast expression on his father's face when he came to him with another half-baked explanation or plea.

Her battle won, Tracy returned to deploring *The Garden Square Journal*'s assault on the Stapletons. "I think you should go see your father and push him—really push him—to agree to that book."

Tracy was a Kentucky girl, with a highly developed sense of family pride, which she had transferred to the Stapletons. For months, she had been spluttering over the snipes at Paul Stapleton by opponents of busing. Driving to work in his Mercedes coupe, Ned wondered if the all-out assault in the paper might change his father's mind about the book. He doubted it. Paul Stapleton had dismissed the idea when Ned suggested it to him six months ago.

Coming off the expressway, Ned crunched through debris in the littered streets for ten blocks. Black faces streamed past him. Downtown was one big ghetto. What did his father think he was doing, trying to solve this mess with court orders? Ned wondered. He parked his car in the garage beneath the new City Hall Plaza, which Mayor Jake O'Connor had built to enrich his Irish contractor friends and supporters, and took the elevator to the twenty-fifth floor.

In the reception room of Stapleton, Talbot, Ned stopped to joke with Teresa Moran, a pert, pretty redhead of about thirty-five. They had a running gag about how many days in a row Ned could go home without a briefcase. "Go ahead, search me, I'm clean," he said, holding up his hands.

"I believe you," Teresa said.

"It's all up here," Ned said, tapping his forehead.

"What's all up there?" growled Walter Ackroyd, coming in the door with his usual bulging briefcase. Walter's lean sallow face, with the bluish pouches of weariness beneath his eyes, had long typified what Ned was determined not to become, a legal drudge.

"What keeps this firm going, Walter. My brainpower," Ned said.

Walter started to glower, but Ned had him by the arm,

strolling down the center hall. Walter had succeeded Paul Stapleton as the managing partner of the firm. "Walter," Ned said, "what are the chances of an advance on next year's income?"

"We've never done it, Ned," Walter said. "It's a very bad habit. How much do you need?"

"Never mind. I'll get it from Pete," Ned said.

"Have you finished that appeals court brief for Slocum's Remedy?"

"No. I sent one of the associates to Washington yesterday to get some more stuff from the FTC."

"Get it done, will you, Ned? We can't ask for another stay. It sounds like we're stalling so they can keep on selling that alcoholic licorice."

"I'll have it by the end of the week," Ned said, realizing uneasily that he had told Walter Ackroyd the same thing last week.

They were at the door of Ned's office. Walter would continue down the hall to the managing partner's corner office. Where Ned Stapleton would never sit, Ned thought for a rueful moment. "What did you think of that lovely story on us in the paper this morning?" he asked.

Walter Ackroyd shook his head. "It made me wish I could change this firm's name."

"You're kidding, aren't you, Walter?" Ned said.

"More or less," Ackroyd said with a sigh. "But frankly, Ned, it isn't going to do us much good. Corporations are getting creamed by juries these days. It's not going to help us hold clients if they think they might be identified with an unpopular judge and a rich family."

"Good God, Walter, do you believe that garbage about our millions?"

It was outrageous disloyalty. Walter Ackroyd's father had been a plant manager at Principia Mills. He had been killed in a bomb explosion during a 1912 strike. The Stapletons had put Walter through college and law school. Paul Stapleton had selected him as the man of Walter's generation—he was almost sixty-five—to be the managing partner.

"Of course not," Walter said. "But a lot of people will consider it gospel truth. People like to believe the worst, Ned. Just between you and me, we can't afford to lose a

21

major client. Our expenses are skyrocketing and our income has remained pretty static. I'm thinking of forming a new business committee, and asking you to run it. I think you'd be pretty good at it."

Walter Ackroyd trudged down the hall to his office, discouragement, even defeat in his drooping gray head and slumped shoulders. Ned found the sight unnerving, dismaying. What the hell was happening? The older generation, his father and his partners and friends, had always been the ones who wore confidence, authority, like armor while Ned had been the one who hesitated, feared, blundered. Ned buzzed his secretary, Mary Wollock, and asked for the Slocum's Remedy brief. She said it was being retyped. He asked her if she had finished the invitations to the New Grange Country Club fall dance. Ned was chairman of the Entertainment Committee this year and he had spent most of last week working on preparations for this event. He wanted it to be the best dance in the history of the club. He had gone to New York in search of a better band. He had spent hours persuading the committee to make it a costume ball. Tracy had reported that they were the rage in Kentucky's hunt country.

Ned gave Mary Wollock another set of names from the membership lists of the Essex Fox Club and the Hamilton County Hunt, to extend the invitation list and hopefully fiance the expensive New York society band. Ned had a habit of combining his social life and his business life. His secretary often spent half her week working on yacht club and country club affairs. Ned liked managing social events. He liked to see people having a good time. But he found himself vowing that this was his last dance.

"Greetings, fellow millionaire."

Ned's brother George was standing in the doorway of Ned's office. Mary Wollock scuttled for cover. She knew trouble when she saw it.

"I loved your poem," Ned said.

"I thought you would," George said.

"Have you heard from Dad?" Ned asked.

"No. Only from Mother. She said she liked the poem She also said she'd pray for me."

"You may need it," Ned said. "Dad told you—"

Under no circumstances ever to reveal that a member of the firm of Stapleton, Talbot wrote poetry!"

George's growl was more a parody than an imitation of Paul Stapleton's voice.

"It makes sense, George."

"I don't think anything he says makes sense any more. And I don't think he's going to do anything. He's too tired. This busing case is killing him, literally."

It was true. Paul Stapleton had aged five years in the last twelve months. The flesh had vanished from his face. His step had become unsteady. He looked his eighty years.

Ned struggled for a moment with two emotions. One was a genuine regret for the way his father was dying. The other was relief at the thought of having enough money to live well without constantly visiting Pete Ackroyd. The second emotion made him feel unworthy to be Paul Stapleton's son. But he had felt this way so often that he had almost stopped worrying about it.

Ned told George what Walter Ackroyd had just said about the firm's finances, and the possible effect on the newspaper story. "Do you think he's right?"

George shrugged. He did not care. He was waiting with unabashed greed for his father to die. Meanwhile, he was doing as little work as possible. This was the first time he had come to the office in a week. Ned barely concealed his disgust. He was twelve years younger than George. Ned was not in the habit of thinking superior thoughts about any of his older brothers. But lately George had become more and more repellent. His brother's contemptuous attitude toward Paul Stapleton infuriated Ned. Maybe he was not worthy to be his son, but Ned was proud of it. He was proud of being a Stapleton even if he doubted he would ever be one of the best Stapletons. He had heard enough about the family's history to know that the annals contained a few Grade C's who had lived agreeable if not heroically admirable lives. He also knew there were a few lulus, like his Uncle Peregrine, to reassure a Grade C who at least was trying to do a few things right—raise his kids decently, love or at least like a sometimes bitchy wife.

"Goddamn it," Ned said. "I'm going to get Dad to

agree to that book on the family. The firm needs it as much as we do. I'm going to tell him what Walter Ackroyd said. I bet it will shock hell out of him."

George shrugged, indifferent here too. "I don't see how it will do anyone any good. If this writer you have in mind—what's his name?"

"Kilpatrick."

"If he told the truth, the Stapletons wouldn't like it. If he dishes out perfumed tripe, no one else will like it."

Ned pounded his fist on his desk. "Goddamn it, George, I say he can tell the whole truth and everybody will like it."

"You don't know what you're talking about, Neddy."

George's smile was so knowing—and so sick—Ned felt his confidence dissolve. But for once he was not going to let an older brother put him down.

"Go to hell," he said. "I'm going to call Kilpatrick and line him up right now."

III

Ten days later, Jim Kilpatrick drove downtown listening to the all-news-all-the-time radio station's resident intellectual emote about whether America had regained its sense of purpose in the Bicentennial year. The savage opposition to busing among white ethnics from Boston to Louisville, the torpid presidential campaign, the unemployment rate, discrimination against the aged, the young, women, homosexuals and ex-convicts, filled the soothsayer's intensely liberal soul with grave doubts.

Exiting at Bayshore Avenue, Kilpatrick inched through heavy traffic for ten claustrophobic blocks. He looked indifferently at the hundreds of black faces on the downtown sidewalks. Except for some aesthetic revulsion, he stared without emotion at the ghetto's scars—the boarded storefronts, the abandoned apartments with their blind sheet-metal windows.

Twenty years ago, in his Catholic prime, Kilpatrick would have been palpitating with pity for these poor people. Five years ago, as the cool but compassionate ex-Catholic corporate executive, he would have pondered programs, alternatives, workfare vs. welfare, brooded

25

over what the private sector of the economy could do to heal this wound. Both lives now seemed so remote they were like other incarnations.

Kilpatrick parked his red Corvette in the tiny executive lot beside the hundred-year-old red-brick factory building that everyone called the glue works. The city's environmental protection agency had forced the company to eliminate most of the noxious fumes previously associated with the preparation of Slocum's Remedy. But the factory's name refused to die because it was also a commentary on the medicinal value of the product.

Halfway up the airless, almost vertical stairs to the second-floor offices, Kilpatrick paused and took a deep breath. It was hard not to think of a coronary on these stairs, when that supposed milestone, the fiftieth birthday, had recently been passed. Opening the door at the top, he stepped into the arctic zone. Air conditioners thrummed in every window. The bullpen typists controlled them. They sat at their desks, smoking their cigarettes and smiling at him, apparently immune to pneumonia as well as lung cancer, thanks to their hormones.

Kilpatrick stalked down a pasteboard-walled corridor to a flimsy office at the far end. Beatrice Norton, secretary to Brad Mulholland, president of Slocum's Remedy, Inc., exhaled enough smoke to cause a pollution alert and greeted him with a buck-toothed grin.

"Hi, Mr. Kilpatrick. Mr. Mulholland is over at Stapleton, Talbot talkin' to the lawyers. He said to leave the speech with me. He'll read it and talk to ya afta lunch."

"Fine," Kilpatrick said, and handed her the twenty triple-spaced pages in praise of Slocum's Remedy that he had written for President Mulholland's exhortation to the salesmen at the company's annual convention.

"By the way," Beatrice Norton said, "did Mr. Stapleton get ahold of you?"

"Mr. Stapleton?" Kilpatrick said, feeling the name strike his face like a slap. "Which Mr. Stapleton? When did he call?"

"Mr. M. Kemble Stapleton. He called yesterday and the day before. He left his number."

She handed him a blue office memo with the Slocum's

26

Remedy motto, YOU'LL FEEL SO MUCH BETTER, emblazoned in red at the top. The number was scribbled on it: 344-4865. Kilpatrick dialed it on Beatrice's telephone. A switchboard operator said, "Stapleton, Talbot, can I help you?" In a moment he was connected to M. Kemble Stapleton's secretary. "Oh yes," she said, "Mr. Stapleton has been trying to get you."

In another moment M. Kemble Stapleton was on the telephone introducing himself as Ned. "You're a hard guy to find," he said in a voice that struck Kilpatrick as too jolly.

"I've been turning off the telephone at home. I'm trying to write a novel."

"A novel?" Ned Stapleton said in a puzzled, even disapproving tone. "Listen, I've got a better idea for a book. A biography of my father. We've decided you're the man to write it."

"Why?" Kilpatrick asked.

Ned seemed startled by the question. "You worked for my brother Randy at National Products. You're right here in the city. You wrote that fine book, *The, The*—"

"*Vanished Battle.*"

"Right. Brad Mulholland at Slocum's Remedy told me about it. I couldn't put it down. Look, this is my idea, really. I've talked Dad into it. Why don't we have lunch at the City Club and kick it around?"

At 1 P.M., Jim Kilpatrick sat opposite Ned Stapleton in the main dining room of the imitation Norman château called the City Club. He sipped a virgin mary and listened to Ned explain why he was so peremptorily invading his life. Kilpatrick was not particularly impressed by Ned. He looked like his father and older brother Randy—the same long head and narrow face and firm jaw. But the head seemed to require a lanky, bony body, instead of the stocky torso nature had given Ned. The incongruity was heightened by Ned's boyishness. He had shaken Kilpatrick's hand like he was an old prep school or college pal and started discussing squash. He had just finished a match and his thick brown hair gleamed wetly. Ned was disappointed to learn Kilpatrick did not play squash. He said he was looking for new partners. A lot of people quit playing the game when they turned fat and forty. At the table Ned told stories about his black maid and Polish secretary, both of whom were screwballs. Kilpatrick barely smiled. He had come to dislike boyish talkative men—largely because he had been one himself. He now made a policy of keeping his mouth shut as much as possible.

Ned finally turned the conversation to the book. He wasn't sure what shape it should take. It could be his father's memoirs. That is what he would like to see. But his father seemed to prefer a sort of family biography. He thought it might be best for Kilpatrick to gather the material and make a recommendation. If he and Paul Stapleton hit it off, he might be inclined to take his advice.

Kilpatrick found himself irked by Ned's assumption that his acquiescence in the book was already a fact. When he abruptly reminded Ned that he was not at all sure that he wanted to write it, Ned was first baffled, then annoyed.

"You'll be very well paid, I guarantee you," Ned said. "In fact, considering what we're prepared to spend, we could have hired a big-time professional writer. I talked to a couple. But I got the feeling there was a lack of genuine feeling for Dad's values—for the family's achievements. Then I remembered that letter you wrote when Randy died. It showed an amazing appreciation of our approach to life. For an outsider."

In spite of the condescension, Kilpatrick felt old emotion grip his throat. "I was pretty badly shaken up by Randy's death," he said.

Ned nodded complacently. A more subtle, cautious man might have tried to connect that extravagant letter to Kilpatrick's present reluctance to write about the Stapletons. He might have discovered that much of what Randy Stapleton had meant to Kilpatrick had been obliterated by history, personal and public, in the last four years.

But Ned was neither subtle nor cautious. He was old enough to be both. Kilpatrick placed him in his early forties. But there was something unfinished, incomplete about him. When he tried for self-assurance it came out as pomposity.

"You left National Products last year?" Ned asked.

Kilpatrick nodded. "I couldn't stand our esteemed chairman of the board, Dwight Slocum."

"I know what you mean," Ned said.

Ned described the abuse Walter Ackroyd had gotten from Slocum when Stapleton, Talbot lost the first round of their contest of an FTC complaint against Slocum's Remedy for fraudulent advertising. Although the parent company, National Products, was now an $800 million enterprise, the old man took a personal interest in the vicissitudes of the patent medicine on which the early Slocums had risen to wealth.

"Slocum wanted me to write speeches for him, using some of Randy's ideas," Kilpatrick said. "I couldn't put Randy's words in that old bastard's mouth."

Ned lowered his eyes and crumbled a breadstick between his fingers. "Randy was fantastic. Dad measures the rest of us against him. We can't match him. Who could?"

For a moment Kilpatrick almost felt sorry for Ned. He heard defeat, pain in those murmured words. But Kilpatrick had stopped feeling sorry for people. He told Ned that he was making a pretty good living as a free-lance speech writer. Kilpatrick thought it would put him in a better bargaining position when they started talking money. Actually, Brad Mulholland and a few other executives at National Products headquarters in New York were his only clients. Most of them shared his dislike of Slocum and were actively looking for new jobs.

The waiter asked Ned if he would like another drink. Ned shook his head. "Never have more than one. Then you never have to worry about having more than two. That's Dad's formula."

Kilpatrick finished his titillated tomato juice and they ordered lunch. Ned began talking about his father's military career. "That's the heart of the story. He was in both world wars, you know. I think there's only two other men who have won three Distinguished Service Crosses in two wars. He and Patton pioneered tank warfare. He made all sorts of contributions to strategy and tactics. I see a separate chapter on each Distinguished Service Cross.

29

The problem will be getting him to tell the stories. He plays them down. He makes each one sound about as dangerous as crossing a street. Do you have any combat experience?"

"Eighth Air Force. Forty-one missions over Germany. Bombardier."

"Mention that the first time you see him. Sometimes I think he's like George Washington, he doesn't respect any man who hasn't 'heard the bullets whistle.' I've never been in combat myself. I was too young to be drafted for Korea and too old for Vietnam. But that's the way I feel too. I've got a major's commission in the active reserves. I spent a month last summer studying armored warfare at Fort Benning."

Kilpatrick was going to tell Ned that George Washington was only twenty-one when he said the bullets made a pleasing sound. But other words slid past the offhand display of historical erudition. "I was that way myself—about the bullets," he said. "Now I'm not so sure. My oldest son was killed in Vietnam."

The obscene truth spilled across the table between them. It was the real reason why Kilpatrick had quit his job and was sitting here now at Ned Stapleton's beck and call. Why didn't Ned's expression change? Why didn't he call a waiter to mop up the mess? Answer: it was not a mess to Ned. It was just one more fact to be added to Kilpatrick's dossier.

No, it was worse, it was another recommendation, further proof that he was worthy to write Paul Stapleton's biography. "Tell that to Dad when you see him," Ned said.

The waiter arrived with a steak for Ned, a chef's salad for Kilpatrick. Ned began carving his steak with short, angry strokes. "I'm not sure I could handle losing a kid in that kind of war. I think I'd turn into a right-wing nut, no matter what Dad's told me about Stapletons avoiding extremism. Your boy—and lots of others—wouldn't have died in Vietnam if this country hadn't let a minority of loudmouths cripple our will to win. It was appalling to discover how many people had no concept of what it meant to be an American."

Five years ago, Kilpatrick had shared Ned's anger. At that time, he too had thought that there was only one acceptable way of being an American. He knew that there were other versions of the idea floating around. He knew that there were negative examples of American leaders in the political and business world. But men like John F. Kennedy and Adlai Stevenson and Randy Stapleton had enabled him to embrace the positive concept of an America that was prepared to dare, risk, sacrifice for freedom while its leaders struggled to make that freedom a creative value at home. America had been his faith, as noble, almost as salvific, as the Catholicism of his youth.

Now, with his dead son an incubus on his back, with Watergate still fouling the television screen in his memory, Kilpatrick responded to Ned's righteousness with evasion, back-pedaling like an aging boxer from a punch he remembered as too painful to take again.

"Who's going to publish this book, when and if I write it?" he asked.

"The county historical society. It's all set up. We're giving them a hundred thousand dollars. They'll pay you fifty thousand plus expenses. Does that sound right?"

It sounds like a bribe, Kilpatrick thought. But he was in no position to play the moralist. "That's very generous," he said.

Ned's answer was an imperious wave. "This is an important book. I see it as a corrective—a historical corrective—to the slanders against the family in the past—and present. This busing mess has revived a lot of old lies. You saw that story in the paper last week?"

Kilpatrick nodded. He did not tell Ned that the paper's attack on the Stapletons was mild compared to the nasty things he had heard about them in his boyhood home. His father had not been an admirer of the family. Snobs, bloodsuckers, legalized crooks were among the less scatological names James Kilpatrick, Sr., had called the Stapletons. Their enormous wealth, supposedly accumulated from the sweat of the poor Irish in their mills, was high on his father's list of rationalizations for his own pursuit of power in the Irish-American political machine that his devious legal advice had helped to construct.

31

"How does the rest of the family feel about the book?" Kilpatrick asked.

"Mother's opposed. My Aunt Agatha can't make up her mind. My brothers, Mark and George, don't give a damn."

"Why?"

"They've never gotten along with Dad. But you don't have to worry about them. You're not going to explore Dad's family relationships. His public career is what counts. His fantastic army record. His success as a lawyer. His courage as a judge. His leadership in the community. His political influence, which has always been aimed at one thing, the good of the country."

Kilpatrick said he would still like to know why Ned's two brothers did not give a damn about their father. Ned became very tense and asked Kilpatrick not to repeat that phrase to anyone. He descanted on the need to define the limits of the book. He said he wanted to keep the story simple.

"I want people to realize the kind of man they've been vilifying in this city for the past year."

Kilpatrick asked why Paul Stapleton had exposed himself to this abuse by taking the job as federal district judge in the first place. "Didn't he have a lot more power and influence as managing partner of Stapleton, Talbot? You're the biggest law firm in the state."

"This is something else that won't go in the book. There was an understanding that he was going to be nominated for the next vacancy on the Supreme Court. He'd be sitting in Washington now if Lyndon Johnson hadn't bugged out on the presidency and handed the White House to Nixon."

The story struck Kilpatrick as eyewash. But he decided to be diplomatic to a man who had just offered him fifty thousand dollars. "I'm beginning to think we're going to leave more out of this book than we put into it."

"I see it as a kind of brief," Ned said. "A brief for the defense."

"My father always wanted me to be a lawyer," Kilpatrick said.

"Was he one?"

"He was corporation counsel of the city for about twenty years. The brains behind the Shea machine. Then he was a judge."

For a moment Ned looked dismayed. The Shea machine had looted the city for thirty years. Although it had collapsed in the early fifties, it was still a lurid memory. "Is your father alive?" Ned asked.

If he said yes, would the deal be off? Kilpatrick wondered. "He died in 1948," he said.

Kilpatrick suddenly remembered how he had felt when he had told Randy Stapleton about his father, ten years ago. There had been something religious about the experience. He had had a sense of confessing a sin with the certainty that it would be gravely, gently forgiven. Which it was. He contrasted Randy's understanding with Ned's barely concealed disapproval. Perhaps more unsettling was his own barely hidden truculence. It made Kilpatrick wonder if this book was a good idea for either party. But fifty thousand dollars was a very good idea for a man who was trying to start a new career at the age of fifty.

Over coffee, Kilpatrick made an appointment to see Judge Stapleton at New Grange Farm on the following Saturday. Ned would phone and tell him the time. After lunch, Kilpatrick called Brad Mulholland at Slocum's Remedy and was told that he liked the speech. The mortgage was paid for another two months.

Kilpatrick swung his red Corvette, a relic of his days of executive glory, onto the expressway and headed north along the city's uptown spine. In ten minutes he was turning into the driveway of his house on a middle-class side street. The house was big and wide, with a broad porch and a shiny bay window. It needed paint on the gray shutters and white trim. Kilpatrick eased the Corvette into the attached garage. The neighborhood had a collection of teen-agers who eyed the car hungrily and probably knew how to jump-start it for a run west on the expressway.

The driveway was in deep shadow, although the sun was still high in the September sky. The entire front of the house lay beneath the engulfing limbs of a huge oak tree. Over the years it had tipped until it now leaned toward the house at a most alarming angle. Several neighbors considered it a menace and wanted the tree removed. They had called City Hall a half dozen times demanding action. But the tree was still there, leaning. Kilpatrick had grown to like it. Lately, he had begun to think he would welcome its fall. Defiantly he had started sleeping in the front bedroom, directly beneath the eaves that were nearest to the massive old trunk. Each morning when he got up he looked out at it. There was a huge spiral knob about forty feet up the trunk that glared at him like a blind, malignant eye. Sometimes Kilpatrick thumbed his nose at it and said, "Fuck you."

The garage door closed automatically behind him. Kilpatrick reached for the ignition. His hand hesitated for a fraction of a second on the key before turning it firmly erect. He heard a voice whisper: *multiple wounds in the chest and head.*

Off. He turned the key off. He would not allow the dead to drag him down into the darkness. Not yet. But he had played with the possibility again. It would be so simple to sit there and let the motor run for thirty seconds, to drowse off in a carbon monoxide stupor and let the coroner figure out how it happened.

Kilpatrick got out of the car, jammed the murderous key in his pocket and strode into his house. He walked hastily through the empty kitchen, which he always found depressing, into the empty living room. It was furnished with a mixture of Grand Rapids junk that had come with the house and good pieces Kilpatrick had brought from New York.

The cost of child support for the five children of his failed marriage had been one of several reasons why he had not married again. For several years he had lived happily with a woman he had met in California. But she got involved in women's liberation and the anti-war movement, two causes which left him unenthused. They had separated a year or so before he quit his job at National Products and retreated to the city of his birth. He had told himself that living was cheaper, he had seen it as a symbolically satisfying place to pursue the suppressed dream of every English major, a writing career.

He had also told himself it would be a chance to reclaim his fatherhood with his four remaining children. He had bought this big house on the supposition that they would visit regularly, if he was living only twenty minutes away. But after ten years of separation, this idea was freighted with disaster. His ex-wife had made sure that the children did not like him very much. Only his second son, Liam, appeared for sporadic visits, which were paradigms of failed communication, studded with the wreckage of conversations that went nowhere. It had been demoralizing to discover that his search for self-respect had divorced him not only from his wife and from the Catholic Church, but from his children, the heirs of this American future that he had thought he was shaping, in his heady business years with Randy Stapleton. A realist would not have been surprised by his children's defection. But Kilpatrick was only a part-time realist. Half his mind, the half he thought of as the American side, was realistic, factual. The other half, which he considered the Irish-Catholic side, was constantly feeding him impossible dreams.

From a shelf in the living room, Kilpatrick took a copy of his first—and only—book and thumbed through it. It was about an obscure battle fought only a few miles from the city at a town named New Salem in 1780, and forgotten by most historians. He had mined the local historical society and come up with gold—reminiscences, letters, diaries of participants. In the British Army Headquarters papers at the Clements Library of the University of Michigan he found more gold—evidence that the British had hoped to make the battle the climax of a victorious campaign. One of the heroes of the fight was a young firebrand named Kemble Stapleton. Kilpatrick sent a copy of the book to Judge Stapleton with a modest inscription. He got a three-line letter of thanks.

Other readers had been enthusiastic. The state historical society gave Kilpatrick a prize and the legislature passed a resolution praising him for adding another tourist attraction to the Bicentennial. But the reading public ignored the book. It sold 3,113 copies and earned Kilpatrick $4,153.

Kilpatrick had written the book about the battle of

New Salem to see what made these primary Americans fight and die. He was trying to link his dead son to these authenticated heroes. It did not work. Instead of discovering on the dead a radiant patina of patriotism, Kilpatrick's hard-eyed research revealed the Americans of 1780 as quarrelsome, discouraged, reluctant to fight. He listed the shocking percentage of each militia company that failed to turn out, the astonishing number of desertions from Washington's army, the vicious infighting over promotions and supply contracts. This was why the book was praised by historians and ignored by the great American public. Who wanted the bad news about the halfhearted, self-interested way the Americans fought the Revolution, on the eve of the Bicentennial?

It was ironic that this book, which he was sure none of the Stapletons had read, had brought him the invitation to write the patriarch's biography. Kilpatrick reread some of it while he cooked his dinner. He liked the part where Kemble Stapleton rallied the Monmouth County militia and persuaded those quitters to turn out and fight for a change. Kilpatrick wondered what Judge Stapleton would say about Kemble's assessment of his fellow Americans of 1780 in one of his letters. *One third cowards, one third traitors and one third profiteers.*

While he read, Kilpatrick ate creamed chicken on cold toast. He had never mastered the art of snychronizing the toast and boiling the frozen chicken in its plastic envelope. After dinner he went upstairs to the room he had fitted out as a study and worked on his novel. It was about an army infantry company in Vietnam led by a young Irish-American whose father had practically ordered him to live up to John F. Kennedy's challenge. Kilpatrick had spent months researching the war. Around him on the shelves were dozens of books on the politics, tactics, strategy of Vietnam. But the novel was going nowhere. Almost every day he ripped up what he had written.

At 1:30 A.M. Kilpatrick went to bed. He hoped he would not dream about Vietnam. He often did. At times the dreams made him wonder if he was going crazy. Once he saw a Chinook, one of the big troop helicopters, flying

36

above the jungle trailing a sign behind it, the way advertising planes flew ads along the beach when he was a boy. But the Chinook was not trailing an ad. Its sign read: MULTIPLE WOUNDS IN THE CHEST AND HEAD. Kilpatrick had awakened with tears on his face.

Tonight, Kilpatrick dreamt he was in a plane. It was one of National Products' Lear jets. The compartment was fitted out as a flying office. There was a typewriter on a folding table, with a pile of papers beside it. He read the title on the top page. THE POWER OR THE PROFITS. It was a speech that Randy Stapleton had been going to give to the National Association of Manufacturers. Kilpatrick had written it. Randy had said it was the best speech Kilpatrick had ever done. It was about what should come first for American business, the power to lead the nation or the ability to make bigger and bigger profits. Randy Stapleton felt that the time was fast approaching when businessmen would have to choose between these alternatives. Randy had taken the speech with him on the plane that had crashed.

Suddenly Kilpatrick was afraid. This plane was going to crash. He was remembering something about Randy Stapleton that he preferred to forget. The man was incredibly indifferent to danger. Some people said he had a death wish. At least a half dozen times, Kilpatrick had been with him when Stapleton insisted on making an instrument landing in dense fog or told the pilot to fly straight into a ferocious weather front or decided to take off in a blizzard that had every commercial flight grounded.

Turbulence. Kilpatrick was flung around the cabin as the plane careened through the sky. He stumbled to the cockpit door and yanked it open. Randy Stapleton, wearing an absurd Lindbergh-style helmet with a dangling chin strap, was flying the plane. He smiled in that calm, slightly mournful way that had made Kilpatrick both envy and worship him.

"It's all right, Jim," he said. "Everything's under control."

Kilpatrick awoke sweating, his heart pounding. It was dawn. He knew he would get no more sleep. He got up and walked through the dark, silent house to the study. From the bookcase he took down a file folder of his work for National Products, Inc. He paged through the speeches and memoranda and annual reports, past pictures of him and Randy Stapleton sitting together on daises at company dinners, debarking from company planes, inspecting the latest smart bomb, the newest guided missile. On the last page was the New York *Times* obituary.

NATIONAL PRODUCTS PRESIDENT
DIES IN CRASH OF COMPANY JET

J. Randolph Stapleton, president of National Products, Inc., was killed yesterday along with two other executives when the company jet in which he was flying tried to make an instrument landing in a heavy snowstorm at a small airport near New Providence, Ohio. Mr. Stapleton was making one of his frequent impromptu inspections of an NPI subsidiary—in this case the Johnson Electric Company. Mr. Stapleton was 58.

The rest was about Randy's career at National Products, how in tandem with board chairman Dwight Slocum, he had built the company into one of the nation's most successful conglomerates.

Opposite this dolorous relic was a carbon copy of Kilpatrick's letter of condolence.

May 21, 1972

Dear Judge Stapleton:

I have never met you but I have heard a good deal about you. In a certain unreal and unworthy sense I feel I am almost a member of· your family. For six years I worked closely with Randy, as his director of corporate public relations. I wrote speeches for him. I traveled extensively with him. I watched him running one of the most important companies in this country. In those six years I never heard him say or saw him do a dishonorable thing. At a time when so many Americans are losing faith in our country's purpose, its business system, its role in the world, this was tremendously important to me, personally. I think it was important to everyone who knew and worked with Randy. His loss leaves a gap in my life that will be almost impossible to fill. He had a unique ability to lead men and women simply by being what he was—a man who combined integrity and compassion and understanding. We worked hard for him. But it was the easiest hard work I have ever done. You will probably get a lot of letters saying these things. But I don't think you will get one that says them more wholeheartedly. I was raised in the same city as Randy. But by an accident of birth I was taught to despise and even to hate the name Stapleton. I suppose this is why learning to know a real Stapleton has meant so much to me. It has changed my attitude, not only toward the Stapletons, but toward America itself. Being able to call Randy my friend as well as my boss made me feel part of this country in a deep, secure way I had never felt before. I'm sure that this feeling of trust and pride is a legacy that I will be able to draw on for the rest of my life.

After saying all this, I hardly need add that I can share to a very small extent the grief you must feel at having lost such a son. Please accept my deepest sympathy.

Sincerely,
James Kilpatrick

There it was, living proof that Randy Stapleton had become part of the mental and emotional apparatus that connected Jim Kilpatrick to his middle-aged American world. Was it his fault that he was no longer able to live on that legacy of pride and trust? Was it his fault that, a month after he wrote it, the phone call from the army officer with the hushed husky voice penetrated his skull like a blunt spear, telling him that Kevin Sugrue Kilpatrick had joined the long list of sons who had sacrificed the future to give America more time to enjoy the present? More time to pop more pills and prong more pussy and rig more prices and chomp more steaks and vroom more horsepower and belt more booze. Was it his fault that a voice kept reminding him that Kevin Sugrue Kilpatrick had died of multiple wounds in the chest and head from a fragmentation grenade, a weapon manufactured by a National Products subsidiary, the Baldwin Firearms Company? Or did the fault line reach out with spider fingers, like the hole a bullet or a sliver of a grenade left in glass or metal or flesh, to include presidents of the country and the company, Randy Stapleton and his esteemed father, Judge Paul R. Stapleton, Ned Stapleton and all the other true believers in the gospel of America, the good, the true, the victorious?

Kilpatrick told himself he did not know the answer to that question. He was not going to sit in judgment on anyone before he heard his story. But a dull anger throbbed in his chest like pain around the edges of a wound.

IV

Through her bare foot Allyn Stapleton felt the pulse of blind, meaningless force as she sent her Volvo 1800E down the dark curving country road at ninety-five miles an hour. Beside her sat Jacqueline Chasen, also immune, as befits the possessor of a bottomless trust fund, to normal emotions like affection or fear. Jacky was high on Valium, her latest kick. Allyn had taken only five, because she was driving. At the top of the S curve just below New Grange Farm Jacky started to laugh. Allyn did not know why until they reached the bottom of the S and saw the milk tanker roaring toward them. She flicked the wheel to the right, then to the left. The Volvo proved it had survival instincts all its own by holding the road.

"I saw his headlights," Jacky said. "I thought about the story it would make. Joint funeral for heiresses. Rabbi calls it an American tragedy."

"My grandfather would insist on a Protestant minister."

"So would my grandfather. But my father would disagree with him for the first time in his life."

"Dreamer."

They were two bored, thoroughly disillusioned rich girls who wished the 1960s had never ended. Allyn wished it because she had spent most of that violent decade being very, very good. Jacky wished it because she had never learned to handle explosives and try urban guerrilla warfare.

Allyn and Jacky had met at a party Jacky's mother had given to whip up enthusiasm for a Bicentennial project she was chairpersoning—the redevelopment of the original section of the city, where the founding fathers had put up their slope-roofed frame houses in the early eighteenth century. These had long since vanished, replaced by brownstones built around several tree-filled parks. Jacky's mother, who was intensely interested in worthy causes and totally uninterested in Jacky, teamed up with Allyn's cousin, the mayor's wife, to persuade them to buy and redevelop one of the brownstones. Allyn had suggested opening an art gallery on the ground floor, devoted to women painters, weavers, potters. She also suggested the name, Artemisia, after Artemisia Gentileschi, the first important woman painter. Why not? Jacky said. It might be good for some giggles.

They each put $20,000 into redeveloping the brownstone. Jacky took the third floor for an apartment, Allyn took the second floor. The fourth floor, the top, they split into studios for deserving artists. On paper it looked inspirational but in reality it was closer to *folie à deux*. They discovered that each had tyrannical grandfathers who set impossible standards of obedience, honor and virtue. Each liked to drive sports cars at suicidal speeds. Jacky had introduced Allyn to pills. Allyn had tutored Jacky on booze. Each liked to swing. They even liked each other a little, but Allyn said she wasn't ready for that. There were times when Jacky was frightening or at least intimidating. She wanted to try everything as fast as possible. She was only twenty-three, but she had had a half dozen serious men and a ledgerful of one-night stands, all carefully recorded in a cryptic diary which she occasionally read aloud to Allyn.

Although Allyn had a discarded husband whose name she disdained to use, Jacky made her feel retarded. At thirty, Allyn had had only one big brainless affair with a muscular young local politician. For most of her life she had been a secret inner rebel, outwardly the model daughter, student, wife, worthy of her Stapleton heritage. Then came the stunning news that Father, the man whose gentle eyes and mournful voice perpetually cajoled obedience from her, had been snuffed. As casually, as haphazardly as a swatted fly or mosquito. Smashed, mashed, incinerated in the wreckage of his company jet. So much for the rewards of duty, kindness, compassion.

Allyn had not visited her grandparents at New Grange Farm since Paul Stapleton's birthday dinner, last January. It was another reason to drive past it at the fastest possible speed. They were sitting there, the two undying paragons, the Great Man and his sainted wife, mourning her. Wouldn't it be nice if they had to do some real mourning, if they had to come out and scrape their beloved granddaughter off one of their trees? She roared past the familiar windows on the hill to the first crossroad beyond them. She took the turn at seventy. The Volvo practically bounded over a little ridge and squealed to a stop in front of her Uncle George's house, a replica of a Mexican hacienda. "I don't get it," Jacky giggled.

"Uncle George loves his mother," Allyn said.

They crossed the floodlit cobblestone courtyard and pushed open the wide mahogany front door with the Aztec symbol, the plumed serpent, inset in gold around the knocker. Paunchy, raunchy Uncle George was in the hall telling one of the black waiters to add another quart of tequila to the punch. Allyn introduced him to Jacky, who was as chic in her tailor-made jeans and Gucci shirt as Allyn was tacky in her soiled tennis shorts and sweat shirt.

"Any friend of my favorite niece is a friend of mine," George said. "What would you like? Uppers, downers?"

He pointed to two large bowls, one full of red, the other full of green pills.

"We brought our own," Jacky said.

"Valium?" George said, recognizing the yellow capsules. "That was last year's around here. Try those." He pointed to the reds. "They should work beautifully with Vals."

43

"Don't put us on, Unc," Allyn said. "You know what we came for. The white gold."

George gave an abrupt angry shake of the head, a Stapleton trademark. "Don't broadcast it. I don't give that stuff away to every nose that walks in the door."

"Hey," Jacky said. "Is he anti-Semitic?"

"Uncle George is anti everything except fucking and poetry," Allyn said. "Come on, Unc. Give us a snort."

George led them down the hall to the stairway to his study, an immense room that took up most of the second floor of the house. The walls were lined with cork for total seclusion when George wanted it. A glittering purple-and-green mosaic of a plumed serpent was inset in the ceiling. One wall had a glassed-in high-fidelity system that George claimed was better than a front-row seat at the Boston Symphony. In splendid isolation in the center of the room was a huge semicircular teak desk with George's red Olivetti electric typewriter on it. The desk had dozens of drawers. George pulled one out and made a magician's gesture. *"Voilà,"* he said.

The drawer was lined with two-gram vials of cocaine. It was the best. George had excellent contacts in Mexico. He went there regularly. He had turned Allyn on to coke about six months ago. She had given some to Jacky last week and she had agreed it was superblow, the best she had ever had. Giggling to conceal the greedy anticipation she felt, Allyn chopped the small white fibers into tiny pieces with a razor that George kept in a silver holder.

"Go kid," she said to Jacky, handing her a silver snorter. Nothing déclassé about George, you wouldn't find a Stapleton lining with rolled-up dollars or plastic straws.

Jacky took two and two and bombed around the room like a pursuit plane. "That stuff is fantastic," she said. "I think the whole frontal lobe sheared off."

"Congratulations," George said. "Why don't you go for a swim or something? I want to talk to Allyn."

"You and your goddamn Wasp privacy," Jacky giggled.

Allyn was leaning over the white magic, about to ride two equally ecstatic lines up each nostril when George caught her hand. "Before you blast off," he said, "a little

44

practical discussion. The Great Man has decided to do the book. They've got this guy Kilpatrick to write it. He'll be at the farm this Saturday. It's the first hunt of the season. Let's both go and try to meet him."

"Anything you say, Unc."

"Listen, you whacked-out bitch. This is important. It's up to you to find out if this guy's as true-blue as St. Randy thought he was."

"St. Randy," Allyn said.

The Valiums jolted her head. She must have been holding them back by an act of the will. She frowned up at George. His face dissolved into the map of Mexico. A snake grew out of his forehead and coiled around his neck.

"I'll be there," she said. "Now stand back."

She took two deep ones on each side. She hunched in the big swivel chair and counted one two three four. Pure light blazed inside her skull and raced down her arms. She held up her hands and saw the brightness gushing from her fingers.

"Oh Jesus," she said. "Oh Jesus. Holy fucking Jesus."

She giggled at George and touched his chin with her fingers. She wanted to bathe that sad, puffy middle-aged face in the same brightness. She loved him. She loved everybody in the whole crazy, crooked world. She called for Jacky, she wanted to kiss her, but she had floated off somewhere. Allyn was stuck with George.

"I heard the Great Man curse like that once. In the barn, when he found out someone had forgotten to feed his favorite horse, Thunder. 'Jesus goddamn fucking Christ,' he said. I ran and told holy Maria. She said he had learned it in the army."

George put his hand on her breast and bit the back of her neck. "When are you going to let me fuck you?"

"I don't know. Maybe I'll make it your Christmas present."

"I keep telling you it is perfectly permissible."

"What isn't perfectly permissible?"

"Bad poetry."

Uncle George was quite a discovery. When Allyn had left New Grange for New York six years ago, George had been little more than a family worry, a Stapleton, Talbot

45

tax drone who had a tendency to drink too much and had divorced one dull wife to marry another one. But the rhetoric of the sixties had apparently been stirring a secret rebellion in his pudgy soul and by the time Allyn returned last winter, sans husband and ready to swing, Uncle George had shed his second wife and was providing the liveliest scene around. He had encouraged Allyn's inclination to think and say the worst about the Stapletons. But his sexual interest in her was new and very unappealing.

She removed his hand from her breast and floated to the door. "I want to dive," she said.

"Okay. Let me put on some music."

By the time she reached the living room, native chants, the wail of flutes and the beat of drums were filling the house. George was determined to unravel civilization, man's greatest mistake, and recreate the primitive soul that the industrialism had destroyed.

"The privacy hour is over?" Jacky called. She was sitting on a couch beside a beefy black man. Allyn knew him, but not his name. He was a poet. George's Lenape Press, named for New Jersey's vanished Indians, had just published his poems. He had his eyes closed, reciting one of them to Jacky.

"They told me you were white, Zenobia.
But I know your flesh was dark like mine."

Allyn began drinking the punch. It was practically straight tequila. She gave some to Jacky, who whispered that it made the black's poetry sound a lot better. People kept coming in. Associate professors from the state university's creative writing department, painters from the school of plastic art, actors from the drama department. Not one of them real, Allyn thought. Everyone had to produce his or her title to prove he or she existed. She saw a woman painter who had contributed several watercolors to the opening exhibition at the gallery. She was a burly, short-haired field-hockey type. Her watercolors had been lousy imitations of Ryder.

Allyn had another glass of tequila and decided it was time to do some diving. The green water looked cold. People around the pool were wearing sweaters. But Allyn knew the pool was heated. She went down to the little

46

adobe house at the end of the pool, where George parked his girl friends, and found a blue bikini in the closet. She came out and climbed the ten-foot diving board. The audience at the poolside applauded. Allyn bowed mockingly. She saw Jacky and George come out of the house to watch.

Up on the toes, three swift steps to the end of the board and up, floating free, back arched, arms out in a swan. It was beautiful. In spite of leering faces flitting like evil birds along the edge of the pool. Diving was the best way to achieve the new consciousness George was always blabbing about.

The pool suddenly receded in a whirlpool of green light. It became a menacing vortex that confused her descent. She hit badly. Pain blasted her face and body. Bewildering. Was it possible she had forgotten how to dive? Or had she ever known how, was it all a dream, floating free, beauty in precious, precarious space between heaven and earth? She could hear her grandfather saying: *I want you to be the best diver in the country. I want you to be the best horsewoman. I want you to be the best student. I want you to be the best wife, best cook, best mother, best.*

She hated him. Beneath the clear green water, the purifying eye-burning chlorine bleached hatred into her skin. She hated his wife even more. That was the secret not even George knew. Allyn also hated his holy mother, Maria, with her prayers and her sad, worried, obedient face.

Allyn climbed out of the pool and strolled dripping into the living room to get some more tequila. The hockey-player painter descended on her and began discussing a one-woman exhibition. She had over a hundred paintings ready to hang. Allyn hadn't seen any of her oils. They were very experimental. She was into de Kooning. Allyn excused herself and wandered into the hall. She gulped down a handful of George's green downers, vaguely hoping they might be fatal.

When she woke up they were in the car and Jacky was driving and laughing she had fucked the black poet or she thought or he thought they had fucked but he was more interested in reciting and she had sucked him off finally and he never stopped reciting not once. But she liked Uncle George. She liked making it with older men. He had invited her for dinner some night should she go?

Allyn smiled at the speedometer needle rocking past 90. "Sure. Go," she said.

She asked Jacky for some Valiums. "In my right tit pocket," Jacky said. Allyn started fooling with the tit and Jacky almost lost control of the car.

Around noon, Allyn was awakened by Clarice Heller, the deadly serious, highly efficient art major whom they had hired to run the gallery. Clarice thought that Miss Stapleton would like to know that they had finally sold a painting. Allyn said that was wonderful. She stumbled into the bathroom to stare at herself in the mirror. Below the tangled hair, the puffy eyes, the ruined makeup, she saw she was still wearing her sweat shirt. Something was written on it in lipstick. She took it off and read: *"Saturday. The Hunt."*

V

A hawk swooped and wheeled in the blue sky above the
white clapboard house. Four dormer windows in the
slanted roof were precisely counterpointed by six windows
on the lower floor, spaced to the right and left of the
dormers. The windows were small. The impact the house
made on the eye was similar to an abstract painting. A
rectangle of glistening white affirming order, simplicity,
basic American virtues. The graceful fanlight above the
wide front door was a nod to beauty.

From the road, approaching New Grange Farm at a
45-degree angle, Jim Kilpatrick could see that the house
had two rear wings. From the front they were invisible.
They had been added with such skill that there was no
trace of a modern intrusion on the eighteenth-century
farmhouse façade. Behind the house were two big red
barns and corrals for exercising and training horses and a
matching red garage for the farm's trucks and family cars.
A half dozen horses gamboled in an upland pasture.
Beyond them, twenty or thirty cows sat in the shade of
some old elms.

A dark-skinned houseboy, who seemed to be Mexican

or Puerto Rican, escorted Kilpatrick down a short hall to the left of the door into a cavernous living room which occupied the entire first floor of the left wing of the house. The furniture was Spanish colonial—oversized chairs and couches with flat arms and slat backs of some dark expensive wood. A group of mounted animal heads—a grizzly bear, an elk, a mountain lion—hung in the corner on the right. The room was crowded with men and women in jodhpurs and red hunting coats. Some were drinking coffee. Most were on booze. Their faces were flushed and their eyes glowed as they talked about the jumps they had taken, the close calls they had survived.

"I cut through the woods and all of a sudden there was this branch a foot from my head—"

"I saw sparks when Frank took that stone wall. It's a miracle he didn't break his neck. That horse hates to jump—"

Kilpatrick stood on the edge of this conversation, a total outsider. He had never ridden a horse in his life. He wondered if Ned Stapleton had deliberately invited him with this in mind. Awe the peasant with a glimpse of upper-class life style.

A long-legged redhead in a well-filled hunting coat strolled up to him. She had a dark brown drink in her hand. Her green eyes were unnaturally bright. The wide, full mouth was much too friendly. Either she thought he was an old friend or she was drunk.

"You look lost," she said.

"I'm meeting Ned Stapleton—"

"He'll show up eventually. I'm Allyn Stapleton."

"Jim Kilpatrick."

"One of the slaves at the Stapleton, Talbot salt mine?"

"No. I'm a—" Kilpatrick was going to say businessman, but changed it to writer. "I may write a biography of Judge Stapleton."

"How interesting. Whose idea is this?"

"It seems to be Ned's."

"That figures. Poor Ned never stops trying."

"Trying what?"

"Trying to win the Great Man's approval."

"You're not an admirer?"

"Just a granddaughter. A disenchanted granddaughter."

"Your father is—?"

"Was the oldest son—he's dead."

Kilpatrick remembered the words in Randy Stapleton's obituary. *He leaves a daughter, Allyn.*

"I know. I worked for him for six years."

"The plot thickens. It's obvious what kind of biography this is going to be. You've been preselected as a safe ceremonious worshipper at the shrine."

The unprovoked nature of this assault made it easy for Kilpatrick to deny the truth. "I'm going to write exactly what I find. I can't believe the Judge wants anything else."

It unsettled him to discover that the moment he said this, he wanted to believe it. Maybe it was a reaction to the scorn curling Allyn Stapleton's red mouth.

"I like liars with broad shoulders. Where do you live?"

"In the city. Boardman Avenue."

"So do I. Maxwell Square."

"In the Old Town?" Kilpatrick said. He had followed the development of the historic district with interest.

"Yes. I'm one of the pioneers. So far the natives have been friendly."

The district was at the foot of the city's south slope, on the edge of the ghetto.

"Hello, Jim," Ned Stapleton said, rounding a knot of hunters. They shook hands. "Sorry for the confusion. I thought all these people would have gone home by this time. But it's hard to hunt a fox on schedule. He has his own ideas about how long the chase should last."

"Ned got the tail today. Isn't that *wonderful?*" Allyn Stapleton said. "I don't think the fox enjoyed it quite as much."

"If you don't like it, Allyn, why do you come? Not that we've seen very much of you."

"Basically, I'm here for the same reason you're here, Ned. To make sure I don't get disinherited."

"That's ridiculous," Ned said.

He seized Kilpatrick by the arm and led him rapidly away from Allyn Stapleton.

51

"I hope that wasn't too unpleasant," he said as they emerged from the crowd of drinking hunt persons and paused beneath the animal heads at the opposite end of the huge room. "Allyn is a very mixed-up girl these days. Her marriage broke up last year. After Randy's death she pretty much went to pieces."

She's still quite a piece, Kilpatrick thought. Ned invited him out on the patio. "Dad should be along any minute. I thought we could chat here for a half hour or so and then have lunch."

On the patio, the two side wings of the house created a secluded rectangle of sunny quiet. There was a free-form reflecting pool in the middle of it, surrounded by a rock garden with a dozen or so cactus plants and several dwarf trees. To the right were metal chairs and a white metal table with a red, white and blue umbrella in the center of it. Blue and white chaise longues were scattered here and there.

"This is Dad's favorite spot. It's where he does his thinking," Ned said.

"Is this our Plutarch?" asked a voice behind them.

Kilpatrick turned to confront a man who did not look like a Stapleton. He was big—a head taller than Ned, but he did not have Ned's squared shoulders and stiff back. He stood loosely, the left shoulder lower than the right one, a potbelly bulging against his jodhpurs, hands casually in his pockets.

"This is my brother George," Ned said. "We finally got him to take a little exercise today."

"Good for the body, bad for the soul," George Stapleton said, smiling and holding out his hand. He had dark hair, a wide relaxed mouth and a round face—remarkably different from the basic Stapleton mold. George looked like an easygoing peasant out of a Brueghel painting.

"I liked your book, the one on the battle. A first-rate job," he said.

"Thanks," Kilpatrick said. "I liked that poem of yours the newspaper published the other day. In spite of the reporter's stupid comments."

"If you thought that was bad, you should have heard what my father said."

52

"Dad doesn't think the law and poetry mix," Ned said with a nervous laugh.

"I keep telling him they're a colloidal solution," George said.

"Why don't you take it easy here, Jim, while we go back and say goodbye to the hunt," Ned said.

"You're better at that than I am, Ned," George said. "I'll keep Jim company."

Ned looked annoyed, but he obviously lacked the authority to give George an order. The younger brother retreated to the party and George sprawled into a chair beside Kilpatrick, sticking his long legs straight out like a Westerner.

"Have you ever met my father?" he asked.

"We shook hands at Randy's funeral," Kilpatrick said.

"Did you really mean that letter you wrote to him, or were you trying to protect your job?"

"I meant it."

"Maybe it wasn't Randy's fault. He was the oldest. There was no way that he could fight the old bastard off. He had to buy the whole package."

"I'm sorry. But I don't understand."

"Do you have any interest in finding out the truth?"

"Of course I do."

"What would you do with it, if you found it out?"

"I don't know. What do you think I should do with it?"

"Write the whole story. It's a juicy exposé, believe me. It's got everything—sex, violence, corruption in high places. If I were you, I'd learn as much as I can now from him, from me, from everyone who'll talk. Dwight Slocum, for instance."

"Why don't you write it?"

George grimaced and tilted his face toward the sky for a moment.

"There's something slightly repugnant about a son assaulting his father's reputation. Besides, I'm a poet. That means I'm unbalanced as far as the public is concerned. You, a former loyal subordinate, with some reputation as a historian, assailed by pangs of conscience, moral repugnance—"

"You're being a little unrealistic, aren't you? I haven't

53

signed anything yet, but I assume there'll be a contract that will tie me up six ways from Sunday. That's the way these books work."

"You can break those contracts with ridiculous ease," George said. "This is the era of the First Amendment. If guys can tell the CIA to shove their contracts, you can sure as hell do it to the Stapletons."

"Why are you so anxious to have me do this?"

George paused to light a cigarette. He took a long, slow drag. For a moment, Kilpatrick wondered if this was a carefully rehearsed performance. But the impact of the next words obliterated this flash of doubt.

"I want to destroy the Stapleton duty machine, once and for all. I want to save the souls and bodies of future generations from being consumed by that historic garbage grinder."

The patio door opened and Ned Stapleton emerged, followed by his father. The Judge was wearing dark brown jodhpurs and a tan open-necked riding shirt. Father and son unmistakably shared the same bloodlines. But there were striking differences, beyond Ned's shorter stature. There was a clouded, somewhat puzzled quality to Ned's eyes. He seemed to be straining to open them a little wider, to understand something that had somehow escaped him. His father's eyes had a clarity, a directness that riveted the attention. These were the eyes of a commander, of a man who had given men hard, perhaps impossible orders. The grim, unillusioned mouth, the frown lines on the forehead, the two deep indentations just above the hawkish nose, suggested he had given the same kind of orders to himself.

Kilpatrick felt an unnerving sense of penetration as he rose to meet Judge Paul Stapleton. Those eyes seemed to be reading, weighing and deciding his net worth as a human being while the slim tapering hand reached out to grasp his moist palm in a hard dry vise.

"Glad to see you again, Jim," he said, his lips parting in a formal, empty smile.

The voice told Kilpatrick something that he had sensed from Paul Stapleton's walk as the Judge came toward him. This was a very tired man. Each step had a slight wobble in it. For a hesitant second it existed as an entity

54

until the will insisted on another step. The voice had a dead spot, a kind of echoed thud at its very center, and the words—even these casual words of greeting—gave the same impression of special effort as the walk. At the same time those fierce eyes seemed to declare that the effort would be made, the necessary words spoken, the steps taken, as long as the body obeyed that commanding will.

George Stapleton stood up and said he had to go. "Stay for lunch, George," his father said. "We could use some literary common sense on this idea even if it's negative."

George shook his head. "I keep telling George that he ought to decide whether he's a poet or a lawyer. Then go all out in either direction," Paul Stapleton said. "That's what his brother Mark did. He decided to be an academic, and he's one of the best. He teaches a course in the corporation at Columbia Law School that gives the guys at Stapleton, Talbot violent headaches. But he's the best. He did it by concentrating his energy. It's how you win in peace and in war. Concentration of force."

"I keep telling him I don't like the metaphor," George said with a smile that struck Kilpatrick as strained. George shook hands with him, murmured something inconsequential about having a good lunch and departed.

A squat Indian in a white coat emerged from the central wing of the house. Paul Stapleton introduced him. "This is Sam Fry. He was with me in both world wars. He knows more about me than anyone else alive. But he's an Apache. That means he can't tell the truth, even if he wanted to."

With a ghost of a smile, Sam Fry shook hands and said he was there to take drink orders. Kilpatrick asked for his usual virgin mary. Paul Stapleton asked for bourbon, and Ned for scotch. When the orders arrived, Paul Stapleton raised his glass and said, "Welcome to the family, Jim. I've felt you've been a part of us ever since I read your letter about Randy."

Kilpatrick nodded. The words stirred seismic tremors in his chest.

"Even today I find it hard to believe he's gone. I find myself thinking that when the mail comes there'll be a

55

letter from him. It must be the way he died. In the plane crash. It's kind of like friends who got killed in the war in another theater. I guess the only deaths you really believe are the ones you see."

A thick-bodied gray-haired woman emerged from the center door, which probably led to the kitchen. At first Kilpatrick thought she was a servant. She was wearing a white apron. But her blue knit dress was clearly not a servant's uniform. Her complexion was dark and her skin rather wrinkled. But it was easy to see that her oval face had once been beautiful. She leaned on a cane as she walked slowly toward them.

"Forgetting his medicine as usual," she said.

"This is my wife, Maria—Jim Kilpatrick," Paul Stapleton said.

Kilpatrick was astonished. He had expected a tall, austere old lady in the classic Wasp tradition. This woman was Spanish and Indian, a Mexican heritage, if he read her physical appearance correctly. That explained where George Stapleton got his peasant looks, where Ned had inherited his short bulky body.

Paul Stapleton looked with distaste at two large pills his wife was carrying in her hand. He gulped them down and followed them with a healthy swig of bourbon.

"Have you ever seen a man who drank whiskey with his medicine?" Maria Stapleton asked Kilpatrick.

"The doctor said it wouldn't hurt me."

"You've got that poor man intimidated, like everyone else," Maria said.

"Sit down and have a drink with us."

"I have a lunch to cook."

She plodded back to the house.

"We can't get her out of that kitchen, no matter what we do," Ned said. "She doesn't believe anybody can cook for Dad the way she does."

"She's right," Paul Stapleton said. He put down his glass and leaned back in his chair. "What do you think of this damn-fool idea, Jim? Writing a book about an old coot like me, who has never done anything important enough to get more than a line or two in *Time* or *Newsweek*. Who's going to read it?"

"That's not the point," Ned said. "We don't want—or

56

need—a best seller. Every library in this city, in this state—would get a copy. Your friends in Washington—in New York—"

"The ones who know what I've done don't have to read it, Ned. The ones who don't know probably don't care."

Ned grew agitated. He was obviously not used to arguing with his father. "Randy would be for it. I know he would. He'd see it as a perfect way to refute the rotten things that people have said about you in the newspapers."

"Nobody pays attention to that stuff. Nobody worth worrying about, anyway. Do you think Randy would have been for it, Jim?"

"I think—he would have wanted to see something written about you. He was tremendously proud of you. He often talked about the three Distinguished Service Crosses you've won—"

"Did he ever tell you about the one he won?"

"No," Kilpatrick said.

"That's just like him, isn't it, Ned? He won his medal for taking on two German Tiger tanks at Falaise Gap and knocking them out, even though he had a shell splinter in his chest about a quarter of an inch from his heart."

Paul Stapleton took a rather large gulp of his bourbon. Kilpatrick sensed that he was unusually nervous. Ned was extremely tense. He was sitting on the edge of his chair, his whole body rigid.

"If there's one thing I've tried to get across to my sons, it's the importance of doing the job right. Who gets the credit doesn't mean a damn thing. If some of it comes your way, great. Randy operated that way in business, you know that, Jim. He was the man who ran that company. But Dwight Slocum got the write-ups in *Fortune* and *Business Week*. Randy didn't give a damn."

"A lot of other people did," Kilpatrick said.

"If they did, that was Randy's fault. He didn't get the message across to them."

"I think it's just human nature," Kilpatrick said. "We loved Randy and we despised Slocum."

A mournful shadow passed over Paul Stapleton's face. He seemed to be far away for a moment. Then he laughed harshly as if he was not really amused.

"I can understand that. I can understand it. Here's what I think about the book, Jim. It can't be just about me. That would contradict everything I've just been saying. I'd look like the biggest hypocrite in the world. It's got to be about the whole family."

"Damn it, Dad," Ned said, "that's not the book I want to see written. You're not just another name in a long procession of Stapletons."

"I appreciate your feelings, Ned, but that's the way I look to Jim here—and the rest of the world."

"Dad, excuse my French, but I've had it up to here with this modesty crap. I think it's about time we blew our goddamn horns—"

"Modesty *crap?* Did I hear you correctly?" Paul Stapleton said.

At first Kilpatrick thought he was censuring Ned's language. But the old man's rage was directed at the idea.

"Didn't you hear what I just said about credit? A Stapleton—a gentleman—doesn't ask for credit for anything he does. He does the right thing because it's worth doing. He accepts responsibility because he was born to accept it. He doesn't look for glory, because he doesn't need it."

Ned nodded mechanically throughout this reprimand. "Yes, Dad, I know. Yes, Dad," he said.

"I'm sure you didn't mean to put it that way," Paul Stapleton said, getting control of his temper. "I think there is some merit to getting the story of the family's achievements down on paper. But it has to be—objective. No horn blowing on anyone's part. If it was done that way, it would put—some perspective on what the newspapers have said recently. Which is nothing compared to what they've said in the past. We had a paper in town during the 1910s and 1920s that used to paint the Stapletons with horns growing out of their heads. The old Hamilton *Record.* It went out of business in 1934. Do you remember it, Jim?"

Kilpatrick shook his head. "I was only eight years old in 1934."

Somewhere inside the house, the telephone rang. Maria

Stapleton came out and said it was Kevin McGuire, the president of the Board of Education. He needed the Judge's advice on some problems that had emerged from last night's board meeting.

"Excuse me, Jim," Paul Stapleton said, and plodded into the house.

"They're trying to wear him down," Ned said. "They won't hire or fire a janitor without asking him first."

"Ned," the Judge said from the doorway of the house. "Maybe you ought to listen on the extension. I don't trust this guy."

Ned left Kilpatrick sitting alone. A few minutes later, Maria Stapleton emerged to ask him if he wanted another drink. Kilpatrick said he'd have another virgin mary.

Maria Stapleton smiled. "It sounds a little sacrilegious. But I'm sure the Virgin doesn't mind for a good cause. You don't drink alcohol?"

"I used to drink too much of it," Kilpatrick said.

Maria Stapleton nodded. "My father's name was O'Reilly. He had a brother with the same problem. It's a terrible thing among the Irish."

While Kilpatrick tried to make sense out of that remark, Maria Stapleton got him his virgin mary. She sat down opposite him and smiled shyly.

"So you are going to write a book about us," she said.

"It looks that way," Kilpatrick said.

"I saw the letter you wrote about Randy. I hope you will write it—the book—in that spirit. You have the power to hurt us. You must know that."

"I don't—I haven't thought of it that way," Kilpatrick said.

"We are not gods. None of us. Try to remember that, Mr. Kilpatrick."

Kilpatrick nodded. What was going on? Were they giving him some sort of test? Each trying to spook him in a different way?

"Randy was a good son. I miss him, even though I seldom saw him. He always found time to write us letters. He wrote me as many letters as he wrote his father. About different things. Do you have children?"

"Yes. Five. Four now."

"What happened?"

"My oldest son was killed in Vietnam."

"Is that why your eyes are so sad? It must be several years ago now."

"I suppose that's the big reason."

"I don't mean to imply you should not be sad. No one can judge another person's grief. The name Kilpatrick suggests you are a Catholic. Doesn't your faith help you?"

Kilpatrick shook his head. "I'm not a Catholic any more."

"I see. And your wife?"

"I'm divorced."

"You have several reasons to be sad. Would you mind if I prayed for you?"

Maria Stapleton spoke in the same casual voice that she had used when she had asked him what he was drinking. Kilpatrick discovered that the question made him angry. He had an impulse to snarl *yes*. But he masked it with a shrug.

"It can't do any harm."

"You never pray? Not even to an unknown god, a guiding spirit?"

"No."

Paul Stapleton and Ned emerged from the house and walked toward them. "More of the same old nonsense," the Judge said as they sat down. "They want me to lose my temper, do something rash, extreme, that they can appeal."

Sam Fry came out the kitchen door followed by two small, Mexican-looking houseboys. The Apache was carrying a big dish of paella. One of the boys carried a cut-glass salad bowl full of sliced fruit, the other a pitcher of iced tea.

The paella was delicious. Kilpatrick praised it.

"That's how this woman has kept me around for sixty years," Paul Stapleton said as Maria gave Kilpatrick a generous second helping. "Basically I think I'm just a dogface or a grunt, as they called them in Korea and Vietnam. Feed me well and I'm happy."

60

"Lately you haven't had the appetite of a flea," Maria said.

"Tell Jim about your first DSC, Dad, the one where you saved this guy's life," Ned said.

Ned pointed to Sam Fry, who was tossing the salad a few feet away.

For a moment Paul Stapleton looked very tired. "I've told you three or four times, Ned, I don't think those medals deserve more than a line each in the book."

"I don't agree," Ned said. "Your war service is the heart of the book, in my opinion."

"Why don't you just tell the story, Paul," Maria said. "I'm sure Mr. Kilpatrick will place it in the proper perspective."

"The whole thing was an accident," Paul Stapleton said. "I was in the Tank Corps in World War I. We were operating near a river called the Rupt de Mad. The Dutchmen were dug into one of those small French woods about two hundred and fifty yards ahead of us on the opposite bank. They were banging away at us with machine guns. Our Apache friend here was my driver. We were putting along at the usual four miles an hour. I was up in the turret shooting back at them. Those old tanks were pretty crude affairs. The driver sat down in the bottom like a man in a coffin. He couldn't see a thing. The officer in the turret gave orders by kicking him. The left foot to turn left, the right foot to turn right, and so forth."

"Two kicks in the head meant back up, right?" Ned said.

"I think so. Do you remember, Sam?"

"Two kicks, back up," Sam Fry said.

"We were moving right along the riverbank. It had been a pretty wet spring and the ground was mushy. All of a sudden the damn embankment gave way and our tank went kerplunk into the Rupt de Mad. The thing sank like a stone. I was in the turret and had no trouble getting out. The Germans in the woods decided I was a better target than the other tanks and started shooting at me. I swam to the opposite bank, where I had some cover from their fire. It was my first time in action and I was pretty

61

upset about losing my tank. Only when I got to the riverbank did I realize that Sam was stuck down in the bottom of the damn thing.

"I knew it was almost impossible to kill an Apache, but when he didn't come up, I began to think I might have succeeded. I couldn't let that happen to the best horseman in the U. S. Army. Sam and I had been in the cavalry together in Mexico, and I had talked him into joining the Tank Corps with me. So I had to give those German machine guns a few more shots at me while I swam back and dove down and got him out of that tank. Frankly, I had nothing to worry about from the machine guns. They can't hit anything at two hundred and fifty yards. I had a lot more trouble getting him out of that tank without drowning both of us."

"And then you had to drag him back through the machine-gun fire to the riverbank again," Ned said.

He had a boyish smile on his face. His eyes were bright with pleasure. Thirty or more of his years had vanished, and he was listening to the story for the first time, probably told by Sam Fry, about the marvelous man called Father.

"Right. The Germans weren't too impressed by my act. But if you want to hit a single man, the last weapon you should use is a machine gun. A couple of riflemen could have picked us off in ten seconds. Anyway, the commander of the Tank Corps, Colonel George Patton, happened to be sitting in his tank watching the show. He decided the outfit needed a medal and he wrote me up for the DSC. Patton had lots of clout. He'd been on Pershing's staff. So I got it."

"You deserved it," Ned said. "My God, how many other men would do such a thing?"

"Ned," Paul Stapleton said, "how many times have I told you that for every man who gets a medal, there are a thousand who do more courageous things and don't get one. Because they get killed, or their commanding officer gets killed, or the CO is having a fight with the general and he couldn't get an overnight pass out of the old bastard, much less a medal. Were you in combat, Jim?"

"Forty-one missions over Germany."

"No kidding. Now you wouldn't get me to do that for

all the gold in Fort Knox. Planes scare the hell out of me. They always have. I fly in them, but I'm sweating all the time. The thought of being up there with ten thousand German antiaircraft guns and a few hundred Focke-Wulfs looking for me would have turned my hair gray on the spot."

"You got used to it," Kilpatrick said.

"I admired our airmen in both wars. Especially in the second one. I remember Italy. We were dug into those foxholes up to our eyebrows. Every day we'd watch the planes come in and take terrific punishment from those German eighty-eights. People say Vietnam was a mess. There was the mess to top them all. That Italian campaign."

"Except we won that war," Ned said.

"The hell we did. We'd still be sitting outside Cassino if the Russians and Eisenhower's army hadn't chewed their way into Germany. The Germans beat the hell out of us in Italy. The Americans have gotten the hell kicked out of them at least once in every war we've been in. Usually it's been our own stupid fault."

Sam Fry removed the remains of the paella and served the fruit. Kilpatrick glanced at Ned. He looked unhappy.

"Ned doesn't like to hear me talk this way," Paul Stapleton said. "He wants this book to be a tract that will restore his kids' patriotism. But nobody can do that for them. I have a different reason for wanting to underwrite this book. I got it from this crazy Indian."

He gestured toward Sam Fry, who plunked a dish of mixed fruit in front of him.

"Last week I went riding with old Rain-in-the-Face here. We got talking about dying. For the first time he told me how it felt when I temporarily abandoned him in that tank at the bottom of the Rupt de Mad. Tell them what you said, Sam."

The Apache ignored the rest of them. He kept his eyes on Paul Stapleton. "I died down there in that tank. I let my soul go. I was outside watching you swim through the machine-gun fire. I saw you go down, pull me out and haul me back to shore like a sack of meal."

"How did it feel to let your soul go?"

"Good. I felt free. I thought I would go home and leap

like a puma from mountaintop to mountaintop. I felt I could do anything. I was angry when you pulled me back."

"Tell them what you said when I asked you if you were still sore at me."

A scowl turned the lined coppery face into a menacing mask. For the Apache it was a kind of play. Kilpatrick wondered if he had rehearsed the words many times before he said them to Paul Stapleton.

"Only when I see you still working yourself to death for no good reason. You would never see an Indian do that. They let their old men sit by the fire and dream back their lives. They purify their spirits that way. When death comes, they are ready."

"I told him I was ready to die right now."

The Apache shook his head, still in the play. "You are ready to die like a warrior in battle. You should die like the chief of a tribe. They summon everyone to listen to them. They tell the story of their lives. The young people learn from the good things they did. The old people help them mourn the mistakes."

"There's my reason, Jim," Paul Stapleton said, riveting Kilpatrick with those intense eyes. "To tell young people—not just members of the Stapleton tribe—some of the good things I think I've tried to do, that the family's done, and some of the bad things. Maybe together we can mourn a few mistakes and praise a few men who deserve more credit than they've gotten so far. They don't include me, I assure you."

Kilpatrick sipped his iced tea and nodded, ostensibly the calm, competent professional writer. Behind this façade, a voice told him it was no longer a question of wanting or not wanting to do this book. He had to do it. He had to dive to the bottom of this man's life and see what he found there.

Paul Stapleton suggested that Jim go see his son Mark first, and then his sister Agatha. "Mark will put us in perspective," he said with a smile. "He won't tell you very many good things about me. But maybe I can convince you that I'm not as bad as he thinks I am. Agatha has a lot of family memorabilia and some pretty interesting thoughts about us."

Paul Stapleton drained his iced-tea glass and put it down on the table with a judicial rap. "What do you think, Jim? Do you want to do this thing? I'm not telling you how to write it. All I want from you is a promise to give us your best."

"You've got it," Jim Kilpatrick said.

Paul Stapleton held out his hand. As Kilpatrick shook it, he thought: *You aren't going to get me, old man.* In a darker corner of his skull, another voice asked: *Is he your last hope?*

VI

Agatha Stapleton Slocum walked swiftly down the curving hall of the Anne Randolph Stapleton Hospice for the dying. The hundred-bed facility was housed in a graceful poured-concrete building shaped like a coil. It rose beside the rigid rectangular towers of the city's Medical Center like an organic creature.

It was five o'clock, time for only one more visit. Agatha spent almost every afternoon here, working as an ordinary volunteer. All the members of the board of trustees were expected to work as volunteers. They took a six-week course from the training psychiatrist to prepare them for the five states of mind through which the dying usually passed: denial, anger, bargaining, depression—and finally—hopefully—acceptance.

Her last patient of the day, Mrs. Malloy, was an obese middle-aged woman with cancer of the liver. She was in the angry stage. Agatha sat and listened while Mrs. Malloy criticized the nurses, the food, even the Catholic chaplain, who she said was smug. "I ast him what I'd done to deserve this and he said only I could answer that question. Ain't that smug, Mrs. Slocum? I call it smug.

Snotty. I tole my pastor about him, when he visited me yesterday. I tole him to tell the archbishop."

"He's a very dedicated young priest," Agatha said. "I'm sure he didn't intend to be smug. But I admit—it does sound that way. I suppose—what he was trying to get you to do is talk it over with God. Accept His will."

"I don't accept nothin'," Mrs. Malloy snapped. Her eyes suddenly filled with tears. "What I really want is to go to my son's weddin'," she said. "It's in November."

Agatha nodded. "Maybe you can," she said. Bargaining for time was a good sign. It was often a turning point.

"Agatha?"

It was her brother Paul. He stood in the doorway of Mrs. Malloy's room. The late-afternoon fall sun pouring through the banks of windows in the outside wall made him look ghostly. Even ghastly, Agatha thought. He was being devoured, day by day, in his courtroom. The harsh natural light made the skin of his cheeks seem papery. His neck, that proud trunk of life that was once as supple as the bole of a birch tree, seemed withered and forlorn. But he still carried himself with the ramrod back and braced shoulders of youth. For a moment she could hear their grandfather's voice snarling: "Stand up straight. Get those shoulders back. You too, Agatha."

"Paul," Agatha said. "What a nice surprise. Come in."

Paul entered, wrinkling his nose with distaste at the odors in the room. All his life he had been a fastidious man. Dirt, stenches of all kinds, repelled him. By an odd reverse, Agatha had been a tomboy who had never been bothered by smells or smears.

"This is my brother, Paul Stapleton," she said to Mrs. Malloy.

The woman's eyes widened with shock, then squeezed small again. "Judge Stapleton?" she said.

"Yes," Agatha said.

"And you're a Stapleton?"

"Yes. Slocum is my married name."

"I don't wanna see you again."

"Now now, Mrs. Malloy. Don't feel that way. Don't let old feelings that are meaningless now distract you from—"

"They ain't meaningless to me. My father worked in your lousy goddamn mills. He went out on strike in '26 and never got his job back. Now you're tellin' us to send our kids to school with niggers. I don't wanna see you again. Get out. Get outta my room."

Paul's face was a mask. He turned and strode into the hall. Agatha did not follow him. She sat quietly beside Mrs. Malloy's bed.

"You hurt him a great deal," she said.

"Good. I feel better than I felt in a long time."

"You hurt me too."

"I'm—I'm sorry about that. You been a friend, a real friend. You probably didn't have nothin' to do with all that old stuff."

"It is old, isn't it?"

"But he did. Him and his lousy rotten brother."

"He was my brother too."

Mrs. Malloy twisted in the bed. "I need a pain pill," she said. "Can you get me one?"

"Of course. I'll send the nurse down. Can I visit you again tomorrow?"

"Sure, if you wanna. Listen. I'm sorry."

In the hall, Agatha tried to explain to her brother that Mrs. Malloy was still in the angry stage. She was treating everyone badly. He dismissed Mrs. Malloy with a wave of his hand. "An ignorant mick," he said.

Inwardly Agatha recoiled from this hard, cold side of her brother's character. It reminded her of scenes she preferred to forget. They walked down the hall together. Agatha took his arm and forced herself to remember the way they used to stroll arm in arm to tea dances at the Fairview Hotel in the spring and fall.

"What brings you here? Do you want an inspection tour to see what we're doing with your money?"

Paul Stapleton had donated well over $250,000 to the hospice. It had not come in a lump sum. Agatha had had to extract it from him, in various-sized pieces. He had not opposed the Anne Randolph Stapleton Hospice. But his support had been distinctly lukewarm. Agatha understood

68

why, and quietly contrived to deal with it, without once confronting the reason for Paul's lack of warmth. She was glad on the whole that they had been able to handle it in the usual oblique Stapleton style. She knew how painful it would have been for Paul to admit that he had hated their mother, Anne Randolph Stapleton.

Now, over a decade of dealing with the dying had made Agatha a little impatient with the Stapleton tradition of intense personal privacy, of noncommunication of ugly emotions. Occasionally she found herself yearning for the kind of brutal honesty she frequently heard at the hospice.

Paul was saying that he would like a tour, but he didn't have the time. He had come down to the hospice to give her a ride home.

"There's something I want to talk over with you," he said.

She knew it must be the book. She felt burdened by her inability to decide what she felt about it. Sometimes she thought Peregrine was right, a dispassionate, reasonably honest account of the family's history would be a good thing. It was time they got down off their pedestals. But she still recoiled from disentangling what was reasonably honest from what could never be revealed to the merciless public.

By a miracle, she remembered to tell the floor nurse to give Mrs. Malloy a Darvon. Downstairs she dismissed her taxi driver with his usual five-dollar tip and said she would see him tomorrow at the same time.

"You still come in every day?" Paul Stapleton asked as they walked to his Mercedes.

"Yes."

"Three times a week would be enough, it seems to me. You're seventy-five years old, you know."

"Good God, do you have to remind me?" Agatha said, getting into the car. She said hello to Paul's chauffeur, Sam Fry, and won a brief smile from his expressionless Apache face.

"Maria's pretty lonely at the farm. It would be nice if you spent a few hours with her now and then."

"Is that her idea, or yours? Ever since Randy's death she's seemed—almost in another world."

69

Paul Stapleton nodded. "I know. But she's better now. A little better."

"Did she see it as punishment of some sort?" Agatha asked.

Paul was honestly baffled by the question. "Why should she do that?"

"She has a very personal relationship with God."

And you don't, Agatha added mournfully to herself.

"I've always felt Maria's religion—everybody's religion—was a private matter," he said.

Agatha knew how much those words omitted. She also knew it was useless to argue with him. "Of course," she said.

They were moving through the midtown traffic toward the expressway. Paul looked out at the familiar streets. "I think I told you at dinner on my birthday that Ned wanted me to underwrite a book. He calls it my biography. He thinks it's time we answered the slanders against us, once and for all. That story in the paper got him heated up on the idea all over again. Now he's got Walter Ackroyd to back him. Walter's afraid all this negative publicity will be bad for the firm."

"I never liked that man," Agatha said. "He's a flatterer."

"Ned says he needs the book for his kids. He's especially worried about my namesake, Paul, the boy who was suspended from Pennsgrove last year. He's pretty cynical. Ned thinks learning something about the family could change his attitude."

"Utter nonsense," Agatha said.

Ten years ago, Agatha mused, I wouldn't have been able to say that. Twenty years ago I wouldn't even have thought it.

For a quailing moment she wondered if it had been wise to think or say it. Paul Stapleton shook his head in an abrupt angry way that reminded Agatha of their grandfather. She could see that terrible old man at the dinner table, feel the curt shake of that death's-head like a blow as she or Paul or someone else was told that they were wrong, wrong.

"I admit there's no point in answering those newspaper attacks. Grandfather had the right idea about them back

70

in 1912. Ignore them. But I think there are some things that might be worth saying to the younger generation. Maybe even someone like Allyn could be helped—"

"How?"

"I'm not sure," Paul admitted.

"Paul," Agatha said. "You know what I think about Allyn. She has to get the anger out of her system. Remember your own—experience. How rebellious you felt once. Remember me in the full flower of my revolutionary rage, fifty years ago."

Again that abrupt shake of the head. "You were imitating Mother. I was—running away. But I knew what I was running from. These kids don't know anything. I've heard you say it yourself. They have no sense of history."

"They're typical Americans."

"Agatha. A Stapleton is not a typical American. A Stapleton stands for something."

Agatha sighed. Suddenly she found herself invaded by Peregrine's iconoclastic spirit.

"Maybe we should stop doing that. Maybe this book you're talking about should explain why we've stopped."

Paul was genuinely, deeply shocked. "We haven't stopped. What I'm trying to do in the city is part of it. Until the day of his death Randy was acting it out, living it out, at the head of one of the biggest corporations in the country."

How could he go on believing that about Randy? Agatha wondered. She wished it were true. It would have meaning, deep meaning for her too. But everything she knew contradicted it. For her as well as for him, it was too painful to argue about Randy. She turned to other evidence.

"I don't think Ned and George are interested in standing for anything larger than the pursuit of their hobbies— yachting, poetry."

"Maybe this book could change them too. It might even change—Mark's mind."

Agatha saw what an effort it cost him even to say Mark's name. "I've told you before—I think you were in the wrong there as much as Mark was. But I don't think the book would tell him anything that he couldn't get

71

from a biography of Louis Brandeis or Oliver Wendell Holmes."

"I don't understand it. I thought you'd be enthusiastic about this book. All the time you've spent on the family's history—"

"I like history—especially the family's history—because I'm nosy. I love to read old diaries and letters because they take me inside people's lives. I've never had any interest in using the past to persuade future generations of Stapletons to imitate us. If you're going to have a book written, it ought to free them from the past. Encourage them to stand for something. But not necessarily what we stood for. Think of what it cost us."

Paul Stapleton frowned into the rush-hour traffic on the expressway. "Agatha. I've never done anything in connection with you that wasn't aimed at your happiness."

"I know you haven't. But that doesn't mean I have no regrets. Any more than you have none."

He did not meet her eyes. For a moment Agatha felt discouraged. At eighty, he still refused to face the truth about himself. That was probably why he was still driving himself, working fourteen hours a day on this busing mess. It was easier than facing the truth.

"I really think the young people only need time," Agatha said. "The country's gone through so much turmoil. The last thing they want is a lecture on how great we were. They just won't believe it."

"Someone needs to show them that no matter how bad things get, a few people have to keep their heads, stand up for the old ideals."

"I think the young people want to find the ideals for themselves," Agatha said. "It's the difference between weaving a design on your own loom and buying it in a shop. You value the one you create more than anything you buy. Just give them time to do a little thinking."

"I haven't got time. I had another one of those strokes at the dinner table the other night."

"Oh," Agatha said, seeing again the enormous weariness on his face.

"I passed out in the chair. I woke up in about five minutes. But the doctor says there's no telling when the big one will come."

72

"I can't—imagine life without you," Agatha said.

Suddenly she was no longer the serene wise sister. She was a woman who needed this strong man. No matter that his strength was contorted and dangerous. She wanted and needed his power. Then she was beyond it, beyond the clutching hand of the past, in the present where old age made the future, that chief source of anxiety, no longer threatening.

"I'm going to try it," Paul said, oblivious to the tremor he had just sent through Agatha's spirit. "Ned's got a writer picked out. I'm so damned busy in court, I hope you can give him some help. The way I see it, the book won't be about me. I'll just come in at the end, with my few flourishes. Father and Grandfather are the really important ones. You can tell him as much about them as I can. Maybe more."

They were leaving the city on the expressway. The meadowlands created by one of the guardian river's several branches waved like golden wheat in the slanted rays of the September sun.

"I disagree with your modesty almost as much as I disagree with your psychology," Agatha said. "You are as important in your own way in your own time as Father and Grandfather were in their time. If you hope to have any impact on your sons or your grandchildren, you must tell your story from the inside, discuss not merely events but their inner meaning. Psychological truth. That's what counts today."

She could see that Paul simply did not understand her. "I'm willing to tell as much of the truth as can be told."

"No one else can tell certain things—like what happened to you in 1913 down on the River of Doubt."

"What do you mean?" he said, tension gripping his voice, deepening it to a hostile growl. "You know what happened."

"As far as you're concerned, I know nothing. You've never discussed it with me. What little I know I've acquired second or third hand."

Again that abrupt shake of the head. "I don't think that sort of stuff is relevant. Basically, we want to make the Stapletons look good. We don't have to tell any big lies. Compared to the rest of the country—"

73

"Everything you've said—about the grandchildren, your sons—requires something much more subtle. There is no point in hiring a hack to grind out a lot of clichés about the Stapletons as great Americans. Dwight Slocum tried to glorify the Slocums that way ten years ago. It was atrocious trash, as you might expect."

Paul smiled in a wintry, weary way. "You make this sound like hard work."

"It will be, if you take it seriously. It will be hard for me too. I will have to collect my thoughts rather carefully. You can't leave Dwight Slocum out of the story."

Again, her brother's reaction was fiercely negative.

"I can't see making that sort of thing public."

"Why not?"

Agatha was feeling more and more reckless. She was enjoying this opportunity to give advice to a man who had tried to run her life more than once. She recognized residues of resentment in her mood, the younger sister against the older brother, the young rebel against the stern voice that had lectured her. But she dismissed this twinge of conscience and plunged on.

"You know what I'd like to see? One book that told the whole truth. It would be put away in the family vault for another fifty or a hundred years. Another book that would tell as much of the story as we want the public to know."

Paul Stapleton said nothing. The idea clearly appalled him. He sat there for a good ten miles, while they hummed past acres of identical row houses in the city's middle-class suburbs.

"I see—some value in your idea of getting at a kind of—inner truth."

He did see it. But she could see that he dreaded trying to do it.

They were silent for another ten miles. "Grandfather," Paul said. "What do we do with him?"

"The truth, in all its horror."

"No. I understand him now. I appreciate him."

"Remarkable," Agatha said dryly.

"And Father too."

"Do you really?" she said.

He did not answer her. He did not ask her for her

opinion. He sensed that she had one. But he did not want to hear it. It was preternatural, the way the Stapletons understood what could be said, what had to be avoided, without violating their mutual privacy.

Another long silence. They swung off the expressway and turned right toward New Grange town center. In five minutes Sam Fry was braking to a stop in front of Agatha's house.

"We haven't really talked about these things," Paul said.

"No."

"I've wanted to. But there's never been enough time."

There was something quintessentially American about that plea, Agatha thought. An eighty-year-old man was telling his seventy-five-year-old sister who had lived less than a mile from him for the past twenty-five years that there had never been enough time to talk about the roots of their lives.

"What's the writer's name? Do I know him?"

"Kilpatrick. James Kilpatrick. He wrote a history book that Ned says won a prize from the state historical society. He used to work for Randy at National Products."

"I know the book. *The Vanished Battle*. Competent. But does it make sense to expect an Irish-American to understand us? I gather that's what Mr. Kilpatrick is, from his name."

"He worked for Randy. He was his speech writer. When Randy died Kilpatrick wrote me a letter, telling me how much Randy meant to him. Kilpatrick said that his father had taught him to hate us. But Randy changed his mind."

"How?"

"I—I don't know. By being Randy, I guess. He was the best of the boys, Agatha."

"He was a good man. But the others have tried to be good men too."

She sensed he was asking her for an explanation of Randy's death. Even a man who believed in nothing but a blind impersonal fate felt a need to see some kind of method, purpose, in its workings. She had an explanation, but she did not think it would help him. He would not believe it. She let the moment pass.

"You may be right about your approach to the book," Paul said. "We certainly don't want a cheap puff. If I'm not around when it's finished, I want you to look it over. You'll have the final authority to decide what should go in, what should be left out."

"I'll do my best. But I still don't like Kilpatrick as the writer. He sounds—unstable."

"No more than any Irishman. They all live by their emotions."

And we don't? Agatha thought. Perhaps that is our fatal flaw. Telling ourselves we don't.

"Kilpatrick can be handled. We'll write a contract that guarantees that you—or even Ned—can handle him."

Agatha saw that he had not arranged this talk to seek her advice. He was giving her orders, as usual. Resentment flickered in her mind. But the negative emotion was countered by the compassion that Agatha had come to feel for her brother, after years of primary hatred. She suddenly found herself wondering if those old spiritual wounds could bleed again. It was not a pleasant thought. She tried to deflect it by telling herself that at least Paul had taken her advice seriously. But there was no way of knowing whether he would act on it. In the end, he would do what he thought best, as usual.

"Would you like to come in for a cup of tea?" she asked.

"No, thanks," Paul said with terse minimal courtesy. He still loathed the sight of their homosexual first cousin, Peregrine. He had violently opposed Agatha's decision to offer Peregrine refuge when he ran out of money ten years ago. Only once a year, at the family dinner celebrating Paul's birthday, would he deign to shake Peregrine's hand.

Sam Fry opened the rear door and helped Agatha out of the car. She mounted the steps to the porch, thinking about what she had heard and felt. She was still disturbed by the extravagance of James Kilpatrick's attitude toward Randy and the family. She did not like the idea of the Stapletons being part of anyone's creed. She disliked all forms of idol worship. *Thou shalt have no other gods before me*, said the First Commandment. Anyone who

76

tried to make gods out of the Stapletons was going to be tremendously disappointed.

Before she could get out her keys, Peregrine opened the door. He looked down the street after the departing Mercedes. "Was that the Great Man giving you a ride home?"

"Yes."

"Did anything interesting transpire?"

"He's decided to do the book."

Agatha did not like the greedy anticipation in Peregrine's eyes. She did not like greed in any shape or form. She let Peregrine know it.

"He's given me the final authority on what goes into it—if he dies before it's finished."

Peregrine was undismayed. He obviously believed, in spite of the years they had spent apart, that he and Agatha were still one in spirit. Agatha found herself wondering if he was right.

VII

"Busing, then," Mark Stapleton said, gathering the pages of his lecture and noting that he was in the final thirty seconds, "is the kind of crude device used by unimaginative judges to solve a social problem that requires finesse and patience. It might be compared to trying to perform surgery on the body politic with a nightstick. Surely the genius of the American people can invent a better tool to make equal education a guarantee for all our citizens."

The applause was satisfying but far from thunderous. The audience was largely fellow legal scholars, gathered at Columbia for the annual fall symposium on public law. Mark Stapleton had no difficulty imagining what they were thinking. He's done it again. Grabbed the lead horse on the great liberal merry-go-round and justified it with dubious logic and impeccable scholarship.

That was good enough for Mark Stapleton. Being first on the liberal merry-go-round was the name of the academic game even if the rider regarded the whole process with contempt. His book, *The Just Society,* which argued that equal rights meant equal economic results, was the most talked-about piece of legal theory since

Adolf Berle's *The Modern Corporation and Private Property*. His course, Public Law and the Corporation, had sent legions of students out to do battle with the big business dragons. A *Newsweek* reporter had called him the most influential legal scholar of his generation.

Mark Stapleton had written *Newsweek* a bristling letter denouncing the reporter for gross exaggeration and asking why the fellow had not quoted his repeated insistence that he doubted all generalizations, including his own. He did concede that the reporter had gotten one thing straight. He was determined to press the premises of American liberalism to their logical conclusions, even if they ultimately proved to be absurd.

Mark limped offstage and went down the hall to his office, ignoring potential critics and congratulators. Performing in public was always an ordeal for him. All his lectures were honed to exquisite precision in long hours at the typewriter, and then delivered in the driest, most offhand fashion. It often took students three months to discover that every word was vital if they hoped to pass the course.

"There's a gentleman waiting to see you, Professor Stapleton," said Hilda Zimmer, his severe blond secretary, as he passed her desk. "He went to hear your lecture. He should be back any moment."

"What's his name?"

"Kilpatrick. He says he's writing a book about your father."

"I'll see him."

In his office, Mark sat down at his bare desk and picked up the latest letter from his father. He held it in the aluminum claw that served as his right hand. The claw was attached to a plastic tube that was in turn attached to the stump of his arm, just below the elbow. The letter was three pages long, single-spaced. It described in detail the problems Paul Stapleton was having with busing foes in the city, the economic and legal woes plaguing Stapleton, Talbot and his personal problems with Mark's brother George. Finally there was a discussion of the objectives of the foundation that he planned to establish with his stock from National Products, Inc., and his hope that Mark would serve on the board of trustees.

It was all in flat, understated prose without any personal adjectives or exclamations of distress. It could almost have been written in the third person.

"Professor Stapleton?"

Kilpatrick stood in the doorway, a big red-headed Irishman with a 1950s haircut and a melancholy mouth. He shook hands and said he had enjoyed the lecture. It had been a surprise. He had not expected to hear Judge Paul Stapleton's son criticize busing as a solution to school integration.

"It would not be an exaggeration to say I've made a career out of criticizing my father," Mark said. "That is *not* for publication in this opus you've undertaken."

Kilpatrick's mouth tightened. For Mark Stapleton, it was a familiar expression. Most people did not like him. He was always at the bottom of every student popularity poll among his fellow Columbia Law School professors.

"Does your father know you've decided busing is a mistake?"

"He'll find out. The lecture is being published this month in the *Journal of Public Law*. Someone at Stapleton, Talbot will send him a copy."

"You won't?"

"We don't communicate very much."

"Why not?"

"Because it's a waste of time. I can't change his mind and he can't change mine."

"Aren't there other reasons to communicate with your father?"

"Not with my father."

Mark paused, wondering how much of the truth he should bother to tell this man. "He does try to communicate with me. For the last few years he's written me a letter a month."

"Do you answer them?"

"Occasionally. But most of them don't really require an answer."

"What does he write about?"

"Family business. All sorts of things I don't want to hear. Sometimes he asks my advice. I sent him a couple of things I wrote on busing, in the days when judicial activism was in flower."

"Now you've sort of left him out on the limb you grew—or shall we say grafted—on the constitutional trunk?"

Not bad, Mark Stapleton thought. Kilpatrick had a few brain cells. He smiled briefly. "That's the way our American world turns. Not even the law is immune to the dynamo of change. Yesterday's wisdom is today's stupidity. Why do you want to see me? I don't have anything very eulogistic to say about the Stapletons."

"Your father said you were the family intellectual. He said you could sum them up better than anyone. He's going to stick to the specifics of his experience."

"My father is a snob. He tries not to be, but he can't help it. He looks down on Irish, Jews, Italians, blacks, Poles—anyone who isn't a member of the Great Race. Do you know what I'm referring to?"

Kilpatrick shook his head. Mark sighed, and looked at his office ceiling. Why did people attempt books which they were obviously unqualified to write?

"The full title is *The Passing of the Great Race* by Madison Grant. It shaped the thinking of my father's entire generation. My father's brother, my uncle, Malcolm, considered Grant divinely inspired, on a par with the four evangelists. He could quote him by the page. My father, being a little more balanced emotionally, has managed to avoid the cruder manifestations of Grant's racism. He'd never dream of joining the Ku Klux Klan or the John Birch Society, but in his heart he doesn't trust anyone who isn't descended from the ancestral stock, as my uncle, Malcolm used to call it.

"Malcolm was only a step away from being a Nazi. Before the war, he'd sit at the dinner table and harangue us on bloodlines. That was when I started to think there was something wrong with the Stapletons. Dad should have thrown the son of a bitch out of the house, even if he was his brother.

"Actually, that's a retrospective opinion. In those days all I got was a feeling of uneasiness. Until I went in the Army, I was as brainwashed as the rest of the family. I blame that on my older brother Randy. He should have given us some leadership. He should have defended us against Dad. Instead, he was the chief collaborator. He and Dad were always incredibly close. It was almost a mystic thing. Randy worshipped him from birth, I guess.

"It was unfair to the rest of us. We could never hope to equal Randy's devotion. He was three years older than I was—just enough to make him unchallengeable. Not that I wanted to challenge him. I liked him. Everybody liked Randy. I don't think I ever met a man or woman who didn't like him. I never saw him lose his temper, though God knows I tried hard enough to get him to lose it when we were growing up.

"I was always the family troublemaker. I liked to argue, disagree, debate things. That wasn't the way the Stapletons operated. As Dad saw it, there was a Stapleton way of doing things—and any other way was wrong.

"Another thing that got me into trouble was religion. I didn't go for it. I think I saw through its essential idiocy when I was about nine. Randy, as usual, was just the opposite. I suspect that he was a secret Catholic. Once I caught him praying in front of a little statue of the Virgin of Guadalupe that Mother kept in a drawer in her bedroom. I think she prayed to it too, in the middle of the night. Randy made me promise not to tell Dad. Religion was a pretty tense issue in our house. Dad was determined not to let any of us become Catholics. He said no son of his was going to take orders from an Irish archbishop or an Italian pope. Mother accepted this decree like she accepted everything else about the Stapletons. But she stayed a Catholic in many ways—her devotion to the Virgin Mary, for instance. She was always telling us stories of the miracles the Virgin performed. I used to laugh in her face. Naturally, this made me something less than her favorite son."

Mark Stapleton fiddled with a pen on his desk. He was talking much too personally. He was annoyed at himself. He had not thought about these things for a long time. In the fiercely intellectual world in which he lived, the personal was an idiosyncrasy, an excrescence. He had no desire to re-examine the dead, irrelevant past.

"The Stapletons were really quite typical of the evolution of upper-class American Protestantism," he said. "Instead of faith, which was really rather vulgar, not to say stupid, and smacked of Catholicism, the religion of

82

the lower classes, the Stapletons had ideals. We scorned graft and corruption, we honored father and mother, respected the purity of women, succored the poor and fought bravely when our country called us to war, not out of some demeaning desire for salvation in another life, or a callow fear of a God of judgment. We did those things because they were *right,* because we were the upholders of the ideal."

"You don't think so now?"

"I hope you're not as naïve as you sound, Mr. Kilpatrick. Read the history of the textile industry. You'll find out how we succored the poor. It should be spelled s-u-c-k-e-r-e-d. Dig into the history of the New Jersey legislature. You'll find us down in Trenton bribing with the best of them. We're part of the unsavory history of post-Civil War America. Perhaps our only difference was, we tried to keep up appearances, which is more than one could say for the nouveaux riches like the Goulds, the Fiskes, the Slocums."

"Are you saying that your father is a hypocrite?"

"Not really. Like most people, he simply doesn't stop to examine the contradictions between his ideals and reality. He's not alone in this tendency. Communists, Catholics, liberals, all do it. They all get very uptight when dissidents like me point out the contradictions. That's what happened between me and my father. After law school, he wanted me to go to work for Stapleton, Talbot. He saw me as the next managing partner. I told him I didn't plan to spend my life defending corporations, cooking up clever dodges to beat the inheritance laws. I didn't want to be an apologist for the very, very rich. We exchanged some rather nasty words and I went into academia."

"Where you've been arguing with him from a distance ever since," Kilpatrick said with a wry smile.

"Let's not take that witticism too literally," Mark said.

"Do you ever visit him?"

"I go home for my mother's birthday and sometimes at Christmas. But we keep the conversation impersonal."

For a moment Kilpatrick looked discouraged. He was not getting very many meaty details. Mark toyed with telling him the truth about his split with his father, telling

83

him about Dawn. But he ruefully reminded himself that the story did not have the right kind of ending. Nor was it the sort of thing he wanted to share with a stranger. It was much too personal.

Kilpatrick began asking him about his career. While Mark gave him perfunctory answers, Dawn's sad face swayed behind his eyes. He was back in New Grange Farm with his black fiancée, challenging his father. While Dawn and Maria chatted in the kitchen, Paul Stapleton paced up and down his study, his face contorted, first trying to deny his prejudice, then trying to explain it.

"The Negro just doesn't belong on this continent. We have to do our best for them. But I can't stand the thought of you, the brightest boy I've got, marrying one of them. It's a question of inheritance, Mark, of brainpower, of adaptation." Then out of this naïve racism came the astonishing personal confession. *"It's better to marry one of your own kind, Mark. I know that from experience."*

"I think it's hypocrisy to live with a woman you don't love," he had snarled. *"The same kind of hypocrisy that sends your oldest son to work for a slob like Dwight Slocum. The same kind of hypocrisy that has you defending corporations that bust unions and sell rotten goods to the public. The same kind of hypocrisy that told us to be heroes and defend the American way of life, and get this for a reward."*

He had thrust his metal claw in Paul Stapleton's face. His father had recoiled for a moment. Then he spoke in the coldest, harshest voice Mark had ever heard. "Your brother John didn't think that way in Korea. If that's the way you think, maybe you better get out of this house as soon as possible."

Those murderous words had tightened hatred on both their faces, like masks. Mark had left the house with Dawn within the hour. He had told her, and later told his mother, that his reason was his father's "racist opposition" to the marriage. He had never told anyone the real reason, the implied accusation that he nurtured a cowardly regret for his wounds.

Mark began explaining the genesis of his book, *The Just Society*. Wryly, he told Kilpatrick that some people considered it the most dangerous book written by an American in this century. Behind his words other memories flowed. He gazed with frustration bordering on hatred at the muscular physique of his stepbrother John, as they ran side by side in the dawn, leaving his father, George, Randy, behind them. Their breath came in steaming gasps as they neared the end of the daily five-mile course. Then John would loose that indestructible reserve of stamina that made him a great athlete. He would surge ahead, stride after stride, and finish a hundred feet ahead of Mark and stand there, grinning, while Mark gasped across the finish line and frequently collapsed. A few minutes later his father and Randy and George would arrive and his father would tell him to keep trying, he'd beat John one of these days. George would whine about the pain in his side and tell Mark he was crazy.

That was where he learned to hate losing and accumulate extra reasons for hating his stepbrother John. Perhaps that was why his father's invocation of John had aroused such savage enmity in him. Once more they were being compared, this time because John had been heroic enough to get himself killed in Korea while he, Mark, had only managed to lose half an arm and half a leg on Okinawa.

Personal, trivial, Mark Stapleton told himself, and continued to discuss *The Just Society*. "We must take equality out of the hands of the politicians," he said. "We must analyze it, measure, quantify it. Then we must decide which inequalities are tolerable, which inevitable, which unjust and intolerable in the light of our supposed ideals. Certain inequalities stand out as indefensible already. Inherited wealth, for instance. It clashes irremediably with the ideal of a meritocracy, where everyone achieves his particular success as the result of his own efforts, his own brainpower. An inheritance, in a just society, would be considered a moral blot."

Kilpatrick smiled. "I can see why your father wouldn't like your book."

"I see the Stapletons as anachronisms, superfluities, in our society. We don't need examples from elites. We generate our ideals from other sources, from books, teachers."

"But to be fair to him, your father isn't opposed to equality. Why would he be spending the last years of his life trying to wrestle the city into desegregating its schools?"

"For him that's a personal issue. It grew out of his World War II experience in Italy. He'll tell you about it. I doubt if my father could think his way to desegregation. He's not much of a thinker. In that respect too, he's a typical upper-class American. Do you want to get some good insights into what makes him tick? Read Emily Post. I learned more about him—and about myself—from her than I ever learned from Freud. There's one line that says it all—where she writes that progress in good behavior is marked by the ability to extinguish all thought of oneself.

"That, as I note in my book, is the ultimate goal of the just society—the complete divorce of personal desire from the acts of service a person performs in his chosen role in the world. It goes back to the Puritans, who taught us to distrust all forms of desire. This distrust permeates the Protestant ethic, and it has been slowly emerging, over the past three hundred years, as an ideal of restraint and self-effacement. It has had to contend with a contradictory American drive for self-aggrandizement, the temptation to exploit this incredibly rich continent. But as the age of exploitation ends, the ideal is going to emerge—is emerging, within the idea of equality."

Kilpatrick looked somewhat staggered by this summary. It was probably beyond his middle-class mind. Mark gave him a copy of *The Just Society*. Kilpatrick thanked him in a much too humble way and departed.

Mark Stapleton resumed his professorial self. He signed a few letters refusing invitations to lecture at various law schools, and left his office with a briefcase bulging with legal and sociological journals. In a few minutes a taxi deposited him in front of his apartment house on Central Park West. Up in the elevator he went to the four empty rooms.

He walked from room to room, turning on air conditioners. In his study, he used his metal claw to withdraw his wife's letter from the top drawer of his desk.

Dear Mark:

It pains me to say goodbye this way after twenty years. But I have to do it. If I tried to tell you face to face, it would end up like all our other arguments, with me admitting I was wrong. For a long time I have felt baffled by you. I asked myself, is there a human being behind that ice-cold mind? If you had agreed to have children, I think I might have been able to find out. That was our first mistake. Our next mistake was cutting ourselves off from both our families. I know you had cut yourself off from your people for my sake. And it made sense, according to the great principle of equality, for me to do likewise, since my parents were no more enthusiastic about our marriage. But it left us isolated, deprived of normal human resources. I think that was why I urged you to answer your father's letters. I felt a need, a desperate need, to force some warmth, some caring into your veins—in the hope that some of it might eventually reach me. Your terrible response—your accusation that I was trying to get us written into the will—hurt me deeply. I began to suspect that you don't really know who I am. I was just another weapon in the war you're fighting with your father. I began to realize how little I really knew about what went on inside you. I began to face the fact that the idea of love between a man and woman was totally foreign to you.

There was probably some truth to those last words, but was it his fault? Unfortunately one did not have the privilege of choosing one's father. He had tried to compensate for his icy inheritance by offering Dawn the companionship of his mind. But she had not grown, intellectually. She had been content to be a "working lawyer," as she so artlessly put it, wandering from the NAACP to the grubby world of the district attorney's office. With irritating protestations of humility, she declined to join his torturous ascent to the real meaning of the law in American life. Was there something about the middle class that made them either impervious to ideas, like Dawn, or overimpressed with them, like Kilpatrick? He recalled for a moment Kilpatrick's awe at his vault from Emily Post to equality. If he had tried that gambit on his father, Paul Stapleton would have smiled and said: "Okay, Mark, now come down from Cloud Nine."

Mark Stapleton sat down in his worn leather chair and switched on his reading lamp. For a moment the memories that had seized him during his talk with Kilpatrick dragged him into the past again. Maybe Dawn was right. She had really been a pretext, a ruse that he had brought home to trigger the argument he had been spoiling to have with his father. The argument that would enable him to limp across the room on his plastic leg and thrust his steel claw into Paul Stapleton's face and ask him why.

Personal, trivial, Professor Stapleton told himself. He opened the *Journal of Sociology* and turned to the first article: "Sociometric Measurements of Success-Failure Ratings in a Middle-Class Community." He began to read the stiff, impersonal prose.

VIII

"I believe there are foreshadowings in life, just as in novels. When we were children, we used to play the Checkered Game of Life. It had a board with white squares on it marked Honor and Ambition, Industry and Idleness, and Ruin and Suicide. You spun a teetotum—a numbered wheel with an arrow—which gave you so many moves up or down the board. The goal was to get from Infancy to Happy Old Age without landing on Suicide or Ruin. Paul always won. I never remember him losing. He was especially good at landing on Perseverance, which jumped you across the whole board to success."

Good God, I am rattling on like a perfect fool, Agatha Stapleton thought. After lecturing her brother on the need for honesty, she was discovering within herself an enormous reluctance to be frank. Jim Kilpatrick was no help. He seemed anything but the worshipful admirer of the Stapletons that Paul had led her to expect. At best he was distant; at worst, surly. She had assumed he was young. This man was at least fifty and there were lines in his face that suggested a troubled soul. His reddish hair, his wide, thick-lipped mouth and high, square cheekbones were explicitly Irish-American. This made him even more un-nerving.

She decided to finish talking about the Checkered Game of Life as quickly as possible. "I still think that was a marvelous game. It prepared you when quite young for the ruder shocks of life. Politics sent you to Congress, which was several steps *backward*. Bravery sent you to Honor, which was also some distance back. A Government Contract sent you to Wealth—but that was even farther back. Wealth was one of the earliest squares—far, far away from Success and Happy Old Age. I remembered all this with particular force during the years I was married to Dwight Slocum."

"I detested that game," Peregrine said. "Honesty let you advance to Happiness and Idleness sent you reeling back to Disgrace. Piffle. Victorian piffle."

Agatha clenched her teeth and forced a smile. Peregrine had inserted himself into this meeting by persuading Agatha that it would look suspicious to omit him. He had promised to let Agatha do most of the talking. But the agreement did not extend to offhand comments. Peregrine had gotten out his favorite cream-colored Saint Laurent suit and shirt of delicate rouge. Agatha had to admit that he looked extremely dignified and had thus far conducted himself fairly well. He had served an excellent lunch of moules, steak tartare and salad niçoise, and then taken Kilpatrick on a tour of his collections, which included some really remarkable eighteenth-century miniatures as well as some dreadful art deco stuff, including a bedroom set once owned by Noël Coward.

Peregrine had proposed this scenario as a way of easing her and Kilpatrick into a formal interview. She would be able to get more information on Kilpatrick's background, Peregrine had argued. But Kilpatrick had been extremely close-mouthed. All she knew was that he was divorced, hardly a sin at which they could look askance. George Stapleton's second wife had left him last year. Kilpatrick's father had been a politician in the dreadful Shea machine but he apparently had very little admiration for him.

At lunch, Agatha had found herself doing much of the

talking, largely about her work at the hospice. She told him how she had gotten the idea for the spiral design from the late Cardinal Matthew Mahan, who had been a collector of rare seashells. One night, at a United Church Fund dinner, she had sat beside the cardinal and he had told her of his fascination with spirals as models of spiritual growth. She thought Kilpatrick might respond to this fraternization with the local head of the Catholic Church, but he seemed utterly indifferent.

After lunch they had adjourned to the living room, where Agatha began lecturing on the Stapletons. She thought it best to begin with generalizations. She told Kilpatrick to abandon such standard categories as liberal and conservative. The Stapletons did not fit easily into molds. During the American Revolution they had been radicals, in spite of their already substantial wealth. On the eve of the Civil War, her great-grandfather, the Commodore (he had been a naval hero in the War of 1812), had been a Democrat who favored letting the southern states go in peace. He was so vehement on the subject, he had inadvertently almost persuaded the state of New Jersey to secede. The Stapletons had been Bull Moosers under Theodore Roosevelt and die-in-the-last-ditch foes of the "other Roosevelt."

"We generally supported what we thought was right, what was good for the country," Agatha said.

"And what was good for the Stapletons," Peregrine said.

Annoyed again, Agatha had retreated to random memories of their childhood, which had degenerated into her monologue on the Checkered Game of Life. Kilpatrick was looking bored until she mentioned Dwight Slocum. For the first time Kilpatrick asked a question.

"When did you marry him?"

"In 1925, when he was worth a mere five or six million."

"How long were you married?"

"Fifteen years. But I don't think it's *terribly* relevant. At best, I am a very minor character in the Stapleton story."

Kilpatrick nodded, accepting this evasion at face value.

91

Agatha had difficulty concealing the dismay she felt at so totally failing this first challenge to candor. If she could not tell this man her truth, what could she expect Paul to tell?

Peregrine insisted that Agatha was too modest. "Your marriage to Dwight Slocum has a great deal to do with our sitting here comfortably wealthy today," he said.

"That's an exaggeration. Don't you think we ought to take a historical approach? Poor Mr. Kilpatrick will be totally confused if we leapfrog all over the twentieth century. Let me try to bring some order out of the chaos we are creating by telling you that I think the most important person in your story is my brother Paul. But you can't understand him without understanding two other people. His father and his grandfather."

"Who is probably in hell, or deserves to be," Peregrine said.

"Really, Peregrine, I don't think we should be so judgmental."

"My dear, I have always maintained that judgments are the spice of life. Mr. Kilpatrick does not have to accept them. But I think we should state them frankly. Don't you agree, Mr. Kilpatrick?"

"Absolutely," Kilpatrick said.

"Let me tell you what the General—our grandfather—was like," Peregrine continued. "He was quite tall—well over six feet. I don't think we've had anyone in the family who was taller. He walked like a soldier on parade, measured strides, with his head projecting forward, as if he were expecting a challenge from an enemy. His expression was a glare. When he smiled—perhaps twice a year —it was ghastly, a caricature of mirth. He dressed like a man going to a funeral, always in black, congress boots— those old high shoes with elastic sides—a negligible string tie, a blinding white shirt with a detachable collar and cuffs. His voice was a rasp—worn out from giving orders above the roar of machinery in the mills."

"He detested my mother," Agatha said, feeling grateful to Peregrine for breaking the ice. "She was a Southerner. He had tremendous prejudices against whole groups of people. He despised the Irish. He thought they had ruined the city. For years he refused to hire them at the mills. He disliked the English even more. As a nation and as a people. He had no use for Americans who doted on everything English. I suppose the Germans were the only group he really liked. He hired them and promoted them. All his foremen were Germans."

"He was a general in the Civil War?"

"At the age of thirty-two. He raised a regiment here in the city. Within a month they made him a brigadier general, and a year later, a major general. They say he saved the Union Army twice, at Malvern Hill and Chancellorsville."

"How long did he live?"

"Until 1918. He was eighty-six when he died. He outlived both his sons. Peregrine's father, Rawdon Stapleton, died on San Juan Hill in the Spanish-American War. My father, George, died in 1914 on the River of Doubt."

"I beg your pardon?"

"The River of Doubt. It's in South America. He went on an expedition with Theodore Roosevelt to explore its headwaters. They were close friends. Paul was with him. They thought it would be a glorious adventure. It turned out to be a nightmare. The river was full of rapids and they had to drag the canoes around them. Everyone came down with jungle fevers. They ran out of food. Father died on the steamer coming back. The whole thing was stupid. Fifty-five-year-old men trying to act like twenty-year-olds. When TR died six years later, I remember someone saying that he'd lost ten years of his life on the River of Doubt."

"How did your father know Theodore Roosevelt?"

"He went to Harvard with him. They were rather close friends all their lives. Father was the leader of the Progressive Party in this state."

"Would you say Roosevelt influenced your father?"

"If anything, it was the other way around. Father was a very thoughtful man."

That wasn't true, Agatha thought, dismayed again. She was in the grip of atavism. Peregrine was eyeing her skeptically. She heard herself murmuring: "I never knew Father well. I was only twelve when he died."

"TR was the stronger personality, you must admit that, Agatha," Peregrine said.

93

"Unquestionably. He was a unique human being. Ideally suited for his age. A natural democrat. We Stapletons have never had that knack."

"A failing for which I have never shed a tear," Peregrine said.

"Except for Hugh Stapleton, our Continental Congressman, I don't think any member of the family has ever been elected to public office," Agatha said. "We have always preferred to work behind the scenes to make sure the right things get done. For about thirty years—from 1830 to 1860—nobody voted for anything in the state legislature without our approval."

"We owned the railroad, you see," Peregrine said. "We had an absolute monopoly on all the transportation in the state. Rather delicious."

"Why did you sell it?"

"Because the big operators, the Goulds and the Harrimans and people of that sort, were getting too powerful to hold off any longer," Agatha said. "So we sold out and put all our money into textiles."

"To our ultimate disaster," Peregrine said.

"Why were textiles a disaster for the Stapletons?" Kilpatrick asked. "From what I've heard, they were a disaster for the city."

"What do you mean?" Agatha bristled.

"Didn't Principia and the other mills pay minimum wages? Which meant slum life for most of the city."

"Textiles were a vulnerable industry," Agatha said. "We had to keep the wages low to compete with European mills. That meant constant labor agitation. But it was a manageable problem until—the Irish came pouring into the city and took over the local government. That was the beginning of the end."

Atavism again? Agatha considered. She could feel the hostility that the word "Irish," used in this context, ignited in her blood. Yet she had no animosity, she could show honest (she hoped) compassion to Mrs. Malloy. It was the truth, Agatha told herself. If Kilpatrick was any kind of historian he must know that she had told him the truth. Unfortunately, he gave no hint of what he thought of it. His face remained expressionless.

94

"All that is pathetic and authentic, Agatha, my dear," Peregrine said. "But I am afraid that the Stapletons themselves, especially the more recent standard-bearers, are as much to blame for the ultimate collapse as our Celtic friends."

"I don't agree with you, Peregrine, you know that."

"Agatha's worship of her brothers Paul and Malcolm sometimes approaches the religious," Peregrine said. "I have struggled to see them more objectively. I have always maintained that we should have gone into the fashion business, perhaps even opened our own retail stores. That way we could have had a say in the selling side of textiles. We could have had a direct impact on public taste, and acquired a share of the market to which we could have adjusted our factory output. But no one listened to me. We stayed in the raw cloth business, at the mercy of the Semites on Seventh Avenue. The family motto seemed to be, what was good enough for Grandfather is good enough for us. So we sat there losing money year after year until the Depression finished us."

"It's more complicated than that, Peregrine, a good deal more complicated," Agatha said with considerable tension in her voice.

"Why did the family go into the textile business?"

"I think it was pride," Peregrine said. "This part of the country has always been a sort of no-man's-land, the middle ground between New England and the South. They were competing with New England. They wanted to prove they could do it better than the Yankees."

"The Yankees were another group Grandfather didn't like," Agatha said. "He blamed them for starting the Civil War. Sometimes, looking back, life with Grandfather seems a series of tirades on his prejudices. But thanks to him, for a long time we did run better, more efficient textile factories than anyone in America."

"That's true," Peregrine said. "He brought in the best engineers in the country to build the factories. You ought to go down to Woodlawn Point sometime and walk through the old raceways that carried the river through the heart of the factory complex. They're marvels of hydraulic engineering."

"The trouble was, Grandfather was all alone," Agatha said. "In many ways it was the Civil War that ruined the family. Three or four of the best of that generation were killed in it. Two of his brothers. Several cousins came out of it spiritual and mental wrecks."

"And the rest of them imbibed the soldier's code: it is a good and glorious thing to die for one's country," Peregrine said. "It's infected the family down to the present day. It doesn't make any sense. The best people shouldn't go out and get killed in something as insane as a war."

"There is a strain of idealism that runs through the family," Agatha said. "Idealism that can run to extremes. But I'm proud of it."

"Oh, please, Agatha dear, don't start on that," Peregrine said. "Agatha has a theory which sees the Stapletons as part of a vast spiritual development, a Hegelian unfolding of the American idea. She got it from her father, who was very influenced by the idealistic philosophers who reigned at Harvard and elsewhere around the turn of the century."

"I thought you didn't know your father very well," Kilpatrick said.

"From his letters," Agatha said. "I have some of his letters."

She was furious with Peregrine for ridiculing her even before she tried to explain herself. For all his effeminate ways, Peregrine had that innate masculine contempt for the thinking woman.

"It's nothing so grandiose," she lied. "Essentially, it's a search for the Beloved Community."

"I've been looking for that all my life," Kilpatrick said with an unexpected smile. "What is it?"

"Have you ever read Josiah Royce? He was Father's favorite. Especially *The Problem of Christianity*."

"I'll get it," Kilpatrick said.

Peregrine was looking rather discomfited. She had succeeded in interesting Kilpatrick, in spite of her resident cynic.

"What was your mother like?" Kilpatrick asked.

"She was a Randolph from Virginia. The great-great-granddaughter of Thomas Jefferson. The descent was through his daughter Martha, who married Thomas Randolph. Mother's family had no money. But they were terribly proud of their bloodlines. Proud of their southern heritage. This led to some rather sharp differences between her and my grandfather. He was as—as inflexible as Mother was headstrong."

"She was a beautiful woman," Peregrine said. "A beautiful gallant woman."

Agatha nodded. "I was born with an inferiority complex. For the first twenty years of my life, all I ever heard was, what a pity, she doesn't look like her mother."

"Was your brother Paul fond of her?"

"Oh, yes," Agatha said. "But I don't think he really approved of her. Mother liked to say outrageous things even more than she liked to do them. I think Paul felt Father did a rather poor job of coping with her."

Was that better or worse than her previous performance? Agatha wondered. You couldn't tell a perfect stranger that your brother despised his mother and had practically scourged her out of the country. But she had at least hinted that there was some kind of alienation.

"No one could cope with Anne Randolph Stapleton," Peregrine said. "She was born to drive men crazy. I thought she was absolutely *spectacular*. We often met in Europe. She was my link with home."

"When did she die?"

"In 1935. The date is synonymous with the Depression for me—both financial and emotional," Peregrine said.

"Would you like to see some memorabilia?" Agatha said, standing up much too abruptly. If Kilpatrick was even moderately perceptive, he must have noticed she was cutting Peregrine short.

Why? What was he about to say? With a surge of shame Agatha knew that she did not want to hear him tell the details of her mother's death. She did not want to hear it because it aroused too many difficult memories.

Concealing her agitation (she hoped), Agatha led Kilpatrick downstairs to the cellar, which was finished in walnut. In the rear was a large oak vault, a sort of room within the room. Agatha explained that behind the wood was four inches of lead and steel, making it bombproof and fireproof. This was where the Stapleton memorabilia were stored. She had spent the last decade organizing it. She gestured to a whole shelf of gray boxes marked Civil War Diaries and Letters. Another half shelf recorded the history of the Stapletons in the Revolution. "Our Continental Congressman kept a diary which gives a rather shocking picture of the politics of the period. I showed it to Paul and he decided it would be best not to publish it. I'm not so sure these things should be suppressed. Perhaps you could do something with it after you finish this book."

She pointed to another shelf. "Here's what I want to show you. The picture album one of our nurses made up. And Paul's Pennsgrove yearbook. He never graduated from college, you know. He left Princeton in his sophomore year, and when he came home from France, he read for the law and went directly into practice at Stapleton, Talbot."

Kilpatrick carried the album and yearbook to the other end of the cellar, overlooking the garden. Fall sunshine poured down on the faded pictures as he turned the pages. Agatha herself had not looked at the album in at least ten years, and she found it interesting. Even as a boy, Paul seemed to dominate every family picture. He stared solemnly into the camera and as the shutter clicked there was an almost eerie resemblance to the penetrating adult stare he had inherited from their grandfather.

The album began when Paul was about five or six. There were no pictures of Agatha or her brother Malcolm for several dozen pages. Kilpatrick asked why.

"Grandfather didn't approve of baby pictures," Agatha said. "He maintained that the human being only got interesting when his or her character became visible."

"There's Mother," Agatha said, pointing to a delicate dark-haired stranger with a cupid's-bow mouth. The picture had been taken in 1902. Agatha found it hard to believe that woman was even related to the imperious egotist she had known. Paul sat opposite their mother at a wicker table in the garden. Father sat between them, unsmiling. Just as well Kilpatrick could not see the way

e concealed tension in the picture was concentrated in
ul's solemn, staring, boy's face.

*Suddenly Agatha was back in that garden, walking
own the path to the same wicker table. What year was
1913. She was twelve years old. She had been reading
lice in* Wonderland *and she had left the book on the
ble. Walking down the path in white organdy without a
re in the world, thinking of herself as Alice, stepping
rough the looking glass and possibly meeting the March
are or the White Rabbit behind a rhododendron bush.*

*Voices. Mother and Father were sitting at the wicker
ble, Mother in a dress like the one she was wearing in
e picture, with flounced sleeves and a wide collar.
ather was in his shirt sleeves. They were arguing. She
d never heard them speak to each other in such an
gry, threatening way.*

"You will not see that man again," Father said.

"I will see whom I please, when I please," Mother
id.

"You will not!" Father said, and brought his fist down
the table.

"I will. I have a right to seek some human consolation,
me innocent, human consolation in return for the abuse
d scorn to which I am subjected in this house. If you
nnot protect me from your father I will protect myself.
will find a spiritual refuge."

"You provoke him. You draw his abuse on yourself.
ve told you that a hundred times."

"As usual, you defend that arrogant old monster. That
urderer."

"Will you stop seeing this man?"

"No."

"I think perhaps we should talk about a divorce."

"I will not be frightened by brutal threats."

"That is not a threat."

"Then let us discuss it now."

"No. When I come back from South America. When
e are calm and collected. In the meantime, you must
omise me that you will stop seeing that man."

"I will promise nothing."

Sixty-three years later, Agatha felt the way she had

that day: on fire. She had fled down the path like a victim of an explosion. In her bedroom, she had lain on the bed for a long time wondering whom she could tell. She knew the answer: no one.

Now could she tell it to this stranger? This Irish American? No.

"Your father looks like a charming man," Kilpatrick said.

"He was. I wish I had gotten to know him better."

There were several dozen more pictures of Paul riding ponies, stepping from old automobiles, standing on the beach in a bathing suit. "He was a marvelous swimmer and diver," Agatha said. "In some ways our summer house at Paradise Beach was our favorite place, growing up. Everyone was more relaxed down there. Even Grandfather."

Gradually, Paul's brother, Malcolm, and then Agatha began to appear in the pictures. Already Malcolm looked angry. Agatha stared at her own homely, solemn little face, the wispy blond hair and saucy eyes and saw double resentment. "I was a rebel already," she said.

"Why doesn't anyone ever smile?" Kilpatrick asked.

"That was Grandfather again. He didn't think anyone should smile when he had his picture taken. He said it made you look like an idiot when you picked up the picture ten years later and couldn't remember what you were grinning about. Mother thought that was nonsense and always smiled."

Agatha turned a page. "Here we are at our city house Bowood, in 1912. It's the mayor's residence now, as you probably know. My brother Malcolm gave it to the city after World War II."

Paul, Malcolm and Agatha stood with Mother and Father beneath the Greek-revival portico, which Grandfather, with typical disregard for aesthetics, had added Bowood's original Georgian front. As usual, Mother was the only one smiling. To Agatha, Paul's face glowed with intense compressed idealism. He was unbelievably handsome.

"He looks like pictures I've seen of the Duke of Windsor when he was Prince of Wales," Kilpatrick said.

"Yes," Agatha said.

"He has an interesting mouth," Kilpatrick said.

"Very," Agatha said, pleased to discover someone else who considered the mouth the seat of character. Paul's mouth had his father's full upper lip. It rose to a kind of central crest, like an echo of his mother's cupid's bow. The lower lip was a hard, ascetic line.

She began telling Kilpatrick how pleasant it had been to grow up at Bowood. "The grounds were much larger in those days. Most of the woods and gardens are now part of Washington Park. We gave that to the city in 1920. But in those days we had a perfect forest to romp in. Grandfather's bad temper was really the only thing we had to worry about. We knew there were people out there who didn't like us, of course. We heard about strikes at the mills. But we were insulated from the grisly details. To this day, I can't decide whether that was a good thing. Paul, of course, was more exposed to the whole situation. Grandfather selected him, as—I guess you might call it his spiritual heir—quite early. He never stopped telling Paul that being a Stapleton was a responsibility. It was up to us to set the city's tone, give it political direction and economic leadership."

That was rather good, Agatha decided. She had come very close to the truth that time. But Kilpatrick utterly missed the point. He began talking about the two cities, the immigrants downtown and the native Americans uptown. What had the Stapletons done to bridge the gap between them? That seemed to him a crucial question. Agatha found it unanswerable. She wanted to tell him that they never felt any great need to bridge the gap. But she was afraid that would offend him. "My father rather favored craft unions," she said. "And Mother helped run Kemble House, one of the biggest settlement houses."

Kilpatrick looked disappointed. That makes two of us, Agatha thought. She opened the 1913 Pennsgrove year-book. "This is my favorite picture of Paul," she said.

The young face was staring into the camera in the same serious, penetrating way as the boy on the beach and the teen-ager on Bowood's portico. This picture was a close-up. Oddly, that made the details of the face almost irrelevant. The ripe upper lip was all the more visible; so was the harsh line of the underlip. But the expression on

the face was what fascinated Agatha. It was unstained
unblemished. This face had never known defeat, disappointment or more than a momentary unhappiness.

"There is the man I have always loved," Agatha said.

The words trembled in mid-air like a prism between
her and the picture. Suddenly the face was evil, hateful. It
came at her like a projectile. Was that the reason, was
repressed forbidden love behind all her envy and hatred?
For a moment Agatha felt panicky. She had to struggle
for self-control.

Beneath Paul's picture were words that beautifully described his unblemished face.

*Stapleton the blameless, Stapleton the brave. Who can
surpass him?*

"That was taken two months before he went down the
River of Doubt. He never looked that carefree again. If
you want to find out the real story—his inner story—
you'll have to find out what happened to him on that
river."

"You told me. His father—your father—died."

"Something happened before he died. Father did or
said something that had a terrible impact on Paul, a
terrible spiritual impact."

She had said it. She had put him on the scent. But did
he have the spiritual nose for it? Did any outsider?

Beside Paul's portrait was his favorite verse. Each
Pennsgrove graduate had to choose one.

Lord, who's the happy man that may to Thy blest courts
repair;
Not stranger-like to visit them, but to inhabit there?

'Tis he whose every thought and deed by rules of virtue
moves;
Whose generous tongue disdains to speak the thing his
heart disproves.

"Who wrote that poem?" Kilpatrick asked.

"I don't know," Agatha said. "It was Thomas Jeffer-
son's favorite. It's called 'The Portrait of a Good Man.'
Mother used to read it to us on Jefferson's birthday.
There are more verses about keeping promises, never

slandering your neighbor, respecting piety, ignoring vice in its pomp and power. I can only remember the ending."

Agatha closed her eyes and recited it, simultaneously seeing Mother in Bowood's April garden (or ballroom when it rained), declaiming it in the histrionic style of her southern girlhood. Agatha spoke flatly, quickly, not trying for vibrations, even in the oratorical last stanza.

"The man who, by this steady course, has happiness insured,
When Earth's foundations shake, shall stand by Providence secured."

"Did you believe it?" Kilpatrick asked.

"Yes," Agatha said. "All of us did. Especially Paul."

"Does he still believe it?"

"You'd better ask him that," Agatha said.

Those questions were a hopeful sign. Perhaps Kilpatrick could or would write the kind of book she wanted to see. She was suddenly tempted to tell him her hopes, her faith: that even in the Stapletons' gritty history, it was possible to discern the struggle for the ideal. She could hear her father, that gentle, ultimately sad man, talking about it at Bowood's dinner table in the poetic language to which he was unfortunately inclined. *You have to look for the golden thread.* The grim gravel voice of her grandfather replied: *Balderdash.*

Peregrine's scorn blended with Grandfather's and with something vaguely forbidding in Kilpatrick's reserved manner to silence Agatha. Instead of confessing her dubious faith, she turned back one page in the Pennsgrove yearbook and confronted a face that was the total opposite of the one Paul Stapleton wore in 1913. It was squarish, with a wide, thick-lipped mouth parted in a faintly mocking grin, dark tufted eyebrows, a beetling brow and small, squinting eyes. A brute was what the face said at first glance. There was a crude sophistication in those small, confident eyes, but not a trace of what used to be called character.

"Dwight Slocum was in Paul's class," Agatha said. "Isn't he detestable? To think that I was once insanely in

love with him. Paul did everything short of arresting me
to stop the marriage."

"What was Slocum like then?"

"Almost as ill-mannered, as bad-tempered as he is
now."

She let Kilpatrick puzzle over that one while she read
the verse beneath Dwight's picture. It was from Kipling's
"If."

> *If you can fill the unforgiving minute*
> *With sixty seconds' worth of distance run*
>
> *Yours is the Earth and everything that's in it,*
> *And—which is more—you'll be a Man, my son!*

Perhaps dropping clues was the way to do it, Agatha
mused. Puzzle, intrigue Mr. Kilpatrick until he asks the
right questions. Stop fretting about whether she could tell
him this or not tell him that. Make him earn the truth.
She rather liked that idea. It enabled her to match the
undercurrent of hostility she sensed in Kilpatrick.

Agatha closed the yearbook. Kilpatrick caught the cue
and stood up. "We ought to talk a bit more about the
hospice," Agatha said. "But I think you should come see
it first. I'd be happy to show you around. I'm there
almost every afternoon."

Kilpatrick said he would call her for an appointment.
In the meantime, would she let him see these letters from
her father she had mentioned?

Agatha became flustered. "Of course. But—perhaps I
should go through them first. There may be some private
matters—"

Her words trailed off as she encountered the irritation
on Kilpatrick's face. He began telling her that he had to
know all the facts if he was going to write an intelligent
book. He did not intend to embarrass anyone. He was
prepared to be reasonable about what he wrote. But he
had to know the facts. Agatha seized the folder of letters
from the vault and thrust them into his hands.

Upstairs, Kilpatrick made a point of thanking Peregrine for a delicious lunch. He had surprisingly good
manners, Agatha thought. Another good sign. She and

Peregrine stood behind the living-room curtains and watched Kilpatrick get into his Corvette.

"What do you think of him?" she asked.

"He has a hard, tough quality. He'll need it to deal with Paul."

"I hope there's some sensitivity there too."

"To look for the golden thread?" Peregrine scoffed. "I hope you didn't get into that downstairs. He'll think we're a pair of old saps."

"I didn't mention it," Agatha said.

IX

A dawn breeze blew through the open windows of Paul
Stapleton's bedroom at New Grange Farm. Deep in his
dream, he felt it touch his cheek and knew it came from
another time. He welcomed it. He wanted to escape this
dream before it reached the unendurable climax. On both
sides of them the jungle was a green impenetrable wall.
They were toiling upstream, against the vicious current.
The dusky *camaradas* in the bow and stern strained at
their paddles, their bodies shiny with sweat. He sat behind his father, staring at the black handle of the .45-
caliber pistol protruding from its holster. The merciless
sun beat on the water. His father hunched forward in the
boat. His once white shirt was gashed and torn in a dozen
places, smeared with mud. He was a dying man. The boy
in the boat knew that, he knew it before they started up
this murderous river. *Don't do it, Father, please*, he
whispered.

Suddenly he was flung out of the boat. Had his father
pushed him? Those words were spoken by the boy in the
dream. The real boy had said nothing. The real boy had
known nothing. He was a pathetic idealistic ignoramus.

But it was too late to say anything. He was swept downstream at an incredible pace. His father, the *camaradas,* never looked back. He caught a glimpse of Teddy Roosevelt's startled face on the riverbank. "I'm sorry," the boy cried, "I didn't mean to say it. I'm sorry." But it was too late. The boat was a mere speck on the glinting river. He was in the rapids. The roar filled his ears, the white water swallowed him.

Paul Stapleton awoke. He was bathed in sweat. The dawn light on the windows told him there would be no more sleep. He got up, shrugged into a blue silk robe that lay at the foot of the bed and turned on the light. The long, narrow bedroom also served as his private study. A bulging rolltop desk filled the far corner. It had belonged to his grandfather. Two plump early Victorian chairs flanked the desk. The sleeping end of the room was simple, even spare. The furniture was American Colonial. Tables with thin, delicate legs, fragile side chairs, two graceful walnut highboys with gleaming brass handles and a painted dresser of even earlier vintage. On the dresser was a picture of a solemn young woman in a wedding dress, beside a handsome, equally solemn officer in a high-collared World War I uniform. Around it were five separate pictures of young boys.

Sam Fry knocked on the door, once more demonstrating that his Apache ears could catch the creak of a box spring. "Can I get you something, Colonel?" he said. It was always wartime in Sam's warrior heart.

"A glass of buttermilk, Sam," Paul Stapleton said.

Sam was back with the buttermilk in seconds, so it seemed. He was ageless. He moved with the same animal grace at eighty that he had possessed at twenty in Mexico. Paul Stapleton wished his own creaking knees and weary legs could match him. He drank the icy buttermilk in one long gulp. In the bathroom he shaved with an electric razor, then stripped off his robe and pajamas and stepped into the shower stall. He turned on the cold water and let it beat against his face and chest. It was spring water, pumped from a well on the farm, brutally cold. Toweling himself dry, he avoided his image in the full-length mirror on the back of the bathroom door. His withered body disgusted him.

107

At the rolltop desk, Paul Stapleton began reading an opinion he would deliver in court that day, rejecting yet another appeal to rescind his Phase 2 busing order. He could not concentrate on it. He kept thinking about the dream. He had not had it in years. Falling in the water was a variation he had never dreamt before. Did it have something to do with seeing this fellow Kilpatrick today?

"Paul?"

His wife, Maria, stood in the doorway of the bedroom.

"You're up so early. Are you all right?"

"I'm fine. I just had a bad dream."

"What was it about?"

"Nothing important."

"I had a bad dream too, earlier in the night. I couldn't get back to sleep, thinking about it. I saw George dead in his swimming pool. Drowned."

"It could happen," Paul Stapleton said. "If he's drinking as much as people say he is."

"There must be something we can do."

"There is nothing we can do. He's fifty-three years old, Maria. He's made a mess out of his life."

"I prayed so hard for him."

"Nothing else will help him."

"If you could talk to him—once more."

"No! I have said all I am going to say to him. He will never get me to say what he wants to hear."

"Paul—he doesn't want that. He wants you—to forgive him."

"I have forgiven him! I've told him that. I've tried to show it in a hundred ways. Building him that ridiculous hacienda. Paying for his divorce. His idiotic printing press. Letting him—"

He saw on his wife's face the pain he was inflicting. An enormous helplessness, weariness, seeped through his body. "Pray for him," he said. "That's all we can do."

"Do you?"

No, never, he wanted to snarl. But he was in control of his temper now. "You're much better at it," he said, and began turning the pages of the opinion.

"What would you like for breakfast?" Maria asked.

"Coffee and toast."

"Nothing more?"

"Sam just brought me some buttermilk."

As Maria left, Paul Stapleton took a letter from one of the pigeonholes of the rolltop desk. It had the Stapleton, Talbot letterhead in bold roman at the top. On the left were the list of partners, with George Gifford Stapleton and M. Kemble Stapleton on it. The letter was from Walter Ackroyd. It began with a lengthy paragraph of circumlocutions about how difficult it was for him to write it. But the firm was having problems, Walter confessed in the second paragraph. Income was down and several seniors were pressing for a re-examination of the partners' shares. Some people were simply not pulling their weight.

> Among these, I regret to say, is George. He comes in late and goes home early when he comes at all. His last two briefs have had to be completely rewritten by other partners. I don't know what to say or do, beyond urging you to speak to him. If some change is not forthcoming, I fear a substantial reduction of his annual share will be in order. Ned, I am happy to report, is a much more positive story. His yachting contacts have brought us some valuable new business. He still tends to let his social life interfere with . . .

Paul Stapleton threw the letter aside. He sat there thinking of what he could say to George. If only Randy were alive, he could send him. If he went himself, it would be worse, infinitely worse than what he had just said to Maria. He felt his face growing hot. He was losing his temper just thinking about it and there was no point, it was useless but he could not stop it. *Jesus Christ,* he cursed. *Jesus goddamn fucking Christ.*

Four hours later, black-robed and impassive, Judge Paul R. Stapleton sat on the lofty hand-carved mahogany bench in the federal district court, listening to Joseph Haggerty, the lawyer for a group called RIP (Restore Independence to the People), argue that the school integration plan ordered by Judge Stapleton five months ago was causing a mass exodus of whites from the city. RIP was seeking to stay the Judge's order implementing the second half of the plan, which had begun busing another 20,000 children three weeks ago.

Haggerty had a labored grunting style and the standard speech pattern of the city's North Slope. He called the Judge "yer honuh" and spouted dire predictions about the city's "fewchuh." He had a gravy stain on his bright green tie and his striped brown suit needed pressing. Paul Stapleton thought about the time and effort his father had spent organizing night school education to teach English grammar and basic arithmetic to the city's Irish. Here was one of them with a law degree, still sounding like a hod carrier, dressing like a slob.

Jim Kilpatrick was sitting in the rear of the empty courtroom, looking mournful, or maybe it was just bored. Paul Stapleton wondered what he thought about Haggerty. It would be interesting to ask him. From what Randy had said, Kilpatrick had cut the ties of ethnic and family loyalty. But a little testing might still be in order.

Haggerty completed his oral argument and Paul Stapleton began his reply. "I find your petition has no merit whatsoever, Mr. Haggerty," he said. He conceded that whites were moving out of the city, but cited statistics from Boston and Denver and Louisville to prove that such moves fell far short of an exodus. It was regrettable that the court had no power to change the limits of the city government's jurisdiction. But it did have the power to do something about the city's failure to give equal educational opportunity to its black citizens. As long as he sat on this bench, he was going to exercise that power to see that justice was done. Haggerty's petition was "herewith denied."

Haggerty rose to request permission to appeal. Paul Stapleton granted it. His gavel fell, adjourning the court until 2 P.M. In his chambers, his clerk, a young Pole named Roman Pignatowski, greeted him with a smile. The Judge had selected Roman not only for his brains but as proof that he had no prejudices against white ethnics. It was a small gesture. Roman did not have much of a

110

constituency beyond his six brothers and sisters, but it was better than no gesture at all.

"I don't think that appeal will ever be filed," Roman said.

Paul Stapleton nodded. "That was a good idea." Roman had suggested denying the motion using language taken from an appeals court ruling on Boston's busing crisis.

He told Pignatowski to find Kilpatrick in the courtroom and bring him into the chambers. On a yellow pad on his desk Paul Stapleton saw six telephone calls from school officials, each probably with a loaded question to ask him. There was no end to this thing. For the time being he would have to see Kilpatrick this way, at lunch, perhaps in the evening at the farm. It was not the right way to work on the book, if he wanted to get at those inner truths Agatha thought were so important. He was not sure he wanted to go anywhere near them.

Roman Pignatowski arrived with Jim Kilpatrick. Paul Stapleton waved him to a seat beside the desk. "I hope we didn't bore you to death out there. Haggerty's the sort of lawyer that makes you think there ought to be a bar exam every five years. Weed out the trash."

"I went to high school with him," Kilpatrick said.

"He was probably trash then."

"Not really trash. Just mediocre."

Paul Stapleton felt a twinge of mistrust. "He's matured into trash," he said. "Like most mediocrities."

Kilpatrick said nothing. Paul Stapleton felt uneasy.

"Do you like this room?" he asked. "It's modeled on a room in Lyme Hall in Derbyshire, where the family got started."

The chamber was a generous square, the walls covered with interlaced panels of inlaid walnut. Opposite the desk was a black marble fireplace with a white figure of Justice in bas-relief above it. The two doors had scrolls and floral carvings in walnut above the lintels.

Kilpatrick nodded. "My father took me through this place when I was twelve or thirteen. He thought it was the handsomest courthouse in the country."

Paul Stapleton had avoided mentioning James Kilpatrick, Sr. Now he felt he had to say something. "I knew your father."

There was an embarrassing pause. What else could he say? He was glad to see Kilpatrick drop his eyes and dismiss the statement with a nod. Paul Stapleton retreated to the previous subject.

"My father had a lot to do with building this courthouse," he said. "He was a good friend of Teddy Roosevelt's. The White House made sure Congress put up enough money to hire a decent architect and add the right touches, the paneling, the carvings, the mosaics in the lobby. Dad had great ambitions for this city in those days. City Hall was another building that he supervised. He knew more about architecture than a lot of architects. That's how he met my mother. He was visiting Virginia to study Monticello and some of the other buildings Jefferson designed. I think he half hoped getting some Jefferson blood into the family might produce a few architects. But we disappointed him."

Paul Stapleton summoned Roman Pignatowski and discussed what to do with the briefs of other motions that had been submitted that morning. Some required opinions, others could be dismissed without comment. He told Roman that he and Kilpatrick would be at the City Club, if some member of the Board of Education or the superintendent of schools got into a frenzy and insisted on reaching him.

The Judge took a gray hat from a rack in the corner and led Kilpatrick through a side door to a marble corridor. They walked along it to a small paneled elevator. It creaked to the basement. A short walk down a less aesthetic cement-walled corridor took them to a sunny parking lot where Sam Fry sat behind the wheel of the purring gray Mercedes.

"I wish I could give you more time," Paul Stapleton said. "But this busing thing is like running a three-ring circus."

They got into the refreshingly cool back seat. Sam Fry always ran the car's air conditioning for ten or fifteen minutes before they went anywhere. Paul Stapleton felt compelled to apologize for the extravagance. "The doctor claims it's good for my heart or some damn thing. Personally, I think this Indian talked him into it. He's gone soft like the rest of the country."

Sam Fry smiled and let him get away with it. He swung onto the expressway and headed downtown. "I think we've got time to do a little sightseeing before lunch," Paul Stapleton said. "Have you ever visited the old mills?"

"No," Kilpatrick said.

Paul Stapleton looked across the charcoal gray tenement roofs, at the soaring white towers of City Hall Plaza, the bold attempt to redevelop downtown launched by the current mayor, Jake O'Connor. He began talking about the Plaza, giving Jake O'Connor a bit more praise than he thought he really deserved. Jake had been the best mayor the city had had in decades, which was not saying very much. Privately, the Judge suspected that his niece Paula, the mayor's wife, was the brains behind the Plaza. But he wanted to show Kilpatrick he was not loath to praise an Irish-American when he accomplished something.

"My father tried to do the same thing in 1910, when we had some real say in the city's politics. He wanted to put up more buildings like the courthouse and City Hall. He brought in top architects from McKim, Mead, and White to give talks to the real estate board on apartment construction. When he died it all fell apart. So much depends on one man. You see it again and again."

Sam Fry left the expressway at the last exit before the suspension bridge across the river. They drove along dockside streets for a while, then the road curved inland past factories and warehouses and finally emerged onto a tongue of land jutting out into the river where the city's guardian hill, angling east, cut off the downtown section. The slope of the hill was covered with the tombstones of Woodlawn Cemetery. On the tongue of lowland stood a dozen rectangular red-brick buildings surrounded by a high wall with an arched entrance that once contained a gate. In the middle of the arch was a hexagonal white marble stone on which a single word was carved: PRINCIPIA.

"There they are," Paul Stapleton said, "the old mills. There was a trolley line that ran out here. Early in the morning they'd put three or four cars together and make little trains. Some people preferred to save their money and walk, at least in the spring or fall. One way or another, six to eight thousand people poured through that gate every morning, six days a week."

They got out of the car and walked through the gate. Vandals had wrecked the buildings years ago. There was hardly a window left. Doors dangled from hinges, the ground was littered with shattered glass. They walked into one of the buildings. It was as empty and dim as a cathedral. Every step echoed. Sunlight streamed through holes in the ruined roof. The floor was covered with puddles. There was no machinery. Paul Stapleton explained that it had all been sold for scrap when the mills moved South.

"You can't imagine how exciting it was to visit one of these buildings when production was going full blast. All those spindles whirling and looms churning. The clatter was tremendous. There was a smell of cloth in the air. You could see it, hear it, practically breathe it being made."

About a hundred feet away a big rat emerged from the shadows and began sipping water from one of the puddles. Paul Stapleton turned to Sam Fry, who was standing behind them. Kilpatrick started slightly, not used to the Apache's noiseless style.

"Get the gun out of the glove compartment."

Sam came back with the army .45. The rat continued to drink. Paul Stapleton released the safety catch. "I got this baby in Mexico in 1916," he aid.

He raised the gleaming black weapon. Suddenly his hand began to shake. He was back in the dream. The rat was a man on the riverbank, begging for mercy. He pulled the trigger. The shot echoed like cannon fire against the high sloping roof. Water sprayed around the rat, who scampered frantically for the safety of the shadows along the wall.

"The old hand just isn't steady any more," Paul Stapleton said.

He put on the safety catch and handed the gun back to Sam Fry. They emerged from the building and Paul Stapleton led them past the other buildings to the water's edge. Some rotting piers drooped from the marshy bank. "We used to have our own dock right here," Paul Stapleton said.

He walked over to a small structure that resembled a sentry box. He opened the door and invited Kilpatrick to look down a ladder into a huge underground tunnel. "That's one of the raceways. For a long time we ran the whole operation on waterpower. There wasn't another mill in the world that could match it for cost efficiency."

They walked slowly past the wrecked buildings toward the gate and the waiting car. The October sun was surprisingly hot. The broken glass crackled beneath their feet as they trudged past the smashed windows.

"I haven't been down here in a good ten years," Paul Stapleton said. "Now I know why. It depresses the hell out of me. We sold these to Dwight Slocum in 1945. It was the hardest decision I've ever made in my life. I took stock in National Products instead of cash. I wound up making so much money it embarrasses me."

In the car they retraced their progress through the warehouses and factories to Dock Street. "It was a perfect place for a mill, when we built it there on the point," Paul Stapleton said. "But other people built mills further down the waterfront. A lot of them were miserable fly-by-night operations. Cockroaches, we called them, paying the lowest possible wages. They were responsible for most of our labor problems. When their workers went out on strike, our people had to run a gauntlet to get to work."

They regained the expressway and found themselves in heavy traffic. All the best restaurants had moved uptown. Most of the city's businessmen, lawyers and politicians headed for them on their lunch hour. Kilpatrick stared out at the city. Normally Paul Stapleton would have let him stare. But he felt a need to reach this man, to reassure himself about him.

"Maria tells me that you had a boy killed in Vietnam."

Kilpatrick's head jerked around and for a moment he glared at him with incredible rage in his eyes. He looked away and nodded. "Near Dak To," he said. "In '72."

"Did he die in battle?"

"No. He got fragged by one of his own men."

"Did they catch the son of a bitch?"

"No."

"What was your boy's rank?"

"Lieutenant."

"That war was a mess from start to finish. All wars are, one way or another. My grandfather used to tell stories about the bird-brained things the Union generals did in the Civil War. I could tell you a few from World War I and World War II. In Korea—"

Suddenly he was there in the tank in Korea. Feeling the smash of the explosive charge, the eruption of flame, hearing the screams.

Maybe there were no screams. Mark Stratton's letter did not mention screams. *I feel like a murderer,* Stratton had written, *sending men into battle against these odds. We're losing the bravest and the best while the goddamn country is busy looking for a better deodorant.*

"Korea," he heard himself saying from a distance. Kilpatrick was looking at him curiously. "We sent our men into action against Russian T-34 tanks without a single weapon that could stop them. Bazooka rounds just bounced off them. It's immoral, to send men into battle against an enemy with better weapons. It's happened in the four wars of my lifetime. My father told me the Mauser rifles the Spanish had in Cuba were twice as accurate as our Springfields. In World War I we had to use British and French planes, tanks, artillery. In World War II our planes were obsolete for the first two years and we never did develop a tank to match the German Panthers and Tigers. They had heavier armor, longer-range guns. I saw a lot of men die in North Africa in burning tanks that never got a chance to fire a shot."

Outraged patriotism. Let Kilpatrick think his emotion was outraged patriotism. It would be the worst possible taste to start telling him about John, now. It would seem like a crude attempt to claim that he had a bigger, better grief. *I had a boy killed in Korea. My adopted son John.*

Adopted son John? Could he lie that way, and still pretend he was searching for inner truths? Maybe this book was a bad idea. But how could he back out of it now? What excuse could he give Ned, Agatha, Kilpatrick?

At the crest of the hill, Sam Fry pulled off the expressway and eased the Mercedes onto the Parkway, the city's fashionable street. Big houses with broad porches and bay windows sat on terraced lawns. "I'd like you to see Bowood, the house where I was born," Paul Stapleton said.

Kilpatrick nodded.

"This street doesn't change much," Paul Stapleton said.

"Except for the names of the owners," Kilpatrick said.

"I suppose most of them are Irish and Italian now."

"Mostly the latter," Kilpatrick said. "The Irish have imitated you Anglo-Saxons and gone suburban."

Paul Stapleton liked the way Kilpatrick said "the Irish." He could think objectively. That was important, objective thinking. Once the emotions got involved, trouble started.

"The Stapletons aren't as Anglo-Saxon as you seem to think. We've got quite a bit of Celtic blood in our veins. My middle name is Rawdon, from a Welshman who married into the family during the Revolution. My grandfather's name was Jonathan. He was named after Jonathan Gifford, an Anglo-Irishman who married one of our Kemble cousins around the same time. I agree with Teddy Roosevelt. A fused race is better than one stock, which tends to thin."

Kilpatrick nodded mechanically. It was obvious that he had never given the subject much thought.

"Have you seen my son Mark?"

"Last Thursday," Kilpatrick said, avoiding his eyes. Paul Stapleton sensed that he had been waiting uneasily for the question.

"What did he say about me?"

"He was pretty tough on you, as you predicted. He said you were a snob. You looked down on everyone who wasn't a white Anglo-Saxon. He said it wasn't your fault. It's the way you were brought up."

Paul Stapleton nodded. It was more or less what he had expected Mark to say. It simultaneously saddened and angered him. Kilpatrick did not realize he was a covert emissary, returning with a report that nothing had changed between Paul Stapleton and his oldest living son.

"I've never been able to get close to Mark. You've got sons. You know what I mean. With some of them, everything seems to click. That's the way it was between me and Randy. But with Mark—"

He struggled to keep his tone casual. "It's too bad, because there's a loss on both sides. Mark's sort of frozen me in his mind at some fixed point in the past. He doesn't want to admit that I've changed. That's one of the things I want to talk about in this book—why I've changed."

He forced a smile. "That sounds like I'm going to produce some sort of earthshaking revelation. Nothing of the sort. It's just what I've learned—from experience. That's the only thing you can trust, Jim."

Trying even harder to make light of it, he added: "On one point I'm still a snob. I think we should insist on the best from everybody, white or black, Irish or Pole or Jew or Wasp. I think it's foolish—and a disservice to the indivual and the country—to demand anything less. I got some pretty sloppy briefs from the local NAACP attorneys in the early stages of this integration case. I got on the phone to their national headquarters and told them to send their best people over here. I don't buy the idea of lowering standards in law, medicine or anywhere else to achieve some sort of dubious equality. It just won't work."

They were approaching Bowood. Sam Fry slowed to a stop before the gold-tipped gate. Paul Stapleton identified himself to the policeman on duty and they rolled up the white-graveled drive, shaded by huge old oaks. "My grandfather planted those trees," he said. "They're just like him. Steady as rocks."

"I've got one in front of my house that looks like it's going to fall on me any day," Kilpatrick said.

"Really?" Paul Stapleton said.

He didn't particularly like the comparison. Was there a hint of antagonism in it?

They got out and rang the bell. A butler with an Irish brogue answered the door. "Hello, Mahoney," Paul Stapleton said. He introduced Kilpatrick and said he would

118

like to give him a tour of the house. Was the mayor or his wife at home? Mahoney said no. They were both lunching elsewhere. He showed them into the center hall.

On the left was a blazing-eyed portrait of Kemble Stapleton. "That's our Revolutionary hero," Paul Stapleton said. "You mentioned him in your book, *The Vanished Battle.*"

"He looks just like I imagined him," Kilpatrick said.

"What do you see on his face?"

"Utter contempt for anyone not willing to die for his country."

"I see pride. A lot of pride. Maybe too much."

Paul Stapleton stalked ahead of Kilpatrick into the library. A massive marble fireplace stood between two tall windows. Above it was a rather primitive portrait of a man gazing across a vast estate. The staring eyes, the rigid mouth inflicted on him by the painter, gave him a hunted look. But it was unquestionably a Stapleton face, the same sharp angles and delicate bones and stubborn chin.

"That's our immigrant," Paul Stapleton said. "Charles. He bought up a lot of land around here for about a cent an acre."

Paul Stapleton walked closer to the portrait and pointed to a host of tiny figures toiling in the fields across which Charles Stapleton was gazing. "Notice those workers. All black. He owned about sixty or seventy slaves, I've been told."

"Is that why you feel strongly about the blacks?"

"No. I don't believe in ancestral guilt. If old Charles felt guilty about keeping slaves, that was his business. A man should only try to even up the things that happen in his own life. That will give him plenty to do, without worrying about what his great-great-great-grandfather did."

"Even up," Kilpatrick said. "That's an interesting phrase. Do you mean expiate?"

"That sounds too religious for me. I think of it as evening up. Are you religious?"

"No."

"Good. That puts us on the same wavelength. I was trained to respect piety—but not to practice it."

119

They returned to their tour of Bowood. On the right side of the center hall they glanced at portraits of other Stapletons. Hugh, the Continental Congressman, was an interesting variation on the standard Stapleton look. There was humor in his eyes, and his face had a comfortable quota of flesh on it. There was no trace of the fervor that glowed on the faces of Charles and Kemble Stapleton. "My father looked a lot like him," Paul Stapleton said, studying the Congressman. Beside him was his son Charles, the railroad tycoon. He looked hard and cool but basically contented. A cautious smile was on his lips. Hardly surprising for a man who had the state of New Jersey in his pocket.

Beside the tycoon was his brother, the Commodore. He was a reversion to the fierce challenge of Kemble and Charles. Behind him a tangle of ships exploded and burned. Kilpatrick remarked that the portraits were a fascinating glimpse of the interplay between genes and experience.

"Maybe a man's life has more to do with shaping his character than the geneticists are willing to admit," he said. "Maybe character isn't fate. Maybe fate is character."

"I like that," Paul Stapleton said. He liked cleverness. But only up to a point. It was hard to trust a man who was too clever.

Opening a door to the right, they stepped into an oak-paneled hall lined with paintings of steamships and steam engines that had once belonged to the Camden & Amboy, the family's railroad. At the end of the hall, another right turn took them into the ballroom. His father had added this wing to the rear of the house, Paul Stapleton explained. On the opposite side was a matching wing which contained a squash rackets court, an exercise room and the servants' quarters. The ballroom was two stories high. From the chaste white ceilings hung two crystal chandeliers, exact replicas of ones Theodore Roosevelt had installed in the White House in 1903.

"Father picked them out. He was chairman of the arts committee TR appointed to give the White House a little class. Father designed this room. See those windows?

120

Jefferson would have liked them. Straight from Monticello's drawing room."

The six tall windows along the west wall were topped by white pediments in a severely classical style containing friezes of ancient weapons and armor. Paul Stapleton showed Kilpatrick how the windows were really French doors that opened onto a formal garden. The walks were lined with boxwood hedges. A weeping willow tree stood like a grieving sentinel in the rear.

"Father planted that tree," Paul Stapleton said. His voice was suddenly husky. He could remember the whole scene. He was eight or nine. It was in June. His mother had recited a poem by James Russell Lowell. His father had said the tree would live long after they both were dead. He said it was a symbol of what he hoped Paul and his brother Malcolm might do for the city, plant spiritual seeds that would create structures, institutions to bring beauty and happiness to the people. How easy it had been to believe in those lofty words, to love the earnest smiling man who said them. Too easy. Paul Stapleton suddenly remembered the dream that had awakened him. For a moment he was overwhelmed by an enormous sadness.

He turned his back on the garden and led Kilpatrick into the ballroom again. They crossed to the huge marble fireplace. Above it, resplendent in the blue uniform of a Civil War major general, was Jonathan Rawdon Stapleton. He was ignoring a battle that was raging behind him on the canvas. He looked capable of ignoring an earthquake if he put his mind to it. An intense disapproval of everything and everyone emanated from his glaring eyes.

"That's Grandfather," Paul Stapleton said. "Old Steady, they called him during the Civil War. His division never broke and never retreated unless they were ordered to withdraw. He died in his sleep in 1918 at the age of eighty-six. Teddy Roosevelt wrote me that if it had happened while he was awake, death would have had one hell of a battle. A year later they were saying the same thing about Teddy."

"He looks formidable."

"He was. Almost too formidable. You'll hear a lot about him."

In the dining room were portraits of two of General Stapleton's brothers, Charles and Malcolm, who had been killed in the Civil War. "They say Charles would have been the genius of the family if he'd lived. He was killed at Gettysburg," Paul Stapleton said.

On the walls of the upstairs hall were portraits of various Stapleton women. Old Steady's wife, Agatha, was small and plump, with a vaguely frightened look in her eyes. "She died in childbirth," Paul Stapleton said.

Kilpatrick was more interested in Paul Stapleton's mother. She was painted on a sun-filled summer porch by someone who had studied the Impressionists. She was wearing a white organdy dress. There was a red book in her hand. Her lips were parted in a small willful smile.

"Your cousin Peregrine spoke of her with great affection," Kilpatrick said.

"He would," Paul Stapleton said. He gazed at the painting for a long moment. "She was a remarkable woman. A delight to be with as long as she got her own way. When she didn't, you realized why a half million men got killed in the Civil War."

Kilpatrick pointed to an eighteenth-century portrait of a red-haired Stapleton woman. "She has an unbelievable resemblance to your granddaughter Allyn."

"Yes," Paul Stapleton said. "That's Kate Stapleton. Bloodlines are remarkable things. You see the same faces again and again."

Kate's bold eyes and willful mouth troubled Paul Stapleton. "Allyn is a handful," he said. "I don't know what to do about her. When did you meet her?"

"At the hunt party last Saturday."

"I didn't see her. I guess she didn't stay long enough to say hello to me."

A door opened a few feet down the hall and a small blond girl peered out at them. She giggled and shut the door. Paul Stapleton went to the door, got down on one knee and slowly opened it. "Boo," he said, eliciting a squeal of laughter from Mayor O'Connor's four-year-old daughter, Dolores.

He looked around the sunny, blue-walled playroom. Stuffed toys, dolls, a dollhouse, a seesaw, a rocking horse. It was not much different from the room he had romped in as a four- and five-year-old. A fat-faced frowning nurse advanced on him and Dolores. "Now what has the little minx done?" she said with the inevitable Scottish accent. All his nurses had been Scottish.

"Nothing at all," he said. "I'm the one who's acting up. I'm her grand-uncle, Paul Stapleton."

"Oh yes, how do you do," the nurse said.

He took Dolores by the hand and led her out into the hall. "Here's an Irish Stapleton, Jim," he said. "The mayor's little girl, Dolores. This is Mr. Kilpatrick."

"Hello," Kilpatrick said with a warm smile.

Paul Stapleton ran his hand through Dolores' hair. "She spent some time out at the farm last spring. But she didn't enjoy herself, did she? This grouchy old judge was always asking her to be quiet. The next time you visit, he's not going to be a grouch. Won't that be a nice surprise?"

Dolores nodded. She was completely at ease. It was easy to envision her in fifteen years, stunning a generation of males.

"She could use more than a bit of correction," the nurse said. "She's the most spoiled girl I've ever seen. Her father does nothing but spoil her."

"That's what little girls are for," Paul Stapleton said. He got down on one knee again to talk to Dolores. "You come out to the farm when I've got some free time and I'll show you what spoiled really means. We'll go horse-back riding every day and have ice-cream sodas every afternoon. How does that sound?"

"Like *fun*," Dolores said.

He gave the little girl a kiss and sent her back to the playroom. His watch warned him that it was time to get moving. He put off reminiscing about Bowood until they were back in the Mercedes.

"My brother and I and Agatha had a good time in that house when we were kids. We used to play soccer in the ballroom on rainy days. One day I kicked a wild ball and it knocked Grandfather's painting off the wall. It landed on an andiron and it put a hole through his chest. We were terrified. But when Mother saw the damage, she laughed and called it the South's revenge. She rushed the painting out of the house before the old boy came home from the mills and told him that it was being cleaned. She had it repaired in New York and rehung without a glimmer of suspicion ever passing through his mind. Then she told all her allies in the family the story so they could go around laughing behind Grandfather's back.

"They were a pair. They kept on fighting the Civil War until the day they died. My mother's father, my southern grandfather, was shot to pieces at Malvern Hill. He was in a wheelchair for the next twenty years. His wife was his dutiful, devoted nurse. Mother always held them up to us as a model of idealism, of pure disinterested love. But she only went to see the poor fellow once in five years and sent him a present at Christmastime. Mother was very southern. Big talk about ideals but not much follow-through.

"You can see I've absorbed some of Grandfather's attitudes. He was never reconciled to the idea of his younger son marrying a Southerner. He'd seen too many men get killed down there in Virginia to look on them as anything but the enemy. Have you ever heard the expression 'waving the bloody shirt'? That's what they used to say Republican politicians did to win votes in the 1880s and 1890s. When you talked to Grandfather, you realized why they waved it. They got a campaign contribution from him every time.

"But he was no abolitionist. He despised that New England crew more than he did the southern bully boys. He used to say that he never saw the point in killing a half million good white men to free the blacks thirty or forty years ahead of schedule. He was proud of coming from the Middle States, as he called them. He used to say that we stood between two sets of fanatics, and it was up to us to save the country."

Sam Fry eased the Mercedes to a stop in front of the City Club. A half dozen lawyers, several of them partners in Stapleton, Talbot, greeted Paul Stapleton warmly in the marble-pillared lobby. Upstairs he led Kilpatrick through the dining room to the reserved table for two in the rear corner. He told him that in his managing partner days he used to preside at a table for six or eight every day for lunch. But a judge had to be circumspect about his public associations. These days he usually ate at this table, alone.

"Most of my friends are dead, anyway," he said as the waiter took their drink orders. He noticed Kilpatrick ordered tomato juice. Maria had told him about his confession of a drinking problem. She cited it as one more reason for not doing this book. He had told her that he wished George had the self-discipline to drink tomato juice.

"I'm doing all the talking," Paul Stapleton said. "What do you want to know?"

"What did it feel like—to grow up knowing you were part of the richest, most powerful family in this city and state?"

Did he hear hostility in that question? Or was Kilpatrick still pursuing Mark's accusation that he was a snob? "My grandfather—and to some extent my father—went out of their way to make sure I didn't get any fancy ideas about being rich and powerful. We were told again and again that we didn't possess any inherited gift that couldn't be taken away from us. Grandfather drummed into us—me and my brother—the necessity, the expectation, that we should *be* the best, that we had to make the effort, no matter what it cost us personally.

"That sort of superiority—the challenge to be the best—played a lot bigger part in my life than anything ordinarily associated with wealth or snobbery. But I'll be honest and admit there was some of the latter. Grandfather did tend to look down on the Irish, the Jews, the Poles, blacks, because they didn't have that tradition of excellence, of pride in being the best. What he said about them came out as prejudice, and it did influence my attitude somewhat when I was young. But the other thing—the pressure on me to measure up to the family's tradition—was a lot more important.

"There were other forms of snobbery that were really just the way people thought in those days. When I was in grammar school, Grandfather refused to let me associate with Dwight Slocum. I was told that the Slocums were—to put it bluntly—beneath us. They'd made their money from patent medicine—which was considered on a par

125

with getting rich from advertising. That was another field that was beneath respectable people in 1905 and 1906."

Suddenly he could hear his grandfather snarling, "Slocum's father is worse than a Jew. He married a Jew to get the money to start that filthy patent medicine factory. The Jews will ruin what's left of this country after the Irish get through with it."

Better leave that out. It was impossible to tell the whole truth about Jonathan Rawdon Stapleton and make him sound admirable. Yet somehow, eventually, he had to explain why he admired, even loved the old man.

Kilpatrick pursued his remark about Dwight Slocum. He was puzzled by it. "Your sister Agatha married him. Your son Randy worked for him," he said.

"That will take more time to explain than we've got today. I don't think I really understand why Agatha married Dwight. You'd better ask her. As for Randy— did he ever explain any part of it?"

"I gather it had something to do with family money being invested in National Products."

"That's the gist of it. We'll go into it in a lot more detail later."

Kilpatrick looked skeptical. He probably thought the old buzzard was avoiding something he didn't want to tell. That probably explained the bluntness of the next question.

"Agatha told me about the River of Doubt. She said it was one of the most important episodes in your life. She said it had a—a spiritual impact on you."

"Agatha's a woman. She's very intelligent but she's a woman. They tend to take—an emotional view of life. They like to think it's some sort of spiritual drama. They talk about—the inner truth. A man finds out those things are—pretty irrelevant. Not completely, of course. But they're not half as important as getting the job done right."

Paul Stapleton took a long swallow of his drink. This was worse than hard work. It was highly unpleasant, confronting this Irish-American face asking questions about the inside of his life.

"Why don't you just tell the story as you remember

it?" Kilpatrick said. "I never even heard of the River of Doubt until your sister mentioned it."

"It's in Brazil. How we got there takes some explaining. My father was active in politics here in the city. He was supposed to be executive vice-president of Principia Mills, but Grandfather was the president and as long as he was around there wasn't much for a vice-president to do. So Father had a lot of time to devote to things like architecture and politics. I don't suppose you've ever heard of something called the New Idea. Nobody remembers it now, but it had tremendous influence in this state starting around 1900. It was an attempt to restore respectability to American politics and give business a conscience. I was only about five years old when my father first got involved with the New Idea, so I didn't pay much attention to it at the time. All I knew was, it took him away from the family night after night and made Mother mad as hell, which was very difficult for all of us to live with.

"Grandfather didn't like the New Idea either, because it split the Republican Party. He maintained till the day of his death that it was the worst thing that ever happened to the country. But for the time being this was beyond me. I was just delighted when I got to be ten or eleven and Father started talking to me about what he was trying to do. A lot of it went over my head but I got the general idea.

"The country was in a hell of a mess. A lot of crooked operators, the railroad barons, the coal, steel and oil boys, had teamed up with the political bosses to run everything their way. They were working people to death, letting them live like pigs in the slums, while they bought up state legislatures and the Congress to get the laws they wanted to run the profits up higher and higher. It was ridiculous because most of the people who were doing it were already rich. If somebody didn't put a stop to it and give the average man some feeling that the government and the people on top cared about him, we were going to have a revolution that would make the Civil War look like a picnic."

Paul Stapleton paused. Should he add what his father

said about Stapletons being part of it? *"Don't ever let your grandfather hear this,"* the quiet voice had said as they sat before the fire at the farm. *"But some of it is our fault. We taught the fat cats how to do it. Back in the days when we owned the railroad, they used to sing a song in the legislature:*

> *"We are all a band of robbers,*
> *We are all a band of robbers,*
> *From the Camden & Amboy State."*

No, Paul Stapleton decided. Let Kilpatrick dig up his own dirt. He resumed his narrative.

"All this was pretty heady stuff. I thought Father was a kind of white knight. I didn't particularly like Grandfather, anyway. He'd decided that I was likely to be the black sheep of my generation. I guess I looked a lot like my uncle, Rawdon, the one who got killed in Cuba. Peregrine's father. That fellow broke Grandfather's heart. He had a wild streak in him a mile wide. He absolutely refused to go into the business. He didn't see any point in spending his life strapped to a desk. He said we had enough money and it was stupid to spend your life trying to make more of it. The idea that we had a responsibility to run a business, to employ people, to be leaders in the city and state, meant nothing to him. He moved to New York and lived there for years, enjoying himself.

"Grandfather was determined that Rawdon was not going to happen again. He was always giving me fishy looks and warning my father that I was developing bad traits. He'd tell me to sit up straight, speak distinctly, give me sermons against smoking, drinking and bad women. It was a trial to live with him.

"I found it especially hard to take because I started out worshipping the old boy. He doted on me until I was nine or ten. He'd sit me on his knee and let me ask him questions about the Civil War. He bought me the best collection of toy soldiers I've ever seen—exact reproductions of Union and Confederate uniforms—and we'd refight Malvern Hill and Chancellorsville and Gettysburg.

"I'm sure Grandfather went on loving me. But when I started looking—and maybe acting—like Rawdon, the general in him took charge. He didn't know how to apply discipline gradually. He just started issuing orders and reprimands.

"My father hated to argue with the old fellow. He hated arguments, period. Instead, he worked out ways to get me out of Grandfather's clutches as much as possible. He bought New Grange Farm and we used to camp out there on weekends. Father loved the outdoors. I think he got that from Teddy Roosevelt. The old farmhouse was pretty much a wreck. We worked on rebuilding it together. In the evenings we'd sit in the living room and talk about what was happening in the country. He knew all the political bosses, Platt in New York, Matt Quay in Pennsylvania, old Sewell here in New Jersey. Sewell doubled as agent for the Pennsylvania Railroad. He used to hold court in the Pennsylvania Railroad office in Camden. Can you imagine that happening today? We've made a little progress, and people like my father and TR were the ones who got it started. It wasn't easy. They were regarded as traitors by a lot of the so-called best people.

"Father thought the best people in both parties would unite in a third party that would change the country. Grandfather just shook his head and warned him against wrecking the Republican Party. He didn't think much of Republicans after 1876, when they sold the Negro down the river. But Grandfather was a realist, a brutal realist. What counted with him was order. He thought the Republicans were a lot better than the Democrats when it came to keeping the country on an even keel.

"Then came the strike of 1912. It wrecked Father's beautiful dream in this state—and a lot of other states. It was national news. Have you ever read about it?"

"No," Kilpatrick said.

"There was nothing new about labor trouble at the mills. Every so often the workers would get sore about something and walk off their jobs at one or two buildings. Father would go down and talk to them and settle things to everyone's satisfaction in a day or two. We paid better wages than the New England mills because we were closer to New York and Philadelphia and other big markets. But the strike of 1912 was something new—it was

129

led by the Wobblies—the International Workers of the World. These fellows weren't out to win higher wages. They were out to change the system so that they ran things.

"The Wobblies were a tough, rough bunch. They believed that in a class war the motto was 'Anything goes.' Bombs, bullets, arson, you name it, it was in their repertoire. They were first-class agitators. They got the workers in a frenzy and shut us down for six or eight months. They beat up anyone who tried to get to the plant to work. The police did nothing. They were mostly a bunch of second-rate drunks and grafters.

"Grandfather took charge of the situation. He met force with force. He got the governor to call out the militia and he took command of them. They went after the Wobblies. There was blood in the streets and in the houses. One of our plant managers and his wife were killed by a bomb that was thrown through the window of their living room. You can imagine the shock I got reading all this in the newspaper at prep school. I got an even bigger shock when I came home for Christmas and found men with loaded guns in their hands standing behind sandbags at Bowood's gates.

"The strike finally ended when the Wobblies got tired of getting beaten up and left town. Without them around the workers came to their senses pretty quickly and we were open for business again. But Father's dream of building a coalition between the best elements in the working class and the best people in the business class went glimmering. An awful lot of people got scared and retreated back into the Republican Party. If it hadn't been for that strike and a few others like it, TR and Father and the other progressives might have been able to take over the Republican Party in 1912. Instead, they got thrown out on the street. TR ran as an Independent, a progressive. That split the Republican Party and handed the presidential election to the Democrats—to Woodrow Wilson, a power-hungry academic phony if there ever was one. The screwball to end them all, William Jennings Bryan, became Secretary of State. Grandfather sat around growling I told you so.

"This left TR with nothing to do until 1916, when everyone was sure the country would get wise to Wilson and swing to Teddy. You can imagine how thrilled I was when Father invited me to join him and a party of TR's friends on an expedition to explore the River of Doubt. No one had ever followed it from its headwaters in Paraguay through southern Brazil to the Amazon. In fact, it had only been discovered a few years earlier. I accepted on the spot. This was a once-in-a-lifetime opportunity to get to know TR. I'd met him a few times during the 1912 presidential campaign when he spoke at rallies around here. Now we were going to spend eight or ten weeks with him.

"No one gave much thought to the problems we might meet on the River of Doubt. TR saw it as a smaller version of the Amazon, flowing serenely through the jungle. But they called it the River of Doubt—Rio da Dúvida—because no one knew exactly where it went. My father knew it might be dangerous. He went along for only one reason. He wanted to maintain his friendship—by then a very close friendship—with Roosevelt. He thought he had some things to offer TR—things Teddy lacked—balance, judgment.

"We went up the Paraguay River on a gunboat-yacht to the border of Brazil, where Colonel Candido Rondón met us. He had discovered the Dúvida four years earlier. He knew more about the Brazilian backcountry than any other man alive. After some hunting along the border, we went up a tributary of the Paraguay to a place called Tapirapuan. There we got on horses and spent a month crossing the Mato Grosso, a fantastically beautiful highland wilderness. It was like an island in the sky after the jungle heat of Paraguay. The air was dry and the nights were so cool you needed a blanket and you could see the bottom of the brooks. But there weren't too many of these brooks. We ran out of water and some of our pack horses almost died.

"We finally got to Utiarity, an Indian village back in the jungle. Three or four more days got us to the headwaters of the Dúvida and we started down it toward the end of February 1914. We had eight canoes manned by sixteen *camaradas*—Brazilian rivermen, big husky fellows of every shade from white to black as ink. Kermit Roosevelt the President's twenty-four-year-old son, was with us. He had been in Brazil for several years building railroads. There was a naturalist named George Cherry, and Colonel Rondón had two junior officers with him.

"So far it had all been a fantastic adventure. I had been able to sit around a campfire at night listening to Roosevelt and my father argue political tactics and discuss history, literature, biology, genetics. I'll never forget the conversation they had on the night before we started down the Dúvida. My father had read a lot of H. G. Wells. Not the novels, but his essays and social philosophizing, and had been very influenced by him. Wells was pretty pessimistic about the future of America and the world in general. My father started wondering aloud if maybe the Englishman was right. Was America a giant childhood or a gigantic futility? Were we going to end up like the society Wells pictured in one of his books, with the workers sinister subterranean monsters and the property owners a bunch of degenerate aesthetes clinging to power with the help of hired barbarians?

"TR said there was no way that you could disprove a pessimistic prophecy of the future. It was all too possible that America would lose the impetus of her ascent, as Wells put it, but TR said that he chose to live as if this were not going to happen. Suppose it all ends in morlocks and butterflies, that doesn't matter now, he said. The effort's real, it's worth going on with, it would be worth it—even then.

"I can still see his face with a kind of friendly peering snarl on it, like a man with the sun in his eyes. He had his hand out and it slowly closed into a fist as he said this. can still hear the words in that peculiar strained voice—'The effort—the effort's still worth it.' "

"I suppose that's had quite an influence on you," Kilpatrick said.

"What?" Paul Stapleton said. Memory had swept him out of the dining room with its hurrying waiters and chatting lawyers and businessmen. The corned-beef sandwich and iced tea he had ordered were in front of him.

Kilpatrick was putting mayonnaise on his shrimp salad. Paul Stapleton had no recollection of the food being served.

"That idea. The effort's worth it."

"I'd been told that by Grandfather about a hundred times. But it was interesting to hear a former President apply it to making America work. I've thought about it more than once lately, with so many people predicting our decline and fall."

He dabbed mustard on his sandwich and sipped some iced tea.

"The next day we were on the river. For the first week it was like something in a dream. The forest was a green wall on either bank. Huge trees leaned against each other with great loops of vines hanging from them. The current was extremely strong. The weather was wet, lots of rain showers, but the sun dried us off in minutes. It was a lark, a holiday.

"With no warning, the river turned ugly. From a quarter of a mile wide it narrowed to an unbelievable two yards in the wildest rapids you ever saw. We had to unload everything from the canoes and lug the baggage and the boats a half mile around these rapids. It was the beginning of our ordeal. Day after day we ran into rapids and had to repeat the portage. Our progress was reduced to zero. We ran low on food and everyone started suffering from exhaustion—particularly my father and TR. They were in their middle fifties. They were in good condition but they were just too old to take so much physical abuse. The insects bit us during a portage until our legs were a mass of swollen sores. We were eating only two very inadequate meals a day. My father jumped into the water to help with an overturned dugout and got a bad gash on his leg. It turned into an abscess and the Brazilian doctor we had with us had to lance it and insert a drainage tube. TR came down with an attack of fever that left him terribly weak. TR actually discussed with Father the possibility of sending the rest of us along without them and dying there in the jungle with the help of a little morphine. Instead of arguing with him, Father took Kermit aside and advised him to tell TR that we would carry him out, dead or alive. It was the last we heard of that idea.

"Everything about the trip began to change from a dream to a nightmare. The thick, hot tropic air made it impossible to get a breath, the sun seemed to be burning the flesh off our bones, and that green jungle on both sides became a sort of monster, perpetually watching us for a sign of weakness. My father's leg swelled to twice its normal size but he insisted on walking on it because he knew we didn't have the strength to carry him.

"The *camaradas* got very unruly. They were on half rations too. One of them, a bad actor named Júlio—pure white, incidentally—grabbed a rifle and killed the best man we had, a black fellow named Paishon, who had caught him stealing meat from TR's pack. Júlio ran into the jungle and—"

No he could not tell him he could not tell this surly stranger with the enemy face he could not tell him.

Kilpatrick was jotting notes on a pad beside his plate. Paul Stapleton looked down the room and saw Walter Ackroyd lunching alone in the opposite corner. A commentary on what was wrong with Stapleton, Talbot.

"Excuse me, Jim," Paul Stapleton said. "I just saw Walter Ackroyd, the managing partner of my old firm, come in. There's a little message I want to give him about one of the partners."

He strode down the room, nodding to a dozen familiar faces, and touched Walter on the shoulder. He started to get up, as if he thought he should come to attention. "I just wanted to say that I got your letter, Walter," Paul Stapleton said. "I'll do something about it as soon as I get some animals back in their cages over at my court."

Ackroyd began telling him how sorry he was to have been forced to write the letter. Paul Stapleton waved aside the apology.

Back at the table with Kilpatrick, he ate some of his sandwich and drank the iced tea. "Where were we?"

"The *camarada*—Júlio—just ran into the jungle."

"Oh, yes. We never saw him again. We went on struggling from rapids to rapids. Finally the Dúvida settled down and we were able to do some paddling. But the crazy river turned out to be fifteen hundred kilometers

134

long. We staggered into Manáos on the Amazon, a bunch of half-starved skeletons. The doctor told us my father's leg had become gangrenous. He amputated it in a little clinic in Manáos but it was too late. Or he was too weak to handle the shock. I don't know. He died three days later on the steamer that took us down the Amazon."

He was back in the stinking cabin of that dirty chugging riverboat, watching his father twist and gasp in the heat. The smell of his unwashed body, with its bowels and bladder out of control in the throes of death, filled his lungs. "Rawdon," his father whispered, reaching out to him in the semi-darkness. "Is that you, Rawdon? You were right. You can't do business with the old man. I tried. You were right. I should have done it your way—"

Paul Stapleton heard his own voice as if it came from a distance, as if he was standing back there in the semi-darkness, sixty-two years ago.

"It was a terrible blow to me. I felt—betrayed, in a crazy, stupid way. As if Father had died deliberately. I guess it takes a long time to realize people don't have any control over when they die. Grandfather was another reason, I felt that way. I felt I had no one to protect me from him now."

"Did Roosevelt say anything to you?"

"Oh, yes. The usual things. What a fine man, even a great man, my father was, in his quiet way. A fighter for the ideal. There weren't many like him."

Paul Stapleton remembered, but could not tell Kilpatrick what he had been thinking as the ex-President said these consoling words, and the seventeen-year-old boy nodded and wiped the tears from his face. *You don't know what the hell you're talking about, you foursquare bully-faced fraud. You can shove your ideals up your fat ass.*

"He talked about San Juan Hill, how Father had showed just as much courage as my uncle, Rawdon."

For a moment Paul Stapleton was on a hill in Italy. It was snow-covered. Around him, saw-toothed peaks and sheer cliffs stared bleakly. He stood there beside Sam Fry looking at sixteen twisted frozen American bodies. *Goddamn it,* he cursed. *Goddamn Jesus fucking Christ.*

"The net effect of all this on me was not too healthy,"

135

he said to Jim Kilpatrick. "I came home from Brazil ready—without realizing it—to rebel against Grandfather."

Paul Stapleton looked at his watch. It was almost two o'clock.

"That's another story. We'll have to tackle it the next time."

Downstairs, Sam Fry had the Mercedes cool and purring. Kilpatrick declined a ride. He was going to do some research in the public library only a few blocks from the club. Paul Stapleton rode back to the courtroom, thinking: *At the end there I came close. It was better than nothing.*

X

"I'm getting drunk," Allyn Stapleton said. "So are you."

"You can't get drunk on a virgin mary," Jim Kilpatrick said.

"The hell you can't. That's no virgin any more than I am. I put two shots of vodka in it."

He had known it, of course. He had felt the alcohol surge in his blood. He had felt the wind of old disasters blow through his mind. But he had struggled to control it. He told himself that she might have done it by mistake, mixing the drinks in the kitchen. She was pretty drunk when he arrived at 6 P.M., the agreed-on hour, and did not try very hard to conceal it. She said that they had had a little party for one of the painters downstairs at the gallery, to celebrate a five-hundred-dollar sale.

Whether it was liquor or will or wish, Kilpatrick did not know, but he felt his grip on himself loosen. It had been a long time, almost two years, since he had been this close to a desirable woman. Allyn Stapleton was wearing a gray flannel skirt and matching vest, beneath a brocaded velvet jacket. A wine-colored ascot was tied at her throat. Her dark red hair spilled down her back in a glowing sheen. It swung, as if it had a life of its own, when she turned her head to say something to him on the way back to the kitchen for more drinks. Her apartment was white on white—white rugs and white contoured furniture with Lucite arms and chrome tubing. She sat on a white leather couch, her long legs crossed, sipped her martini and insisted on hearing his life story, the compound of accident and impulse that had led him to Randy Stapleton's door.

He tried to make it sound funny, and apparently succeeded. She laughed into her drink and once almost choked on it. He used his talent for imitation to resurrect the jerk Catholic intellectuals with whom he had spent his college years. He did an especially good job on Esther, his ex-wife, her wide-eyed upper-nasal intonations of the virtues of poverty and large families, which persuaded him to ignore his father's urgent advice to get a law degree. He did a first-rate parody of his discovery that the white-collar dragon which was supposedly going to corrupt and destroy him was largely composed of people like himself, semi-bright young guys hustling bucks to stay two steps ahead of the banks and finance companies. It had slowly dawned on him that holy poverty was a gimmick created by jerk Catholic intellectuals who were too lazy or too incompetent to make it in the real American world and needed an excuse to despise it.

He had trouble making that one sound funny. He could hear old rage pulsing in his voice. But he regained his stride with expert mimicry of the accents and grammar of the candy-store owners he had endured on his soft-drink sales route. He acted out a few of his choicer imbroglios with evasive prospects during his career as a life-insurance salesman in Bridgewater, the mostly Irish-American suburb to the north of the city. He described his sales-motivated martyrdom as a Little League coach, his tour as a Knight of Columbus factotum, complete with cocked hat and sword, his later career as a health-insurance salesman with a company that used the "cold canvass" approach. This required the gall to barge into an office and convince total strangers that their salvation depended on the purchase of his brand of coverage. He parodied the pep talks he was ordered to give himself

138

each morning to build up his confidence, the mental energizers he was supposed to administer to himself in one-sentence doses throughout the day.

After these merry travails, it was mere jokery to abandon his wife and children and flee to the West Coast to drink himself to death quietly, perhaps ending it with a swan dive off the Golden Gate Bridge. Instead, for reasons needless to describe, he had chosen life with dignity, gotten himself a job in a National Products subsidiary and done so well that he had attracted Randy Stapleton's attention.

Allyn replied with a merry version of her own adventures in New York, designing industrial exhibits for the clients of a big advertising agency, dodging passes from horny account executives and corporate vice-presidents. After Vassar, she had wanted to go to the Columbia School of Architecture, but Paul Stapleton disapproved of women in the professions. He was too shrewd to say so openly. Instead, he found a career counselor who convinced her that she lacked the mathematical background. Since she returned to the city, Allyn had gotten the man to admit that he had been paid five hundred dollars for this lie. Meanwhile, her grandparents, with whom she had lived since her mother's death in 1952, had worked tirelessly to warm a tepid romance between Allyn and the son of one of the Stapleton, Talbot's partners. Allyn called him "Boola Boola" because he was always humming Yale songs.

"Boola Boola finally proposed and we moved to New York, where he planned to get five or six years of seasoning on Wall Street before joining Stapleton, Talbot. Of course, we went home every weekend, either to the farm or his parent's place, about two miles away, so Boola Boola could keep all the connections oiled. Without telling him or anyone else, I started taking the pill. I enrolled in Peter Cooper and got some design training. But I was supposed to be having babies. Maria was saying prayers and Boola Boola was going to doctors to check his sperm count and sending me to doctors and suggesting special diets. He had his whole life planned, and he couldn't stand it when his prime brood mare failed to produce on schedule. In the end the only thing holding us together

139

was Randy. I knew a divorce would make him feel horribly guilty. He felt so damn responsible for me, because he never married again. When Randy's plane crashed, I became a liberated woman. Guilty as hell, of course, but liberated."

The reference to Randy short-circuited the merriment. Or had it short-circuited much earlier? Kilpatrick was finding it hard to keep track of sequences. It made him uncomfortable to hear Allyn calling her father Randy, as if he were her older brother. It sounded vaguely disrespectful. Somehow, it also made her more desirable, permissible.

He had seen girls like Allyn Stapleton in New York, svelte, chic, with glossy expressionless faces, sophistication worn as a mask. More than once he had undressed them, fantasized stripping away the mask, conquering the msytery of the blasé world they represented, knowing it was probably trivial, preoccupied with hairstyles and hot name designers and who was sleeping with whom, things he as an ex-Catholic moralist disapproved. He had told himself that he would let his sons have the glossy girls, especially his oldest son, Kevin, who had the cocky self-confidence of his paternal grandfather, Judge James Kilpatrick, Sr. Kevin would take what he wanted from their swinging sex and cool style and go on to more serious things. Instead, Kevin had gone on to a military cemetery in Long Island. He had never gotten to the glossy girls. Maybe a few bar girls in some smelly Saigon alley.

Allyn kept talking about Randy. Kilpatrick started to find it irritating. He had not come here to talk about Randy. He had come ready for a jolt of truth about the Stapletons past and present. Maybe that was why he took the vodka in the tomato juice without mentioning it. He had been listening and he had been reading and he already suspected that the old folks were not telling him the truth. The letters from Paul Stapleton's father that he had pried from Agatha's grasp revealed him as about as influential with Teddy Roosevelt as Polonius with Hamlet. Kilpatrick had spent the afternoon in the library reading books about the progressive Republicans in New Jersey. There had never been more than about 1,200 of

140

them and their pathetic revolt lasted less than five years. The bosses had ground them to mincemeat and gone back to business as usual.

Before he could get Allyn off the subject of Randy, she started mourning him. She recited a litany of the kind and thoughtful and loving things Randy had done for her. No matter where he was, Singapore or New Delhi or Buenos Aires or Madrid, Randy called her long-distance at least once a week and always returned from a trip with an unusual present, a piece of jewelry, or a dress, or a book that she still treasured, and on her birthdays Randy flew from anywhere, once from Tokyo nonstop, to take her to dinner and when she was little he taught her to ride at the farm and he called her a special nickname Tiz short for Tizzie because she was always having temper tantrums.

Suddenly Kilpatrick was in it too with his own mournful memories, the time he had stayed up two consecutive nights to finish the annual report and perfect the president's speech to the stockholders and Randy had given him a thousand dollars in cash and told him to take a long weekend in the Bahamas; the time that Randy had paid his son Kevin's tuition to Pennsgrove for his senior year and had helped him get into Princeton and the time that he had promoted Kilpatrick to vice-president in charge of corporate public relations and told him to bring order out of a chaotic overstaffed department and had patiently listened to his problems and ignored the political infighting and quietly backed every decision he made but insisted on budgeting $10,000 for each man fired to give him the counseling he needed to find another job.

Allyn started again, almost weeping now. Through the haze of alcohol, Kilpatrick saw her guilt but it vanished like a housetop glimpsed from a plane landing at an airport in thick fog, heartstopping but quickly forgotten. "Jesus, Christ," Kilpatrick said. "I know Randy was a goddamn *saint*. But he's dead. You said on the phone you could tell me some juicy stuff about the old man."

"That's right," she said with a reckless smile. "Let's have another round and I'll tell you everything."

Quickly she multiplied the martinis and the bloody marys and Kilpatrick took the Japanese tape recorder out

141

of his briefcase. He did not remember turning it on but when he played it back it was all there, Allyn Stapleton's story in one long, drunken sentence.

"Randy my father was a marvelous man a goddamn saint like you said, smart, gentle wise he could've been great but his father wouldn't let any of his sons escape him each had to *worship* yes worship his supposed greatness all part of his bullshit about family tradition and service to the country every son had to bow down and kiss the Great Man's feet every morning of his life or he was kicked into outer darkness like the Jews banished apostates in the old days there was no way of satisfying him no way of getting his love except this total *devotion* and the tragic thing about Randy was the *willingness,* the way he *loved* and explained and defended the bastard he wasn't satisfied until Mother and I believed too until we worshipped at the goddamn *shrine* Mother fought back the poor bitch in the only way she knew she used the only power she had the power to destroy herself she became a drunk but that didn't change anything they took me away from her and put her in a sanitarium until she finally died and I spent most of my time at the farm with Holy Maria and the Great Man until they shipped me off to Miss Porter's but they didn't trust me or the school they dragged me home every other weekend to make sure I was saying my prayers and remembered I was a Stapleton they never said a word against Mother but I knew they were glad she was dead she was from the wrong class you know common a nurse Randy met her in Germany it was just as well she died they would have destroyed her the Stapletons destroy every woman they turn us into *them,* knights in goddamn armor, with no feelings every time I think of it I have to take a drink or smoke a joint or fuck somebody or go to a movie and sit through it three times until my mind is empty again maybe you know the rest of it what Randy was doing at National Products he was minding the family money what there was left of it thanks to the stupidity of the Great Man and his halfwit brother it didn't matter that Randy had to sell his soul and his body to one of the vilest characters in the history of the country Dwight Slocum it didn't matter that he ended up running one of the most murderous companies in the military-industrial complex it was all for the greater good and glory of the Stapletons and the survival of our imperial democracy those tanks and missiles enabled the apostles of capitalism to go on raping the world of its raw materials and its dignity but that was okay because the Great Man said it was right his approval justified Randy spending seven out of every eight weeks flying around the country or the world while his daughter sat home trying to remember what he looked like nothing mattered but the honor of the Stapletons the security of A-M-E-R-I-K-A go see Mark Stapleton in New York with half an arm and half a leg, ruined, the poor bastard, and George, finally revolting now with his life two thirds over and Ned and his bitchy little Kentucky wife sitting there in that imitation of Bowood trying to pretend it's still 1910 while their kids are getting stoned on marijuana and Christ knows what else each is tormented or frozen or powerless because he hasn't been able to match the paragon and all the time the son of a bitch has the morals of a mafioso when he was young he fucked everything that walked he had an illegitimate son he raised in his house John a beautiful guy that he turned into a professional killer he went to West Point and got incinerated in a tank in Korea and you know how we made our money don't you by starving workers and breaking strikes and bribing politicians and hiring spies what he does now is nothing but an extension of the same system lying for corporations in the courtroom and probably bribing senators and congressmen and IRS men I tried to accept it while Randy was alive he used to explain it to me as part of history or some goddamn thing but when he died I started asking myself why I was married to a nice straight stupid lawyer who was going to work for Stapleton, Talbot and build me a house in the country and join the hunt and make sure I had sons to send off to the next decade's wars for the first time I started listening to the voice inside me that said it all stank Maria is the only one I can't figure out Agatha is easy she's an old maid by instinct on some sort of spiritual trip but Maria should *hate* him for what he's done killing her oldest son and destroying her other three sons and fucking other women behind her back and bringing his bastards home for her to raise how in Christ can she love him there's only one explanation she's afraid of him like I was like I still am she's one of his *possessions* something he picked up in his travels symbolic like so many other things about him she's his Spanish servant or conquest of Mexico and that Indian Sam Fry is another one, an Apache, from the wildest of the tribes reduced to a valet and you his Irish bard hired to hymn his glory all the conquered peoples do you like to fuck I'm in the mood if you are."

Of course Kilpatrick was in the mood. What middle-aged man could refuse such an invitation? Answer: a middle-aged man without eight or nine ounces of vodka deliquescing his brain.

He let her lead him to a sea-green bedroom with interesting fabrics, full of bright geometrical designs, framed on the walls. They undressed and took a shower together. Slowly, drunkenly, succulently he soaped her dark red pubic hair and let his finger move up her vagina while she played similar games with his smooth swelling cock. Beside the bed, then, toweling those small firm breasts, coned like he always imagined the twin roes in the Song of Solomon, not full and pudding soft like his California girl friend's or disappointing snubs like his ex-wife's. There was pride and defiance in the way they lifted their nipples to him. But no pride, only pleasure in the open mouth and something beyond desire, something darker and more profound in the silken cunt, the hot wet vagina.

"There's nothing, absolutely nothing, that I don't like to do," Allyn said.

Kilpatrick let the significance of that double negative slip by him while he liquefied that hot vagina with his tongue. But he heard it, he felt the darker spirit beyond desire invade him as he entered her from behind and she gasped and said it was her favorite position except for the mouth she loved it in the mouth. He was entering between two moons of youth of time into the past and future his hands on those breasts were father hands and son hands and brother hands he was part, part of this man who had changed his life, this man who was son and father like him. The old man had said: *I've felt you were part of the*

144

family ever since I read your letter. Was that all he wanted now?

But not this way, from behind. He wanted not merely to be part, not merely to enter but to belong, to remain, to hold. From behind was the way they had taken the whores in London's East End during the war. He turned her and kissed her and she whispered, "Let me suck it," but he shook his head and stretched her on her back and entered her again and felt enormous unreal love flow out of him as he came.

She did not like it. At the very last she did not like it. She turned her face away from him and he kissed her neck and tasted cold dry flesh and heard her whisper, "No," as he came. He thought he had come too soon and apologized. But she said it was all right. She seldom came. She kissed him and said she liked it. She said he was fantastic. She started to suck him off.

Suddenly he remembered a story he had read about a marine in Saigon who had gone to a whorehouse for a blow job and was killed by the Viet Cong in the middle of it. He watched her take his cock into her mouth and she transmuted into the nameless faceless rich girls on the streets of New York and he wanted her without love, as meat, desirable flesh, the lust of youth, in his dead son's name. He was entering her, entering all the Stapletons in Kevin's name, in search of revengeful truth.

He came in her mouth, hot, tight, sending a pulse of pain through his testicles. At the same moment he sank two fingers deep into her hot vagina, wet with his semen. For both spirits, in the name of truth in the name of revenge in the name of lust in the name of love, whispered a cacophony of voices in his head.

She smiled up at him. "My God," she said, "I came."

He cradled her in his arms. The bone line running from her neck to her shoulder was as delicate as porcelain. "Let me help you write the truth about them," she said.

Far gone as he was, Kilpatrick knew that was a bad idea. He knew, for instance, that her version of Randy Stapleton's business career was ominously distant from reality. But balance, judgment, faltered in his alcohol-sodden brain. Maybe she was right. Maybe nothing in the

145

Stapleton world was what it seemed. Maybe even Randy wore a mask that concealed the hatred and rage that was destroying his daughter.

"All right," he said. "But we need proof."

"I'll get you proof," she said.

XI

Star
In the heart of darkness
Star
On the ribbon of empire
Star
In the priest's eye
In the eagle's talon
In the snake's coil
Dark star calling us
Out of the north
Summoning us to the violated south

George Stapleton took two Dexedrines and studied the poem. He turned up the volume on his stereo to maximum. From Africa crashed the chant of another time. "UM-MALI UM-MALI UM-MALI" was what it sounded like. He did not know what it meant. Drums boomed through his flesh. He was escaping the prison of age and memory. The words were coming. He was almost happy.

The phone rang. It was Allyn. "I think I've got Jim

Kilpatrick, Unc. But I didn't like doing it. There's something about the guy that gives me bad vibes. He's not the simpleminded Irish slob you described."

"Leave the definitions to me. Did you fuck?"

"Yes."

"Tell me about it."

"Go to hell."

George returned to the poem, less happy. Ten minutes later, he was unhappy. Eddie Osborne, the stocky black editor in chief of Lenape Press, smiled uncertainly at his patron. Lately, George had begun to dislike Osborne. He had been a poet when George hired him. But he had started trying to make a business success out of Lenape Press. He had taken a night course in publishing procedures at the state university and started talking about the need for cookbooks, children's books, how-to books, to create a "balanced list."

"What do you want?" George said. He left the stereo on full volume.

"George, I've been trying to talk to you for two weeks. You don't answer my calls. We got bills to pay, George. We got returns from last season's list like you can't believe."

"What about the grant?"

Osborne had applied to the National Council on the Arts for a grant.

"It doesn't look good. You were going to ask your father—"

"I didn't. I thought your application was so good I could avoid that ordeal."

Osborne rolled his eyes toward the cork ceiling. "There's three or four hundred small presses like us trying for those grants. With the friends that man's got in Washington—"

"Maybe your application wasn't as good as I thought it was."

"That could be. But I need to know, George. How do we pay those bills? We've only got enough money to pay salaries for another month."

One more year, his father had snarled. *I will pay for one more year. Publishing is a business. You should be able to make money at it.*

148

How did you explain to that graven face, those blind eyes, that merciless mouth that poetry was not a business, it was a spiritual revolution aimed at undoing the wounds he and his kind had inflicted on the world? How do you explain that you want to take his money and undo his pride, this smoking industrial nightmare that he had created, with its compartmentalized lives and its dead souls and lost tribes?

"Another month may be all Lenape Press has to live, Eddie," George said. "The old man told me last year that he wouldn't pay for another year. He said we had to show a profit, like all Stapleton enterprises."

"Maybe you could show him that plan I worked up, projecting our potential sales, if we take on some of those books I mentioned to you."

"That plan produced instant nausea," George said. "I didn't get into this to make money. I got into it to publish poetry. Good poetry. If the goddamn country won't buy good poetry, fuck it!"

"Yeah, but—look, George, I put in three years on this thing. So did the other people at—"

"You got paid. You all got paid pretty well."

"That isn't the point, George. We've got some pride. We worked hard to make it go. We produced beautiful books. We don't want to see it fail because—it's us failing."

"No one has failed but me, Eddie. I take full responsibility."

"Bullshit!" Osborne said. "I don't buy that trip, George. I can't believe your father—with what he's doing in that courtroom—"

"Eddie, he doesn't give a shit for you or anyone else. It's all principle. He doesn't really think it's going to work. He doesn't really think you're worth the time and effort. He thinks you're nigger trash. You should hear him talk about the 92nd Division in Italy. I told you about it. You go down there and ask him for help, and he'll look at you and shake his head and say, 'What else can you expect, you people are worse than the Irish and the Jews.' Do you want to buy that trip?"

"I don't believe you."

"I don't care whether you believe me or not, you're not

149

going down there to beg money from him in my name!"

Eddie seemed to shrink in front of his eyes. His chest sank, his shoulders drooped. "So we got a month," he said.

"A month," George Stapleton said.

Eddie departed. George stared numbly at his unfinished poem. He went over to the bar and poured himself a tumbler of straight gin. He wandered around his empty house, past the huge beaten silver and gold plates from his mother's home, the Hacienda Gloriosa, in Mexico, past the bright Indian rugs, the Aztec and Mayan stone gods that he had paid thousands of dollars to smuggle across the border.

The telephone rang. He answered it and a familiar voice said, "George, this is your father. I tried to get you at the office."

"I've got a cold."

"I want to have lunch with you today in my chambers. Can you and your cold make it?"

"I'm working on a poem."

"George, this is important. I don't want to talk about it on the telephone. Switchboards have big ears."

"Next week, maybe."

"Goddamn it, George, this may not be able to wait until next week. Will you be home at six o'clock tonight? I'll stop by."

"I've got a dinner date in town."

"You can take your cold to dinner but you can't take it to work? Or to lunch?"

"I'm in bed right now loaded with antihistamines."

"I'll call you tomorrow."

George hung up and finished the gin. Smooth, he was as smooth inside now as the skin on a black ass. Outside he heard the thrump of the diving board, the splash of water in the pool. He went out on the patio and found Jacky somebody swimming toward him. She flipped on her back and smiled up at him.

"I didn't bring a bathing suit," she said. "Allyn told me not to bother."

"I don't even own one," George said.

"That was great last night," she said.

150

"What did we do? I don't remember a thing," George said.

"Neither do I. But it must have been great. I wouldn't be here, with this head."

"How does it feel?"

"Like bubble gum."

George watched the dark V of her pubic hair undulating under the green water. "Do you think we should start calling it public hair?" he said. "It might change people's attitudes."

"Write a poem about it."

"Pubic went public today. The market in disarray—"

George shook his head. "Too much gin."

"Join me?"

"Which way?" George said, pulling off his polo shirt and shucking his blue jeans.

"Your choice," she said.

They played goosey grab-ass for a while. Then she tried sucking him off underwater. Nothing much happened. "I guess I gave it all to you last night," George said.

"Try the finger," she said. "I'll never know the difference."

He exercised his finger for a few minutes. They talked about Allyn. "She says she never comes. What is it with you Wasps? How did you get those ice-cold genes?"

"We use nothing but the best frozen sperm."

"I wish I never came. That's how I decided I was really Jewish. I cream my pants every time a man looks at me."

"The other way is more interesting, don't you think?"

"Definitely. I'm working on it. That's why I like making it with old farts like you. A little repugnance goes a long way."

She was still high. She still had a license to say exactly what she felt. But he was no longer high. With one finger still in the vagina, he shoved her head underwater and held her there until she started to struggle. Another sixty seconds and the little Jew bitch would never call anyone an old fart again.

She got both lithe legs against his chest and shoved.

They broke apart and she surfaced, gasping. "Hey, Uncle George. I didn't like that."

"I didn't like what you just said."

"What's the matter? Can't you face reality?"

Reality. The word echoed and reechoed in George Stapleton's brain. Reality. Reality therapy. He was in the sanitarium talking to Dr. Nathaniel Kane again. *You must face reality, George.*

"Get the fuck out of here," he said. "Get out before you get hurt, you goddamn fucking Jew cunt. The next time I won't let you up. The next time I won't think it's funny. I was only kidding, but you weren't. You're like every goddamn Yid I've ever met, the sensibility of a slob and the morals of a whore."

She swam to the other end of the pool and vanished into the adobe cottage where she had spent the night. George retreated into the house and poured himself some more gin. The telephone rang. He picked it up and heard a secretary telling him that Dwight Slocum was returning his call.

"Mr. Slocum? I'm George Stapleton—Paul's son. Randy's brother. I think I met you once. When I was in New York on business. That tax matter with the Caribbean Investment Company."

"I remember," said the old throaty voice. "The goddamn IRS was trying to ruh-rape me. You did a nice job. Saved me a good million."

"Listen, Mr. Slocum. My father's having a book written about him. By a guy named Kilpatrick. He used to work for Randy."

"I re-remember him. He qu-quit two years ago. A good speech writer."

"Yeah. But the things my father's telling him about you. They just make me sick. He's smearing you. I don't know the whole story, but—I don't get along with Dad— my father—very well. That explains why I'm calling you. That and my feeling that a man should have a right to defend himself. Why don't you talk to Kilpatrick? I'm sure you can get him through the Remedy office."

"I'll call the son of a bitch today."

George took two Quaaludes and drifted into his favorite state of consciousness, half asleep, half awake. Images surfaced from the depths of his mind and he could banish or play with them. His first wife with her earnest plain Protestant face rode naked on a huge horse. Her sagging breasts flopped menacingly. His Cuban second wife sat in the middle of a barren plain eating a plate of roses, while a bearded man, presumably Fidel Castro, sliced off her right breast. Castro pulled off his beard and revealed he was really Pancho Villa, who took off his mustache and revealed that he was George. Blacking his face, George began doing a soft-shoe dance in a snowstorm. Suddenly he was wearing an army uniform, a helmet. There was blood on his face. A half dozen other black soldiers surrounded him. One carried his head under his arm. Another walked on stumps of legs. A third had no eyes. George ordered them to vanish but they refused. They drew gleaming .45s and formed a bizarre firing squad.

"No," George heard himself saying. "No."

Fighting panic, George struggled back to full consciousness and stumbled into his study to work on the poem. He sat and stared at it for a half hour. He put on his favorite tape: "Mushroom Ceremony of the Mazatec Indians of Mexico." He listened to an old woman and an old man cackle, chant and sing in a nightmare language. He thought about the trip he had taken to the village of Santa María in the Mexican Sierras last year, where he had tried drug therapy with Dr. Salvador Blanca. First LSD, then Ketamine. It had been a disaster. He had gone berserk and tried to kill Blanca, certain he was at last killing his father. It had taken a dozen Indians to control him.

Nothing works, George thought. Nothing will work until that monstrous hypocrite. that murderer, is hounded from the earth. He shoved aside the typewriter and took a letter from his desk. In his years as a tax lawyer, he had made a number of friends at the Internal Revenue Service. He found the comfortable tone of this letter reassuring.

Dear George:

I have your letter, which of course I will regard as completely confidential. The issue you raise is complex, and I understand perfectly why your conscience is troubled. At this point in our social development, the IRS might severely question the propriety of a foundation created by a man whose money was made by fraud or violence. If a Mafia boss, for instance, created a foundation in his will I think we would look very hard at it and perhaps decide that those involved lacked the good moral character needed to run a charitable enterprise. We would probably insist that the money be regarded as taxable under the inheritance laws. This John Doe you describe, a lawyer and investor, poses a trickier question; Rockefeller, Ford, even Kennedy money is not without some historical taint, yet they have been permitted to erect foundations. But the abuses of these organizations, particularly the Ford Foundation scandal in 1969, when they got caught handing out money to ex-Kennedy gurus for European vacations, inspired Congress to pass a much tougher foundation law in 1972, giving us a lot more authority over the creation and operation of the whole field. If you could give us hard evidence to disprove this man's supposed integrity, we would certainly challenge the will, and bring the whole matter under the most rigorous scrutiny. I need hardly add, although I am sure it does not interest you, that you would get the usual 10 percent of any tax monies that accrued to the government.

Cordially,
Ron

Three cheers, George murmured, three cheers for the onward march of the liberal conscience. Fools like you, Ron, fools like Kilpatrick, freaks like Allyn, are my unwitting witless servants. In the end the poet is the master man of the master race. He dangles white whales before the eyes of the witless. Ron's white whale is the landmark tax ruling. Kilpatrick's is honorary membership in the Noble Order of Certified Americans. Allyn's is the ultimate fuck, the dong that will scour Stapletonism from her mind like hot steam sears the grime from downtown buildings.

Ron was a bonus, a gamble. It might work. It was like a huge land mine under the whole system. Kilpatrick's book would be the trigger, to set the fuse burning. The IRS ferrets were the flame racing down the wire to the mine, the confidential tax records of National Products,

Inc., which George had been stealing from the offices of Stapleton, Talbot for over a year. It was all legal, every maneuver, like everything Stapleton, Talbot did, but the IRS could do wonders quoting from the right document, slightly out of context. And the IRS was ready to do wonders, when it smelled a thirty- or forty-million-dollar tax windfall. If it worked, George Stapleton would walk away with three or four million secret IRS reward dollars, in addition to his legal money under the inheritance tax law.

Then Mexico would beckon. The Hacienda Gloriosa could be reconstituted. Perhaps his mother would see at last the stupidity, the gross evil of her devotion to her husband, and join him there.

George put the letter away and chose another tape for his stereo: "Sleep Gently in the Womb." It was cool otherworldly electronic music. From a chamois bag in another drawer of his desk George drew a solid-silver tube. He took a two-gram vial of his 90 percent pure cocaine, unscrewed the cap and dumped a little mound of white particles onto the small mirror beside his typewriter. He chopped them with the razor blade set in its silver holder. The clicking of the metal on the glass was a reassuring sound, mathematical, mechanical. Then came the ritual. George carried the pulverized particles on the mirror to the big bed in the far corner of the room. He lay down on it and assumed the fetal position. Quickly, expertly, he snorted two deep lines in each nostril and rolled over to wait for the impact. In less than ten seconds, it hit, a blast of fire like the breath of an angry god. The skin, the flesh of his face, seemed to be peeling off, spewing power, poems, prayers, against the mosaic of the plumed serpent on the ceiling.

Suddenly he was back in Italy. There was the smashed village, with the shells sending up great geysers of plaster and stone. There was the rising sun like a bleeding eye on the eastern horizon. They were out of the foxholes now. They were going forward, a swaying brown and black line in the muddy snow. The German machine guns chattered. The mortar shells plopped and boomed. Men were screaming, falling. But he was going through, he was running down the main street throwing grenades and his

155

black soldiers were following him, their eyes wild with bloodlust, their pink mouths wide with screams of triumph. The machine guns could not touch him. He chanted poems at them and their bullets fell at his feet. He aimed his black .45 at them and the words it spoke left the gunners speechless. Peace, beauty roared his gun and the Germans wept and begged his forgiveness.

He was on a political platform, speaking to an immense crowd on a huge map of America. Smiling in conscious parody, he pumped his arm Jack Kennedy style and said, "My fellow morons, ask not what your country can do for you, but what your country has done to you." George laughed. That was brilliant wit. The gonging, crooning electronic music poured over him. He was being born again. He and the world were being born again.

It was time for another tape. He put on "Hitler's Inferno in Words and Music." He strode up and down the big room, thinking about what he could do with fifteen or twenty million dollars in Mexico. The room trembled with the crash of massed bands, the thunder of hobnailed boots.

From another drawer of his desk George took his black army .45. There was the final solution. If the plan failed, if the fools refused to hunt their white whales, there was always this alternative. He rubbed the gleaming gun with the chamois bag. The study became a control tower, the typewriter a console. His mind, pulsing and triumphant, remained here, guiding his body with consuming intelligence, unfaltering courage.

He would put the gun in his Mark Cross briefcase, with its built-in alphabetical file. He would put it under A for assassin. Downstairs the blue Porsche would be waiting. To the federal courthouse he would drive. He would park beside the gray Mercedes in the reserved section of the lot. Upstairs to the courtroom, striding past guards to the rail while the ancient hated face glared at him. Then the gun, huge in his hand, speaking the ultimate poem. Finally, turning, a bow, shouting to the assembled morons, the body politic. "I DID IT FOR THE PEOPLE."

While the mind, serene, secure at the console, smiled triumphantly.

Shrill then guttural, the voice of German madness

156

raged through the room. "Sieg heil! Sieg heil!" roared the worshippers.

Why not now? whispered the mind. But there was a tremor in the assurance. The cocaine was starting to fade. The vision was still there but it was no longer participatory. It was no longer being done. The view was clinical, philosophical. The poem as object, rather than subject. T. S. Eliot's abominable objective correlative instead of D. H. Lawrence's octopus dragging the victim down, down into the primal darkness.

George turned off the stereo and put the .45 back in the drawer. He lit a cigarette. Only a fool would make a move now and George Stapleton was not a fool. He pulled the poem out of the typewriter and read it. Great. All it needed was a climactic line, reaching up to the dark star. Like a life reaching up to one supreme obligatory act. George Stapleton was sure his life was a poem. Even though the poem in his hand was shaking, and his nose was beginning to drip like a toddler's on a cold day. Even though the room was hot. Even though the air conditioning was on full.

Now was not the moment. But the moment would come. George was sure of it. For the present, he would launch another white whale. Quickly he dialed the familiar number. "Hello, Peregrine?" he said. "I think we have Kilpatrick on our side."

XII

It was not intelligent, it was not even sensible, but Kilpatrick was drinking again. Sipping scotch on the rocks in his empty house, he watched and listened while two ghosts fought over Allyn Stapleton. From a distant corner of his skull, Randy Stapleton spoke elegiacally. In the foreground, Kevin Sugrue Kilpatrick strutted exuberantly. Most of the time he wanted Allyn for Kevin. He wanted her without love, with the careless flamboyance of young desire, the cool acrobatic lust of the Eighth Air Force flyboys. Randy's voice warned him that this was gone forever. More than that, he insisted that something better had replaced it. Allyn was his chance for fathering love, that compound of tenderness and care which fate had prevented Kilpatrick from giving his own children. Rescue her, Randy whispered, rescue her from the hatred and lies that were destroying her. *But what if it's all true?* chortled Kevin's ghost from Saigon. *Have another drink and fuck her one-two-three for me.*

Allyn had called the next day and said she wanted to see him again. She could hardly wait, she said. Maybe she should move in with him. They could work and play together. The gallery practically ran itself. She was looking for some place to hide from the dozens of third-rate painters who were pursuing her. Kilpatrick said that sounded like a great idea. He would call her in a day or two. Meanwhile, where were those people she had told him about, the ones who were going to give him the evidence he needed?

"You'll hear from them," Allyn said.

That night, while the scotch bottle fell like a barometer, Kilpatrick started reading the book that Agatha Stapleton had recommended to him, *The Problem of Christianity,* by Josiah Royce. He found it difficult but fascinating. It reawakened the moribund intellectual self of his college days. Royce's central idea was the lost state of natural man, a wandering atom in a world of equally irrelevant atoms. Only by joining a community and committing himself to its purpose and truth could he find meaning for his life. One passage struck Kilpatrick with particular force. It practically summed up the book.

This is the root and core of man's original sin—namely, the very form of his being as a morally detached individual. Until the beloved community itself appears in his life, he is a stranger in his father's house, a hater of his only chance of salvation, a worldling and a worker of evil deeds, a miserable source of misery.

The telephone rang. Kilpatrick groped his way downstairs in the dark empty house to answer it. "Jim," said Brad Mulholland of Slocum's Remedy. "I'm sorry to call you after hours like this. I've had a rough day. The old man wants to see you."

"Who?"

He was too involved with one old man to remember there was another one lurking on the edge of his life.

"Dwight Slocum," Mulholland said impatiently.

"Why?"

"It's got something to do with this book you're writing about Randy Stapleton's father. You know the place—the thirty-fourth floor of the Waldorf Towers. Be there at eleven tomorrow morning."

Kilpatrick gave himself two full hours to get to New

York. He parked his car in the Waldorf garage at 10:30 A.M. after taking twenty minutes to crawl across Manhattan in the midtown traffic. His pulse quickened at the sight of the crowded streets, the gleaming glass-walled office towers. Power was at the heart of New York's surging vitality. Although Kilpatrick had savored its beat, he had never been part of it. He thought of Josiah Royce's beloved community and his youthful angry shame at the rapacious botch his father and his cronies had made of governing the city of his birth. Was love the source of his shame? If Royce was right, by instinct every man sought a beloved community. But it was impossible to love New York. The city had no particularity. It was, in the words of William Carlos Williams, "too much a congeries of the entire world's facets."

Maybe even New Yorkers needed to come from a beloved community. To be from a family, a city, a state you despised, that was the destructive thing, that exposed you to all the torments, the terror of New York's grid. But to look back with pride, to bring gifts of place and person to this congeries of the entire world—that made New York possible, that was why Randy Stapleton had been able to traverse New York's grid with such careless poise, such smiling grace, without a trace of Kilpatrick's sickening fear that a misstep meant annihilation. Or worse, the dread that the surges of the grid were its only meaning, the endless hustle around it the only purpose.

Up in the elevator, the old exultant, soaring sensation. Irrelevant, Kilpatrick told himself. Meaningless memory. The door to Dwight Slocum's apartment was opened by a woman in a nurse's uniform. Her gray hair was set in an unappealing pageboy; her small pursed mouth had a permanently sour expression, as if she had spent too much time seeing or doing unpleasant things.

The nurse nodded when Kilpatrick introduced himself. "He's not having one of his better days. The secretaries went home about an hour ago."

Kilpatrick waited in a living room that revealed nothing but money. The undoubtedly genuine Louis XVI furniture, the cushions of delicate blue and green, the yellow Chinese wallpaper, the Aubusson rugs, had obviously been selected by a talented decorator. But there was not a single personal touch in the room. Not a picture of a wife or a son or a friend, not even a book or magazine.

Kilpatrick thought of the first time he had met Dwight Slocum here, about a year after Randy Stapleton's death. He had sat in this antiseptically beautiful room wondering if he was going to be fired—half hoping it would happen. He had been vaguely curious about meeting Slocum, who had spent most of his time abroad while Randy Stapleton was alive. On Slocum's rare visits to New York, Randy had dealt with him here at the Towers apartment. After Randy's death, Slocum had returned and immediately started throwing the company into chaos with his foul temper, his contradictory orders, his crude attempts to play favorites. By the time Kilpatrick received his summons to the apartment, the old man had alienated or fired a dozen top executives at headquarters.

That first time (also the last time), Slocum had limped into the room, huge, bald, a gouty foot swathed in bandages. He had started telling Kilpatrick that National Products' public relations department was not worth shit, they were no fucking good. After five minutes of obscenity from the thick-lipped, sneering mouth, he got down to the reason they were no good. They had not been able to interest *Fortune* magazine in how Dwight Slocum had come home to rescue the company from disaster. Maybe it was time to try another approach, a speaking campaign. He wanted a series of speeches using the bullshit that Randy used to hand out about corporate social responsibility and executive sensitivity.

That was when Kilpatrick had begun to plan his departure, when those words, *multiple wounds in the chest and head,* transmuted from grisly mockery to an imperative snarl, a demand for an expiatory act.

A door opened at the far end of the room, twenty feet away. Kilpatrick stood up. A man wearing blue pajamas and a blue silk robe came toward him in a motorized wheelchair. It was a different Dwight Slocum. He was still huge and completely bald. But his right arm dangled uselessly. His right shoulder slumped, and the right side of his face was crumpled, twisting the right corner of his mouth into a snarl. The collapse also twisted the right eye slightly out of focus. Brad Mulholland had said something about Slocum having a stroke. Its seriousness was obviously a well-kept secret.

"Kuh-Kuh-Kilpatrick?" he said. "The one who's wri-writing the book on Stuh-Stuh-Stuh-Stapleton?"

Kilpatrick nodded.

"How is he?"

The words exploded from the thick, veined throat. There was nothing in them but loathing.

"He's fine."

The buzzing wheelchair stopped a foot from Kilpatrick's ankles. Slocum waved his good arm toward the couch. Kilpatrick sat down.

"Wha-wha-what's he been telling you about me?"

"Not much. He mentioned selling Principia Mills—"

"Selling!"

The massive frame shook with savage laughter. Phlegm drooled from the twisted right corner of the mouth. He sopped it up with a handkerchief he pulled from the pocket of his robe.

"Selling. They didn't sell. They su-su-surrendered. I went in there and tu-tu-took it away from the ga-ga-god-almighty Stapletons. Dwight Slocum. The gu-gu-guy they wouldn't invite to their ga-ga-goddamn dances. Never invited my mother to Bo-Bo-Bowood's famous afternoon teas. Slocum took it away from them. A hundred-million-dollar company for ta-ta-ten million. Back in 1945 when a hu-hu-hundred ma-ma-million was worth something."

"He didn't mention the price," Kilpatrick said. "We're just beginning—"

Slocum was not listening. "He'll tell you about it. He'll make himself the hu-hu-hero. He sacrificed his cu-cu-cash value. Gambled on Slu-Slu-Slocum. Su-su-some gamble. Now he's worth a hundred and fu-fu-fifty million dollars. National Products Class A stock."

"He did say he was embarrassed by how much money he'd made on the deal."

"Embarrassed!" The ravaged face pulsed with rage. "Embarrassed! The arrogant su-son of a bitch. Did he tell you how we did it?"

"You moved the mills to North Carolina."

"That didn't gu-get us off the hook. Some stockholders

sued us for twenty muh-million in damages. Stapleton told me not to worry about it. He said the fuh-fix was in with the judge. I didn't believe him. The bastard was a Democrat, part of the goddamn Shea machine. I figured he'd want a million at least. But we guh-got it for a hundred grand. If we'd lost that suit, Pra-Pra-Principia's stock wouldn't have been worth shit. I didn't have a nu-nickle. The ten million was all bu-borrowed money. They didn't know that—the Stu-Stapletons."

Another pause to sop up drool.

"B-beating that goddamn union. He was in on all that. I didn't know what to do. I was half crazy when they followed us to Carolina. I was a W-Wall Street man. I didn't know anything about unions. These were a bunch of b-bastards. Cr-crooked as hell and v-vicious. St-Stapleton went down to Carolina and took charge of the whole thing. He br-brought in some people he knew in the Army who were just as t-tough as the union's goons. They had a regular p-pitched battle about t-ten miles from the mill. They found five or six of the goons stinking in the woods about a week later. The rest of them just disappeared. I th-think he killed them all. He told me I could stop worrying about the union."

Dwight Slocum was breathing in labored gulps like a distance runner. Kilpatrick winced at the pulsing veins in the raddled neck. He was sure the man was going to collapse and die in front of him. "Ca-Campbell," Slocum said. "Go down there to Carolina and find a black guy named Campbell. I remember that name. He helped organize Stapleton's pr-private army. I remember his name because of the song, 'The Campbells Are Coming.'

"That su-son of a bitch Stapleton poses as a guh-goddamn symbol of integrity. You know he's got twa-twenty or thirty congressmen on his puh-payroll, ready to vote his way on any ish-issue you want to name? How the fuck duh-do you think we got all those duh-defense contracts? The bastard suh-set it up to make his little boy Randy luh-look good. When I fuh-found out about it I went through the goddamn roof. I told them I didn't guh-give a fuck for the United States of America. I wasn't guh-gonna ruin my company to kuh-keep the world safe

163

for Stapletons. Here's five or six of them, the only ones I can remember. Go down to Washington and ask them why they always voted Stapleton's way. I don't give a shit what it does to the cuh-company's defense contracts. I've been trying to get us out of that crap work for a good ten years now. You remember the trouble it caused during the Vietnam mess."

Slocum handed Kilpatrick a piece of paper with a half dozen names scribbled on it. He recognized them instantly. They were men with whom Randy Stapleton had regularly conferred to discuss new weapons systems or iron out problems in defense contracts. Kilpatrick had carried confidential letters to them by hand, more than once.

"What else did he tell you about me?" Slocum asked.

"He said he liked you when you were boys. But his grandfather wouldn't let him associate with you because your money came from patent medicine."

"Bullshit. It was because my mother was Jewish. That was the only goddamn reason. Ask him about that. Ask him about his attitude toward the Juh-Jews."

A pause to sop up more drool. "Did he tell you about prep school, Pennsgrove?"

"Not yet."

"The su-son of a bitch ran the fucking school. Just the way his family ru-ran the city. The Stu-Stapletons couldn't be wrong. You were wrong if you disagreed with them. You were cut, ignored. I didn't like it and I let them know it."

The nurse came in. "Mr. Slocum. The doctor said ten minutes and no more."

Slocum told the doctor to perform an anatomically impossible feat.

"Did Stuh-Stapleton mention Muriel Bennett?"

"No."

"She was his favorite girl. I tu-took her away from him in Pu-Paris in 1918, while he was out getting his head blown off. Go talk to her. She's here in New York now. She'll tell you pu-plenty.

"She was a great lady, Muriel. I always su-said Stapleton was never right for her. He was a jerk Galahad with

164

women. A cunt like Muriel only wants one thing. Or maybe two things. A good fuck and lots of money in return. I wanted to marry her. But she told me she was only interested in someone who was going to the top. Ask her what she thinks now."

More explosions of choked laughter. Then the menacing anger returned.

"Listen, Kilpatrick, you write this book my way. You pu-put in it what I tell you to put in it. You do it my way and I-ll take care of getting it published. I understand they're puh-paying you fifty grand. I'll tr-triple that price and for a bonus I'll hire you back at any reasonable salary you n-name. I don't remember why you quit but it must have been salary. When I came back I thought Randy was paying too goddamn much money to everybody. Maybe I roughed you up. If I did, I'm sorry. I need suh-someone at headquarters with Randy's gift for smuh-smoothing things out. I've never been mu-much of an operations man. I sh-should have known someone Ru-Randy kept close to him had t-talent. Randy was as d-different from his father as d-day from night. He wasn't a f-fucking snob. When he first c-came to work for me, he was lu-like a son. Then the old mu-man started wu-whispering things in his ear and the next thing you know he started giving me the fr-freeze like a typical St-Stapleton, but I never held it against him. I knu-knew he couldn't help it and he was a hell of an executive. He—"

Slocum shook his head as if he was remembering things he wanted to forget. "The hell with Randy. He's du-dead. I want this b-book to tell the truth about Paul St-Stapleton the blah-blameless, the br-brave."

Slocum pressed a button on the wheelchair. It spun around. He pressed another button and purred away from Kilpatrick toward the door at the far end of the room.

"Mr. Slocum?" Kilpatrick called.

"Yeah?" he said without turning around.

"You didn't mention Agatha Stapleton. Weren't you married to her?"

The wheelchair spun and Slocum came back down the hall. "We leave her out of it. Not that she doesn't deserve to be put in it. She—"

165

He choked for breath. He seemed to be grappling with a ghost there in the shadowed hall. "We leave her out of it," he snarled.

Kilpatrick left him in the hall, sopping up the drool. In a moment, he was in the elevator, going down, down, down from the tower of power, his stomach, that putative seat of courage, sinking with every rushing foot.

XIII

Waves of pleasure curled up Allyn Stapleton's belly, along with a mindless panic. Awake, she could see nothing taste nothing smell nothing but dark perfumed hair. The pleasure was still there but the panic vanished. Jacky Chasen was going down on her. That big black beautiful Jewish pussy was obliterating the whole world while that clever Jewish tongue was giving Allyn a better time than any male of the species had managed to do. She began to return the favor, remembering last night, bombing around the apartment after grooving on George's white gold, letting Jacky take off her clothes and starting it right in the middle of her white rug in the living room, while Johnny Carson told jokes.

Giggling, they had gotten out the dildo Jacky had bought one night in a downtown sex shop and took turns trying it while Johnny and Ed McMahon sat down with their guests, Doris Day and Paul Lynde and the little bitch who had starred in *The Exorcist*. They accepted the yocks and occasional applause as tribute to their stylized fucking. They finally decided they liked sucking better

167

than fucking and this was why Jacky was at it again, more or less where they had left off after killing a bottle of gin.

"Excuse me, miss, are you sure you're in the right apartment," Allyn said after getting Jacky's clit between her lips for five or six minutes and tonguing it until it was hot and swollen.

"Shut-up-you-sisterfucker," Jacky gasped.

The telephone. Allyn answered it, wedging the receiver between her mouth and Jacky's cunt. Jacky went right on sucking. The caller was Jim Kilpatrick. He started telling her about his visit to Dwight Slocum. He had gotten an earful. He wanted to come and tell her about it.

Jacky chose this moment to start playing games with the dildo. Allyn started to get a little excited. She flipped over and Jacky kept on doing it from behind. "I'm a little—busy right now," Allyn said as one stroke went almost to her tonsils. "But it does sound *tremendous*. Give me an hour, no, make it two."

"What's going on?" Jacky said, stroking away.

"A Wasp conspiracy," Allyn said.

"Are you coming?" Jacky said.

"I told you, I never come," Allyn said.

"You came last night on the rug," Jacky said.

"That was the coke," Allyn said.

"Shit," Jacky said, and threw the dildo across the room. "You've got an answer for everything."

"What does coming have to do with it? I can love you without coming."

"Yeah, the way you love Uncle George. Speaking of him, do you remember what I told you about our little ducking game in the pool? That guy's dangerous."

"Fucking, sucking, ducking, it's all dangerous," Allyn said. She was sure Jacky was exaggerating the incident. She had been high, George had been low. George was ugly when he was low. But he was no murderer.

"Why don't you go to work on my uncle Ned? He's in much better shape than George. He's the family athlete."

"Introduce me to him," Jacky said.

She had confessed to Allyn that her secret ambition was to fuck her way through the Wasp upper class. The emphasis was on *through*. Then she would do the outstanding ethnic groups and finish with the Jews. In the end

168

she would marry some nice straight Jewish grind from Brandeis who had no idea that he was getting the most thoroughly fucked cunt in America. She would become chairman of Hadassah and gush over rabbis and raise money for Israel. She might even have a baby.

Allyn shoved Jacky upstairs to her own apartment and cleaned up the place. She took a shower and picked out a pale blue silk dress by Halston. It was perfect for her Wasp princess act.

Kilpatrick arrived about noon, looking much more relaxed than the last time she had seen him. He liked her choice of martinis and said he would be the bartender. He reminisced about being stationed at an air base in southeastern England during World War II with an Australian bomber group. They liked his American martinis so much they fired the base bartender and refused to drink each day until the "Yank leftenant" showed up to mix them. He said he was drinking again with no apparent damage to his modus operandi. But he had seldom been a sloppy or outrageous drunk. Most of the time in the past he had used liquor to lift his chin out of the slough of despond. It was a sort of fuel.

"Of course," he said, raising his glass, "above a certain altitude I get a little turbulent, as you may have noticed."

"I do seem to remember some sort of outrageous behavior," Allyn said. "But I blamed it on lack of oxygen. God knows what might have happened if you didn't have the marvelous little device that pops up in an emergency. I just put it in my mouth and stopped worrying."

The remark seemed to make Kilpatrick uneasy. He abandoned humor and began telling her about his visit to Dwight Slocum. He wanted to know if she had arranged it. She told him George had handled it. Kilpatrick shook his head and said it certainly was a new way to look at Stapleton the blameless, Stapleton the brave. Was he really anti-Semitic? Draining her martini, Allyn said the old bastard was always mouthing off on the Jews, the blacks, the Irish. She listened, admiring her own performance, while Kilpatrick talked about corrupting senators and congressmen, busting unions.

"Have you seen Muriel Bennett yet?" she asked. "George says she has a really juicy story. I won't spoil it by telling you what I heard. But she's been his big secret love for years. They used to meet in Europe."

"Slocum mentioned her to me," Kilpatrick said. "I plan to call her. Meanwhile, I've got another date with your grandfather."

"What's he been telling you?"

"Pretty standard stuff. Family tradition, I guess. About his father being Teddy Roosevelt's right lobe. As far as I can see, the old boy was more like the court jester. But he died pretty tragically on the River of Doubt."

"I've heard that dolorous tale."

Kilpatrick nodded. The uneasy look passed over his face again. "His father meant a lot to him."

"Whose father doesn't? The trick is to outgrow them."

"Easier said than done," Kilpatrick said.

The more he drank, the less cheerful he got. "Hey," Allyn said, pouring him another martini. "This is supposed to be a celebration."

"Okay, Ms. Brighteyes," Kilpatrick growled. "You're now lip to lip with Jimmy the K., investigative reporter. You got exactly one minute to get to the bare facts."

"What's the world record?"

"With or without girdle?"

"I'm insulted."

"Twenty-two seconds. Held by Brigitte Bardot."

She took off her dress, kicked off her shoes, and let him take off her stockings. "I'm not in an olympic mood," she said.

"What do you think about while you're doing it, champ?"

She took off her slip and let him unhook her bra. "Whether I can break Roger Maris' record, before age forces me to the sidelines."

He stretched her on the couch and pulled off her pants. "You mean you'll be satisfied to hit the big one sixty-two times a year?"

She watched him take off his tie and shirt. She reached up and unzipped his fly. "Was it sixty-two a *year?* I thought it was sixty-two a month."

"Close your eyes," he said. She obeyed. When she

opened them he was naked, consulting his watch. "Not bad for a warmup," he said. "I think we could play olympic doubles someday."

"At forty thousand feet?"

"Sure. But we haven't finished the interview. What's your opinion of the multiple orgasm?"

"I'm hopeful that it can be eliminated in the next round of SALT talks."

"Could you give us a demonstration of how this might be done?"

She sat up and took his cock in her mouth. It swelled enormously and she looked up at him planning to smile. But he was not smiling. He was ecstatically serious, on a trip that was coming from a place she had never been. He held her face between his big hands and whispered, "Don't Allyn, you don't have to do that."

He lay down beside her on the couch and kissed her in a deep possessive way that she found somehow threatening. She wanted to say, *I'd rather have it in the mouth* but she never had the chance, his tongue filled her mouth and he rolled on top of her and entered her. She sank into the couch feeling absorbed, consumed by his body, the penis moving in her seemed to be twice as large as any she had ever had which was absurd it was big but not gigantic but it was opening her in a way that she had not felt for years, not since the first few times with her husband while she was still in the brainwashed stage of obedience and thought love was possible. She started to gasp and her pulses were pounding. *Come,* she whispered in her head, *come and get it over with come and we'll just forget the whole goddamn thing I'll tell George to shove it come.*

He came with a great rush of hot semen. A terrible trembling power surged up through her belly. Not the mere sensations that Jacky's tongue induced but a presence that opened her to pleasure and fear. It was six, seven, eight on the Richter sale, *coming.* For the first time she understood the word and hated it refused it but it was no good he was doing something forbidden to her, he was loving her because he did not know he could not know that Allyn was de facto unlovable that was the name of the whole game to make Allyn unlovable and free.

"Holy shit," she said. "What are you doing to me?"

"Falling in love with you," he said.

"Don't do that. Don't let that happen to you."

"Why?"

"Because—I'm afraid I'll end up hurting you. I don't want to do that."

He said he understood the risks. He was not expecting her to love him. He would hope for it but he knew she was young. She said thirty wasn't young, that was not the point. He only shook his head and said he would avoid singing "September Song" but he understood the way she felt.

That was so far from what she was thinking, she almost laughed. Or wept. She was close to both. She was slightly hyterical. She tried to stop the process once more.

"It's not your fault, it isn't anybody's fault but I get bad vibes from you. It scares me. I'm afraid of what we'll do to each other."

He shook his head again. He said that he liked the vibes he got from her. Allyn told herself to let it happen. It was not her fault. It would give her more control over him. Again she swam naked through the green water and the old voices bleached hatred into her skin. Hurting Kilpatrick, possibly even loving him, was a risk she would have to take.

XIV

The courtroom had been a chaos of shouting, sneering lawyers all day. But that was not why Paul Stapleton felt especially exhausted as he sank into the back seat of the Mercedes. He had been planning to have lunch with Jim Kilpatrick. Morris Teitlebaum had called and asked him "as a fellow grandfather" to see him as soon as possible. He had canceled Kilpatrick and lunched with Teitlebaum instead. They were old friends from the textile years. The Teitlebaums had bought control of Forstman and Hauffman, one of the biggest mills in the city, just after World War I.

Morris was about his age, maybe a year or two younger. He was looking trim and fit in his usual British tweeds. He had been born in Russia but he looked and acted like a retired British colonel. He had a white brush mustache, carried himself like a Grenadier guard on parade and even affected a faint British accent. But Paul Stapleton respected him. He was a tough, honest businessman and he had fought as an infantryman in World War I.

After reminiscing for a few moments over the textile

173

wars, Morris got to the point, which Paul Stapleton had been uneasily anticipating from his fellow-grandfather remark. For some time Morris had retained a private detective to keep track of his only grandchild, Jacqueline Chasen. He had been encouraged when she and Allyn had become business partners in the Artemisia Gallery. But in recent weeks the detective's reports had turned gloomy again. Jacky and Allyn had been spending a lot of time at George Stapleton's house. The detective had crashed one of George's parties. What he reported almost defied belief. Naked swimmers in the pool, pills of every type being handed out as casually as after-dinner mints, and for the insiders, cocaine.

Paul Stapleton remained calm through a massive act of the will. He said he was sorry. George had had a history of emotional instability. He would try to do something about it. But he could not promise any miracles. George was fifty-three years old. George could tell him, he could tell anyone, to go to hell.

For the rest of the lunch Paul Stapleton listened to Morris Teitlebaum lament the state of the nation and his family. Once he had been a major giver to the Democratic Party. Now he gave everything he could spare to Israel. He was still an American patriot but patriotism was now considered either stupid or immoral. His son's only interest was chasing girls. His daughter spent her time pursuing liberal causes which were either dangerous to law and order or a waste of time. His son-in-law was a nebbish.

Ruefully recalling this monologue, Paul Stapleton consoled himself that he had done a little better with most of his children and grandchildren. But not well enough to be smug, much less satisfied. Stapletons should be surpassing Teitlebaums by light-year distances. Instead, he had to sit and listen to one of his sons being described as a corrupter of young girls. He was going to have to land on George with both feet.

And Allyn? Paul Stapleton could only sigh with baffled helplessness. He had tried to avoid the mistakes his grandfather had made with him. He had never said a harsh word to her. He had tried to accentuate the positive, to challenge her to compete in the male world, to have a career as an architect, a weaver, a fabric

174

designer—whatever she wanted. But she seemed, with dismaying perversity, to rebel against every choice, even the ones she made herself, like her marriage.

He had spoiled her when she was young. He admitted it. He had been prepared for sons and grandsons. A granddaughter had turned him to putty. But spoiling a little girl was not synonymous with ruining her, in his lexicon. Maria insisted that his penchant for showering her with presents and privileges was the source of Allyn's erratic life. He suspected the trouble lay in some hidden female quarrel between Allyn and Maria about which he knew nothing. Maria had always been severe with Allyn. With her sons she had been the kindhearted excuser, constantly interceding to mitigate a punishment, relax a rule of discipline. Why she had changed with Allyn was a mystery to him.

"You still want to pick up Mr. Kilpatrick?" Sam Fry said as they rolled up the Parkway in the rush-hour traffic.

Paul Stapleton knew Sam was telling him that he looked too beat to do any more work. He got stubborn and said yes. He wanted to finish telling the story, however badly he did it. He found himself thinking about it in bed at night, in the courtroom. He wanted to get it out of his system, once and for all.

Kilpatrick was waiting on the porch of his house. He got into the car with his usual brief smile and handshake. Once more Paul Stapleton felt a certain discomfort at the distance this man seemed to put between them. It did not connect with that emotional letter about Randy's death. He pretended to relax and asked Kilpatrick where they had stopped the story.

"After your father's death. You were about to revolt against your grandfather."

As Kilpatrick said this, he put a small tape recorder on the seat between them and turned it on. He said something about wanting a complete record.

The tape recorder bothered Paul Stapleton. He started explaining why his father's death left him feeling exposed to his grandfather. For the first time he realized that this was what Allyn probably felt. Randy had always been able to reason with her, to calm her tantrums and control

175

her willful ways. It pained him to discover that he was so absorbed in the present that he had not noticed how the past was repeating itself. It intensified the memory that surged into sight as he began talking.

"My revolt really started on the lawn at Pennsgrove, the day of my graduation."

He was striding across the green grass in the hot sunshine. Grandfather was sitting there in his black suit and string tie and high black shoes, the same suit he wore to work, and Mother and Malcolm and Agatha were sitting beside him and suddenly Paul Stapleton was someone else, Uncle Rawdon, the brother that his father had talked to in his last delirium. "Rawdon," he had called, "Rawdon, maybe you were right. I've been wanting to tell you." He became this rebel spirit who had tormented the old man who was now tormenting him.

But he could not tell something like that to Kilpatrick. The man would consider him a nut case. Maria believed in spirits inhabiting and influencing people. Kilpatrick would get enough of that from her.

"I told Grandfather that instead of going to Harvard, I was going to Princeton—which he considered a school for drunks and loungers. He wasn't far wrong and I was soon keeping company with the best of them. But we had something else besides women, liquor and cards to keep our minds off studying. By the time I got to Princeton in September of 1914, World War I was going full blast in Europe. We spent most of our time arguing about whether we should get into it or not. TR was calling Wilson a coward and a liar in the newspapers almost every day. I agreed with him one hundred percent and couldn't wait to smell some gunpowder. Grandfather had precisely the opposite opinion. He thought it was insanity for us to go anywhere near the thing.

"He said it wasn't a war. It was a continental-sized slaughter pen. He'd resign his commission before he'd send men against massed machine guns and artillery the way the French and British and Germans did for the first three years. Grandfather didn't think much of the British. He was different from most of the people we knew on that point. They were all Anglophiles. Mother was abso-

176

lutely passionate for everything English. She had dozens of friends in England and would frequently come down to dinner weeping because she'd just heard that so-and-so's son had been killed on the Somme or at Ypres. At Princeton we thought it was just a question of us getting over there and showing these dumb Limeys, stupid Frogs and moronic Krauts how to fight a war. We were sure that an American army could clean up the Western Front in a month and a half.

"In the summer of 1915 I went up to Plattsburg, New York, and got some military training at a camp that the Anglophiles had organized up there. Three of TR's sons were there. There were about twelve hundred of us and six hundred army regulars to make us soldiers. TR came up and gave us a pep talk. He attacked Wilson and all the people he called hyphenated Americans who wanted us to stay neutral. In the middle of it a big Airdale walked up to him, rolled over on his back and put his paws in the air. TR pointed to him and said, "There's neutrality.'

"We saw ourselves as apostles of preparedness. But looking back on it now, I think a lot of Republicans like TR were more interested in making Wilson squirm. Hotheads like me just wanted to see some action. A few people like General Leonard Wood knew their business and were sincere about getting a decent army ready to fight.

"In the spring of 1916, Pancho Villa and his thugs started raiding across the Rio Grande. Villa was hoping to start a war between Mexico and the United States. Wilson had to do something about it or look like a complete idiot. So he sent Pershing and six thousand regulars and National Guardsmen down to the border. This was my chance. I had gotten friendly with several cavalry officers at Plattsburg, in particular a captain named Mark Stratton. He was on Pershing's staff and he got me a commission in the 13th Cavalry. Without telling Grandfather or my mother or anyone else in the family, I decamped from Princeton and the next thing they heard from me I was in El Paso getting ready to invade Mexico with Pershing's gang."

177

*How incredibly remote, unreal, that stiff young lieuten-
ant looked on his black horse, riding at the head of his
troop of mostly Irish veterans as they plodded south from
Columbus, New Mexico, toward the border. He remembered civilians cheering them from a nearby train, which
had been stopped to let the column pass. An hour later
they were in the brutal heat of the Mexican desert, the
yellow alkali dust searing their lungs, filling their boots,
making their eyes feel as big as soup kettles. Behind
them, gasping infantrymen collapsed by the dozen. It was
the first disillusionment for the young lieutenant, who
was in search of death or glory, the discovery that war
was mostly a plodding, boring, exhausting business.*

"The big problem in Mexico was the terrain," Paul
Stapleton continued. "You went from desert heat to
snowstorms in the Sierras in the same day. We had a
couple of troops of black cavalrymen. Half of them came
down with pneumonia. We never caught Villa himself but
we whacked hell out of him a couple of times. He was
some hero, always the first guy off the battlefield.

"Something a lot more important than catching Villa
happened to me in Mexico. I met Maria Teresa O'Reilly
and I fell in love with her. I remember my first reaction
when I was introduced to her. It was at a dance the army
gave as a gesture of friendship to the civilian population
in Casas Grandes. O'Reilly? What the hell are the Irish
doing down here? I didn't think much of the Irish in those
days. No one in the family did. They cost the city a
fortune in poor relief, they came to work in the mills
drunk half the time or didn't show up at all for the same
reason. Here I was looking at one of the most beautiful,
cultivated young women I had ever seen. I was totally
confused, but Maria straightened me out pretty quickly.
She had gone to school in San Antonio and spoke perfect
English.

"Her people were descended from one of those aristocrats who left Ireland under the terms of the Treaty of
Limerick in 1691. They became professional soldiers for
the Catholic kings all over Europe. The original O'Reilly
and his son and his grandson had been generals in the
Spanish army. Believe it or not, the grandson fought in

the American Revolution. He commanded a regiment in the Spanish army that captured Florida from the British in 1780. He settled in Mexico and bought a huge ranch in the state of Chihuahua.

"I was amazed to find out that the O'Reillys were a lot prouder of their lineage—and maybe had more reason to be—than the Stapletons. I got an even bigger shock when I was invited out to the Hacienda Gloriosa. I thought the Stapletons were pretty important back home. But Carlos O'Reilly was the ruler of a kingdom. He could ride for two days in any direction without reaching the borders of his ranch. Behind the house was the most fantastic rock garden, with desert cactus and dwarf trees and a waterfall. O'Reilly called it his hanging gardens. He was a big cheerful guy, always joking.

"O'Reilly had no use for Pancho Villa. He supplied us with a dozen or so scouts who knew the country and helped us keep Villa on the run. We promised to protect the hacienda by stationing a platoon there. But the orders got mixed up in the army bureaucracy—"

Paul Stapleton stopped and stared out the window at the peaceful suburban landscape. He was back in a stinking Mexican village, going from house to house in the heat, dragging bleary-eyed unshaven troopers out of bed, apologizing to the half-naked women they were kissing one more time. *You can tell some of it,* he decided.

"I contributed my share to the delay. I let my men loaf on the way out there. It took us a day and a half when we should have done it in five or six hours. I was a pretty green shavetail, and those old army types sort of intimidated me. We stayed overnight at a village and had a wild old time.

"No one knew that Villa had split his men into a half dozen small groups and swung north again. By now he was like a mad dog who wanted to do nothing but kill. His special targets were Mexicans like Carlos O'Reilly, gringo lovers, Villa called them. He shot O'Reilly in his own courtyard. I felt pretty damn guilty about it, and spent a lot of time at the hacienda in the next few weeks. That's when Maria and I fell in love. We were married on Easter Sunday, 1916, in the church at Casas Grandes.

179

Stratton persuaded Pershing to leave me in the town with a cavalry troop to protect the army's line of supply. That meant we could live at the hacienda.

"I began to think I would spend the rest of my life down there. Maria's mother wanted me to take over the hacienda. Then the mail caught up with me. I got about thirty-five letters from Grandfather in one package. He wasn't going to let me escape him, no matter what I did. Every day he dictated a two- or three-page letter to me, filling me in on everyone in the family, going into all sorts of detail about the mills. I read about twenty-five of those letters and got so furious I threw the rest of them in the fire. I was rotten to Maria and everyone else for the next few weeks.

"When more letters arrived, I tried to burn them. But Maria wouldn't let me do it. She asked me if she could read them. I gave them to her. She read them and told me I had to go back to him. That was the last thing I expected to hear. For a couple of days I hated her almost as much as I hated Grandfather."

Paul Stapleton sighed. He wasn't even coming close to the inner truth.

"I was a very dangerous fellow in those days," he said.

He remembered how Mark Stratton's jaw had dropped when he told him that he had proposed to Maria Teresa O'Reilly. "Are you out of your goddamn mind?" Stratton had roared. "She's a fucking Mexican. Lay 'em and leave 'em, Paul. That's all they expect."

How could he explain to Stratton, to anyone, what had happened? He had found Maria Teresa O'Reilly brooding beside the reflecting pool in the hacienda's rock garden. The witty laughing girl who danced the tango with a mocking blend of sensuality and innocence had vanished. A black mantilla shrouded her somber face. It was twilight. He stood for a moment watching the water splash down the dark-veined rocks. Without speaking, guided by nothing but a sudden wish, he had kissed her. There had been a conqueror's swagger in the gesture—and a kind of anger. The girl had been so melancholy since her father's death. It was time for her to enjoy life again, courtesy of Lieutenant Paul Stapleton.

"What do you want from me?" she said. *"I have no father to protect me. I have only a mother who tells me I should give myself to you and hope for the best. She has learned from others in your army that you are rich. If you want me only for tonight and tomorrow night, tell me. But I am prepared to love you for the rest of my life."*

Not even the ghost of Rawdon Stapleton could resist those words. But it was impossible to recapture the subtle blend of desire and guilt and pride that made him tell her that he would try to do the same thing, love her for the rest of his life.

He continued with the easy part of the story.

"Then all sorts of things started happening that made a private quarrel small beer. Maria got pregnant, Wilson recalled the army from Mexico and within six weeks—before volunteers like me could even get discharged—he declared war on Germany. I got promoted to captain, took Maria to Bowood and introduced her to Grandfather and left her there to have the baby. They liked each other on sight. Don't ask me why. I never have figured that one out. Mark Stratton got me aboard the *Baltic,* the ship that carried Pershing and about two hundred staff officers to France in May of 1917. I was the only officer below the rank of major in the party.

"Pershing was a bear for detail. He looked over the manifest list after we sailed and he spotted my name and rank. 'What the hell is he doing here?' he growled. Stratton told him that I was very fluent in French. Actually I had barely passed the damn subject in prep school and had flunked it at Princeton. Pershing said, 'Great I'll use him as my interpreter.'

"They were giving brush-up classes in French to colonels and majors. But I couldn't go to them after Stratton had made me Pershing's interpreter. We twisted one of the French teachers' arm and we paid him five dollars an hour to stay up half the night giving me a cram course in conversational French. But it was no good. I just didn't have the vocabulary.

"When we got to France, Pershing called me in. Stratton was in a frenzy trying to figure out some way to save my neck and his, but I got us both out of it by telling

181

Pershing I had deceived Major Stratton. I couldn't speak a word of French. I just wanted to get over to France and see some action as soon as possible.

"I could tell Pershing liked that attitude, but he wouldn't admit it. He chewed me out for a good five minutes about the importance of an officer being a man of honor. I had to stand at attention and take it. But I knew I had him. I swore I'd never tell another lie, and he sent me over to his chief of staff, General James Harbord, to serve as his aide.

"There was a wonderful man. He was all the things Pershing wasn't—relaxed, easygoing, always ready to laugh and joke. He had risen through the ranks—not an easy thing to do in the army in his day. Pershing had served with him in the Philippines and knew Harbord was the man he needed to get along with the French and English. It reminded me of Grandfather and my father. Pershing was a lot like Old Steady. He had the disposition of a surly grizzly most of the time, but he'd let you get away with almost anything if he saw that you wanted to fight. He knew you couldn't win a war without killing people. Sometimes I think that kind of man is the most misunderstood of all.

"As long as we worked twelve hours a day for him, Harbord didn't care what we did with the other twelve. I had a good time for myself there in Paris during the last six months of 1917. Our headquarters were on the rue Constantine. I was billeted in a little French hotel around the corner. The French treated us like we were ten feet tall and were going to win the war for them the day after tomorrow."

You owe me an explanation.

Paul Stapleton heard the words as clearly, as explicitly as if Kilpatrick had said them. He glanced at him, momentarily shocked, and was nonplused to find he was only listening politely. Paul Stapleton knew who had spoken. He could see Muriel Bennett on the corner of the rue Constantine, her blond hair gleaming like an aureole in the Paris sun, the crisp Red Cross uniform clinging to her long lean body.

For a moment he felt unstrung. What were all these women doing to him with their demanding eyes and

182

mouths? Standing outside time, spectators demanding inner truths, explanations, faith in God, while he grappled with the brutal exhausting details of living his life. With a rush of anger he told himself he did not owe anyone an explanation.

"I grew up a lot during those six months in France—especially after I got a cable from Grandfather telling me Maria had given birth to a son and asking me what I wanted to name him. That was a shock, believe me. I was so absorbed by what we were doing, by the frantic pace we were living, that for weeks at a time I practically forgot who I was and what I'd left behind me.

"I felt so out of it, I told them to pick any name they liked. The next cable told me my son was now Jonathan Randolph Stapleton, which made me think Mother and Grandfather were fighting the Civil War again. I felt horribly guilty, leaving Maria at the mercy of two such strong-willed characters. A couple of years later I found out that the name was Maria's choice, not theirs.

"About January 1918 we heard they were going to form an American tank brigade. Stratton volunteered for it and so did I. They made George Patton colonel and Stratton second in command. He made me commander of A Company. If you're not familiar with cavalry tactics—tanks were an outgrowth of cavalry—A is the lead company. It meant I would head up all the attacks. This suited me perfectly. By now I had seen enough of the Western Front to have become a complete fatalist. I was more or less resigned to getting killed.

"We spent months training with British tank specialists near Bourg. We used French light tanks. They broke down almost every time they hit a bump in the road. We'd go out on a maneuver with ten tanks and come back with five. Patton tried to overcome our lack of confidence in our machinery by insisting on having the best-trained officers and men in the AEF. Every man and every officer in the brigade had to know how to drive a tank, assemble a Hotchkiss machine gun in the dark, learn how to fire it and the thirty-seven-millimeter cannon, and know how to make maps as well as read them and interpret aerial photographs.

"Attention to detail. That's the secret of success in war

183

and practically everything else in life. Grandfather used to tell me this three times a week. It was a shock to discover a flamboyant guy like Patton following the same rule.

"Early in September 1918 we were ready for action and so was the AEF. Pershing had a million men in France by now and we launched the first American offensive at St.-Mihiel. It wasn't much of a fight. The Germans weren't interested in holding the territory and started retreating the moment that we attacked. But we ran into all sorts of problems operating the tanks under fire. Taking prisoners, for instance. There was something about a tank that discouraged surrender. People either ran away from it or kept on fighting until you rolled right over them. This didn't make much sense. It was easier for everybody concerned if they surrendered. So the officers were always getting out of the tanks to round up prisoners.

"We were outside the tanks most of the time anyway because of another problem. The tanks had no radios in those days and it was impossible for them to communicate with each other. At first we thought we could do it with signal flags. We found out that this was pretty silly at St.-Mihiel. The first time I stuck some signal flags out of my lead tank, we were under heavy machine-gun fire. In about ten seconds I was left with nothing but a couple of splinters in my hands.

"There was only one thing to do. I had to get out of the tank and deliver my orders on foot. This sounds like suicide tactics. But it wasn't really that dangerous. It got hairy only when they had the range with artillery. You couldn't dive into a shell hole because the tanks were under orders to keep moving. A stopped tank was a sitting duck for artillery. So you had to keep walking out there with the shrapnel all around you until a runner arrived with orders to stop advancing.

"An awful lot of runners didn't make it through the shellfire, which meant sometimes we'd keep advancing while the infantry and most of the tanks had stopped. Near the end of the St.-Mihiel show I found myself out there in no-man's-land with three tanks left and shells falling like hailstones. Up ahead we could see an artillery battery that was giving us hell. I got in my tank and we

184

charged the sons of bitches. The supporting German infantry ran away when we got close enough to open up on them with our machine guns. I knocked out one gun with the thirty-seven-millimeter cannon on my tank. It was a wild show there for a few minutes. By the time the artillerymen realized we were attacking them, it was too late to depress the guns low enough to give us pointblank fire. So their last few rounds went over our heads.

"I got out and took the breechblock off the gun we'd disabled to prove what we'd done. When I got a look at the trenches and the gun emplacements I saw these weren't the makeshift fortifications we'd been overrunning at St.-Mihiel. It was the real thing, the Hindenburg Line, the main German defenses. Without realizing it, we'd knocked a hole in it. If I had had thirty tanks, or better, three hundred with me, we could have gotten in the German rear and torn them apart. Mark Stratton with his West Point training saw this possibility the moment I told him about it. He and Patton sat down and spent half the night talking about it.

"That's how I made my accidental contribution to the theory and practice of armored warfare. I don't mention it to brag—but to underscore how quickly our military leaders adapted to the tank. It fitted naturally into the basic American military strategy of fire and movement, wide-open fluid warfare, where casualties are low. It opened up the possibility of using machines instead of human bodies to break through an enemy's defenses. But what did we do with the tank after World War I? Nothing. In 1920, Congress cut the appropriation for the Tank Corps to five hundred dollars. We ignored the tank and let the Germans develop it as the great offensive weapon of World War II.

"We didn't have enough tanks to bust things open in France in 1918. We had to try to do it with infantry in the Argonne. That battle was the real thing. The artillery barrage alone would make you remember it for the rest of your life. It started at one A.M., and the sky was bright red until dawn. I don't know how those artillery men did it. They must have dropped in their tracks when they got the order to cease fire. I don't know how the Germans took it without breaking. But they were there, fighting like demons when we jumped off. Our tank brigade was supposed to lead the advance of the 28th Division, a Pennsylvania outfit. It was hard to tell where anything or anyone was located. Between ground fog, the dawn's feeble light and the powder smoke from the artillery barrage, it was like groping your way through a hotel corridor full of dark gray smoke with people shooting at you from the doorway of every room. We had planned to cross a ravine and go up a hill to attack the Crown Prince Division, one of the best outfits in the German Army. I was in the lead tank as usual. About three quarters of the way up the hill I saw something strange through the fog and smoke. It looked like a big black hole in the ground. It was. The Germans had blown off the top of the ridge with a couple of hundred land mines. I got out to take a look at it and got shot in the head. Mark Stratton felt sorry for me and wrote me up for another medal I didn't deserve."

Maybe that was the best way to tell it, leave out the heroics, maybe it will make up for the inability, the impossibility of telling the whole truth.

"When I woke up a month later, I began to wish I had been killed. I was in terrible shape. If the bullet had gone an eighth of an inch to the left, it would have killed me instantly. Instead, it tore apart all sorts of control centers in my brain. I couldn't walk more than five or six feet without staggering. I couldn't get out more than three or four sentences without stumbling all over myself, spitting and stuttering like a man with cerebral palsy. It was hell. I kept trying to walk and I'd fall down or lurch into people. Once a general thought I was drunk and tried to arrest me. I couldn't concentrate on anything for more than ten or fifteen minutes."

Ta-ra-ra-ta-ra-ra. He could hear the merry-go-round music from the park across the street from the hospital in Savenay. The name still made his flesh crawl. It was the hospital for the permanently disabled, waiting for a ship home from St.-Nazaire. Everywhere men hobbled on crutches with dangling stumps for legs. The blinded tapped their way with canes, the armless sat and waited to be fed. He remembered when Pershing visited them. The iron face never changed expression. He had thought of

Grandfather and understood a little more of what it took to be a general.

Pershing had asked the man in the next bed, a New Yorker named Sullivan, were he was wounded. Apparently misunderstanding the question, Sullivan had replied, "Near Beaurepaire Farm, sir. Do you remember, sir, just where the road skirts a small grove and turns to the left across a wheat field and then up over the brow of the hill? Right there, sir."

In his memoirs, Pershing told how touched he had been that the man thought his general had been so close to him in battle. Pershing never knew that after he left, Sullivan had wept. He could not tell the general that he had lost both his legs. He could not tell himself.

Paul Stapleton had felt the same way. He could not admit that the body in which he had always taken such pride was now his mocking, humilitating betrayer. He would never trust that body again. Henceforth it would be ruled by the cold, resolute will.

"They moved me to a big base hospital at Savenay, where my mail caught up to me. I found out that Grandfather had died in his sleep on the same night that I was hit. My brother Malcolm was only twenty—still at Harvard. I was the oldest living member of the family—except for Mother—and I was a wheelchair case. I also had a son I'd never seen and a wife I barely knew by now.

"Every man has times when life looks bleak. The first six months of 1919 were my bleakest. I was transferred to a hospital in Paris. The French were supposed to have the best neurologists in the world, and they had had tremendous experience in treating wounds like mine. They tried drugs. They took a thousand X rays. They prescribed special exercises. Nothing worked. Several times I considered suicide. I couldn't stand the thought of being a burden to—to anyone, everyone for the rest of my life."

Did Kilpatrick catch the hesitation before "anyone"? Of course not, he was still listening politely. Paul Stapleton lowered his eyes and continued his narration. He felt like an infantryman, slogging through the cold clinging mud of France.

"That's when I found out what the word love really

187

meant. Maria and my mother came to France to take me home. I told Maria I was ready to give her a divorce. I wasn't the same man she had married in Mexico. Half my brain was scattered across that ridge in the Argonne. There was no reason for her to spend the rest of her life pushing some stammering cripple around in a wheelchair.

"Mother thought a divorce was a good idea. Hell, I might as well say it—she suggested it to me as the only honorable thing to do. She was dying to get her hands on me and turn me into a tragic drama that would occupy her old age and give her a chance to imitate her mother's devotion to her father. Except, of course, knowing Mother, she wouldn't have spent much time nursing me. She would have let the servants do that and dropped in to see me ten minutes a day when she was in town and spent the rest of the time talking about her shattered wreck of a hero son in Newport, Deauville, Baden-Baden and those other places where she liked to spend most of her time.

"I'll always remember the day I told Maria to get a divorce. We were in the Tuileries Gardens. I was in my wheelchair. She had pushed me down there from the hospital. There were children playing all around us. She looked at them and I knew she was thinking of Randy. She asked me if I was telling her this because I didn't love her any more. I told her it was *because* I loved her. Because I couldn't bear the thought of inflicting myself on her. I told her I didn't even know if I could be a husband. I'd lost all confidence in my body.

"Maria told me that none of that mattered. She knew what I was like when she married me. She knew I was a wild Yankee who was ready to live and die with a gun in his hand. She knew something like this might happen. That didn't stop her from loving me then. Why should it stop her now?

"Besides, she didn't believe I was going to be a wheelchair case for the rest of my life. The first time she saw me in Mexico, she had had a kind of prevision, a flash of insight or foresight, intuition, whatever you want to call it, that she would marry me and never regret it, no matter how much grief I caused her, because together we'd serve a purpose in this world—a purpose that we could never achieve separately. She still believed it. In fact, she be-

188

lieved it more than ever now that she had met Grandfather and become a member of the family. She was going to pray to the Virgin of Guadalupe to make me well again. She was sure the Virgin had gotten me out of the Argonne alive. The Virgin always answered her prayers.

"I didn't believe in the Virgin. I didn't believe in much of anything at that point. But I saw I had a responsibility, Jim, a responsibility to respond to that—love. At least to try. It was crazy. Grandfather had preached responsibility to me until I hated the word. But he never talked about being responsible to another *person*. It was always to the country, to duty. Yet now I know, thanks to Maria, that he was really saying, be responsible to me, don't fail me. He was trying to say he needed me. But he couldn't do it. He wasn't that kind of man.

"Maria had spent hours discussing me with Grandfather. He knew me. He knew us all. He'd spent his life studying men, deciding how good they were. He told her more about the—the inner life of the family than he ever told anyone else."

"I hope I can—talk to her—to Mrs. Stapleton," Kilpatrick said.

"She's a little shy with strangers. But I'll try to arrange it."

What would Maria tell him? Paul Stapleton wondered. Almost everything that mattered to her was too private to tell anyone. He continued the story, feeling more and more weary.

"I went home to Bowood with Maria. But I couldn't stand the place, with Mother trying to elbow Maria out of my bedroom and bringing in quack doctors that her New York friends recommended, and all the servants running to help me every time I fell down, and looking solemn whenever I lost control of my vocal cords.

"Maria saw I was miserable and moved us out to the farm. The nearest house was a good mile away. We had the place to ourselves. I could walk, fall down, get up, walk, fall down, get up again all day if I felt like it. Maria got Sam here to leave the reservation and be my keeper. Then Maria suggested I start riding.

"At first I thought she wanted me to break my neck so she could get rid of me. But it was a brilliant idea. The

189

balance control in my brain had been destroyed. Somehow I had to relearn it—transfer that ability to another part of my brain. The doctors in Paris had told me it could happen, but they didn't know how or why or when. Walking didn't seem to do it. Or at least it did it so slowly I would be eighty years old before I could cover a hundred yards. I had failed so often I expected to flop, and I did. A horse was a new challenge. I could go someplace, cover some territory, and if the whirlies hit me, I could fall on the beast's neck and hang on like a beginner.

"So I started riding again. I took a couple of pretty bad falls. But I knew we were on the right track. After a couple of weeks without falls, I started jumping. Nothing too formidable. Just low farm fences. I took a couple of more falls. But it was working. By the end of the summer I was able to walk a straight line without veering to the left or right for a hundred yards. By Thanksgiving 1919—a year after the war was over—I could start thinking about what I was going to do with the rest of my life.

"That was when Maria gave me Grandfather's marching orders. About a month before he died, he had told her how he thought we should operate. Malcolm should run the business and handle local politics. I should study law and handle national politics. Not run for office. Grandfather considered holding a political office a waste of time. But operate as a man of influence. Between the two of us, we might add up to the Commodore—his father.

"The Commodore had been a power in state and national politics for forty years before the Civil War. Grandfather spent his life trying to emulate him. But he didn't have enough money or power to influence people beyond the borders of New Jersey, and sometimes he had trouble inside the state. He had no access to the stupendous amounts of capital accumulated by the coal and oil and steel and interstate railroad interests.

"I was furious at Grandfather's directive to study law. I had no desire to go back to college, much less to law school. But Grandfather had figured that one out too. He had arranged for me to read law in the office of his cousin, Garfield Talbot, for a year or so. Old Garfield would then tutor me in the fine art of passing the bar exam and we would be in business.

"I still didn't like the idea. But it was either accept the plan or get involved in a nasty quarrel with my brother Malcolm, who had just graduated from Harvard and thought it was a good arrangement. He didn't relish the idea of running the business with me as a supposedly equal partner. He knew I was a born boss like all older brothers and within a year I'd have my own way on everything.

"Maria was pregnant again, with Mark. She told me that it was time for me to face facts, face my responsibility as a Stapleton. I couldn't run away from it any longer, I couldn't use a war or my health or my state of mind or my unenthusiasm for learning to escape it. Pretty soon I'd be the father of two children. Two sons. She was sure the new baby would be a boy. What kind of a father was I going to be? She could understand my feelings about Grandfather. Something had broken my spiritual connection with him. She didn't know what it was. Maybe it was his fault. Maybe it was someone's dark angel seeking revenge on him. But she could not believe I would let this happen between me and my sons.

"That was decisive. The next day I reported for duty at Garfield Talbot's office and started becoming a lawyer. I was surprised to discover I liked it."

They were turning into the gravel road of New Grange Farm. They crunched up the hill and Paul Stapleton apologized for not being able to give Kilpatrick more time. "They're trying to chew me into little pieces in the courtroom, Jim," he said.

You owe me an explanation.

Was that Kilpatrick this time? No, he was only nodding, and turning off his tape recorder. It was that other face, that knowing, mocking female face speaking those words from the Paris of 1918.

191

XV

Kilpatrick got in the front seat with Sam Fry for the ride back to the city. They said nothing for the first mile. The Apache's leathery dark red skin and coarse black hair made an incongruous picture behind the wheel of the Mercedes.

"That must bring back memories," Kilpatrick said, "listening to the Judge talk."

"It does," Fry said.

"Is that an Indian name, Sam Fry?"

"They gave us Christian names when they sent us to Florida. They exiled our whole tribe to Florida. I'm a Chiricahua Apache. My Indian name is Naiché. Does that mean anything to you?"

Kilpatrick nodded. "He fought with Geronimo." Kilpatrick pronounced it correctly, "Heronimo." He had been waiting for a chance to talk to this man, and had spent a day in the library reading about the Apaches.

Fry looked pleased. "Not many people around here know that. You spend some time in the Southwest?"

"I like to read history," Kilpatrick said.

"My father was one of Naiché's warriors."

They talked for a while about Naiché's exploits and about Red Sleeves, the Mimbres Apache who declared war on the White Eyes at the age of sixty and ran them ragged for the next ten years, about General George Crook, who fought the Apaches for a decade and then became their staunchest defender in Washington, D.C.

"How did you wind up working for Judge Stapleton?" Kilpatrick asked.

"You heard how he saved my life. After the war I went to a reservation in New Mexico. I was getting drunk every day like most of the other Indians, when Mrs. Stapleton shows up. She said she'd prayed and the Virgin of Guadalupe sent her my name in a dream. She said the Captain—that's what I called him then—needed help. So I came to the farm and helped him get better from his head wound."

"How?"

"Mostly by following him around and picking him up when he fell down. I had to do it maybe two hundred times a day for a year."

"He was in bad shape."

"The doctors gave up. It was her magic that healed him. She used to go into his room and pray over him while he slept. She'd put her hands on his head and pray. She'd take a little statue of the Virgin she brought from Mexico and touch his head with it. If he ever caught her doing it he would have smashed it to pieces. But her magic protected her."

"Do you believe in the Virgin?"

"I believe in Mrs. Stapleton's magic."

"What happened in the Argonne? The Judge didn't get a medal for getting shot in the head."

"Of course not. He always leaves out his part of the story. That's the difference between him and an Apache. If an Indian does something brave he talks about it. He inspires other warriors. That's one of the first things we noticed about white men. They think it's wrong to talk about being brave. I still say they're crazy."

"What did the Judge do in the Argonne?"

"The bravest thing I've seen him do, anywhere. And I've seen him do a lot of things. Cochise used to say that Apaches carried their lives on their fingernails. That's the way the Captain was. He told you how the Germans had set off a couple of hundred land mines and blown off the crest of the ridge in front of us. Well, the Captain gets out of his tank and walks along the hole, with half the Crown Prince Division shooting at him from the other side. He finds a hunk of the crest that the explosion had missed—a sort of bridge big enough and solid enough—he walked out on it to test it—to hold a tank. He came back to our battalion and told us to follow him. I was a sergeant by then, working the guns in the rear tank. I heard people yelling that they couldn't see him. The fog and gun smoke were so thick, people disappeared at ten feet.

" 'I'll fix that,' the Captain says, and takes out a white handkerchief and ties it on his arm. We could see him all right, but so could the Crown Prince Division. They're all still shooting at him. He guides us down to the bridge, and stands there like a traffic cop waving us across. Just as my tank reached the turning point, one of the Crown Prince sharpshooters got him in the head. I jumped out and dragged him to a maintenance tank that was following the attack tanks into action. They got him to an aid station and then to a hospital. General Stratton saw the whole thing and wrote him up for another DSC."

"Is General Stratton still alive?"

"Sure. He lives in Washington, D.C. He comes up here to visit about once a year."

They drove in silence for a mile or two.

"He makes it sound like everybody got out of those tanks and walked around no-man's-land under shellfire. At first no one did it but him and Patton. And the Captain started it. Then Patton had to do it. He couldn't let a junior officer get away with being braver than him."

"Did anybody else try it?"

"Yeah. Mostly they got killed."

"You were with him in World War II?"

"All the way. But I didn't see him win his third DSC. He got it in Morocco, in the first American tank fight of World War II. I fell into our landing craft and smashed my leg. I didn't catch up to him until he got to Italy. Stratton was in command in Morocco. He can tell you about it."

Sam was silent for several miles.

194

"Between the wars I used to train his polo ponies for him. He doesn't talk about it much any more because his son Mark decided polo was a rich man's sport and nobody should play it. I'd go down to Texas and Oklahoma and buy the ponies and train them. In polo, you know, the horse is half the game. The other half is nerve. You and some other guy go for that ball and he's swinging a mallet that can knock your brains out and coming straight at you on about a thousand pounds of crazy horseflesh. Nobody plays that game without nerve.

"He was up there with the best of them, seven or eight goals. He probably would have been a champion like Cecil Smith or Tommy Hitchcock if it wasn't for his head wound. It threw his timing off a hair. That damn wound ruined him as a marksman too. Down in Mexico, he won a pistol match from regulars who'd been competing all over the world. Stratton says he was the best shot he's ever seen."

As they approached Kilpatrick's house, Sam Fry groped for a summation of what he was saying. "It's not easy to find a White Eyes who shoots like an Apache, rides like an Apache and fights like an Apache. I guess that's why I've stuck around all these years."

"Why don't his sons like him?" Kilpatrick said.

"Some of them do, Ned—Randy," Sam Fry said, disconcerted by the question. "It's funny but a man like him has trouble with his sons. It's true in the Apaches too. The best warriors, men like Naiché, had some bad sons. There's only one explanation, I guess. You don't inherit bravery. Each man has to find his own."

Kilpatrick saw it would be a waste of time to try to probe deeper. He thanked Sam Fry for the ride.

XVI

Don't think about it, Kilpatrick told himself. Just get the data and think about it later. He poured himself some scotch and spun back his Phonemate. He discovered Muriel Bennett had returned his call. He had pursued her at Allyn's urging, and kept missing her. She apparently had a busy social life. He dialed the New York number again.

A silken voice came over the wire. "This is Muriel Bennett. What can I do for you?"

"I'm writing a book about Paul Stapleton. I understand you knew him."

"Paul Stapleton? Why in the world would anyone want to write a book about him?"

"I can explain that if we get together for an hour or two."

They made a date for 10 A.M. the following morning. He drove to New York and parked in Ms. Bennett's underground garage. Her apartment building was on the corner of Park Avenue and Seventy-third Street. It had art deco bronze doors and stone carvings. A maid led him through a center hall tiled in striking green and white into the living room. Kilpatrick braced himself for a possible repetition of Dwight Slocum's drooling decay. It would be more repulsive in a woman.

The living room was a pastiche of furniture that Muriel Bennett had obviously collected in her travels. There were Chinese chests and Spanish armchairs, an Italian Empire couch. The rug was an authentic Persian. A huge Russian samovar stood in the corner. On end tables, on the grand piano, on the walls, were dozens of autographed pictures.

His fears of decay proved to be superfluous. A tall white-haired woman with amazingly smooth rounded cheeks and a very determined mouth strolled to meet him. Muriel Bennett was wearing a purple dressing gown clasped to her slim waist by a wide leather belt. She stood as straight and held her head as erect as Paul Stapleton. Her eyes appraised him in much the same direct way. But his eagle's stare was replaced by a mocking gaiety which seemed to say: I hope this will be very amusing.

"Kilpatrick," she said. "I've been looking you up in Who's Who. I don't find your name. What have you written?"

"Only one book so far," Kilpatrick said.

"Oh." Her smile declined perceptibly. "I find it hard to understand why any writer would want to do a book on Paul Stapleton. He's not a successful businessman. As a lawyer, he's achieved nothing but local influence. He's—I won't call him a nonentity—but—"

"I see him as an interesting figure. Symbolic, in a way. The public image of rectitude, patriotism. I want to get behind it. That's where I've heard you can help me."

"I'm not sure—after all these years—" Muriel Bennett said with a wave of dismissal.

"The first time I met him, he impressed me tremendously," Kilpatrick said. "But everything I've found out about him since has gone in the opposite direction."

She nodded, still sparring with him. "He always had that knack of impressing people. I think he inherited it. A very deceptive gift in the long run. He made you think you were important. You gradually realized the truth.

197

Behind that proud stare, the autocratic bearing, the ridiculous sense of noblesse oblige, there was nothing but mediocrity."

"Several people in the family are cooperating with me," Kilpatrick said. "So is Dwight Slocum. He told me Stapleton was in love with you in France, and he took you away from him."

The shrewd mouth lost its mocking smile. He saw grief, bitterness on the downturned lips, heard them in the cold words. "That's good for a laugh."

Kilpatrick sensed she was wavering. "That's why I'm here. To straighten things out."

"How much did Dwight offer you to write the book his way?"

"Not enough—yet."

Muriel Bennett laughed and sat down on her blue Empire couch. She lit a cigarette and gestured Kilpatrick to a chair. "I like your style. I think I'll tell you everything. The whole truth and nothing but. They say it's good for the complexion."

Kilpatrick took out his tape recorder. Muriel Bennett ignored it.

"How's Dwight Slocum? He was one of my few mistakes. I could have done a lot with him. I remember one night about three years ago he called me up. I hadn't heard from him in twenty years.

" 'Muriel, I can't sleep,' he said. 'I haven't been able to sleep for a week.'

" 'You must have a dozen call girls ready and eager to solve that problem,' I said.

" 'No,' he said. 'It's got to be somebody I can talk to, Muriel. I just want to talk.'

"I couldn't sleep either, so I said what the hell and went down to the Waldorf and talked to him. We sat there watching the dawn come up over Manhattan, talking about dances, parties, the dopes we knew back home."

"The Stapletons?"

"Of course the Stapletons. You can't believe how important they were in those days. The Stapletons and their goddamn Kemble and Talbot cousins. I used to say it was all incest. They'd been intermarrying so long it was incest.

198

But the Stapletons, the ones with the name, they were the white-hot center of it all. I can remember my mother rushing into my father absolutely breathless because she'd been invited, finally *invited* to Anne Randolph Stapleton's Easter tea. That was the summit of social acceptance. To earn that reward Mother worked about forty hours a week in one of the downtown settlement houses, teaching the Irish to take baths. There were other teas during the year that didn't rate as high. One in June for the wives of the mill managers, for instance. But the Eastern tea was for the inner circle. Mrs. Stapleton actually poured *herself*. Honest to God, that's how they reacted. Being invited to Bowood was like an invitation to Buckingham Palace.

"Looking back, I wonder how they did it. It wasn't just the money. My family had almost as much money. My grandfather had founded the locomotive works. For a while they were making half the locomotives in the country. But Grandpa was a newcomer. He hadn't arrived here until 1865. By that time the Stapletons had been here two hundred years. That was part of it. They were always reminding you of that in little ways. But the other thing, the important thing, was their instinct for power.

"No one could run for mayor without their approval. No one could get to be president of a bank or head of the Bar Association or the Chamber of Commerce without their permission. Governors, congressmen, everyone had to go down to the mills hat in hand before they dared to be candidates. My father was like my grandfather, basically just an engineer, one of those mousy men who let the women do all their living for them. He was more comfortable with machinery than he was with people. He never dreamt of challenging the Stapletons. He just contributed his hundred or two hundred thousand dollars to the Republican Party war chest each year and let the Stapletons decide where to spend it.

"My mother was very middle-class. Her father had been a shop foreman at the locomotive works. She would never have dreamed of disagreeing with anything Mrs. Stapleton said or did. Instead, she imitated her. If Mrs. Stapleton bought a Russian pony-skin car coat, Mrs. Bennett bought one. If Mrs. Stapleton rode around in a

Stevens-Duryea seven-passenger special or a Daniels Town Brougham or a Stoddard-Dayton Knight—she changed cars every year—so did Mrs. Bennett.

"There wasn't anyone else with the money to challenge them except the Slocums and they were so incredibly vulgar no one took them seriously. Dwight Slocum's mother came from the Lower East Side of New York. Her family put up the money to launch Slocum's Remedy, and wrote marrying her into the contract. Her idea of a stylish dress was purple with bright green ribbons. Her husband spent most of his time chasing girls, trying to spend the incredible amounts of money he made with that rotten patent medicine.

"I made a decision, very early in my life, when I was ten or eleven, that I was going to get the hell out of that city as fast as possible. I thought it was ridiculous playing big frog in a pond that everyone else considered a puddle. I wanted to spend my time with important people, with men who made things happen—

"Then Paul and I discovered each other. We'd been going to dancing classes and parties for years. We were the same age. But I was always cool to him. I guess even then I resented the fuss everyone made over the Stapletons. Anyway, at that age girls usually prefer someone a year or two older than they are. Men don't mature as fast as we do. I know several who are still maturing at eighty. But my attitude toward Paul changed when he came back from that trip he made with his father and Theodore Roosevelt—the one to South America where his father died. My father died around the same time. That was another bond between us. Poppa left me half his money, which made me independent of Mother and her fuddy-duddy ways.

"I was naturally fascinated by anyone who'd spent three months sitting around campfires with a former President of the United States and I decided to make a play for Paul. But I found out I couldn't stand his personality. I decided to be blunt. I told him to his face that he was an insufferable goody-goody and a bore in the bargain.

"It was my first try at changing a man and it worked so well I could hardly believe it. Paul dropped his big-brother approach to life and turned into the liveliest man I'd ever met. Maybe we were both young and that explained it. But we did have a time during those two years he spent at Princeton—1914 to 1916. I was at Bryn Mawr, and I could come up at the jangle of a telephone. I don't think I missed a weekend. But contrary to a lot of rumors, we did not have a love affair. Sex was the great no-no in those days and all we did was spoon, as they called it. Lots of smooching and squeezing and dancing. God, did we dance. And drink. And roar around the back roads along the Delaware in Paul's car, a yellow Hudson Super Six. He drove like a man in search of an early death.

"We talked a lot too, He couldn't understand why I wanted to leave the city. He wanted to marry me and take me back to Bowood and install me as the next Mrs. Stapleton. We would have a great time shocking the plebs, as he called them. I told him I didn't want to die of boredom. I wanted to go to New York, and I wanted him to come with me. I wanted him to go into politics there. TR would help him. When you were somebody in New York, you were somebody in the country. You could make things happen. He couldn't or wouldn't understand me. That basic Stapleton stubbornness, which makes it practically impossible for them to take advice from anyone, became very visible. I got infuriated and called him and the family some nasty names. We stopped seeing each other.

"The upshot was he did what heartbroken lovers have done since time immemorial, I suppose. He joined the army. Pershing's expedition to Mexico gave him a perfect excuse. He said he wanted to get as far away from me as possible. I told him it was good riddance as far as I was concerned. But we were still insanely in love with each other. We couldn't get close to each other without instant intoxication. He was incredibly handsome in those days, and I wasn't exactly decrepit. Let me show you some pictures. Come into the library."

Kilpatrick followed her into a small, book-lined study. She pulled a scrapbook from a lower shelf and flipped it open. Silently she turned the pages while a nearby de-

201

humidifier whirred. There was Paul Stapleton, the ripe upper lip dominant, standing with a cocky smile on his face beside the Hudson Super Six while Muriel Bennett sat in the front seat. He was wearing a white blazer. His white cap came down over one eye. Other pictures showed them standing in front of Nassau Hall, picnicking in a field along the Delaware.

"Were you blond?" Kilpatrick asked.

"Honey. My hair was the precise color of fresh honey."

The faces radiated happiness, confidence, cheer. They were certain that the world awaited their arrival with bated breath.

"F. Scott Fitzgerald was at Princeton in those days. He was always trying to get into our crowd. But we didn't have much use for anyone with an Irish name. I got to know him rather well in Paris in the twenties. There's a picture of him on the bookcase."

Fitzgerald stood beside the Seine wearing white shoes, a striped suit and a rakishly tipped straw hat. The inscription on the bottom read: "To Muriel. Long may she 'mu-tate.'"

"I loaned him the money he needed to finish *Tender Is the Night*."

They returned to the living room. She summoned the maid and ordered tea.

"I really loved Paul. When he left Princeton, I was miserable for weeks. It was the last time I ever let a man do that to me. You can imagine the shock I got when my mother wrote and told me that he had married some Mexican girl. I was enraged, horrified, sickened. I couldn't believe that someone I loved could do such a stupid thing. Maria Teresa O'Reilly. It was so unreal, I could only believe that he had been forced into it at the point of a gun or a machete.

"Then we got into World War I. Every interesting man in America was heading for Paris, and I decided to go with them. I joined the Red Cross and talked my way into a job at Paris headquarters. Guess who I met coming out of a house on the rue Constantine?

"Paul looked handsomer than ever in a captain's uniform. At first, neither of us knew what to say. We just

202

stood there looking at each other. I think it lasted a full five minutes. Then I said, 'You owe me an explanation.'

" 'I know,' he said.

" 'I'm free for dinner,' I said.

" 'I think I'd rather go over the top,' he said.

"We went to dinner at a restaurant near the Bois. He told me about Mexico, how much he hated it, how miserable he was down there without me. He fell in love with this girl and married her as an antidote to me. Those were the precise words he used. An antidote to me."

She raised her blue teacup to her delighted mouth. Kilpatrick watched it rise, heard the swallow, watched the mockery glitter in those eyes above the cup's gold rim.

"I told him I was the only antidote to me. I told him he had made the greatest mistake in his life. He had married a woman not merely from the provinces, but from the provinces of another country. A woman who would be a drag on him, a liability for the rest of his life. This is precisely what has happened, of course.

"He agreed with me. The war had finally gotten him out of that parochial state of mind—the Stapletons' tragic flaw. You couldn't spend much time at army headquarters without seeing where and how the power flowed in this country—along the Washington-New York axis and nowhere else worth mentioning.

"That night—that was a night—we went back to my flat near the Quai St.-Michel and became lovers. During those first four months of 1918 he spent almost every night with me. We agreed not to argue about what he'd do or wouldn't do after the war. It was enough—what we had together.

"Besides, in Paris there was another reality—the Western Front. That changed our feelings about everything. There was hardly a single French family who hadn't lost a son or a brother or a father. The whole country was in a kind of agony of mourning and despair, especially after the last German offensive started, and it looked like they were going to steamroller all the way to Paris.

"Paul was certain he was going to get killed, and I wasn't at all sure he was wrong. That was the real reason we didn't argue, we didn't do anything to spoil what we had. We just made love and danced away the night in that little flat beside the Seine. Slow dreamy dances, blues. Our mood was blue. But not dark blue, more cerulean.

"We couldn't go out. It was too dangerous. Paul's commanding officer, General Harbord, was a pretty straitlaced character and Pershing was the original Torquemada. A lot of people knew Paul was married. They'd been in Mexico with him. Only his friend Mark Stratton knew about us. But he was the sort of guy who could keep his mouth shut. A couple of times, Paul got a few days' leave, and we went to the south of France. Mark covered for us. He and Paul pretended to leave together, luggage in hand. I'd be waiting for them at the train station. Mark would take himself and his suitcase over to my flat and spend the weekend there. He had a French girl he was seeing and they didn't care where they spent their time as long as there was an empty bed around.

"I won't deny it, they were the happiest four months of my life. I loved him, and I know he loved me more than he ever loved Maria Teresa O'Reilly. The last week we were together, before he went off to tank training school, I decided I wanted to have a child by him. I had become convinced that he was going to be killed. I stopped douching. I just ran the water when I went in the bathroom after we made love. He never knew the difference. It worked. I got pregnant, and I carried his baby during those horrible months when he was at the front. It was a marvelous consolation.

"Then Mark Stratton called to tell me Paul had gotten most of his head blown off in the Argonne. I found the best neurosurgeon in Paris and drove him down to that disgusting base hospital myself. He supervised the operation that took the bullet out of Paul's brain. For a month he was in a coma. A couple of times he sank so low he had no life signs at all. But he came out of it.

"When I went to see him at the hospital, I was horrified. He was almost a paraplegic. He drooled out of one corner of his mouth. His eyes rolled around in his head. He could barely pronounce one coherent sentence without going da-da-da. I was six months pregnant, but he didn't even notice it. He just turned his face to the wall and told me to go away.

204

"I didn't know what to do. I am not by nature a maternal type. The thought of taking on an invalid like that for life overwhelmed me. I went to see the neurosurgeon and asked him if there was any hope. Practically none, he said. I asked him if he knew a good abortionist. I didn't see what else I could do with Paul's baby now. But the doctor told me I was too far gone for an abortion without risking my life. So I carried the baby to term and gave birth at La Maternités in Paris like a good little peasant. I hired a wet nurse in the countryside and left the baby there.

"I went to London and ran into Dwight Slocum. We had quite a time together for three or four months. It was like having sex with a grizzly bear. It suited my mood. I wanted someone who didn't know the meaning of the word affection. I just wanted to get laid again and again and again until Paul Stapleton and his baby and his dumb ideas about honor and duty were erased from my life.

"I went back to Paris with Dwight. He was on the staff of some rear-echelon commission—the sanitation engineers, I think. He was too smart to get his head shot off in the trenches. We went for a walk in the Tuileries. It was a beautiful day in April. Who comes down the path being pushed in a wheelchair by his devoted Mexican wife but Paul Stapleton. It was the only time I ever met Maria Teresa O'Reilly. She was damn good-looking, I'll say that for her. A little cameo face and jet-black hair. Not a bad figure either. Did you ever see Goya's Maja? That sort of body.

"We stopped and chatted. Paul slobbered all over himself, but he managed to introduce me. We talked about home. I was surprised by how good Maria Teresa's English was. She told us that old General Stapleton was dead. Paul was going home to take charge of things. That was almost good for a laugh. He looked like he couldn't take charge of getting himself a glass of water. But apparently they found some very good doctors in this country or some sort of miracle occurred, because the next time I saw him, in 1928 when I came home to settle my mother's estate, he was riding to hounds and playing polo and fathering children.

"I saw him at Stapleton, Talbot. He was the managing

partner already. They handled Mother's will—and every other will in town worth mentioning.

"But there was something missing. I saw it the moment I looked at Paul. The gaiety, the wildness, the fun that had meant everything to me, that made him so extraordinary, was gone. He was just a dull, plodding lawyer.

"By now, our son John was nine years old. I told him his father had been killed in the Argonne. In a sense, it was true. I kept him in Paris, where I spent most of my time. I was having a lot of fun running a little magazine and bankrolling various writers. I knew them all—Ezra, Jimmy Joyce, Scott, Ernest, old garbage-mouth Henry Miller. A nine-year-old kid just didn't fit into my life style. Artists are impulsive types. They like to go to bed at the most unexpected hours of the day and night. So with a little malice aforethought, I told Paul about John.

"I have never seen a man go through such a transformation. He had obviously steeled himself to see me. When I told him there was someone named John Bennett, but who really should have been John Stapleton, going to school in Paris, he almost collapsed. He started to cry.

"He wanted to know what I was going to do with him. I said I didn't know, but he was getting too old to be amusing.

"'I'll adopt him,' he said.

"'How are you going to do that without ruining your marriage?' I said.

"'I don't know,' he said, 'but no son of mine is going to grow up in an orphanage or in—'

"I knew what he had left unsaid. A whorehouse. I had become a little notorious by that time. A mistake which I soon rectified.

"Usually I don't hate people. It takes too much psychic energy. But I hated Paul Stapleton then. That Mexican woman—or the ghost of his grandfather—or his own ridiculous ideas about duty had destroyed the man I knew. It was like looking at an automaton wearing his face. No, even the face had changed. It looked like it had been plasticized. The mouth didn't work the same quick, wonderful way. When he tried to smile it was ghastly.

"He brought John to America and adopted him. But it never worked. The kid was too old, too French. He didn't get along with his half brothers. I don't know what Maria Teresa O'Reilly thought of him. Paul told everyone he was the son of an old army friend. Maria Teresa probably swallowed it like the dumb little Mexican that she was.

"They sent John away to prep school when he was fourteen. I don't think he ever came home again. He knew they were getting rid of him. He used to write me letters now and then. I've got them around here somewhere. You can have them. He didn't like me very much. I can't blame him. He remembered being happy in France.

"I suppose I shouldn't have done it. But a person can't help what she is. I'm not a mother. I wasn't meant to be a mother. The whole goddamn thing was an accident. An emotional and physical accident. I wish I could have explained it to Johnny. But it wouldn't have been very helpful, would it?

"The poor kid never got much chance to think about life. He got drafted in 1940, numero uno. He was exactly twenty-one, the guy they wanted most. Paul got him into officer's training school, but he flunked out like he flunked out of everything else. I think he went to about four prep schools and colleges. But he turned out to be a tremendous soldier. He got two or three decorations and Patton promoted him to lieutenant in the field. He was a tanker like his father. I hope you try to do something with that Stapleton fascination for tanks. I think it's part of their basic approach to life. Armored against the slings and arrows of outrageous fortune—and against feelings.

"I guess it shouldn't be surprising, but Johnny loved the army. He decided to make a career of soldiering. I told him if he was going to stay in the goddamned military he should go to West Point. That was the only way you got to the top. Paul agreed and got him into the Academy. He struggled through four dreadful years in the bottom third of his class and graduated in 1950. Wham. We were in another war. He went to Korea and got killed. End of story.

"Paul was terribly shaken by his death. He wrote me a long letter about it. I'll dig it out for you. I was back in Paris with my second husband, the ambassador. I took a taxi to the Quai St.-Michel and found the little flat where Paul and I lived during those first months of

1918. I tipped the landlady, and she let me go upstairs to sit by the window and read his letter, while the winter sun went down over Paris. I had a good cry. Then I went home and entertained twenty people for dinner.

"My motto has always been, let the dead bury the dead. The past is for those who lived in the past.

"When I look back on Paul's career, all I can see is waste and more waste. He had everything—the charm, the looks, the war record—to be a big name in America. Instead, what did he do? He went back home and went to work for that moldy old law firm and watched his brother run the mills into the ground and finally had to swallow the humiliation of selling the business to Dwight Slocum, of all people.

"Then he goes back into the army in World War II instead of heading for Washington, where he might have parlayed his war record and his independence in politics into something important. And comes home to that fat little Mexican wife after World War II. Diddles around with some obscure commissions on integrating the Army, things that didn't even get his name in the papers, as far as I know. Finally, he takes a federal judgeship just in time to get himself involved in the busing mess.

"His whole life is a study in mediocrity. What in the world can you say about him that anyone would want to read? What he needed, what he always needed, was someone like me to put some life into that essential Stapleton dullness, doggedness, stupidity, if you will. As a tribe, they're not very bright, they really aren't. They just happened to be in the right place at the right time and got their hands on a lot of money early in the game. They used it to get a stranglehold on their little corner of the world and just sat there while time passed them by. They're anachronisms, they have been for fifty, maybe even a hundred years.

"I sometimes think of Paul as a machine that I electrified, a machine that's been running down, down, down ever since, like everything else in that city, that whole state. A backwater. I remember what my third husband, the Secretary of the Army, used to say about it. New Jersey's a state that never should have happened."

She lit a cigarette and leaned back against the yellow

cushions at her end of the couch. "If he'd listened to me, Paul could be sitting here, surrounded by those pictures. Look at them—there's Kennedy, there's Johnson, there's Eisenhower, there's FDR—all inscribed to me. They could be inscribed to him too.

"There's hardly one of these guys who hasn't paid old Muriel a visit where it counts. Why don't you write my life? It's a hell of a lot more interesting than Paul Stapleton's. I've had several writers approach me. But I put them off. You can't play kiss and tell and retain any influence. It's quite a story, and it'll sell, my friend. It's got sex in it. That's a lot more than you can say for Paul Stapleton. Once I left him, I think he went neuter."

Suddenly the apartment was underwater. This leering female face in front of Kilpatrick belonged to a gigantic shark who had lived in these depths forever, devouring, devouring, devouring unwary swimmers like him, slashing flesh, crunching bone with those executioner's teeth.

"Could I have those letters?" he said.

"Sure. I'll be glad to get rid of them. I don't think I'll include Johnny in my autobiography."

After several minutes of rummaging in a desk in the study, Muriel Bennett found John Stapleton's letters. But she could not find the letter Paul Stapleton had written to her when John was killed in Korea. If she found it, she said, she would send it to him.

In return, she asked Kilpatrick to put his literary talent to work and suggest a title for her autobiography. Kilpatrick said he would think about it. He stuffed the letters in his briefcase and fled Muriel Bennett's carnivorous underwater world.

XVII

December 10, 1929

Dear Maman,

My stepfather says I ought to write and thank you for the sweater you sent for my birthday. He says writing to you will do me good and help me practice my English writing. I still have a lot of trouble writing in English.

My stepmother, Maria, is nice to me, but I don't think she likes me. For a while I wouldn't call her Mother. I really missed you. But now I decided I will call you Maman and call her Mother. Father says I'm lucky to have a French mother and an American mother. I'm not so sure. I've had a lot of trouble in school. I understand the language, but I have trouble writing and reading English.

Father sends you his regards.

Love,
Johnny

December 10, 1931

Dear Maman,

Father still thinks it's a good idea for me to write to you on my birthday even though you forgot to send me a

210

present this year. I don't have to practice writing English any more. I can do it pretty well by now. I've almost forgotten how to write in French. But Father gives me French books to read. He says he wants me to keep in touch with it. It may get me a job someday.

I'm on the school baseball team. I play centerfield. I hit two home runs in the last game. Father gave me a dollar for each one.

I miss my brother Randy. He went away to prep school this year. He's a nice guy. I don't like my other brothers very much. They gang up on me and give me a hard time. Father gets very angry when he catches them doing it. The one I really don't like is Mark. He's ten. He's a real wise guy. The other day I heard him telling George that I was a bastard. I caught him in the barn after we went riding that afternoon and punched him in the stomach. I don't think he'll call me that again.

I hope you are still in Paris at your old address so this letter gets to you. Give my regards to Colette, if she still works for you.

Love,
Johnny

December 10, 1933

Dear Maman:

Pennsgrove. What a lousy miserable place to spend a birthday. I hate this school. I hate everything about it. They expect you to study day and night. The older guys are a bunch of rats who beat up younger guys like me. Randy is here and he tries to do his best to protect me. But there isn't much he can do. It's a tradition in this school to give the Third Form guys a hard time.

The only subject I'm passing is French. I hate math and English is a bore. We had to read *A Tale of Two Cities*. I liked that because some of it happened in Paris. But the rest of Charles Dickens stinks.

I made the freshman football team and its looks like I'll make the freshman basketball team. Baseball is my best game, so I should have a pretty good time on the playing fields, as they call them, if I don't flunk out.

I've told Dad I wish I could stay home and go to the

public high school in the district. I miss the horses, I miss him, I even miss my ratty brother Mark.

I saw your picture in the paper the other day with your husband. He looks like a pretty flashy guy. Did he pick out the sports coat you sent me? It makes me feel like a movie star.

Love,
Johnny

December 10, 1938

Dear Maman,

Here I am in a new school again. They accepted enough credits from the other two disasters to let me enter the Fourth Form, so nobody will try to push me around. I'm getting too big for that sort of thing anyway. I had to leave Peddie last year, not because of my marks but because I broke a senior's jaw when he started hazing me. I've grown a lot in the last year. I'm five feet ten and I weigh a hundred and sixty pounds. Every day I do the exercises Dad makes us do all summer. I can chin myself ninety times, do a hundred and fifty push-ups with my right arm and a hundred and forty with my left arm. I broke Peddie's record for the shot put and hit .680 for the baseball team. The coach practically cried when I got thrown out.

I think I can settle down and study in this place. There won't be any hazing for me to worry about personally. But I'm not going to let anyone make the Third Formers' life miserable. Dad agrees with me completely. He said he felt the same way when he was in prep school.

I'm sorry about your divorce. I read all about it in the paper. You should have hired a better lawyer. The way it came out in the trial, the whole thing sounded like your fault. Dad says that he's amazed that people in your position would let things like that get into the papers. It's a shame.

Sincerely,
Johnny

September 10, 1941

Dear Maman,

He's in the Army now
He's in the Army now

He'll never get rich
Poor son of a bitch
He's in the Army now.

I didn't get an answer to last year's birthday letter. I guess you're busy with your new husband. But I still trust you have some faint interest in my doings. I've finished basic training, and I'm at Fort Benning, Georgia, for officer's training. I'm hoping I can get through this thing for Dad's sake. He can't picture a Stapleton who isn't an officer. But I've had so much bad luck in school, I'm not sure how things will go. I don't particularly care whether I'm an officer or an enlisted man, as long as I get into armor. We'll be at war within a year, everyone down here's convinced of it, and armor is where the action is going to be. Generals like George Patton are putting together an American blitzkrieg that will make the Nazis beg for mercy. My brother Randy just graduated from OCS and is going into armor too, naturally. If he doesn't get assigned out of here, he will give me a lot of help with the books.

Wish me luck in the OCS grind.

Sincerely,
John

December 10, 1943

Dear Maman:

I don't know whether you'll ever see this letter. Some fish may wind up reading it while dining on me. We're en route to England where we expect to go into training for the invasion of Europe. Sicily was a great show. Typical army snafus all over the place, shooting down our own planes, Christ knows what else. But the big news as far as I'm concerned is a battlefield promotion. General Patton made me a lieutenant on the spot for leading an attack on a village that blocked the road to Palermo. It was jammed with Germans firing antitank guns out windows, throwing Molotov cocktails. We just worked our way up and down the main street, blasting them with every gun we had. It was the most fantastic show. Flames, smoke, bullets everywhere. I loved every second of it. It only lasted about ten minutes, then the Germans ran for their lives. They thought our tank was haunted or charmed or something. When we evacuated one of their wounded, he pointed at it and called it a "teufel tank"—a devil's tank. About ten minutes later, General Patton came roaring up in a jeep. He looked at the village which was a burning wreck and told one of his officers to find out how heavy our casualties were. When I told him we hadn't had any casualties, he almost fell out of the jeep. The colonel of the infantry regiment we were supporting came running up and told him what we'd done. Patton asked me my name. When he heard it, he started laughing. "Like father, like son," he said. "Why the hell aren't you an officer, Sergeant?" I told him I'd flunked out of OCS. He said, "Well, you're an officer now." He took the bars off an infantry lieutenant and pinned them on me right there. The first thing I did when I got to Palermo was find Dad and tell him about it. I told him I'd finally done something he could be proud of. I was surprised how choked up he got. He said I shouldn't think that way. But it's a fact. I have been the family screw-up. I think things will be different if I get out of this war alive.

Sincerely,
John

December 10, 1947

Dear Maman:

I missed writing you last year's letter like I missed a lot of things thanks to the dubious pleasures of a West Point plebe's life. But I still have that classy wallet you sent me. I like this place. It's making me shape up in ways that I have fought and evaded all my life. I've had a few problems. I didn't take too kindly to the plebe hazing and got called out by the upperclassmen. That means you have to fight the toughest guys they can find. After they lost a few teeth, it dawned on them that maybe plebes with combat experience should be treated a little differently. Now I'm a yearling, which means I'll enjoy myself a little more. But not much. I've got to beat the books very hard just to stay at the top of the bottom third of the class. That is where George Patton finished, so I'm not writhing in self-abasement. The only thing that worries me now is the probability that the country is going into a pacifist phase that will practically eliminate the army. This could mean I'll spend ten years as a lieutenant and five as a captain and ten years later I'll retire on a cane as a major. Frankly, I want to be a general and I expect you to pull all the strings in your repertoire to get me those stars.

Fondly,
John

Nov. 5, 1950

Dear Maman:

This is your favorite war correspondent reporting from a new theater. Korea is a fun place. When it's hot, it's sizzling and when it's cold it makes West Point in January seem balmy. From a tanker's point of view it's been a pretty lousy war. Half the country's uphill and the other half is downhill, not the best terrain for armor. I don't think there's been a single tank-to-tank fight since it started. Which is just as well, I suppose. The Reds are using Russian T-34s that can pierce our armor at 2,000 yards while our .75s bounce off them at that range.

They only had about 50 or 100 tanks and air or artillery got all of them down on the Pusan perimeter. Now we're rolling north with no armor left to fight so they use us as mobile artillery to encourage or protect the infantry. MacArthur says it will all be over by Christmas but I'm not so sure. I've got a buddy in intelligence who told me in Seoul that there are a couple of million Chinese massed on the other side of the Yalu making ominous noises.

As Dad has no doubt told you, a tank is a hell of a lot safer than the infantry. But I keep getting an eerie feeling that I've used up my white points with the man upstairs. If I'm right, I don't want you to shed any guilty tears over me. I've had a better life than most Americans. You had to do what you did. You couldn't have picked a better stepfather for me than Dad.

I hope I can read this and laugh when I visit you in Paris as the beribboned war-weary aide-de-camp of the next NATO commander.

As ever,
John

Kilpatrick stood on the corner of Park Avenue and Seventy-third Street reading the letters in the October sunshine. The intense white light hurt his eyes. He walked down to Lexington Avenue and had two quick scotches in the nearest bar. He told himself to rejoice, to be hard, cold, exultant. Allyn was right. Paul Stapleton was a hypocrite of the rankest, raunchiest kind. Kilpatrick re-read the letters in the gray light of the bar. Wisps of regret curled along his nerves, twisting exultation into ambivalence.

All the way home in the car, the two ghosts argued in Kilpatrick's head. Randy Stapleton asked him if he was prepared, much less qualified, to cast the first stone. Kevin Kilpatrick leered and urged him to ask Randy about the first bullet, or to be more specific, the first fragmentation grenade. *Multiple wounds in the chest and head.* Ask him about that. Ask him about the guy who got out of their tanks in no-man's-land imitating Paul Stapleton and got killed. Ask him what he's done with his goddamned bravery except kill people.

As Kilpatrick turned into his driveway, he noticed a red Volvo sports car parked in front of the house. Several teen-agers were ogling it. Sitting on the top step of his porch, smoking a cigarette was Allyn Stapleton. She was wearing blue jeans and a red sweater. He gunned his Corvette into the garage and skipped his act with the ignition key.

He strolled around to the steps and eyed her for a moment, hands on his hips. "What are you doing here?" he said.

"I'm part of a new city service. I decorate houses."

"Where do you start?"

"Usually in the bedroom. But I can start anywhere."

His eyes roved up her legs to the tight crotch of her blue jeans. Desire stirred in him. With it came an ability to tune out Randy's ghost, to listen only to the questions Kevin was asking.

In the house, he mixed double scotches while Allyn looked around the living room. "Jesus," she said. "This really could use a decorator. Who perpetrated this? Someone from the home of the blind?"

"It's bachelor modern," he said. "Designed to keep decorators on the job for days, weeks, possibly months."

She laughed, flicked her tongue at him and asked him what he had found at Muriel Bennett's.

"Our first jackpot," he said.

He showed her the letters. He got out the tape recorder and let her listen to Muriel Bennett's husky arrogant voice. He saw the hatred glow in Allyn's eyes and knew it was wrong. He saw the way the afternoon, the evening would go. Maybe revenge was the only way to heal multiple wounds inflicted by fragmentation grenades. Revenge in the name of truth.

Ambivalence, promises, love, whispered a fading voice that he refused—or the booze refused—to recognize.

Kilpatrick raised a double scotch on the rocks. "To celebrations," he said.

XVIII

At the hospice, Agatha Stapleton spent the last hour of the afternoon with Mrs. Malloy. She had passed through anger and bargaining and was now in the depression stage of her journey to acceptance. She talked about what a rotten hand life had dealt to her. No matter how hard they worked, she and her husband had never gotten together enough money to buy their own house. He was a bus driver who liked to gamble. She had been a waitress, a short-order cook. She had had to support her parents for the last ten years of their lives. Her father had been a textile worker at Principia and several other mills in the city. He had had brown lung from breathing the cotton lint in the air. He had died by inches, coughing his lungs out piece by piece. Now she was dying in a similar way, little by little, in some ways worse, with more pain.

Agatha listened, her mind focused completely on this little life, trying to enter it, trying to offer her a tiny piece of her self, even though the story was as foreign to her experience as the life of a Chinese peasant. She reminded Mrs. Malloy of some of the good things in her life. She had three loyal sons who came to visit her regularly. She had three devoted daughters-in-law. When Agatha left, Mrs. Malloy thanked her and hoped she would visit again tomorrow.

Downstairs, she stopped in the office of the fund-raising director, Harry Flanagan, and picked up a copy of the prospectus they had developed to raise two million dollars needed to double the size of the hospice. He knew where she was going tonight. "Good luck," he said.

"I'll probably need it," she said.

Outside, her rented limousine was waiting, with the usual driver, a short, husky Slovak named Claude Krasko. He smiled and waved her into the back seat and she was on her way to dinner with her ex-husband, Dwight Slocum. The hospice had gotten her back in touch with Dwight, ten years ago. She had written to him after his last and messiest divorce from a twenty-six-year-old Greek airline stewardess, expressing sympathy and suggesting the hospice as a better way to spend some of his money. Paul had growled his disapproval but she had ignored him.

Dwight had responded with a check for fifty thousand dollars, which Paul felt constrained to double. Dwight had also expressed a cautious wish to see her again. Why not? Agatha thought. They began having dinner two or three times a year, when he was in New York. He invariably gave her a hefty check for the hospice. He also used her to communicate with his only son, Dwight, Jr., whom he had totally alienated. Agatha had managed to build a shaky truce between the two of them. It was about as stable as the truce between Dwight and Paul.

It was curious, the way the lives of the two men had been intertwined, in spite of their antipathy. She had played a large part in the twining, and that was one reason why she had tried to play the role of peacemaker between them. Over the years they had had a curious exchange of sons. In the late thirties, while she had been married to Dwight, she had arranged for Dwight, Jr., to spend several summers at New Grange Farm. He had been mesmerized by Paul. For a while, the boy became a manageable teen-ager. But his father's crude and constant interference in his life soon revived his worst instincts. Not until four years ago did he quit being a playboy and win election to Congress with Paul's backing. Dwight was now running for the U.S. Senate.

After World War II, Randy had gone to work for Dwight Slocum, Sr., at National Products and become his faithful lieutenant, a phenomenon about which Agatha had mixed feelings. She had never liked the idea of this sensitive, gentle, young man at Dwight's beck and call. But he had apparently considered it his duty to put up with Dwight to make sure the family money was not recklessly flung away on some chancy scheme that caught Dwight's fancy. He was a gambler by inclination and had made and lost two fortunes while Agatha had been married to him.

She let the doorman at the Waldorf Towers push the bronze revolving door for her and ascended to the thirty-fourth floor. An unpleasant-looking nurse showed her into the living room of the apartment. As usual, Agatha felt again an involuntary womanly satisfaction. Dwight had not allowed his succeeding wives to replace the Louis XVI furniture and Aubusson rugs that she had selected. It was like stepping into a time machine.

The illusion ended when Dwight came down the hall to her in his motorized wheelchair. She gasped at the sight of his stroke-ravaged face, the drooping, useless arm. "Hu-hu-hello, Aggie," he said.

"Oh, Dwight. I'd heard about the stroke. I didn't know it was this bad."

"I'm taking ther-therapy. I get a lit-tle better each day," he said.

He examined her, the small eyes full of his old brutal energy. "You're still looking pretty good," he said. "Remember I used to tell you that you'd be better-looking when you got older?"

"Thank you. I feel fine, thank God. Hardly an ache, except a twinge now and then in my wrist."

An error. Dwight glowered. In their last fight before they had permanently separated in 1940, Dwight had broken her wrist. Or rather, she had broken it, hitting him in the face with her fist.

"What would you like to drink?" Dwight said.

"A little vermouth, perhaps."

220

"They won't let me drink anything, except water. With all the medicine I get, it tu-tastes like piss."

Agatha said that was a shame. It was not much different from listening to Mrs. Malloy at the hospice. Except that Mrs. Malloy had better manners. A maid served Agatha vermouth and they talked about the hospice. Dwight seemed uninterested. He fiddled with his wheelchair, with the strap on his blue robe.

With no warning, he snarled at her like the Dwight of old. "You're not guh-getting a fucking cent from me while your brother sits over there writing a book that's going to make a fool of me."

Agatha was so astonished she asked a stupid question. "How did you find out about it?"

She sounded like a conspirator, which only intensified Dwight's rage. "Nu-never mind how I found out. You're not going to guh-get away with it. I'm going to buy up that guy Kilpatrick. I'll pay him suh-six times what you offer him if necessary to get my version of the stu-story told. If you're in on the scheme it'll include a blow-by-blow of our fifteen years of unholy matrimony."

"There isn't any scheme, Dwight. So I can't be in on it."

"Don't bu-bullshit me. I had this guy Kuh-Kilpatrick sitting right where you're sitting. He told me everything. He agreed to take my price. How can you su-sit there and lie for that fucking bro-brother of yours after what he did to you? I always knew if you went home he'd get his self-satisfied hooks into you. Remember the last thing I told you, before we split? Stu-stay in New York."

"Dwight. I assure you that I am not lying."

He only became more enraged. "I kn-know you," he shouted. "You've rejoined the goddamn Stapletons. I bu-bet you'd suck my cock right now if I said that was my price for dropping this guy Kilpatrick."

"I think we are past those antics, Dwight," Agatha said.

"Maybe you are. That nurse I've got is pretty good at it. Doesn't that fruitcake Peregrine ask you for a little servicing now and then?"

"I'm not married to him, Dwight."

221

"That never stopped you from doing it for other guys when you were married to me."

"I've caused you a great deal of pain, Dwight. I've told you several times how much I regret it."

"Yeah. Now I find out how suh-sincere you were. I feel the way I felt the day you laughed in my face when I came home from the University Cl-club and told you about the guy in the steam room talking about this dame who'd do anything."

"And you punched him in the teeth before you realized he was one of the vice-presidents of the Stock Exchange. That was what I thought was so funny, Dwight. You were as upset by that as you were by what you'd heard. As I recall it, a night or two later you were asking me to repeat the performance."

"Why the hell not? Why wasn't I entitled to it? I was paying for it."

"Dwight. I have tried to explain to you more than once. I thought marrying you was a license to do anything. I thought you didn't care. I never dreamt you expected us to be more respectable than my grandmother."

Agatha sipped her vermouth. She was feeling lightheaded. It was not the alcohol. It was facing the past that she had miraculously survived. She was also facing a present that she was not sure she would survive. Her heart was beating much too fast and her stomach was churning. While her demeanor was trying not to take Dwight seriously, the rest of her was going in the opposite direction.

Dwight continued to rant. He dredged up all their old grievances. "How would you like to see in print the truth about the first loan for the mills? How Agatha Stapleton peddled her cunt to get ten million dollars for her marvelous brothers."

Agatha started to lose her temper. Sick as Dwight was, maybe he deserved some abuse in return.

"I could tell the world that Dwight Slocum was so fascinated by the charms of Agatha Stapleton that he was prepared to loan her brothers ten million dollars in return for Agatha's agreement to remain his faithful, loving wife, instead of getting the divorce she so richly deserved."

"You bitch! I'd tell—"

"Oh, Dwight, stop acting childish. Neither of us could prove anything after all these years. Besides, I made that agreement with as much sincerity as I could muster at the time."

"Yeah. But when you tried to take me seriously, when I was your husband and not some guy you shacked up with to prove you could do anything, the Stapleton ice water started running in your veins again. I bla-blame you for that problem I've had ever since. A kind of panic inside me and then I can't make it with anyone."

"Nonsense. You had that problem almost every time the stock market went down. But I admit there's some truth to what you say. The word wife was bad for me. I froze when I heard it. I won't try to explain it to you. It has a lot to do with my mother."

Agatha sipped her vermouth. She was no longer light-headed. She looked around the apartment she had furnished so long ago. Her body was dross, heavy with the guilt, the failures of the past.

Her confession calmed Dwight. He buzzed for the maid and refilled her glass. He said he was having dinner sent up from the Waldorf's kitchen. He had ordered cold lobster for her.

"There's no need for you to get mixed up in this thing, Ag. I told Kilpatrick I wanted to leave you out of it."

"Dwight. Will you please tell me what you are afraid Paul is going to say about you, if I am left out? How can he denigrate you? Without you, he would be a well-off attorney, nothing more. You've made him a rich man. And you took his favorite son away from him in the bargain."

Dwight looked angry again. "You know," he said. "You've guh-got to know."

Agatha shook her head.

"Paul never talked to you about the cor-corporation?"

"Except for some cryptic communications about my net worth, as National Products stock went up, no."

Dwight struggled for a moment, the veins in his neck working, as if he was spitting something foul from his mouth. "They tu-took it away from me. That's wha-what he's going to put in this goddamn book. He's going to tell

223

the wor-world how he and Randy took National Products away from Dwight Slocum and made him a stupid, meaningless fuh-figurehead."

Agatha was too astonished to do more than stare. "How?" she finally said.

"Step by step. Randy was a bu-born leader. He performed fantastically everywhere I put him. Pretty suh-soon he was vice-president in chu-charge of the defense division. He mu-made it the most profitable division in the company. The next thing I get is a letter from Paul, saying he thinks I ought to ap-appoint Randy president and chu-chief operating officer. He su-said I just couldn't huh-handle people. I realized he was right. So I did it."

Dwight reached over and took a slug of Agatha's vermouth. "The next year, Randy doubles the profits. *Doubles* them. After that, they had me. I couldn't fire a president who delivered that kind of dough to the stockholders. The next thing you know, Randy's telling me to concentrate on overseas investments. He's dreaming up private deals for me, like a Caribbean resort company. Su-suddenly I realize that I haven't given an order to anybody at National Products in twelve months. When I try to give one, I'm told that Randy's out of town and the decision will have to wait until he gets back. Finally, in '69 came the cru-crunch. I wanted to sell the defense division. We were guh-getting a lot of heat from the anti-war protesters. It was hurting sales of other divisions. Randy says no. A letter comes in from Paul, telling me he'll start a stockholder's suit and challenge me for control. I backed off. A fight like that inside a company between the two biggest stockholders would turn our stock to fuh-funny money overnight.

"That's the way it was until Randy's plane crashed. I was out of it. I did what they tuh-told me, signed what they sent me. Now it's too late. I'm too old. I can't deal with Randy's people. They all hate me. All I do at headquarters is fuck things up. I bet they celebrated for a week when I had this stru-stroke."

Agatha could hear Dwight's pain, his grief over his lost power far more clearly than she had heard any similar mourning for their lost love. It was beyond her, this hunger for power, control. But she knew it was not

224

beyond her brother Paul. She had thought it was beyond Randy. She thought he had abandoned that old Stapleton desire for more personal spiritual goals.

She felt childishly ignorant, womanish in the worst sense. She heard herself saying she would do her best to prevent Paul from telling the story. But the scorn on Dwight's face made her realize how feeble she sounded.

"I'd appreciate anything you can do," he snapped. "Bu-but I'm going to duh-do a little preventing on my own. You tell him that unless this bu-book is dropped, Kilpatrick will write it my way. Wu-with all the dirt in it."

Again, Agatha was engulfed by a helpless, bewildered ignorance. She simply did not know what dirt Dwight could tell. It was humiliating, to be forced to sit there concealing this void in her mind, while Dwight rambled on about a crooked lawsuit in some way connected with the sale of the mills, a violent clash with a union in North Carolina, members of Congress whom Paul had supposedly bribed. The lobster arrived and Agatha picked at it disconsolately, while Dwight slopped some sort of special gruel. She finally managed to get him to talk about his son Dwight, but this too proved to be a negative topic. His campaign for the Senate was going badly. She abandoned hope for a check for the hospice and left early.

Riding home in the dark rear seat of her limousine, Agatha felt old anger stirring in her veins. She started remembering things about her brother that she had labored to forget. When she was twelve or thirteen, he had caught her reading a supposedly racy novel by Elinor Glyn and thrown it into the fireplace. After their father died he assumed it was his responsibility to approve each of her pitifully few boy friends. When she had decided to marry Dwight, Paul had written her a curt letter, telling her that under a clause which Grandfather had included in his will, he had the power to buy out her shares in Principia Mills for next to nothing. He was going to permit her to retain them because he suspected she would soon need them. But if her husband attempted to influence the operation of the mills in any way through her, he would instantly invoke the option.

Frigidly correct, Paul had escorted her up the aisle at

225

her wedding and given her away—then pleaded the pressure of an important law case to skip the reception. She remembered sitting in the Princess Hotel in Bermuda, drunk and weeping with rage, writing him an insulting letter, vowing never to forgive him. She had returned his wedding present, a silver tea service, saying it was an anachronism, like him.

But there were good memories too. In 1919, still barely able to walk, he had insisted on coming to her debut. Wasted and pale, he had stood by the fireplace in Bowood's ballroom, with the glaring portrait of Grandfather in his Civil War uniform above him. It had been a paradigm of family patriotism. She had never been so proud of him, so proud of being a Stapleton. She had canceled her last dance, and walked to his side, declaring he was the only man in the room she really wanted to dance with. She had kissed him, everyone applauded and the band had played "Hail Columbia."

Even then she could see the change, the new severity in his eyes, the new harshness around his mouth. The way he walked was different, more rigid, contorted. She had blamed it on his wound. Only when the severity, the harshness, invaded her personal life did she realize that the change was spiritual.

At the beach in 1915, the last summer before he joined the army and went to Mexico, that was perhaps the best memory. He used to take her to the Yacht Club junior dances at Mother's insistence, even though she was a bony, incredibly unattractive fourteen. He would stalk around the room, all calm self-assurance, corralling partners for her. No one ever refused Paul Stapleton, no matter how ugly they thought his sister was. Even then he had had an air of command. Only after her card was full, and his responsibility met, would he find Muriel Bennett and start dancing.

How he danced. With the grace of an athlete, the intensity of a perfectionist. The Tango, the Maxixe, the Hesitation—all the dances condemned by the middle-class fuddy-duddies. The upper classes accepted them eagerly, recognizing them as immense advances in grace and romance over the Two-Step, the Bunny Hug and the Turkey Trot, with their shuffles and twists and wriggles

226

and jumps. She would never forget the night that Muriel Bennett and Paul danced the Innovation, which had been introduced only a few months before by Vernon and Irene Castle at a dinner dance given by Mrs. Stuyvesant Fish of New York.

The Innovation was a Tango in which the dancers did not touch each other. The man danced with his hands in his pockets, conveying his directions to his partner with his head, his eyes, his feet. It required absolute mastery of the Tango's intricate steps—the Cortez, the Media Luna, the Promenade, the Scissors, the Charron. Muriel was wearing a blue chiffon dress with a split skirt and a pleated petticoat underneath it. Paul wore a white dinner jacket. Within minutes, everyone had stopped dancing to watch them. Agatha had stood on a chair to get a better look at those two lithe, gliding, swaying figures, while the sensuous South American music swirled around them.

It had been Muriel Bennett's idea to learn the Innovation, of course. She always knew the latest rag, the newest hit song. Agatha had watched, simultaneously admiring and hating her. She instinctively hated every female who attracted her brother Paul.

She suddenly remembered what she had said to Kilpatrick while they were looking at Paul's picture in the Pennsgrove yearbook.

There's the man I really loved. Was it true? she wondered. Was a dark forbidden love the reason for what Dwight Slocum called Stapleton ice water in her veins? She knew, perhaps better than anyone, the inverted centripetal pull of her blood, the wish to plunge deeper, to possess and be possessed on a level more profound than belonging. But she had told herself that her failure as a physical woman was part of her fate, sealed by her mother's disdain for the flesh. *Only nigras really enjoy it, a lady never does.* That had been Mother's creed, the tradition of southern gentility that curiously condoned tight bathing suits and plunging necklines, all the accouterments of passion, romance, until the moment of pleasure.

Her fate, Agatha thought. But not necessarily her doom, not a final burden but the gate to her spiritual mission, to the Stapletons' purpose. She had read Freud

227

and rejected him. She would not allow herself to be reduced to competence or incompetence in the bedroom, she would not, she had not accepted that as the boundary of her life. On the contrary, she had come to see her failure as two-sided, with a bright as well as a dark perception, like almost everything else in human experience. It had opened her to the life of the spirit, it had put her in touch with that sad, earnest man she had never really known, the man who vanished on the River of Doubt, her father. It had given her a new view of her brother Paul, enabling her to recapture her old love for him, purified, ennobled.

The limousine stopped. Agatha looked out the window. They were waiting for a red light in the center of New Grange Township, at the main intersection. The street was empty and dark, except for a half dozen illuminated storefronts and several antique lampposts. A block away, a sports car emerged from the side street on which she lived and drove slowly to the intersection. Her limousine's headlights illuminated the face of the man behind the wheel. It was unmistakably the squarish, heavy-boned Irish-American face of Jim Kilpatrick. Agatha glanced at her watch. It was ten o'clock. Usually she got back from her dinners with Dwight Slocum about eleven. But tonight's had been so unpleasant she had left a full hour early.

Kilpatrick had been to see Peregrine. He had sent him home well before her presumed arrival, his head stuffed with negative facts and artifacts about Paul Stapleton.

Agatha sighed. It was time for her to have a long frank talk with Mr. Kilpatrick.

XIX

"I don't know what the ol' faggott'll tell you," Allyn had said, drunkenly dialing Peregrine's number. "But he knows *plenty*."

Kilpatrick laughed and twiddled her nipples. She grabbed his pulsing cock. *Whorehouse,* whispered Randy's voice. *You are turning the place where you hoped to renew father love into a whorehouse.* Kilpatrick shook his head, appalled-amused, amused-appalled at what was happening. He was out of control like a truck rolling down a mountain road with severed brakes. They had spent the afternoon drinking and screwing.

He listened while Allyn told Peregrine she was in conference with the noted author James Kilpatrick, Jr. She said he was a great guy and had Dwight Slocum's backing to write a book about the Great Man that would even all the scores.

She handed the telephone to Kilpatrick and began sucking his cock. "Your call couldn't be more timely, my dear fellow," Peregrine said. "Agatha's gone into the city to cadge money from Slocum for her hospice. Would you like to come for dinner?"

229

Kilpatrick said he would love it. Peregrine asked him what he would like, Cornish game hen or tournedos. Kilpatrick took the tournedos and said he would be there at six. As he hung up he came in Allyn's mouth.

Don't whispered a voice. He let it reverberate in his skull. Was it his Irish conscience speaking? Was this the last forbidden pleasure for him? Or was it the voice of poor old Randy, the faltering father-ghost, growing as ghastly, as futile, as the father he was faulting? Go away old man, Kilpatrick said. Don't you know a failure when you see one? Why do you keep interrupting the swordsman-spokesman of slaughtered youth, of John Stapleton and Kevin Kilpatrick in their patriotic graves, by order of Paul the Blameless Stapleton? He went down on Allyn and sucked her clit until she was laughing ecstatically, begging him to stop.

He showered and felt almost sober. He drove carefully out of the city to New Grange Township. A cold October twilight was gathering as Kilpatrick parked in front of Agatha Stapleton's elongated old house. Peregrine greeted him wearing a bright green silk jacket and yellow slacks. Every gray curl was precisely in place.

Peregrine served a dry white wine and a shrimp mousse from a recipe given to him by the chef at the Ritz in Madrid. Not the Ritz in Paris, which he considered a tourist trap.

"Let us understand one thing. I am prepared to tell you a great deal. But if you quote me, I will deny it. I am penniless, you see, and utterly dependent on Agatha's bounty. Your source must be unnamed, in the best tradition of contemporary reporters."

"Agreed," Kilpatrick said.

"The inner secret of the Stapletons," Peregrine said, his head tipped wryly to the left, his wine held elegantly aloft, "is incest. Spiritual and occasionally physical incest. We have been inbred for so long, marrying cousins and worshipping fathers and grandfathers and hero brothers, we are incapable of loving someone who is not one of our own. We may couple with them, as Paul has done with his pathetic little Mexican wife, but we don't love them. Love, intimate love, is reserved only for Stapletons.

"If you are anything of a reader in psychology, you must know that the emotion closest to love is hate. That is the other Stapleton passion. Let me also make clear to you that I hate Paul Stapleton. I hate the things he stands for, duty, honor, patriotism, integrity. Others may tell you that he's a hypocrite, that he doesn't live up to his code, may not even believe in it. I go a step further. I think he does believe in it, no matter how often he may have failed it. That is precisely what makes him a monster, an enemy of freedom, a destroyer of the human spirit. It is what I hate most in him.

"Paul and I are approximately the same age. I am older by about four months. My father's death and my mother's timidity made it inevitable that I would occupy an inferior place in the family. I was a sickly child, and my mother, regarding me as her only claim to the Stapletons' bounty—she was a Kemble whose father had lost his money in the Panic of 1893—hovered over me with frantic solicitude. I was never allowed to play any of the rough games that Paul played so well. Each summer my mother dragged me to Europe with her. She did not make friends easily, and I soon became her favorite companion. This suited me. I loved Europe. I devoured its museums, its cathedrals. I remember at the age of nine standing for two hours gazing up at the rose window of Chartres, ignoring my mother's repeated supplications to depart. I was entranced by the color. As the sun went down, that shade of rose became part of my soul.

"When I was ten or eleven, my grandfather, who, you will recall, was also Paul's grandfather, noted certain tendencies in me which alarmed him. He decreed that henceforth I was to spend more time with Paul and his friends. Paul regarded this as something less than a pleasure, for which I could not blame him. I was ineptitude personified on the baseball field, and football I simply refused to play. His reports to the General only intensified the old man's determination to make me a typical American boy. In spite of her lamentations, my mother was ordered to prepare me to join Paul at the Pennsgrove School. That is where we both began our torturous emergence into adulthood. I don't think anyone else can tell

231

you about our life at that shrine of rote learning and saccharined religiosity except Dwight Slocum or one or two other survivors of our class.

"In those days I had dreams of becoming a poet. I kept a journal of my impressions which I hoped to turn to verse. Let me read you what I wrote on our first day there to set the scene for you."

He picked up a pocket-sized diary and began to read from it.

"September 10, 1909

"Pennsgrove is an ugly place. One brooding gray building at the head of a broad sloping lawn guarded by dark woods. Looking at it, I felt like Byron on the Bridge of Sighs without a Venetian palace to console me. I could only hope eventually I may say:

> Chillon! thy prison is a holy place
> And thy sad floor an altar ...

"Perhaps arriving in the rain has cast this gloom upon my mind. But inside I found little to alter my dolorous first impression. All was confusion and rampage, insult and humiliation. Third-formers are apparently the scum of the earth. They must run hither and yon at the summons of the sixth-formers who are the kings of this peculiar world. They badgered us incessantly all afternoon to make sure we understood their rules. At dinner came a most unpleasant episode. Because I am the smallest in the class, I was forced to put on a white nightgown and baby's cap and sit on the lap of a bruiser named Caldwell, sucking my thumb and making baby sounds. This is apparently a school tradition to make the third-formers realize they are mere infants. If Cousin Paul were not here with me, I would write Mama this very night and ask her to come take me home. But Cousin Paul bore the ragging, as they call it, good-naturedly, never once losing his composure, to the vexation of sixth-formers, I suspect. They take pleasure in snarling a half dozen contradictory commands, all to be fulfilled in the same five minutes. Paul organized us into two cadres which made things go much more expeditiously. It pained me, though, to see him laughing along with the others at my baby role. I do look like an overgrown baby with my puckered-up face and pipestem arms and legs. The food is vile but I forced it down. I am determined to eat and eat and grow and grow. In four years' time I hope to be a bruiser like Caldwell."

Peregrine put the journal aside and sipped his wine.

"You see how important Paul was to me. You may say it was only natural. It was necessary to cling to something in that strange world. Pennsgrove was a typical American prep school which had imported all the traditions of the English public schools, from piety to homosexuality, intact. While the chaplain and the headmaster—both Episcopal priests—breathed sweetness and light on us at chapel each morning from their ethereal upper-world of nobility and faith, the students lived in the brutal reality of their underworld. Let me read you another passage from my journal, November 10, 1909.

"What am I to do? Caldwell and his friend Hoffman appeared in our room last night with their candles at 1 A.M. and forced me and my roommate to perform the same unspeakable acts. Poor Collins is as terrified and as ashamed as I am. If only there were someone I could tell. But how can I dare confess to doing such things? I have prayed to God for forgiveness and help. I am so distracted that I cannot study or eat. At dinner tonight, Cousin Paul asked me if I were sick. I could not look him in the face. I will never again be able to look in the face anyone whom I respect, from whom I hope to earn respect."

Peregrine paused again to pour more wine for Kilpatrick.

"That was my introduction to homosexual love. They returned regularly and got us down on our knees to say our prayers to them. That is what they called it. Finally they ordered us to bring butter from the dining hall and that night they buggered us. I tried to resist what I considered an ultimate indignity. They pounded me around the room and one of them held me while the other penetrated me repeatedly. The next day I could barely walk. Blood oozed from my rectum. Paul asked me where I had gotten the bruise on my face. I burst into tears and ran into the woods. He followed me and made me tell

233

him what had happened. He became ferociously angry and said he would protect me if they came back that night.

"I was frankly terrified when Paul appeared in my room and sent my roommate, Collins, to sleep elsewhere. Paul was armed with a hockey stick. I told him that Caldwell and Hoffman would take it away from him and kill him with it. They were brutes who outweighed him by thirty or forty pounds. He said he did not intend to let them take it away from him.

"We went to bed. An hour later, Caldwell and his friend, Hoffman, appeared. They called on me to get out of bed and prepare to receive another hosing. Paul sprang from my roommate's bed and smashed out the candle Hoffman was carrying. Paul then laid it to the two of them with the hockey stick. They fled in terror, sure they were being assaulted in the darkness by a half dozen fiends. I told Paul they would come back with a mob of sixth-formers and beat us to death.

"But Paul had anticipated this possibility. He went to Sutherland, the president of the sixth form, and told him what he had done and why. Sutherland returned to the room with Paul and confronted Caldwell and Hoffman when they came back, as I had predicted, with a half dozen burly friends. When Sutherland told the reinforcements what Caldwell and Hoffman had done, and informed them that Paul, a mere third-former, had sent them flying with his hockey stick, the two culprits were treated with the utmost contempt. Paul became a hero to the whole school.

"I, alas, became a subject of subtle scorn. Similar things were going on in a dozen other rooms at Pennsgrove, I assure you, but the other third-formers said their prayers, even took their buggering in penitential silence. By publicizing my affliction Paul made me the target of smirks and the subject of leering remarks from my classmates. He also aroused in himself that paternal authoritarian instinct which he had inherited from our grandfather. His role as an older brother had intensified it. He began to see me as someone in danger of another moral lapse and seemed determined to prevent it.

"I remember once he came into my room and gave me

234

one of his hard policeman stares. I was reading Swinburne. He took it out of my hand, read a few passages and told me it was trash. I told him I thought it was the most beautiful poetry I had ever read. He insisted it was trash and said I would be better off joining him to watch the football team practice. Swinburne, he said, was a queerie and if I kept on reading him I would turn into one.

"Remember that Oscar Wilde's trial and conviction for homosexuality was still reverberating through the English and American world. Paul may have had some conversations with his grandfather or father about it and its possible relation to me. I replied with some heat that he might do well to read some of Swinburne himself. It might open his eyes to the world of beauty. Watching a bunch of behemoths bash each other around the football field might be entertainment for apes but not for human beings. If it was queeriness to appreciate great poetry I was guilty of it and I might as well admit it. Thanks to him I already had the reputation.

"I had no interest in homosexuality. Paul's suspicion that I *was* one planted the seed of the possibility in my mind. The following summer I went to Paris with Mother, as usual. While strolling in the Louvre I paused to admire da Vinci's 'Last Supper.' A young German standing beside me began discussing in the most offhand brilliant way the composition of the painting, da Vinci's ability to encompass the human figure as plane and mass. His name was Georg. He was two or three years older than I. He asked me if I had seen much of the new painters, Picasso, Matisse, Braque. I blushed to confess I had never even heard of them. Mother's appreciation of painting did not extend much beyond Raphael. We spent the day wandering through the Latin Quarter, finding the small galleries where the moderns exhibited. I had never met anyone like Georg before. We had coffee afterward at a café on the boulevard St.-Germain, and I poured out my soul to him, describing my misery at Pennsgrove surrounded by cloddish Americans my age who cared for nothing but football and baseball. As a climax I described my sexual experiences.

"Georg frowned and said my schoolmates were

brutes. Love between men was as old as Socrates and as potentially beautiful as the other kind of love. He invited me to his rooms on the Left Bank to show me what he meant. We bathed together in his huge tub like two nymphs. Then he powdered and perfumed me and we came together in a kind of ecstasy which I never thought possible in this world.

"My passion for George lasted for a month, until Mother dragged me with her to Baden-Baden. I returned to America, desolate. I endured my next two years at Pennsgrove only by reminding myself that at the end of the spring term, summer, Paris with George, awaited me. I managed to conceal my loathing for Pennsgrove and most of my classmates, as well as satisfy Paul's scrutiny. I began to think of him as my self-righteous, somewhat stupid keeper, whom I was artfully deceiving. He participated wholeheartedly in Pennsgrove's program to form noble-spirited young Protestant gentlemen. He was ready to rescue damsels in distress, to pity the poor and kill the enemies of his country without a tremor of remorse. The Pennsgrove school song was set to the tune of 'Onward, Christian Soldiers.'

"Adding to my delicious sense of superiority was some spicy information I had inadvertently picked up from Mother during the summer of 1911. I was seeing George again, as well as two or three others, and it was difficult to spare Mother much of my time. I suggested that she continue her tour with Aunt Anne—Mrs. George Stapleton—Paul's mother. I received a withering answer. Respectable members of the family did not approve of the company Aunt Anne kept in Europe. They were all outré men and women, gamblers and adventurers, bankrupt dukes and barons, the sort of men that her father-in-law, General Stapleton, would not allow in the door of Bowood. I was warned not under any circumstances to repeat this startling information to anyone.

"How delicious it was to discover I had an aunt who was essentially doing the same thing in Europe as I was doing—and that she was the mother of my keeper, Paul the blameless, the model Pennsgrove hero. One might have thought I had sufficient psychological ballast to carry me through the remainder of my sentence at Pennsgrove, blasé and self-satisfied. But events both within me and far beyond my sphere were to shatter my complacency.

"When we returned as puissant sixth-formers, Paul was promptly elected president of our class. It was a foregone conclusion. He was captain of the football team, the star halfback of the previous year. He promptly made a proposal to ban all ragging, hazing, fagging, as we called it, of third-formers because it was always abused by a few who had a fondness for inflicting pain on others. It was not a popular proposal. Dwight Slocum became the leader of the opposition. He had been a nonentity for his first two years in the school, but in our fifth-form year he matured into a hulking clod who became a mainstay of our football line. I spoke in favor of Paul's proposal. We put it to a vote. It was carried by a bare majority, thirteen to twelve.

"My support of Paul's program enhanced his opinion of me. He also had been impressed by my apparent good behavior in the previous two years. More important, he had encountered Muriel Bennett, an independent spirit who was not afraid of telling him that the Stapletons were far from gods. Muriel considered them grossly deficient in their appreciation of art and literature. Since the books we were given to read at Pennsgrove were thirty or forty years out of date, Paul turned to me to give him some advice on modern literature. I set him to reading Stephen Crane, whom he loved, Dreiser, whom he hated, and Edna St. Vincent Millay, who bored him. He wrote to Muriel discussing these and other writers, after carefully rehearsing his opinions with me, and, I might add, largely accepting my judgment of them. If there is one thing Paul Stapleton has always dreaded above all else, it is being made to look foolish. I think it comes from the enormous stress our grandfather placed on appearances.

"But the decisive event in our rapprochement was the death of Paul's father. Paul returned from that voyage down the River of Doubt an utterly changed young man. The death of his father, whom I regarded as a rather ineffectual man, shook him enormously. I felt a throb of

237

sympathy when I saw his grief—and something else I could not define—on his face at the funeral. I had never had a chance to mourn my father, who died in Cuba when I was only an infant. Perhaps a wish to mourn him blended with the sympathy I felt for Paul.

"At school Paul avoided me, in fact avoided everyone. He abandoned the leadership of the class to Dwight Slocum, who made the last three or four months of the year an orgy of abuse and exploitation of the third-formers. One day in late April I went to Paul's room. I yearned to talk to him. I dimly perceived that I also yearned for something else. I found him staring dully out the window at the spring sunshine. I suggested a walk in the woods. He shook his head. I asked him if he was going out for the baseball team. He shook his head. I asked him what was wrong. He shook his head.

" 'You should tell someone what you feel,' I said.

"He shook his head.

" 'May I tell you what I feel, Paul?'

"He looked at me uncomprehendingly.

" 'I feel very close to you now. Closer than I have ever felt to any human being.'

"It was true. He stared at me and I could see perception dawning in his eyes. I felt an enormous desire to put my arms around him, to press my body against his—I know he felt it too, felt it with that intensity which perhaps only a Stapleton can appreciate. He had belonged to his father, been part of his life. His father had belonged to him. Now death had amputated him and while the wound throbbed he sensed a need of another self to which he could turn in the narrow cage of his own soul. He needed someone to love him and be loved by him in return. He knew, as he looked into my face, that this person could only be a Stapleton, that there was no one else with whom he could achieve this union of self and other.

"Who else was more qualified than I to fill that place? Both fatherless through the blind accidents of circumstance. I told him in an anguished voice that I had often thought we were part of the same person. This had a terrifying effect on him. His face turned a ghastly white.

238

He stood up, literally shaking. I began to weep. I held out my hand to him, the tips of my fingers reaching toward his lips. 'I love you,' I said. 'Let me love you. No one else knows how you feel.'

"He looked at me for a long moment. I saw the wish play across his face. He knew what I meant. He saw it in all its dimensions and he said something that I will never forget, that I will hear on my deathbed like a knell. 'Love you?' he said. 'I will never love anyone again in my whole goddamn life.'

"I felt more devastated, more horrified than if he had punched me in the face. I believe this was a crucial turning point in Paul Stapleton's life. I am not suggesting, I do not believe that if he had loved me in return that day, he would have become a homosexual. I do not believe we are so clearly divided into hetero and homo. But I do believe in the transcendent value of love as the way out of the cage of the self. He chose to remain inside that cage when he turned his back on spontaneous sympathetic love, the experience that liberates the personality. Whatever had happened to him on the River of Doubt had wounded his soul and made him incapable of such freedom.

"The experience was also immensely significant for me. I had seen in Paul the possibility of a deeper, darker, more consuming love than I had ever imagined, a blending of spiritual and physical ecstasy. It was the beginning of my journey to disaster.

"The year that we graduated from Pennsgrove, the First World War began. It utterly disrupted my pattern of summer love in Europe. I went to Harvard on Grandfather's orders and remained a celibate. Something about America suppressed the normal flow of my desire. Perhaps it was a dread of Grandfather's wrath if I ever got caught. I spent my summers with the family at Paradise Beach. We owned a big house on the dunes outside of town, only a mile or so from the Yacht Club. I followed Paul's career at Princeton with more than ordinary interest. I was not at all surprised when he broke off his affair with Muriel Bennett at the very moment Muriel was expecting a proposal. I saw her at the beach in the

239

summer of 1916, not long after Paul decamped for Mexico. All she needed was a black dress and veil to pass for a young widow. She was devastated.

"I saw it as part of the fundamental incapacity for love that Paul had revealed to me. You can imagine my surprise when he arrived home seven or eight months later with a pregnant Mexican wife whom he left to the tender mercies of his mother and Agatha and the old General while he sailed for Europe. At first I thought that my theory had been blown to atoms. I was furiously jealous of Maria. But my feelings, which I managed to control and conceal, were nothing compared to the wrath with which Agatha and her mother greeted that forlorn woman. The General tried to protect her, but she was vulnerable to a thousand secret humiliations at their hands.

"I had heretofore admired Anne Randolph Stapleton. I wish to say some kind things about her before we part. But her conduct—and I might add Agatha's—was disgraceful during Maria's first year with us. They spied on her, and when they caught her praying to a statue of the Blessed Virgin in her room, descended on the General like a couple of triumphant inquisitors to demand action from him. The old boy told them to shut up and mind their own business. After watching the drama for a while at Paradise Beach in the summer of 1917, I decided Paul's marriage was not at all inconsistent with my insight into him. It was in a sense an admission of his inability to love anyone but a Stapleton. He chose this woman, who was as strange and foreign as any creature he was likely to encounter, as someone with whom he could mate without any concern for the intricacies of a love of union, sharing, blending.

"To the General's immense disgust, I received a draft number which enabled me to delay my entry into the U.S. Army until the war was almost over. I never got to France. After the Armistice I returned home to a new scene. The General was dead. Paul, the executor of his estate, looked like he might be a permanent invalid. I felt liberated by both events. By now it was clear to me that I lacked the talent to be a writer, but I might become a painter. I moved to Greenwich Village and began daub-

240

ing, living on what my mother sent me. She and everyone else in the family except Agatha were appalled by this new ambition.

"By now Agatha was twenty. She was extremely bright, even brilliant, having graduated magna cum laude from Radcliffe with a major in philosophy. She had thoughts of being a poet. She found me in Greenwich Village and suggested that we pool our resources and share a flat. Her offer was heaven-sent as far as I was concerned. Mother had been trying to starve me out of painting by sending as little money as possible.

"For the next year we lived together as brother and sister, went to parties as a couple, danced the Charleston, drank bathtub gin, sniffed a little cocaine and generally comported ourselves in the style of the beautiful and damned.

"One night, coming home from a party a little drunk, we got drunker in my studio. As a sudden tribute to *veritas in vino,* Agatha pointed to my paintings and said, 'You know something, Perry, they're not very good.'

" 'I know,' I said. 'Neither are your poems.'

" 'But we're having fun,' she said. 'I have fun with you.'

"We sat in silence for a moment. The night sounds of the city filtered faintly through the walls. I looked at Agatha and saw the possibility that I had seen with Paul, the dark, deep sharing of inward-turning love. I reached out and touched her cheek with my fingertips.

" 'I think I love you, Perry,' she said.

" 'I know I love you,' I said.

"For a moment I hesitated. I yearned to tell her the truth about myself. I was afraid it would disgust her. I only kissed her tenderly and then we began to make love. I found her body rather beautiful. But it was the thought of entering her, of joining my Stapleton flesh to her Stapleton flesh, mingling seed and blood, that was the real stimulant. We began a very passionate affair.

"It might have lasted for a year or two. Then we might have drifted apart. But with no warning, Paul arrived on our doorstep to find out what we were doing. To everyone's astonishment, he had recovered from his wound and assumed his old air of command and authority, to which he added a certain gloomy harshness that reminded us both of the General. He wanted to know if I was going to spend the rest of my life as a dependent. I had been painting for three years—by now it was 1922—and had not sold a single canvas. Why not face the facts and get a job? As for Agatha, he said it was neither respectable nor sensible for a single woman to be living in the immoral atmosphere of Greenwich Village. It was time she came home and began considering marriage.

"'I have considered marriage,' Agatha said. 'I am going to marry Perry.'

"Paul was stunned beyond words. He whirled on me. I saw no hint, not the faintest possibility, of love in his eyes now. Only contempt.

"'What the hell is she talking about?' he snarled.

"'It's true,' I said. 'We've decided we don't have much talent as artists. We're coming home. I plan to take a job at the mills. We will be married as soon as the arrangements can be made.'

"I got my job at the mills at a comfortable salary, but Paul furiously opposed the marriage. He persuaded his mother to delay announcing the engagement for six months. He claimed modern genetics was against the marriage of first cousins. We pointed to half a dozen previous matings within the family with no obvious ill effects. Neither of us was anxious to have children, anyway.

"Perhaps I should have seen that most of the power was on Paul's side. At the mills I was given nothing to do. My ideas on marketing were ignored. Agatha said that once we were married, she would join me in a lawsuit to demand a voice in Principia's affairs. By inheritance we could claim a third of the company.

"Then came Paul's moment. In September of 1922, about three months after we returned home, my old friend Georg appeared in the city. He telephoned me and we had dinner. His family, who once owned a quarter of the Ruhr, had been ruined by the war. He had little interest in working. He had compiled a list of his American lovers and was touring the country collecting contributions for auld lang syne. He had several boyish letters of mine, which he dangled in front of me. I agreed to pay

242

him five thousand dollars. I borrowed the money from the Merchant's Bank, and went to his room at the Garden Square Hotel to pay him and get the letters. The next day I received a call from Paul Stapleton, demanding that I visit him immediately in his law office. I arrived to discover him and his brother Malcolm reading a letter which Paul had written for me to sign. It was an agreement renouncing all my interest in Principia Mills, in return for ten percent of the annual profits or twenty-five thousand dollars—whichever was larger. This sum would be paid to me as long as I remained in Europe. Beside the letter was a report of a detective whom Paul had hired to spy on me. It described my meetings with Georg and listed several other men who had visited Georg in his room, all known homosexuals, whom he had picked up in local bars."

Peregrine finished his wine and stood up. Kilpatrick had emptied his glass a long time ago. "It's time for dinner," Peregrine said.

He led Kilpatrick into the dining room. The big round table was set for two. For the first course he served a cold cucumber soup. He said it could be made in a blender with such ease it was almost obscene. Kilpatrick said it was delicious. They drank it in silence for a few minutes.

"So you went to Europe?" Kilpatrick said.

"I had no choice. If I had fought them in court, I'm sure Paul would have had no hesitation about bringing in evidence that I lacked the moral character to be an executive at Principia Mills."

"And you became a homosexual?"

"Exclusively. In Paris there were too many memories, too many temptations, to be anything else. I worked as a fabric designer. I was rather successful until World War II. Thereafter, I slid downhill. It was a gentle slide. It took me three or four years to discover I was bankrupt. That was in 1961 or '62."

"Didn't Agatha try to stop him—Paul?"

"The Agatha you see today was not the Agatha of 1922," Peregrine said. "Homosexuality was not an acceptable vice or a tolerated habit. Her brother Paul told her the brutal truth about me, putting it in the worst possible light, of course."

Peregrine removed the soup plates and retreated to the kitchen. In five minutes he returned with the tournedos, a leek-and-watercress salad and a bottle of Châteauneuf-du-Pape.

"The only person who tried to defend me was Anne Stapleton, Paul's mother. She had apparently had a woman-to-woman talk with Agatha and decided I was reasonably normal, sexually. More important, she was convinced that Agatha loved me and I could enrich her life culturally, spiritually. She was disgusted by the way her sons had turned out, hard narrow businessmen in the image of the old General.

"She asked Paul if he was ready to take the responsibility for ruining Agatha's happiness, for wrecking my life. He said that he was trying to rescue Agatha's happiness and my life was my problem. Then he attacked his mother in the most brutal, vicious way. He said he knew exactly what she was doing, she was trying to play the same game with him that she had played with Grandfather and was looking for allies. He called her a hypocrite for this sudden display of maternal affection for Agatha when all she had given her before was bad example."

Peregrine gripped the edge of the table. The knuckles of his liver-spotted old hands turned white. "It was a moment I will never forget. I don't think I have ever seen another human being inflict pain so coldly, so deliberately on a person he had once loved.

" 'I loved you once,' Paul said. 'When I was a son. But now I'm a husband and a father and I see you for what you are. A woman who cares about nothing but your own pleasure, your own whims. I've found a different kind of woman for my wife, a woman who knows how to be a mother, who loves her husband for something more than his checkbook. I'm speaking for that woman and my sons when I tell Peregrine Stapleton to get out of the city and country. If you disagree, maybe you should go to Europe with him and stay there. Then I won't have to worry about you ruining my children's morals.' "

Kilpatrick had an eerie sense that Peregrine was speaking the exact words Paul Stapleton had spoken, that the man before him was blending, had blended in this savage memory with the cousin he both hated and loved.

It took Peregrine several moments to return to his usual wry self. At first his voice was elegiac, muted, as he continued.

"Paul wounded his mother more deeply than she ever admitted to anyone, with those words. She left for Europe with me and never returned. Malcolm visited her every summer in the Twenties. He was very devoted to her. As far as I know, Paul and she never spoke again.

"The scene remains vivid to me because it was a glimpse of a man altering his soul, steeling himself to destroy a woman who he knew was essentially innocent, a victim of Stapleton narrowness, coldness, hardness, that he himself had resisted and despised, partly in her name. I'm sure he will give her no credit for it in his telling, but it was his mother who taught young Paul to be a rebel, who gave him his soaring ideals. Basically, the Stapletons take a dim view of ideals. Power is what they want and they have always been ready to bend, stretch, and if necessary, abandon ideals to hold on to it. The old General was as corrupt in his aloof patrician way as any robber baron. He thought nothing of bribing a state legislator or a congressman.

"Anne Randolph Stapleton possessed what every Stapleton male has abysmally lacked—the quality of mercy and all that it implies—warmth, kindness. She added to this gift a spirit of independence, of vigorous impudent speech that reminded you—I am sure it was her intention—that she was the great-great-granddaughter of Thomas Jefferson. She never submitted, not for one moment, to the Stapleton imperium. But she understood it, oh dear God, how she understood it. She was the only one who dared to mock it, at least in her day. Mock it to its face.

"She maintained that somewhere, back in those murky days when Englishmen still painted themselves blue, an icy wind froze the first Stapleton's heart. Some of them struggled to escape that frigid inheritance. But others, like General Stapleton, rejoiced in it. She used to call him the Ice King and Bowood the Icicle Factory. They often went for a year—once for two years—without speaking to each other.

"The General considered her the quintessence of

southern decadence. Pure prejudice, of course. He had acquired a hatred of Southerners that was as mindless as his detestation of unions or anything or anyone else who dared to challenge the privileges of his class. He was a lonesome old man. He spent his entire life trying to convince himself and everyone else that he was a man of destiny.

"Anne often used to say that she had married the wrong man. It was my father, Rawdon, who was her true soulmate. My mother was one of those pale, repressed women that Protestantism specialized in producing in the nineteenth century. She was handpicked by the General and I gather my father married her as an act of expiation during one of his fits of repentance. He had several of these. But he soon went back to playing the prodigal and treated her outrageously. I think she was glad he got that bullet in his head on San Juan Hill. Anne once hinted to me—I want to be very scrupulous and tell you no more than the truth—it was only a hint—that she had once had a liaison with my father in New York. She intimated that she was not entirely sure that Paul was her husband's son.

"Anne didn't make a habit of such tête-à-têtes, at least not here in America. She was much too clever to give the General an excuse to declare war on her. In Europe, she was always escorted by handsome men—retired French colonels, exiled Russian aristrocrats, wandering South American tycoons. But even there she was discreet. She was convinced that the General was not beyond hiring private detectives to watch her."

"Agatha never tried to see you again?"

"She didn't want to spend the rest of her life in Europe. She went to New York and got involved with Dwight Slocum. She was determined to marry someone of whom Paul disapproved, the more violently the better. She was also fascinated by Dwight's total amorality. She never dreamt that, for Dwight, she was the personification of the Stapleton mystique. He thought he was finally arriving when he got her into bed. I gather that she soon disabused him of that illusion."

"What brought her back here—and then you?"

"A religious experience. It enabled Agatha to rediscover the ideal. It has something to do with Maria, Paul's wife. I don't pretend to understand it. I'm not religious. By and large, Stapletons have never been religious. At Pennsgrove, Paul was idealistic, not religious. Two very different things, as I am sure you know. After I went bankrupt, I fell into rather dolorous straits in Paris. I wrote Agatha, asking for a loan. She invited me to join her here. I accepted with alacrity. Though I continue to believe my lifelong pursuit of beauty and love is more satisfying than the cold world of power and profits in which Paul has lived, I cannot deny the need for the commodity his way so amply provides: cash."

Peregrine pointed to a painting over the fireplace. "Perhaps that portrait of me by Picasso says it all. Do me the honor of drinking to it."

Picasso had put Peregrine in a Pierrot costume and given him a blue face. A clown both bold and sad stared at them.

XX

This constant remembering, even when he was not talking to Kilpatrick, was like a disease, sapping his strength, Paul Stapleton thought. Night after night, he found himself dreaming about the past. Last night it had been his brother Malcolm, lecturing him on the peril to the great race. "They're all around us," Malcolm had shouted. "Can't you see they're all around us, just waiting for the chance to overrun us?" The night before last it had been John. He was with him in the doomed tank in that shadowy valley in North Korea. He was firing the machine gun at the flitting Oriental figures, knocking them over like toy soldiers, and John was yelling congratulations for his shooting and firing the 75-millimeter cannon, splashing Chinese all over the landscape. But the figures flitted closer, carrying their improvised explosive charges. The night before that it had been Agatha, standing beside their mother's open grave in the cloche hat and long clinging skirts of 1935, glaring at him.

He decided it might be best to get it over with, to tell the rest, as much as could be told, in one long effort. Perhaps then he could find the strength to deal with

George. Morris Teitlebaum had called to tell him that his granddaughter Jacky had spent the night at George's house. Paul Stapleton had felt a flicker of the anti-Semitism his grandfather and brother Malcom had preached so vociferously. He was ashamed of himself. He promised to see George immediately. But he had put off the confrontation, unable to summon the energy for it.

Last night he had called Kilpatrick and told him that Sam Fry would pick him up at noon tomorrow, Saturday. They would have lunch and spend the afternoon together. That night he had slept dreamlessly. He awoke feeling less weary than usual. It was a bright, cool October day. The oaks and maples on the surrounding hills were turning golden yellow, dusky red, burnt orange. Kilpatrick arrived on schedule and they had a light lunch, chicken salad and iced tea. During lunch he tried to disabuse Kilpatrick of any notion that he had been a distinguished lawyer. He described himself as an organizer of other men's brains. He told how he had taken his cousin Garfield Talbot's prescient advice and specialized in tax law in the early twenties, when few firms considered it worth much attention. From friends who worked for New York innovators like Paul Cravath he had taken the concept of a law factory employing dozens of attorneys, ready to give a corporation every conceivable kind of legal service. When the Depression exploded, and brought to power in Washington men who regarded corporations as enemies, Stapleton, Talbot had been ready to offer defensive strategies, sorties against destructive laws and potentially ruinous regulations on a scale and with an expertise that few firms, even on Wall Street, could match.

"I picked the men, I organized them into combat teams," he said. "Sometimes we'd turn twenty lawyers loose on a single case. These days on Wall Street it's as many as forty. Now they call it the Chinese Army approach. Basically, it's just good military tactics. Concentration of force.

"You've talked to my son Mark. You know he thinks all this effort is misdirected, we've been working for the wrong people. That was a shock to me, I won't deny it, a shock and a disappointment, to find the son I considered

249

the brightest, the one with the best temperament for a lawyer, sitting in judgment on me.

"Then it dawned on me that my father had done the same thing to his father, my grandfather, but in a more muted, indirect way. That made me feel a little better about it."

But not much, he added silently.

"I tried to tell Mark—and I still believe—he was unrealistic. Not about the big picture, but about me. I don't have any illusions about corporations. I know they aren't run by saints or patriots. But Mark was unrealistic to think that someone named Paul Stapleton could have suddenly started practicing law on behalf of labor unions. Or gone into government as a New Deal trustbuster. I was born on the other side of those battle lines. There was no way that a labor union in this state was going to trust Paul Stapleton as their attorney. There was even less chance of a Democratic politician appointing him to any job with real power.

"It so happens that experience has convinced me that my side of the battle line is no worse than the other side. You won't find many saints or patriots in the ranks of the labor unions or the politicians. As I see the history of the last fifty years, it's been a struggle for power, not between good and evil, but between two groups of people, business types and political types—labor union officers are basically politicians—each potentially dangerous in his own way. Each side has used violence occasionally, and discovered that the other side could be just as violent. So most of the battles have been fought in the legislatures and in the courts. I think that's why I've enjoyed the law so much. It's been at the white-hot center of this fight."

He wanted to tell Kilpatrick what he liked most about the struggle—the comradeship in fierce effort that it produced. It was your brains and stamina—your own and those of the men you had hired and led—against the other side. How many nights in the Twenties and Thirties had he driven home in the dawn, barely arriving in time to join his sons for their daily exercise. And the really herculean efforts, honing a Supreme Court brief to perfection, asking men dazed from exhaustion to catnap and stay on the job for another twelve hours, joining them of course, remembering his grandfather's axiom, never ask a man to do what you're afraid or unable to do yourself. When the last page was typed for the thirtieth or fortieth time, the exhilaration of reading the brief, knowing it was the very best they could have done, there was not an argument unexplored, a possibly useful citation unresearched. They would sit there, he and the dozen or two dozen partners and associates who had worked on it, sipping twelve-year-old scotch or bourbon, admiring their child.

Kilpatrick's sour expression short-circuited this nostalgia. Paul Stapleton suddenly remembered trying to explain these feelings to Mark a long time ago. He had failed. Maybe it sounded like bragging. Anyway, it was time to tell the story of Principia Mills.

When the houseboy took the dishes away, he stretched out on the chaise, facing the autumnal hills beyond the reflecting pool, and began. It was delicate. He did not want to embarrass Kilpatrick. The story was very involved with the history of the city, the impact of the Irish political machine in which Kilpatrick's father had been a chieftain. He tried to explain how his brother Malcolm, assigned by his grandfather to run the mills and attend to local politics, had grown fanatic as the machine won election after election with ever more massive majorities.

"They raised the taxes on Principia and the other mills in the city by fifty million dollars. We got the increase repealed by the state tax commission and they used that as an issue in the next gubernatorial election to win the statehouse and appoint a tax commission that made the increase stick. It slowly dawned on us that we had a new situation in the city and state. The Shea machine was different from the ones we had dealt with in the city since the Civil War. Most of those early pols, whether they were Irish, German or native American, just wanted a piece of the action. We'd arrange for them to acquire an insurance company or a brewery or a water company and bring them into the business community.

"But Dave Shea and his boys had figured out ways to make more money out of politics than anyone could ever have made from running an honest business. They organized the city's gambling, they shook down every saloon, real estate broker, anyone who needed a license or did business with the city. They did it systematically, like an army fighting a war. This gave them tons of money and made them practically unbeatable on election day.

"But my brother Malcom wouldn't quit. He had those marching orders from Grandfather and he was determined to fight it out if it took the last dollar we had in the till. Pretty soon it began to look like it would take that and then some. The Twenties are supposed to have been a boom time, but it wasn't true for textiles. We'd have one good year and two terrible ones. We tried to carry our workers in the lean years, cutting them back to half time. But this caused terrific unrest, wildcat strikes."

"I've been doing some reading about the textile industry," Kilpatrick said in a cold, rather nasty voice. "The hearings of the Senate Committee on Education and Labor in 1926."

"I remember them well. They were chaired by a Democrat from Illinois, Herbert Coe. He was out to murder us and did a very efficient job."

"According to a man named Jett Lauck, a former high official in the Wilson administration, most of the people who worked nights in the mills were women. They kept on working when they got pregnant, right up to the day of delivery, and they'd go back to work a week or two later. As a result, the city had the highest infant mortality rate in the state."

"Jett Lauck was a professional lobbyist who testified for every congressman and senator with a committee even remotely connected with labor. At Principia Mills, we never let any woman work after she became visibly pregnant. But it was hard to stop them. They wore loose dresses to hide the bulge. Other mills, particularly the vicious little cockroach operations, didn't give a damn."

"I hope you don't mind me making this a little more of an adversary proceeding," Kilpatrick said with a brief smile.

"Hell no. I'm glad to see you're digging deep. I don't want you to take my word for anything. You need background to put us in perspective. I'm ready to admit that even at Principia conditions were far from ideal. The mills were old and so was the machinery. My brother Malcolm spent a lot of the money we could have used to modernize them fighting the Democrats for control of the city and state.

"That meant Principia was far from ready for the Depression. For a year or so after the crash of '29, we weren't too disturbed. Principia had weathered other panics, '93, 1907, 1921, and this one didn't seem much different at first sight. But Grandfather had always been careful to keep a fat cash reserve. My brother had used ours up in the political wars. Pretty soon, when banks started collapsing and sales kept sinking no matter how much we cut the prices of our cloth, we realized that this was a new situation.

"I didn't have anything to do with the day-to-day operations. Stapleton, Talbot's business doubled every six months as the brain trusters moved into Washington. But my brother kept me well informed about the bad news. In 1933, he had to start borrowing money to stay afloat. Pretty soon the local banks told us we had to go to Wall Street. They just couldn't handle the kind of debt we were building up. Nobody on Wall Street wanted to touch us. We had failure written all over us—like a lot of other textile companies.

"As my sister Agatha may have told you, she was married to Dwight Slocum, who had been one of Wall Street's big bulls in the Twenties. She brought Dwight into our troubled financial picture. He offered to loan us ten million dollars. All he wanted for collateral was our stock, which was selling for about a dollar a share. I'm sure Dwight saw, even then, in 1935, that he was going to pick up a hundred-million-dollar company for not much more than that ten million.

"My brother Malcolm said he'd rather go bankrupt than do business with Dwight Slocum. I argued that the devil you knew was better than the devil you didn't know, and if we went bankrupt we'd be in the hands of all sorts of unknown devils, a lot of them receivers appointed by judges that the Shea machine controlled. I damn near had to twist my brother's arm off but he finally agreed and we borrowed Slocum's money.

"Dwight construed the loan as a gesture of friendship.

253

He started inviting me to go on hunting trips to Alaska and Africa. That's how I got those heads on display in the living room. I put up with Dwight, literally making friends with the mammon of iniquity, I guess, to keep him quiet in the boardroom. The mills kept losing money and Dwight could have raised hell about the way things were going.

"Looking back at our situation in the 1930s now, forty years later, I can see that we were kidding ourselves. Any man with common sense could have seen that Principia wasn't going to pull out of its nose dive. The unions were beating on our gates. The market was still a mess. We were in the wrong business at the wrong time and in the wrong place. But none of us could see it, even though the truth was staring us in the face. We had been at the center of the state's life for over a hundred years. Our power came from ownership, first in the railroads, then in the mills. None of us could see how we could retain that influence—at a time when we felt it was terribly needed—if we lost the base of our power.

"None of us could see that we had already lost most of our power and a lot of our influence because we had that base, because we had to run a business out there in the open market, which meant we were targets for every social critic and loudmouth politician who was willing to play loose with the truth at our expense. We paid the highest wages in the textile business—but they were low wages compared to other industries. My brother ran the mills just the way Grandfather ran them—with army-style discipline. These were the things that had ruined us, as much as the passing of the great race."

"Your son Mark mentioned that book. I've read some of it. That guy Madison Grant was a certified nut."

For a moment anger flickered down Paul Stapleton's nerves. He was ready to snarl: *He was like hell.* But other memories canceled the impulse. He could see the maddened face of his brother Malcolm reciting passages from the book.

"I guess he was," he said. "But when you were in the middle of the Depression, some of his prophecies looked pretty sound. For a while I saw us fighting a sort of rearguard action in defense of our class, our civilization.

We had a sense of doom haunting us between 1933 and 1940. It influenced all parts of my life.

"You probably find this hard to believe, after thirty years of prosperity. But in 1933 we saw the Communists march to City Hall, ten thousand strong, and demand free gas, electricity and coal, free clothing and food, the use of schools and public halls for meeting places, the distribution of unemployment relief through boards they would control, in the name of the workers. The cops beat hell out of them—but we didn't know how long we could depend on politicians like Dave Shea and Franklin Roosevelt. They had no principles or morals that we could see. They'd make a deal with anyone to stay in power.

"I started to think Grandfather had the right approach in peace as well as in war. I got terribly tough with my sons. I wanted to make them hard physically and psychologically. Each morning we got up and ran five or six miles. Then we'd do push-ups, chins, sitting-up exercises, for another hour. I insisted on tremendous performance in school. The Stapletons couldn't rely on prestige, on money, on tradition. All those things were vanishing in front of our eyes. We had to go back to fundamentals.

"I overdid it. I see that now. But I had to do something, I had to make some attempt to cope with a world that seemed to be destroying us. I thought it was necessary at the time and I still think it was a good idea in essence. I gave those boys a sense of pride in their bodies, a sense of the strength that comes from disciplined effort. Maria thought I was too hard on them. But I still think it was the best way to remind them that we had obligations to fulfill."

For a long moment, Paul Stapleton remembered those years. He saw the four boys, Randy cheerful and smiling even at 6 A.M., John swearing under his breath at the cold but ready to outrun, out-push-up them all, Mark padding his skinny frame with an extra sweat-suit in a hopeless attempt to match John's muscles, George stumbling around half asleep, trying to beat the game by claiming that someone had stolen his sneakers. Ned, born in 1935, never really shared in this strenuous decade. Paul Stapleton sometimes suspected that was one of his problems.

No matter how much any of them, even George, had pretended to complain, they had loved it, loved the challenge to their manhood, the comradeship, the sense that they were special, not merely in their inheritance, but in their daily lives, in the strength of their bodies and their wills.

But the years, what had the years done to those smiling faces, so full of young promise? Two of them were dead, two of them were wounded, in body or spirit. For a moment he hated the whole idea of this return to the past. It was more than a waste of time, it was dangerous, it broke hearts.

He heard a throb of emotion in his voice as he continued the story.

"At the same time I wanted my boys to be men of integrity. Grandfather's approach was too brutal for me. He was totally disillusioned by the way America developed after the Civil War. He used to say the country was like Darwin's jungle, except it wasn't survival of the fittest, it was survival of the worst. He thought there was only one way to cope with the situation. You had to be as ruthless and as indifferent to ideals as everyone else. I didn't go that far. I agreed with the old boy, you had to be realistic, you couldn't be like my father—expect to reform a bunch of skunks by spraying perfume around. But I still thought ideals were important. I wanted my boys to have access to them. Once a year, I used to read them a poem that Thomas Jefferson sent young men when they wrote to him for advice."

Looking past Kilpatrick through the opening at the end of the patio toward the western hills, Paul Stapleton recited "The Portrait of a Good Man." He paused for a moment, then repeated the fifth stanza:

"Who to his plighted vows and trust has ever firmly
            stood;
And though he promised to his loss, he makes his
            promise good.

"That's the hardest part."

Kilpatrick nodded. "Your sister Agatha told me about the poem."

256

"Yes. She heard it as often as I did."

"Let's go back and finish the story of the mills. What happened in 1945 when the loan came due?"

"We had to deal with Slocum," Paul Stapleton said, hearing his voice go dry and cold. "Even during the war, my brother Malcolm didn't show a profit. They'd finally unionized us in 1939. The union leaders were a bunch of thugs and racketeers. Malcolm wouldn't pay them off and they called one strike after another. The government canceled the army contracts we'd gotten. In 1945 we were still broke.

"Practically over my brother Malcolm's dead body, I negotiated the sale of the mills to Slocum. Malcolm insisted on cash. I took stock, largely because Slocum didn't have the cash to buy me out. I was the principal stockholder by far. I'd put my profits from the law firm into Principia to keep it going."

"Wasn't there a stockholder's lawsuit?"

"Yes. A pretty serious one. But we won it."

"Someone told me that you paid a judge a hundred thousand dollars for that decision."

"Who told you that?" Paul Stapleton asked.

"I can't reveal that."

"You don't know who the judge was?"

"My source didn't remember," Kilpatrick said.

"It was your father."

Paul Stapleton watched pain and shame and astonishment mingling on Jim Kilpatrick's face and regretted telling him. It might have been simpler to deny it. But maybe there was a little retroactive equalization coming for the pain he had felt when he journeyed to Supreme Court Justice James Kilpatrick's chambers in Trenton and handed him the white envelope with a hundred thousand-dollars bills in it. Somewhere in his head he had heard his Grandfather chortling: *I told you that you'd have to do it someday. Choke it down, Paulie. It'll do you good.*

"It was one of the hardest things I ever did, Jim. If I didn't pay, the decision would have gone against us and everyone would have been bankrupt, my brother, Agatha, all sorts of cousins and aunts who had their money in Principia. I'll say this for your father, he apologized. He said that on the law we had a perfect case. But Dave

257

Shea had ordered him to collect a hundred thousand dollars for the decision. That was the way they operated."

Kilpatrick nodded. "I know—how they operated," he said woodenly.

"Your father and I weren't friends. But we weren't enemies either. Within the limits of the way he played the game, I trusted him. He kept his word. He did me a few favors, like tipping me about the time that my fruitcake cousin Peregrine started playing around with queers in hotel rooms.

"Of course, that isn't for publication any more than the story about me and your father is. I hope that doesn't discourage you, Jim. Finding out that we're sort of in this together."

Kilpatrick shook his head. Paul Stapleton could see that he was very discouraged. Better to deal with it later, he decided, and finish the story now.

"Another reason I tried to toughen my boys up was the situation in Europe. It didn't take a giant intellect to see there was going to be a war, and from what my army friends like Mark Stratton told me, we were pretty certain to get into it. My brother and I parted company politically over it. He sided with the isolationists. I thought they were a bunch of damn fools and said so. It was a reverse of the situation in 1915, 1916. Then the President was a fool who couldn't see any point in preparedness. In 1939 and 1940 it was the so-called best people in the country. I browbeat a couple of our Republican congressmen into voting for the draft. You'll remember it passed by a single vote.

"I took Randy out of law school and got him into OCS. I let Mark stay in Harvard until June of '41, when he graduated. As usual, he insisted on doing things his way and joined the Marine Corps as a private. I pulled some strings he doesn't know about until this day to get him into their officer's training program. George was only eighteen—a freshman—I let him stay in Harvard until Pearl Harbor. I got him into one of those A-12 programs and then I joined up myself. Mark Stratton got me into the 1st Armored Division in his usual style. He called in his medical officer and told the poor guy that if I

258

didn't pass the exam, he was getting a new medical officer. I passed it all right, except for a little hearing difficulty. But I finessed that one by arguing that you can't hear anything in a tank anyway.

"I commanded a tank battalion when we landed in Morocco in 1943. Most of my tanks never got ashore the first day, the weather was so rotten, and the Vichy French launched a serious counterattack against our beachhead. We beat them off with no trouble but some of the brass got excited because their tanks outnumbered us two or three to one and decided I deserved another DSC.

"War is a funny business. It's amazing how much people forget or never learn. Most Americans are convinced that we won the second war with our superior equipment. But tell that to any tanker who fought in North Africa and he'll laugh in your face. Or maybe cry. Outgunned, outarmored, outmaneuvered, that's all we heard from our men after Sidi-bou-Zid, Sbeitla, Kasserine Pass. We couldn't match those German Mark IV tanks in armor or firepower. The tanks we had, General Grants, had guns with a thirty-degree arc. That means you had to turn the whole tank to shoot it most of the time, while German tanks could swivel their guns three hundred sixty degrees. Our tanks were riveted instead of welded, which meant a glancing shell could rip off the outside heads of the rivets and send them ricocheting inside the tanks like bullets. I hate to tell you how many boys I saw lying inside their tanks, bleeding to death or dead already from those damned rivets.

"The Germans had armor-piercing shells that set our tanks on fire. We didn't have anything like them, until the very end of the war. But the worst thing we did was send men up against German tanks in half-tracks with 75-millimeter guns mounted on them. We called them tank destroyers. They were nothing but rolling deathtraps. They had no armor. All they could do was get off a few shots at the Germans and then run like hell. The Germans splashed them all over the desert."

"How did we beat them?"

"Sheer weight of numbers. In North Africa, between us and the British, we had about five times as many men, ten times as many planes, tanks, artillery."

259

"What was it like, fighting inside a tank? How did you feel?"

Paul Stapleton paused for a moment, remembering the scene at Sidi-bou-Zid, in the valley that everyone kept comparing to Arizona, with its brown sand and shoulder-high cactus and tiny square stucco Arab houses. Across the desert were the green trees of the oasis and high bare hills where the Germans waited. All around him were the tanks of his battalion and hundreds of other tanks, half-tracks, ammunition trucks, stretching out in a vast semi-circle as far as the eye could see. They looked like an irresistible host, an unbeatable juggernaut of metal. Pride was what he felt, then. Pride in America's technology, energy. What other country could have produced this legion of machines and weapons so swiftly? Pride in America's courage. In the next hour, some of these men were going to die. They sat there calmly smoking, talking, ready for the challenge.

He remembered what that valley looked like two hours later, as they retreated across it, sullenly obedient to frantic orders from brigade headquarters. Behind them the pristine sand was ugly with the smoke of burning tanks and half-tracks. From below him in his own tank came the reek of cordite mingled with the stench of vomit. Fear had emptied the stomach of his gunner, Joe Christy, when he saw that direct hits from their .75 did not stop the German Panthers. Rage was what Colonel Stapleton felt now, rage and shame. They had been defeated, thrashed, smashed. The rage was not at his men, who had fought fiercely and well. It was at the fools in Washington who had given them tanks with armor too thin, guns with ranges too short, shells too small. He was shamed by his helplessness, his inability to change the policies or challenge the power of these fools. From the darkness of another war, Muriel Bennett's voice taunted him: *you could have had the power, if you listened to me.*

What had happened in between those two memories? Nothing that could be connected, that added up to that single, elusive word, *feel.* Between had been nothing but performance, acts, noise. Switching radios to speak to the crew in his own tank, to a four tank troop, to his battalion. Giving orders for flank attacks, covering fire, calm responses to cries of distress, panic. Selecting targets for his gunner, who depended on his colonel's eyes above the lip of the turret far more than on what he could see through his narrow scope. Zigging, zagging, stop: *fire*. Zagging, zigging, stop: *fire*. His foot was Christy's foot, stepping on the solenoid trigger of the .75. His arms were his driver Walsh's arms, wrestling with two tiller bars and a set of clutches he could not see. While the motor roared and the sprockets clanked and dive-bombers whined down from the sky and armor piercing shells screamed past and chunks of deadly shrapnel clanged against their steel skin.

"An officer's too busy to feel much of anything in a battle," Paul Stapleton said. "But there was a kind of pride, a special excitement about fighting inside a tank. When shrapnel or machine-gun fire slammed against your armor, you knew if you were fighting in the infantry, you'd be dead. No matter how confusing the battle got, you felt fairly calm, steady, cool, inside a tank. You didn't hate the enemy or even get angry at him. Most of the time he was five hundred or a thousand yards away. It's impersonal, your machine against his machine, your marksmanship, your training and teamwork, against his. Sometimes when you hit an enemy tank and the crew abandoned it, you'd be sort of surprised to see men coming out of it."

"You like war, don't you?"

Paul Stapleton was amazed by the question. "Like it? Good God, no. When I think of what it's done to me, to my sons—"

"All right. You don't hate it."

"That's always struck me as rather pointless. It's like hating crime or fires or earthquakes or floods. A country has to know how to deal with all these things if it's going to survive. I think we've had too many wars in my lifetime, but that's the luck of the draw. You can't control those kinds of things any more than you can control the weather or stop the earth from shaking. People don't like war because it seems irrational, unjust. Brave men get killed by random shells, bullets. The same sort of things happen in civilian life. I ran a law firm for forty years. I could tell you two dozen stories about gifted men who died of heart attacks at forty-five, got hit by cars, took to drink over a woman. War concentrates these kinds of accidents into a few days or even a few hours. The comparison holds in other ways. Your plans go wrong, the enemy is tougher, smarter, better equipped than you thought. Somebody messes up, bugs out. You have to start coping all over again, trying to impose some kind of order on things that have gotten out of control.

"Look at Principia Mills. We spent seventy years struggling to keep it alive. We fought competition from Europe, from New England. We fought radical strikes. We fought politicians. In the end, we lost. You ask yourself why, and you can find a dozen reasons. If my father hadn't died on the River of Doubt. If my brother had been a little older, a little wiser, a little healthier, if we had been able to control the political situation in the city. If—if—if.

"If I hadn't gotten my third DSC, I might have stayed in the 1st Armored Division and gotten killed in France like a lot of my friends. Because I got a medal I didn't deserve, I got derricked out of a battle command after the Sicily show and made personnel officer of IV Corps of the Fifth Army in Italy. The brass thought a guy with three DSCs would inspire young officers.

"I spent the last eighteen months of the war in IV Corps. I was in charge of assigning all replacement officers. I tried to talk to every man before I sent him into the lines. In those eighteen months I got to see a tremendous cross section of the young men of this country. I never believed in Madison Grant's theory of the great race the way my brother did, but I sort of flirted with those ideas. What I learned from those young men disproved that racist junk once and for all for me. It also made me pretty proud to be an American. Those officers came from every state in the Union, from all walks of life, from just about every religious and ethnic group you can imagine. Most of them did a tremendous job under terrible conditions.

"The Italian campaign was war at its most frustrating. You kicked the German off one mountain and there he was, two days later, dug in on the next mountain, pouring shells and bullets down your throat all over again. Tanks were useless. Even jeeps and trucks weren't much good. We had to use pack trains of mules to supply our troops, especially in the winter. The men had the feeling it was a forgotten war, that the guys in France were getting all the glory. Talk about hating war. You should have heard what men would say to us after they got chewed up in a German counterattack or lost half their company clawing their way up one lousy hill.

"But our biggest problem was the 92nd Division. This was a Negro outfit. Grandfather told me blacks had fought pretty well in the Civil War, and my father had seen them perform very well at San Juan Hill, where the 10th Cavalry, one of Pershing's old outfits, fought dismounted.

"I guess the blacks had some scores to settle against the Rebs in the Civil War, and those horse soldiers at San Juan Hill were regulars who had been fighting Indians on the frontier for twenty years. The colored boys in the 92nd Division didn't have any grudge against the Germans and they didn't have much motivation to be soldiers in the first place. They were products of our goddamn segregated society, the one Woodrow Wilson canonized in his eight years in the White House. That was something TR never would have done. He was very conscious of the need to bring the Negro into the mainstream.

"In an army, there has to be a sense of solidarity, a feeling that the battle is worth winning, even if it costs your individual life. Above all, there has to be some feeling of confidence in the command to go forward. A soldier needs to believe that the general isn't throwing his life away. Those black soldiers just didn't have that confidence. They thought the white general was perfectly capable of letting them get slaughtered in some diversionary attack while he made his real push somewhere else. We lost so many fights there in Italy and a couple of times we did get slaughtered—crossing the Rapido, for instance—you didn't have to be black to think that way.

"So there we were in Italy fighting some of the toughest, meanest soldiers in the world with troops who didn't want to fight at all. For a while we thought the blacks would get sore at the Germans because the Dutchmen never took any prisoners—black prisoners, I mean.

They'd talk them into surrendering and then shoot them. But that terrified them. I did everything I could. I'd go up in the lines and give them pep talks. The other senior officers, even the commanding general, Willis Crittenberger, did the same thing. But nothing worked. Nine times out of ten the attack would go nowhere, and half the officers leading it would get killed.

"I turned down a lot of applications for transfers from white officers in the 92nd Division. About a third of the officers were white. I spent a lot of time talking to boys who started to come apart up there in the lines, once they realized the situation. Sometimes a few days later I'd go up to an outpost to bring back the body of a kid I'd talked into doing his job a little longer.

"On one of those trips, for the first time I remembered something my father had told me about Grandfather. Something I'd deliberately forgotten, I suppose. He was one of the few general officers in the Civil War who went out with the grave and medical teams to pick up the dead and help the wounded after a battle.

"For the first time I realized that Old Steady's record in the Civil War wasn't built on pure stubbornness, meanness. Those men in his division never broke, never disobeyed an order to advance because they knew he cared about them. He didn't make speeches about it. He showed them he cared. He was also capable of personally shooting dead a color-bearer who turned and ran. But even that could be seen—men could see it—as a kind of caring.

"I started going up to every outpost, every position where the Germans had wiped us up there in Italy, and personally bringing back the dead and wounded. I wanted the men to see that the staff officers weren't a lot of heartless, mindless automatons who just kept the replacements coming for the next slaughter. I saw a lot of defeat in Italy. A lot of dead men. Almost always, we lost because someone had quit, run away, surrendered, left his part of the perimeter unguarded. Panicked when the man next to him got killed. In war and in peace, a lot depends on one man. Or to put it another way, every man counts."

The field telephone kept ringing and ringing. No one paid any attention to it. They were too busy handling the screams for help from the company radios. The 366th Regiment's colonel ran out in the drizzling rain and ordered the trucks to move up with the reinforcements. He stood beside the colonel and heard the lead driver refuse to move onto the road. Up ahead they could hear the German shells hitting. Paul Stapleton took out his .45 and pointed it at the driver's round black face. "Get that fucking truck onto the road, soldier," he said.

He had stumbled back to the command post and slumped against the dirt wall, groggy with exhaustion. The attack had become another fiasco. A lieutenant shook his shoulder. "Colonel Stapleton. General Crittenberger would like to speak to you."

"Paul?" said soft-spoken Willis Crittenberger. "I gather the news isn't good in your ball park. It isn't good anywhere. I've canceled the offensive. I'd like you to return to headquarters immediately. There's—a private matter. Your son George."

"Is he dead?"

For months he had been expecting it. He had been almost praying for it. Nothing else would satisfy the guilt that was tormenting him. But it was not the dreaded words.

"No. He's alive. But he deserted under fire, Paul. He deserted his men under fire."

He had no memory of Sam Fry driving him to the bank of the Cinquale Canal, of crossing it to help reorganize George's company and beat back a German counterattack. He only found out about it later when other people told him some of the wild things Sam Fry had done with a Browning automatic rifle which apparently inspired equally daring leadership from a black sergeant named Campbell. He did not even remember driving back to headquarters in the dawn. His one memory was facing George in Willis Crittenberger's tent. George's face, his uniform, were covered with mud. "Please forgive me, Dad, please," he kept sobbing. The only thing Paul Stapleton could say was "Your great-grandfather would have shot you down like a dog."

"Judge Stapleton?" Kilpatrick said.

"What?"

He stared at Kilpatrick as if he were a stranger. It took him another moment to remember where he was, what was happening. "I'm sorry," he said. "Italy has some—rough memories for me."

The autumn sun was glittering on the red and gold trees on the hillside. The boys used to ski down that hill in the winter. George had been a poor skier. He had been a poor athlete. No coordination, not much will to win. Why? Privately, Paul Stapleton suspected he had inherited too much of Carlos O'Reilly's temperament. But he had never said it to anyone, and he never would say it.

"I saw a lot of deaths that seemed meaningless. I remember going up a mountain one morning in November of 1944 and finding a lieutenant and all sixteen men in his squad dead. One black boy had surrendered and let the Germans through his part of the perimeter. They'd shot the surrendered kid in the head, and left him there in front of the command post. All the rest of those soldiers were lying in their foxholes, their faces to the enemy, shot from behind. They didn't advance the cause by dying that way. But they didn't disgrace it, either. Whenever I hear someone talk about wasted deaths in other wars, I think of those boys."

Paul Stapleton shook his head, fighting tears. "I haven't thought—talked—about this for a long time.

"There's something else—I want to say here. Something I should have said a long time ago.

"Some of those young officers couldn't handle it. I understood—I understand—why. I understood why they asked to be relieved, why they cracked up, why some of them even broke under fire. But I couldn't be—the father to them I wanted to be. I had to do my job. Even though it almost tore me apart."

He was silent for a full minute, struggling to control himself. He brushed tears from his cheeks with a jabbing clench-fisted motion.

"I don't want anything I've said to suggest a low opinion of blacks as soldiers. They had plenty of brave men in their ranks. A lot of black officers died just the way white officers did, taking reckless chances to encourage their men. Ray Campbell, the head foreman of Principia Mills, down in Carolina, was a sergeant in the 92nd Division. When we were attacking across the Cinquale

266

Canal in Italy, I saw him do things under fire that made my hair stand on end.

"Around the time I wrote my three hundredth letter to the parents of one of my officers who had been killed trying to inspire his black troops to follow him, I made a vow that if I lived long enough I was going to do something to change race relations in this country. I'm glad to say I've been able to make a few contributions along that line.

"After the war I devoted God knows how many hours to working with generals and politicians to desegregate the services. It was quite a battle. We had to fight the Army General Staff and the southern barons in Congress. We kept up the pressure from all directions. When we wrote a new constitution for New Jersey in 1948, for instance, I made sure there was a clause stating that the militia—which meant our National Guard division—had to be integrated. The Army tried to cut off federal funding. By the time the uproar died down, the Guard of almost every northern state had been integrated. I served on the President's Advisory Committee on Military Training and made sure that report had a total repudiation of segregation in it. It also recommended replacing the draft with universal military training. Neither idea got through Congress. But all this pressure had a lot to do with that executive order President Truman wrote in July of 1948, ending segregation in the military. Then I served on the Fahy Committee, which spent another year making sure the Army obeyed the order, and on the Gesell Committee in 1962, where we fought out desegregating the National Guard divisions in the South. That didn't happen until 1965, when Johnson wrote an executive order.

"Maybe now you can see why I have refused to give an inch on desegregating the schools in this city. It's a very personal issue with me, part of my life—

"There's another reason for this commitment. I had a stepson, John. He was the son of a—a—close friend who was killed in the Argonne. I knew his mother too. She came from the city. John was a tanker in the 2nd Armored Division during World War II. After the war he decided to stay in the Army. I got him into West Point

and he graduated in 1950. He was stationed in Japa
with the 303rd Armored Brigade when the Communist
invaded South Korea.

"John's tanks were with the leading elements of th
Eighth Army when the Chinese attacked across the Yal
in December of 1950. You remember what a mess tha
was. The Chinese achieved complete tactical surprise
The Eighth Army dissolved into fragments. There was n
artillery, no air support. The infantry depended on th
tanks to protect them. John took up a blocking positio
on a road south of the Chongchon River, where the 2n
Division tried to make a stand. The Chinese came ove
the river in seven columns and ripped them apart. The
went after the tanks with explosive charges, bazook
rounds tied to a stick of TNT and a friction cap. Towar
dawn on November 26, the last time anyone saw Joh
alive, there were about twenty dead Chinese within
hundred feet of his tank. His guns were still firing, hol
ing the road to give the infantrymen a chance to ge
out.

"He didn't even get a medal for it. Too many other
did the same sort of thing in that retreat. Maybe now yo
can understand why I don't rate my medals very high."

Paul Stapleton felt tears on his cheeks again but he di
not care. Maybe tears were the nearest thing to the trut
that he could offer Kilpatrick.

In a choked whisper, he continued: "I feel John'
death was wasted in Korea just the way you probably fee
about your boy in Vietnam. But I've tried to mak
something out of it, in my own way. I've tried to deepe
my commitment to America. I've spent a lot of mone
backing the right kind of men for Congress. It didn
matter to me whether they were Democrats or Republ
cans, as long as they believed in doing the job right, i
keeping this country strong and reasonably true to it
ideals.

"That's the only way to bear that kind of loss, Jin
Even if you fail, the effort—the effort's still worth it."

Paul Stapleton let his head fall back against the cush
ions of the chaise. He felt drained, utterly exhausted. H
could not finish the story. It was not his to tell. The res
belonged to Randy, his steady, patient, finally triumphar

ears at National Products restoring the wreck of the
tapleton fortune. He would give Kilpatrick the letters
ley had exchanged. It was all there, the step-by-step
rocess by which, blending Grandfather's realism and
.andy's idealism and Stapleton, Talbot's corporate ex-
erience, they had outmaneuvered Dwight Slocum and
uilt a great modern company with over a hundred fac-
ories around the world.

Looking back on the rest of his life since World War
I, it now seemed a calamitous futility. John's death had
egun it, then Mark's defection, his transformation from
on to critic, enemy. Then the realization that George too
as gone, that no psychiatrist was going to heal the
ound he had inflicted on himself. Finally watching
.merica writhing from similar self-inflicted wounds in
ietnam, Watergate. Spiraling into hysterical disillusion.
.ll these things, the personal and public agonies multiply-
ig his helplessness, making a mockery of his private
fforts to reverse the process, regain the momentum of the
scent. America was too huge to influence. His pathetic
andful of congressmen and senators almost always po-
tely ignored his letters. His struggle for the blacks
eemed to be ending in his own city in an obscene out-
urst of hatred.

"That's enough for now, Jim," he said. "I feel like I've
een in combat for a month."

XXI

Take this body. Take my beloved son.
Father, forgive me
Teach me how to bear it

Words like these spoke themselves in Kilpatrick's mind as
he stumbled to his car. They had begun when Paul
Stapleton was describing his son John's death. Kilpatrick
had tried to stop them. He had tried to break the grip the
old man was fastening on him. But Kilpatrick could not
stop what was happening. The old man became holy, the
spirit of America speaking, and he, Kilpatrick, was his
desecrator. His stupid, guilty desecrator.

Dazedly, Kilpatrick started the motor and drove slowly
toward home. He felt dropsical, leaden. Paul Stapleton
had filled his veins with mud. Kilpatrick saw that his
image of a dive into the depths of the old man's past had
been as naïve as the previous presumptions of his discon-
nected life.

On the expressway in the city, he drove numbly past
his exit. Before he knew it he was downtown, rolling
along the river, staring at the familiar gray mass of house

nd buildings on the crest of the ridge. The ruins of 'rincipia Mills flashed by on his right. He turned to climb he hill that would carry him uptown. On a sudden mpulse he took the exit that led down the Parkway to Kenmore Avenue. In a moment he was double-parked efore his boyhood home.

Except for the addition of aluminum siding, it was the ame house, spacious and sedate, with its bulging bay vindows and wide porch. Like the other houses on the treet, it still retained its aura of affluence. Judge James Kilpatrick had believed in living well, which was one of he reasons why he died with only eight thousand dollars n the bank. He thought of his father and the humiliating nformation that he had just been told by Paul Stapleton. He remembered the coruscating shame, the condescension of his Catholic intellectual friends in college, as they ssured him that it was not his fault that his father was a rook.

The past was for those who lived in the past, Muriel Bennett had told him with typical American carelessness. But it was also for those who lived in the present. Those who tried to escape it became fools or liars. He gazed at he house, asking himself what the façade said to a tranger, an outsider. Comfort, good cheer, security. These had unquestionably been part of his life in that ouse. But he had also known bitter disillusion, rage, atred. He remembered the stunning moment in his senior ear in college when his sister Faith had told him that heir father had a mistress. No, worse than a mistress, a econd wife, another woman he had secretly loved for the previous decade.

Truth behind the façade. Kilpatrick thought about the ruths he had found behind the Stapletons' façade. He rove down the block to West Side Avenue and stopped n a bar called Kasey's Korner for two double scotches. Maybe that was the way to deal with both truths, both açades. Oblivion.

Somewhat drunk, he drove carefully home through he twilight. He parked the Corvette in the garage. For the first time in a week he played his pause game with he ignition key. Why? He did not answer the question. n the living room, Allyn was waiting for him, wearing blue

271

jeans and her red pullover. Her reckless smile disheart
ened him. She looked so young and confident.

"How did it go?" she asked.

"The usual," he said.

"He played 'The Stars and Stripes Forever'?"

Kilpatrick nodded. He could not tell her what had
happened. He could not bear another diatribe from her
about Paul Stapleton's rottenness. He poured himself a
drink and sat down. Allyn was feeling ebullient.

"Aunt Aggie has called you three times. She seems
desperate to get in touch with you. I pretended to be a
secretary."

"Anyone else?"

"George. He's ready to talk. Go over everything you've
found and add his story."

"What will that be?"

"I don't know. Something about Italy during World
War II. He was there with the Great Man. I gather he
was the butcher to end them all. Ordering frontal charges
against massed machine guns."

"He talked about Italy today. He didn't even mention
George. I guess he didn't make any of the charges."

"Oh, he probably had George counting ammunition a
couple of miles back. He's not the hero type. That's
always been his problem. By the way, you got a letter
from Muriel Bennett."

She handed him a square blue enevelope. He opened it
reluctantly, feeling like a member of the police bomb
squad. In it, unaccompanied by any note, was the letter
Paul Stapleton had written after John's death.

Dec. 10, 1950

Dear Mu:

I have terrible news for you. We have lost John. He
was killed fighting a rearguard action against the Chinese
in North Korea. It seems like such a waste. After seeing
him struggle through those four years at West Point
knowing how much he hated school work, and then to go
out there and get killed fighting in a war that never would
have happened in the first place if we hadn't dismantled
our army and pretended we were living in a peaceful

272

world while the other side went on expanding their forces, researching and developing new weapons. All my life I've struggled to keep faith in this country, in spite of knowing rather intimately its worst tendencies. But this thing has really undone me. I can't work, I can't sleep. I keep thinking of you and those siren songs you sang about turning me into a presidential candidate. I laughed in your face then, and I still think it wouldn't have worked, the raw material just wasn't there, but I almost wish now that we had tried. it. Maybe I wouldn't be sitting here wondering why my son has died for a country that doesn't have the guts or the brains to give its fighting men the best weapons and strike back with maximum force when another nation launches a vicious sneak attack on our troops.

I know this is raving. But I can't say it to anyone else. I hold out my hand to you, Mu, in grief, in memory.

As ever,
Paul

Kilpatrick handed the letter to Allyn. "Jesus," she said, "it really tore him apart, didn't it? But the only thing he can think of is striking back with maximum force, killing."

Right on, chortled the voices of the dead young soldiers in Kilpatrick's head. But the other ghost, the one with Randy Stapleton's voice, whispered opposite words. It reminded him of what Paul Stapleton had said about effort, commitment. It asked him to remember what had happened while he was listening to him. *You became part of that anguish, that grief. Don't deny that now.*

"Maybe he's tried to do more than kill people. He's a very private man. He doesn't boast. But I'm beginning to think it's all connected. What he's doing as a judge, other things. But he doesn't—he can't talk about them. There's a kind of reticence bred into his bones."

"Hey—are you defending the old bastard?"

"No. I'm just trying to be realistic."

"Let's go see George. You need a little truth serum."

Passivity consumed Kilpatrick. He saw the impossibility of changing Allyn's mind now. He was her conspirator-lover. To tell her another truth was to fail, to betray her. They went in her Volvo 1800E. He sat beside her, indif-

273

ferent to the reckless way she drove. Even on the curving country road to New Grange Farm, she seldom let the speedometer fall below 70.

They screeched to a halt in the cobbled courtyard of George's imitation hacienda. He met them at the door wearing jeans and a beaded Mexican vest. While Allyn trailed along looking bored, he gave Kilpatrick a tour of the premises, pointing out the authentic Mayan statues, the Indian art on the walls. He stopped before a rectangle of gray wool with an interesting red, blue and yellow geometric design. "This is my only piece of non-Indian art," he said. "Executed by that gifted young weaver Miss Allyn Stapleton."

Allyn looked embarrassed. "Former weaver. I gave it up," she said.

"Tell him why," George said.

"The Great Man didn't think Stapletons should be artists."

"No money in it," George said. "If there's no money in it, no self-respecting Stapleton should be interested in it."

They sat down in the living room and George laid out a bottle of tequila, limes and salt. It was not Kilpatrick's favorite drink. Allyn and George liked it. They were soon on their way to killing the bottle.

George became expansive. He was the impresario of this caper. He wanted to know whom Kilpatrick had seen, what they had told him. Kilpatrick said that he would rather not go into it. He had come to hear George's story. George glanced uneasily at Allyn, who shrugged. George said that he had hoped that they could work on the book together.

"I'd rather work alone," Kilpatrick said.

He took out the tape recorder and put it on the round coffee table. George was disconcerted by Kilpatrick's lack of enthusiasm. He asked where he should start. Kilpatrick suggested the beginning. George took a slug of tequila, frowned, scratched his ear and began talking to the tape recorder.

"By the time I was old enough to think about my father and me as separate human beings—when I was about nine—that would be about 1933—he was a voice

274

giving orders, a pair of legs running, a pair of arms doing push-ups. He seemed angry about something and was taking it out on us—especially me. I wasn't very athletic and I didn't like exercise.

"But Randy explained it all. About the Depression, the danger of a revolution in which only the tough would survive. Randy was the perfect oldest son. He was like a Prime Minister with a special gift for rationalizing the tyranny of the Tsar or Kaiser or King. My mother thought the whole thing was an abomination but she couldn't stop it. She's never been able to stop the Great Man from doing anything. Only once in a while, when things got desperate, could she intervene. Like the time he wanted me to get out of bed and run with them in late December, when I had a temperature of 102.

"Then came World War II. I had the wrong build for the Tank Corps. So I went into the infantry. I made lieutenant in the A-12 program. I got assigned to Italy. My father might have had something to do with that. He's never admitted it. But I wound up in IV Corps of the Fifth Army, commanding a company in the 92nd Division the Negro outfit.

"He knew what I was going into. He didn't lift a finger to get me out of it. He didn't even tell me what I was facing. Instead, when I walked into his tent in November of 1944, he gave me a lecture because there was mud on my boots and uniform. As if anyone could keep mud off himself in Italy. He blatted about discipline and example. Then he shook my hand, wished me luck and said, 'I expect you to be the best lieutenant in this division.' "

George was glowering at the tequila bottle, his hands were opening and closing on his thighs as if he wanted to take someone by the throat.

"It was idiocy, the whole goddamn thing was idiocy. The Germans had all the high ground. You couldn't drive a jeep down a road without getting shelled. The Germans had these portable steel pillboxes that could take everything but a direct hit from a howitzer. We'd blast them for five or six hours with planes, artillery, and when we jumped off they'd be there, the machine guns tearing us apart. It wasn't war, it was organized slaughter. I didn't

275

blame the blacks for hating it. The white divisions felt the same way.

"In the first month, the captain and the other lieutenant in my company were killed. I was promoted to captain. In February of '45 we were ordered to get ready for an attack across the Cinquale Canal on the Mediterranean coastal plain north of Rome. It made absolutely no sense. The Germans were on the mountains to the east. On the plain they were dug in to their teeth with those steel pillboxes and poured-concrete bunkers every ten feet. We knew the goddamn war was ending, the Russians were in East Prussia, the Third Army was over the Rhine. The whole thing was an exercise by the white generals to make the colored boys fight.

"I wrote a letter to the corps commander protesting the orders. I said the attack would end in a slaughter, a needless loss of life. I was hauled down to GHQ and chewed out as a goddamn traitor. Crittenberger—that was the general—ripped up the letter and told me to remember who I was—Paul Stapleton's son.

"I went back to my company. On the night before the attack, I went around talking to the men, giving them the standard bullshit. I got along well with them. Then I went down to the canal. I could see some of the steel pillboxes on the other side. Suddenly I couldn't do it. I couldn't let them get slaughtered. I went back to Crittenberger's headquarters and said I was resigning my commission. I told him what I thought of him and his attack. Crittenberger put me under arrest and called my father. He arrived in a jeep about three A.M. We talked until dawn, but he couldn't change my mind. He went back to Crittenberger and recommended I be tried for desertion by a general court-martial.

"That's right, desertion. If I was convicted, it meant the firing squad. He was ready to send his own son to the firing squad.

"They made the attack without me. It was a fiasco, just as I said it would be. They wound up with 560 killed and wounded and not a foot of ground gained. I got shipped to the rear, found myself a lawyer and prepared to fight the charges. The war suddenly picked up steam and roared to a climax inside Germany. I was forgotten and

276

by the time anyone remembered me, nobody wanted to go into the details of that idiotic attack. Over my protests, I was given a medical discharge.

"That was thirty-two years ago. In those thirty-two years, my father has never said one word to me about it. He's tried to treat me like it never happened. But his opinion of me, his contempt, his disgust, have been visible to me during every one of those thirty-two years."

"Why did you go to work for him? Why didn't you split, like Mark?" Kilpatrick asked.

"I suppose—somehow, sometime, I thought he would come to me and admit he was wrong, say he was sorry. But he never has and now I know he never will. That's why I've decided to tell the truth about myself and about him and derail the Stapleton duty machine. When he dies—which I suspect will be very soon—I plan to take my inheritance and head for Mexico, where I hope to find a new wife and a new life. Mexico draws its energy from a single source—the sun. There are no complications, no splits between duty and pleasure, real and ideal, spirit and flesh. The Aztec plumed serpent. There's a symbol that means something. What have we got—the eagle. A perfect symobol of the family and the national malaise. We soar high—for prey."

George Stapleton smiled triumphantly at Kilpatrick, like a man who had just given a very successful speech. Was it true? Kilpatrick wondered dazedly. Nothing Paul Stapleton had said this afternoon contradicted it.

"George," Allyn said. "That was fantastic. Wasn't it, Jim?"

Kilpatrick nodded and turned off the tape recorder. Beyond the numbness in the center of his body, all he could feel was weariness, defeat. Allyn's glowing face, her applause for this paean of possible true hate, only made him realize again how hopeless it was for him to respond to Randy's voice, urging him to rescue her from this ruinous bitterness. Earlier today, Paul Stapleton had given Kilpatrick a glimpse of another response to defeat and death, another way out of the labyrinth of revenge and regret. In a supremely ironic reversal, love was blocking his hope of reaching it.

George began telling Kilpatrick about the hoard of

papers he had stolen from Stapleton, Talbot detailing the tax maneuvers of National Products over the past twenty years. Kilpatrick would need some coaching from a professional like George to grasp their significance, but once he saw how tax avoidance blended into tax evasion, he would have a chapter in his book that would have the IRS and the SEC turning handsprings. It would make the book must reading in law firms from coast to coast.

"The IRS will undoubtedly go to court to demand millions in back taxes from my father and Dwight Slocum, the principal gainers from these tactics. If they win, it would reduce my inheritance by millions. But I'd gladly part with the money, to see a little justice done."

"We let Slocum pay for the book and then double-cross him too," Kilpatrick said.

"It's an amoral world," George said.

"Hey, George," Allyn said. "Do you mind if I—" She ran her finger along her nose and gestured upstairs.

"Sure," George said.

George returned to the intricacies of the corporate income tax laws. When Allyn came downstairs, Kilpatrick signaled his disinterest by packing his tape recorder into his briefcase and standing up, ready to depart.

Allyn had looked rather bored when she went upstairs. Now she was giggling over some secret joke, practically floating a foot off the floor. She gave George a big kiss on the mouth and reaffirmed that he was fantastic. Kilpatrick remembered Peregrine Stapleton's observations on incest and did not like it. George asked Allyn when he was going to see her again. She wrapped a leg around Kilpatrick's thighs and said she was a working girl.

Outside, she handed Kilpatrick her car keys. "You better drive," she said. "For the sake of the cause."

"What the hell's going on?" he asked, feeling more and more out of it.

"Just a little sniff of Uncle George's white gold," she said as they pulled away. "A little pick-me-up for your little lay-me-down-roll-me-over-fuck-me-again girl."

"Cocaine?" Kilpatrick said.

"Right. Angel dust."

She began telling him about George's great cocaine.

Kilpatrick was appalled. All his middle-class Irish-American instincts rose out of his past to condemn drugs as the ultimate self-abuse. But how could he say anything, when he was pouring a quart of scotch down his throat almost every day?

Back in the city, Allyn wanted to continue celebrating. Kilpatrick said he had work to do. Allyn asked him if he was almost ready to begin writing. He said he was not sure. They ate a hurried frozen-food dinner in the kitchen and Kilpatrick retreated to the study. He spent the next three hours typing up what Paul Stapleton had told him that afternoon. On tape, the old man's voice had a sad, labored sound. The effort of memory, the pain of regret, were audible. The way he spoke in rushes of words, then patches of tired breathing. Kilpatrick listened with special attention to what he had said about the officers who broke down in Italy. He wondered what George Stapleton would think if he heard it.

It was after midnight when the last words faded from the tape. The house was silent and dark. Kilpatrick went down the hall to the bathroom, stripped and showered. Wearing only a robe, he continued down the hall to his bedroom. Allyn was lying in the double bed, naked.

"You should have been a lawyer. You like to work Stapleton, Talbot hours," she said.

She flung her long legs off the bed and walked slowly across the room to kiss him. She was wearing a strong perfume. Her tongue went deep into his mouth.

Nothing happened.

Kilpatrick placed the palms of his hands on the nipples of those proud yet suppliant breasts and slowly rotated them.

Still nothing happened. His body remained mud, detritus.

Pretensions were falling off him like the emperor's clothes. She made the metaphor real by untying his bathrobe and pulling it off in one commanding gesture. Her tongue tasted his nipples and roved down his belly till she was on her knees slowly sucking the nub of flesh that remained a nub.

Nothing is going to happen, the mocking voice of

279

reality whispered. Nothing is going to happen because you are no longer a man, you are a no-man's-land, a wounded landscape in a war between ghosts.

Allyn looked up at him, bewildered. "What's the matter?"

"Middle age," he said.

She retreated to her bedroom. It was interesting. Kilpatrick thought in another burst of useless insight, that she had chosen a separate bedroom. In unspoken acknowledgement of the distance between them? Or was it an attempt to people his house for him, an instinctive attempt to please the failed father in him? He didn't know, he didn't care. He put out the light and crawled beneath the sheet and lay there for hours while anxiety churned through his belly.

He finally got up and pulled on a pair of slacks and a T-shirt, and found the car keys. In recent years, when he was assaulted by anxiety, he had found turnpike driving the best tranquilizer. He walked softly through the silent house. In the distance he could hear trucks humming on the expressway. In a few minutes he would be with them rolling down the empty concrete miles beneath the unnatural yellow lamps, letting the American distance devour his anguish, the American wind whisper that it did not matter, the American night remind him that the pangs of a single soul were trivial in the immensity of America's space.

Kilpatrick walked through the kitchen and across the breezeway to the garage. In the distance a police siren howled. He turned on the light in the garage. The car sat there, a somnolent red monster, silent, indifferent, the perfect American friend. He opened the front door and got behind the wheel. He inserted the key in the ignition. Then he knew that he had not come down here to ride the midnight turnpike.

Turn the key. *Vroom*. All will be as quiet as a percolator, thanks to his well-tuned engine. Death would come on little mouse feet, pocketa, pocketa, wearing its own breath and nothing else, naked as an unsubtle slut. What would he think about as drowsy oblivion enveloped him? The look on Paul Stapleton's face when he hears the news? On Ned Stapleton's face? On ex-wife Esther's face? On his children's faces? Tears there, please.

Looks, faces. Allyn Stapleton's face, when she opens the garage door. Did he owe her an explanation? No, what she saw would explain everything. She would handle it. She would sniff some of Uncle George's white gold and go looking for another writer, with a bigger, more reliable cock. Maybe Uncle George himself.

Kilpatrick flicked the trunk key with his finger. He watched it swing back and forth, back and forth on the pendulum of pure chance, obeying the irresistible laws of science; above all, the second law of thermodynamics, inertia, the ultimate goal of all matter. Whatever mattered once no longer matters in the end. Everything-comes-to-a-dead-stop-stop.

Kilpatrick thought about Paul Stapleton in his bed at New Grange Farm. Was he lying awake too? Was he thinking about his life? With each sentence he spoke was he trying to unload the burden of it on this stranger, this unperson, this man without a heritage, a father, a faith? Somebody ought to tell him that he had been pouring his history into a sewer. Or did he think that his life was being extracted from him yard by yard like the coils of his intestines by this evasive stranger? That was probably closer to the truth.

But at least Paul Stapleton had a past worth extracting. By the light of a bomber's moon, Kilpatrick surveyed the shattered landscape of his life. He saw failure as a father, failure as a husband, failure as a lover. He saw the concatenation of bad moves, each one designed to reduce anguish, each inexorably adding to it. All flowing, he saw now, from the original wound, the original choice, the bitter rejection of his father and his mocking realism, his brash corruption. This afternoon he had rounded the final curve of his pathetic circle and confronted that smiling Irish face again, giving him the horse laugh one last time. *That was the way they operated,* Paul Stapleton said. *I knew it but I didn't know,* said Sappyjim. It was time to end Jim's ridiculous pursuit of the unattainable in the name of the ineffable. Sic transit idealists.

The police siren was coming closer. In a few minutes it

281

would be passing the corner. That would be the moment to turn the key. The city's standard wail of distress would drown out the *vroom*. A perfect coda to a life of ironies.

"Jim. What in God's name are you doing?"

He looked into Allyn Stapleton's stunned staring eyes, watched the determined jaw, the Valkyrian nose, the confident mouth sliding sideward into horror.

"You were going to do that? You were going to let me find you here?"

He flicked the dangling key again. It swung back and forth, back and forth on its pendulum chain. "Go to bed," he said.

"Why? Because of what just happened? It happens all the time—"

He shook his head. "It's the whole thing. George, your father, your grandfather. I can't handle it."

"Why? What do you care about him? About any of us?"

"It's not worth explaining."

"Is it me? You're looking for love and all I want is good cocaine?"

"You have helped me recognize my essential asininity."

"I told you not to be dumb enough to fall in love with me. I'm an ice girl. Straight from the North Pole like all the Stapletons. I'll tell you what a bitch I am. I started fooling around with you for only one reason—to get you to write this book our way. It was George's idea."

"Say that again," Kilpatrick said.

"It was George's idea. To feed you the dirty parts of the story. Add a few touches, to make it sound better. Like my mother being an alcoholic. I barely remember her. She died of cancer when I was five."

Kilpatrick stared at the ignition key. It had stopped playing pendulum. "Jesus Christ," he said. "Jesus Christ." He felt a river rising in him, a roaring thundering foaming flood of anger. He glared at Allyn Stapleton. She was wearing his old blue bathrobe. It was a very romantic sight. Miss Stapleton in a bathrobe six sizes too big for her sitting in the plush front seat of his Corvette, her lovely breasts glimpsed in the neckline plunge, persuading James Kilpatrick by the glow of the overhead dome light that he should refrain from self-murder. Why? Because the lovely immediate cause of his despair was a double-talking double-crossing bitch. Herself.

He grabbed the bathrobe's lapels in his fists and began roaring at her. "How could you do it? How could you fuck around with another human being's life that way? I loved you. I told you."

"I told you not to love me. I warned you."

"What kind of a monster are you? Do you think everyone can fuck without caring? Did you ever hear the words making love?"

"It doesn't mean that to me any more."

She twisted free and fled into the kitchen. He followed her, still raging. "I wanted to help you. Stop you from destroying yourself. What a fucking idiot I am. While you're destroying me."

"Why?" she screamed. "Why am I destroying you? Most of it's true. What you heard from George is true. From Muriel Bennett. From Peregrine. Why does that destroy you? Why don't you want to destroy him? Doesn't he deserve it?"

"No," he roared. "As of this moment my answer is no, he doesn't deserve it."

"What happened to you? You hated the old bastard just as much as I do. I felt it. I saw it."

The question ripped into his flesh like a hand grenade. Suddenly he could not stop it, the truth was spilling out of his belly like his own blood. "You want to know why I hated him? For Kevin, my son Kevin. I haven't mentioned him to you. That's one part of my story where it's practically impossible to get a laugh. Kevin went to Vietnam in 1971, when the war was on everybody's shit list. Except true-blue patriots like me, guys who worked for Randy Stapleton and heard stories about his hero father with his three Distinguished Service Crosses. I talked Kevin into going. I told him about the big future that was waiting for him at National Products if he came back with a good war record. I told him his country needed him. I gave him the old American one-two, the appeal of realistic greed and idealistic need. He went. Now he's under a cross in a military cemetery on Long Island."

"Oh, Jim," Allyn Stapleton said.

What was on her face? It looked like genuine sympathy. But who could tell what was genuine, what was phony on that face now? Kilpatrick went into the living room and poured himself a tumblerful of scotch.

"Why didn't you tell me?" Allyn said, following him. She looked like she was ready to cry. She was a hell of an actress.

"Tell you? Why the fuck should I do that? It's not funny. That's all you want to do is laugh, right? It's a gag, to fuck a fifty-year-old man and listen to him say he's falling in love with you. You know who was really fucking you. It was Kevin. I was doing it for him, for all the times he'd never do it. You never had me, you never had Jim Kilpatrick. You were fucking a ghost, Miss Stapleton. How do you like that? Good for a fucking laugh?"

She was shaking her head in that abrupt Stapleton way. Any second she expected him to collapse, to deny everything, to beg her for sympathy, love. But he was not finished with her. He looked down at the empty tumbler of scotch and threw the glass against the wall on the other side of the living room.

"That wasn't the only ghost who fucked you, Miss Stapleton. There was another one, whispering love her, protect her, that first day in your apartment. And the second day. Do you know who he was, Miss Stapleton?"

"I don't believe you," she said.

"It shouldn't surprise you. I was his ghost writer, Miss Stapleton. I put words in his mouth and he put thoughts in my head. That's how ghost writers work."

"Stop it, please," Allyn said. "I loved him so much. If I thought his love, even a piece of it was in you, and I destroyed it, I'd—"

Tears streamed down her face. She was shaking with grief, fear, horror. Kilpatrick stared drunkenly at another failure. Or was it some weird perverse success, to discover a fragment of caring in this red-haired bitch's cold Stapleton soul? Then he saw what it had cost him. He saw his own starved love, standing naked between the two ghosts, betrayed, denied, for this moment of revenge.

"Get out of here," he said.

"I won't go until I'm sure you're all right. Until I know you won't go back into that garage."

"You've cured me," he said.

The words were spoken with cold, calm clarity. The liquor in his brain and blood was isolated, frozen by his will to not love, not think, to become as impersonal and indifferent as a robot in a tank. He waited while she packed her single suitcase. She came back downstairs in her blue jeans and red sweater.

"What are you going to do?" she said.

"I'm going to finish this goddamn book, my way," he said.

"I'd still like to help you," she said.

"I don't need any more help from the Stapletons," he said.

"I mean—honestly."

"I don't think you know the meaning of the word."

The front door slammed. He listened to her go down the steps, start her car and back into the street. He was alone in his empty house again. Now it was truly empty. That snarled confession had driven his favorite companions, the ghost of Randy Stapleton and the ghost of Kevin Kilpatrick, into a kind of netherworld.

Kilpatrick went upstairs and started packing for a departure of his own. On his way out, he stopped to play back his automatic phone-answering machine. He heard Agatha Stapleton's voice: "Mr. Kilpatrick, will you please call me at 885-9876? This is the fourth time I've phoned."

Kilpatrick shook his head. He was through talking to Stapletons for a while. He was going to talk to strangers. After that he would think for a while and decide whether he agreed with his shouted confession that Paul Stapleton did not deserve to be destroyed. After that, who knows? Maybe a call to Dwight Slocum. Maybe another garage, where no one would interrupt him while he watched the ignition key swing on its pendulum to—a—dead—stop.

XXII

On Monday, Ned Stapleton read the finished copy of his appeals court brief for Slocum's Remedy and sent it down the hall for Walter Ackroyd's approval. It was a bit humiliating, at forty-one, to have his briefs read by the managing partner. Ned wondered if it was on his father's orders. It was time he talked to Walter about it. In the past month, as head of the New Business Committee, he had brought two clients into the firm, with potential for a half million dollars in fees.

At 5 P.M. Ned crawled uptown in the rush-hour traffic and parked in the space reserved for his father's Mercedes in the federal courthouse lot. He had been summoned to Judge Stapleton's chambers without an explanation. But he was advised to tell Tracy that he might be late for dinner. Was it going to be an extra-long lecture? Ned felt resentful in advance. He had worked hard all summer. He had barely seen his sloop, *Principia II*. Fall had been more of the same nose-to-the-grindstone act.

In his chambers, Ned found his father conferring with Kevin McGuire, the pudgy, flashily dressed president of the Board of Education. McGuire looked unhappy. The

Judge had obviously been giving him hell. "All right, Mr. McGuire," he said. "I'll give you one more chance. You go up there and tell the principal and the faculty of that school if I hear of another incident in which a teacher makes a racial remark I'll put the whole school in receivership. Uncle Sam will be their boss, and I'll be their principal. I won't slap them on the wrist if they pull this stuff. I'll hold them in contempt of court and put them in jail."

"Yes, your honor, I understand," McGuire said.

"Hello, Kevin," Ned said. "Get any sailing in this summer?"

McGuire was one of the most successful lawyers in the city. He had a half dozen unions among his clients. Last year he had bought a sloop and applied for membership in the Paradise Beach Yacht Club. The mayor's wife, Paula Stapleton O'Connor, had persuaded Ned to sponsor him.

McGuire shook his head glumly. "I'm afraid to get more than ten feet from a telephone. Something goes wrong and I get blamed for it."

"That's what responsibility is all about," Paul Stapleton said. "I know you've got to make a living as a lawyer. But you took this job and you're stuck with it. Just like me and the mayor. None of us are getting paid what these headaches are worth. You've got to think of it as something you're doing for the country."

Kevin McGuire nodded. There was no sign of a glow of patriotism. Ned was sure that McGuire thought of the integration plan as something the Judge was doing *to* the country. Ned half agreed with him.

McGuire departed and Ned felt guilty. His father looked frail and old today. He sat straight in his swivel chair in his usual semi-military way. But the shadows under his eyes, the mournful cast of his mouth, communicated weariness, exhaustion.

"Bad day?" Ned said.

"No worse than usual."

"I wish you'd consider resigning at the end of this year. You deserve a rest. Mother wants you to do it."

"I know. But I'm going to see this thing through."

His father began packing papers into his briefcase for his usual four hours of night work. "I called you over

287

here to talk to you about a family problem. George. I haven't talked frankly to you, Ned, about him or a lot of other things. You're so much younger than the other boys, maybe it's been hard for me to realize you're a grown man and then some. Maybe I didn't want to burden—disillusion you. But you know George has had a lot of personal problems."

Ned nodded. "I never have figured out why you let him get away with stuff that would have had me on the carpet for a week."

"Because I didn't know what to do about him, Ned. That's the truth. You're old enough to know what that means. You faced it last year when your boy Paul got suspended from Pennsgrove. How is he, by the way?"

"Good, as far as we can tell," Ned said, relieved to see that his father continued to regard Paul's marijuana smoking as a boyish prank. "He won the tennis championship at camp this summer. He's made halfback on old Peegrove's JV football team."

There was a momentary flicker of disapproval at Ned's use of that derogatory nickname for Pennsgrove. But Paul Stapleton only nodded and said, "Like father, like son."

He closed his bulging briefcase and snapped the locks. "I wish George's problem was a little youthful experimentation with marijuana. But it's a lot more complicated."

In a flat, hard, tightly controlled voice, his father told Ned that George had "broken under fire" in World War II and had never really recovered from the failure. Ned knew, had known for a long time, that George's problem was connected with the war. When he went into a sanitarium after he was graduated from Harvard in 1950, their mother had hinted at the war as the cause. Ned had thought it was shell shock, battle fatigue. In 1960, George had had another breakdown, after the collapse of his first marriage.

For most of the next decade and a half, George had been fairly well behaved. He drank too much, but he came to work regularly and did a good job. He had been one of the best tax lawyers at Stapleton, Talbot. But the past three or four years had seen a steady deterioration. His second marriage had broken up. He had started to keep very elastic hours. Ned did not know much more than these general facts. He had avoided his brother in recent years, because they quarreled repeatedly over George's attitude toward their father.

"I've tried to be understanding," Paul Stapleton said. "Maybe I've even felt a little guilty about it. You've heard me talk about Italy, Ned. It was a terrible time for me. I had to send an awful lot of young officers into battle knowing their chances of survival were poor. When my own son turned up in the replacement pool, I had to treat him like the rest. I couldn't have lived with myself if I did anything else."

Ned nodded. He agreed with the principle, even though he felt a twist of sympathy for George. Ned suspected that he too might have felt his father should have intervened, done something to protect him. It was hard to shake off a son's habits of feeling, especially with a father like this man, who never stopped asserting his fatherhood over you. Would he be able to give those kinds of orders to his own son? Ned shuddered and had to confess to himself that he was not sure.

"But now the time has come to take George in hand," his father said. "I told him a long time ago that he ought to quit the law and tackle poetry—whatever he wanted to do—full time." He picked up a letter from his desk. "Walter Ackroyd tells me that George is practically a permanent absentee. Other friends tell me that he's throwing parties at his house with drugs like cocaine on the menu. He's got young girls—the granddaughter of one friend—and maybe my own granddaughter—taking the stuff."

"Babe?" Ned said, using the family nickname for Allyn.

"Yes, Babe," his father said. "I'm going out there now to see George. I want you to come with me, Ned. He's always liked you."

Once upon a time, Ned thought sadly. George had been nice to him when he was five or six and George was in his mid-teens. George had been an easygoing, guitar-strumming joker then. He used to call himself the Caballero. Ned remembered that he had had trouble pronouncing it. But a different George had come home from the war. A

289

man who was more often moody and withdrawn than friendly and amusing. The guitar had collected dust in a closet.

"I'm going to make George resign from the firm and move away from here. His only chance—and I admit it isn't a very good one—is a fresh start somewhere else. He's talked for years about going to Mexico. Maybe that's the right place for him. I hope you'll be willing to go with him and help him get settled."

They went out to the parking lot and got into Ned's Mercedes coupe. In a few minutes they were on the expressway, leaving the city. Ned found himself wondering exactly what the words "broke under fire" meant. He wanted to ask but his father obviously found the subject so painful Ned decided to remain ignorant.

"Have you made any progress with Jim Kilpatrick on the book?" Ned asked.

"I don't know, Ned," Paul Stapleton replied. "I'm half inclined to drop it, and let him keep what we've paid him. There are so many things—family feelings—that you can't discuss with a stranger, you can't explain to the rest of the world."

"I don't understand," Ned said. "What's there to hide?"

"There's not much that has to be hidden," he said. "But there's a lot that might be better forgotten. Your uncle Malcolm, for instance, my brother. He's a sad story. He tried so damn hard to make a success of the mills and stop the Irish pols in the city. He lost both fights. He wound up a bitter, viciously prejudiced man. He wouldn't even go to his own daughter's wedding because she married an Irish-American. Do we want to tell the truth about him?"

"I suppose not the whole truth," Ned said. "But couldn't we skip the bad parts, leave out the prejudice and picture him fighting in vain for clean government? A heroic loser."

"I guess so. But it would be like describing me as a military genius."

"How many reserve officers get made general?"

"They gave me that rank after the war, Ned. It was a sentimental gesture by a few old pals in the Pentagon."

Ned writhed. He and Sam Fry and friends in the Hunt had tried to call Paul Stapleton General but his father had asked them to stop it. "I bet you didn't even bother to tell it to Kilpatrick," Ned said.

"I don't think I did."

They bumped up the hill and down the opposite slope to George's hacienda. "Does he know we're coming?" Ned said.

"I called and told him. He said he was going out. But I think he'll be here."

Ned did not have to try too hard to imagine the phone conversation.

Ned knocked several times on the big mahogany door. No one answered. He pressed the latch and it swung open.

"George?" Ned called.

"Upstairs, Father almighty," George shouted.

Paul Stapleton did not hear that sneering invitation. He was rounding the fender of the Mercedes and approaching the door, which Ned held open for him. Ned told his father that George was in his study and strode ahead of him up the short flight of stairs to the huge room with the exotic plumed serpent on the ceiling. Ned found George seated behind his big semicircular desk with a broad smile on his face. He was either drunk or high on something.

"Neddy," he said. "I should have known the Great Man would send you as his errand boy. What's the message? I'm fired from the firm? I'm going to be put on a dollar-a-week allowance?"

"Dad's here," Ned said. "He's coming up the stairs."

Paul Stapleton paused in the doorway. "I don't think you could make those stairs any steeper, George," he said, "without turning them into a ladder."

"You're getting old," George said.

"No kidding."

Paul Stapleton sat down on a low couch at the far end of the room, below George's glass-enclosed stereo set. It was the only seat in the room, besides George's swivel chair. Ned sat down on the windowsill, nervously folding and unfolding his arms, waiting for his father to begin.

"George," Paul Stapleton said, "I take it you've re-

291

signed from the firm. You just forgot to send them a letter."

"I have no intention of resigning from the firm," George said.

"Well, I resigned for you. Today. That's what I'm here to tell you."

"You have no right, no power, no authority to do that," George snarled.

Ned sensed something false, posturing in his anger, as if it was artificially created to mask another emotion.

"I did it to save you the humiliation of getting kicked out," Paul Stapleton said.

"Save who the humiliation?" George said. "There's only one person, one thing you're trying to save. Your goddamn reputation."

"There's some truth to that," Paul Stapleton said. "I'm getting shot at by half the city. The last thing I need is someone leaking stories about my son losing his job because he's too lazy or too drunk to come to work."

George crashed both fists on his desk. "I don't come to work because I'm sick of it," he shouted. "I'm sick of wiping corporate asses, sick of playing games with the tax laws."

"George, I told you a long time ago that I didn't think you had the right temperament to be a lawyer. You insisted on being one. Maybe you thought it guaranteed you a free ride at Stapleton, Talbot. I don't know. Now I'm here to tell you that you ought to face facts and quit. Go to Mexico or California—someplace far away from here—from me—and concentrate on being a poet. I'll put up the money."

Ned was amazed by the transformation on George's face as Paul Stapleton said this. George's mouth twisted from rage to a strange crafty contempt. "There's only one explanation for this generosity. Allyn's told you."

"Told me what?"

"About our little game with Kilpatrick. She was out here around lunchtime, practically wetting her pants, telling me we had to stop it. I told her to get lost. I'm telling you the same thing, telling you to go fuck yourself the way you've fucked me all my life. Because now I've fucked you back. I've given you the ultimate fuck. I've ruined Paul Stapleton's reputation. And I'm going to finish the job. I'm going to stay here and finish the job, if I have to go on welfare to do it."

"What have you been doing with Kilpatrick?" Ned asked.

"Oh, little Neddy brown nose wants to know what's happened to his bright little idea," George said.

"Yeah, I want to know," Ned said, feeling his own temper rising.

"I arranged for that hired hack to find out the truth. From a lot of people. The Great Man here knows who they are. Muriel Bennett, Dwight Slocum, Peregrine. Kilpatrick's on his way to Washington and points south to see a few more. When he comes back I'm going to give him a thousand pages of documents about the tax practices of National Products, Inc. When I'm finished the name Stapleton will have about as much integrity as Capone."

Ned had never heard of Muriel Bennett. He could not imagine what Dwight Slocum or Peregrine could tell Kilpatrick that would damage his father. But the thought of showing the IRS ferrets confidential documents from Stapleton, Talbot's files left Ned gasping. "You're out of your goddamn head, George," he said.

"I'm afraid you're right, Ned," Paul Stapleton said. He sighed. "I wanted you to go away, George. I thought you could handle it. But now I'm afraid it's the sanitarium again."

"No," George said.

"You're not making sense, George," Paul Stapleton said.

"That's the sort of thing you said when I applied for a transfer in Italy. You sent me back to those stupid niggers and told me to be a hero. A lot of other people were dumb enough to think you were the voice of God, standing there with your three Distinguished Service Crosses and still alive. But I saw how many came back wrapped in their ponchos after trying to imitate you."

Paul Stapleton continued to sit on the edge of the blue-covered couch, his back straight, his arms folded on his chest. "I asked everybody to do the same thing George."

"You asked everybody to commit suicide," George screamed. "Including your own son. You're a fucking goddamn murderer."

Paul Stapleton shook his head. "I had orders too, George. I was a colonel. There were generals planning those attacks."

"Your friends. Your hero-worshipping friends."

Paul Stapleton shook his head. Ned had never seen him look so weary. "It's a waste of time, George. I'll call the sanitarium. We'll go down tonight."

"No, we won't," George said.

He pulled open a drawer beneath his red Olivetti. His right hand dove into it and came up with a big black army .45.

"That won't solve anything, George," Paul Stapleton said.

"It will solve things my way. I've thought about doing this a hundred times."

Ned looked at his father. He was still sitting on the edge of the couch, his hands on his knees now, his face expressionless. The gun in George's hand seemed unreal, absurd. He remembered being George's little brother, trying to pronounce Caballero. When George was in Italy, he, Ned, was ten years old. Was it possible that he was going to die now from evil born in that distant time? The answer was yes because he was Paul Stapleton's son. It was the same incredible tangle of reason and unreason George had confronted in Italy.

"You don't think there's any justice in this, Ned," George said. "I didn't want to kill you. Your death will be accidental, part of the fortunes of war. But his death is justice. He's done enough to die a dozen times. He's violated his so-called ideals so often he should have died fifty years ago. But he sits there, proof positive that there is no God. I made one mistake and spent the rest of my life paying for it. He turns his back on his crimes, and goes on eating, sleeping, pretending to be this paragon of patriotism and respectability."

"George," Paul Stapleton said. "A son doesn't know what goes on in his father's life. If he thinks he does, he's a fool. I don't think any man, father or son, son or father, knows how another man evens things up—or why."

"What was your mistake, George?" Ned said. "I'd like to know."

"I ran, Neddy. Shortly before dawn on the morning of February 5, 1945, I advanced to the rear from the northern bank of the Cinquale Canal. I saw a German counterattack coming at us from three sides. Half my company of black heroes was already in the canal, swimming for the other side. I grabbed the last available rubber boat and paddled my precious ass out of there."

Ned shook his head. For a moment he felt like weeping. Would he have done the same thing? He didn't know.

"I couldn't tell Ned that, George. I've never been able to tell anyone, even your mother."

"You lying bastard. You told her. All these years, I've tried to get a word, a gesture of sympathy, forgiveness out of her. No, she stands by her hero husband. She watches her son dying of despair in front of her eyes. She participates in his crucifixion."

"Ned," Paul Stapleton said. "Call the Brompton Institute. Tell them George will be arriving later this evening."

The words were spoken in the same sad, matter-of-fact voice that his father had been using from the start. But it was an order—an order that disregarded the existence of that black .45 in George's hand. Now Ned knew what all the stories meant, all the awed talk he had heard from Sam Fry and from visiting army friends about his father's utter disregard for danger and death. Now Ned Stapleton was going to find out if he was the same kind of man.

Ned did not look at George. He sensed that if George saw fear in his eyes he would pull the trigger. The white telephone was on the desk in front of the red Olivetti. Ned strode over to the desk and picked up the receiver. He was now standing between the gun and his father. Looking down, he could see the dial of the telephone and beyond it the gun with George's finger on the trigger.

"What's the number?" he said. He was amazed to hear his own voice, apparently quite calm.

He glanced down the room at his father. Paul Stapleton

was flipping through a small book of telephone numbers that he carried in his wallet. "It's in Monmouth County. 678-8876. Ask for Dr. Kane."

Ned dialed and got a switchboard. He gave his name and asked for Dr. Kane. The gun and the telephone remained the two major objects in Ned's vision. The gun was pointed at his chest. If George pulled the trigger it would be quick and painless.

Dr. Kane came on the line. "Doctor, this is Ned Stapleton. My brother George is having some problems. My father was hoping you'd have room for him."

Dr. Kane said there was room.

"Good. We'll bring him down tonight."

Dr. Kane asked if George was violent. Staring at the gun, Ned said, "Not at the moment."

Ned hung up. George emitted a weird cry. He sank into the high-backed swivel chair and began to weep. "You cold-blooded little bastard," he said. "You cold-blooded little bastard."

For a moment Ned almost collapsed. He understood all the sadness, the accusation, in that cry. But he willed calm into his body. Methodically he walked around the desk and took the gun away from George. He slipped on the safety catch and pulled out the magazine. It was loaded. Ned handed the gun to his father.

"Thanks," Paul Stapleton said. He emptied the magazine and put the gun in his pocket. He told Ned to go to New Grange Farm and find Sam Fry and tell him what had happened. Under no circumstances was Ned's mother to know anything about it. He was to tell Sam to bring the car down to George's house immediately. They would drive George to the Brompton Institute.

"Are you sure you'll be all right?" Ned said, eyeing George, who had his head down on the desk, sobbing.

"Of course," Paul Stapleton said.

As Ned went down the stairs, he heard his father say, "George, for the hundredth time, I'm sorry."

XXIII

Saturday. Saturday morning.

Mark Stapleton lay in his bed, drowsily remembering Saturday mornings in other years. Dawn beside him, fragrant, fresh from a bath. They would make smooth wordless love. The best time, the morning, when the mind was unbothered by the inevitable irritations of the day, the inexorable accumulation of small failures. He had dreamt of Dawn last night. She had been weeping behind a window in some vast stone building that vaguely resembled the Butler Library on the Columbia campus. The thick glass had nullified her words. All he saw was the tearful contorted face, the gentle mouth moving.

He had read his Freud. He knew that the dream was his personal production. Not sent, as his mother believed, by some spirit messenger from heaven or hell. It was what he wanted to believe—Dawn was regretting her decision to leave him. It was only natural for the blind, hungry id to have these wishes. It was necessary for the intellect to strike them down.

Mark turned his mind to the tasks of the day. A list of

dreary bachelor chores confronted him. Cook breakfast, shop for the week's food, take suit to cleaner, shirts to laundry, demand a new bulb for the refrigerator from his building's elusive handyman. Life without a wife was a debilitating affair. But one could not pick up the telephone and say, "I miss you. I'm sick of shopping. I hate supermarkets." Which was all he could honestly say.

He endured the usual struggle with his artificial leg, rose and began his exercises. He did 100 push-ups with his good right arm. On the bar across the bedroom door he chinned himself 90 times. Then came 100 half curls, 100 knee bends, 100 trunk twisters. He found himself wondering if anyone else in the family still did these exercises. Probably not. Ned had never had a chance to join the group, Randy and John were dead, and George had almost certainly abandoned them. Maybe the old man was doing them, at eighty. It would not surprise him.

The telephone rang. He walked toward it, certain it was Dawn. It was an even more unexpected voice. "Mark? This is Ned. Your brother. I wonder if you could come out to the farm today. We've got a family crisis on our hands."

"What does that mean?"

"This fellow Kilpatrick—the one who's writing the book—seems to be planning to do a job on Dad. At least, he's been prodded in that direction by some of the family —especially George."

It was disconcerting, this calm, mature voice belonging to his little brother. In Mark's mind, Ned was still the callow college boy he had last seen in 1956 or '57.

"What do you need me for?" he asked.

"It would help to know what you told Kilpatrick. What sort of signals you gave him."

"I told him as little as possible. The only signal I gave him was a hint that he wasn't qualified to write the book."

"That's helpful. Even hopeful. Look, Mark. I know you and Dad haven't gotten along. I don't really know why. But I can't believe you don't have some respect and affection for him. We could use your advice. But more than that, I think it's a time when he needs his sons beside him. It's a hell of a thing to discover one of them —I mean George—has been trying to stab him in the back."

Didn't Ned realize how incongruous those words sounded? The Paul Stapleton that Mark knew never needed a son. Need, necessity, was always on the other side. The obligation to obey, to kow-tow, to imitate his towering example—or be banished from his affection. How had Ned managed to survive within that claustrophobic fatherhood without dwindling into a cipher?

"Is this your idea or his—to call me?"

"Mother's, actually. But Dad knows I'm doing it. There won't be any unpleasant scenes, Mark. I don't think he's had any hard feelings toward you for a long time. You should have heard how he talked about you to Jim Kilpatrick. He'll probably never admit it to your face, but he's proud of you, Mark."

"What time should I be there?"

"Come for lunch. We'll talk afterward."

"One?"

"Perfect."

He drove out in his gray Volkswagen. Once past the industrial belt bordering New York, with its ugly factories and miles of dreary houses, it was a pleasant ride. There were still touches of autumnal fire on the hills. Beyond the Watchungs, the city became visible on the northern horizon. Closer, it loomed beside its guardian river like some gray slumbering beast out of prehistory. But it was part of history, part of the Stapleton past, his own past. Its real problem was how to escape history, resist the heavy hand of the past, discover new answers to the old questions and new questions for the old answers. That required the most difficult effort for the human animal: thinking.

His watch told him he was early. He decided to drive around the city and kill fifteen or twenty minutes. He turned off the expressway at the first exit beyond the suspension bridge and found himself in the black ghetto. He was appalled by the pervasive decay, the sagging tenements, the closed stores. Even the housing projects built in the 1950s and 1960s looked battered. The city was old. Within it, Mark had a profound sense of its

299

weight, mass. Questions and answers became muted, even tentative, perhaps presumptuous here.

From behind him came the growl of a police siren. A green-and-white cruiser appeared on his left. A beefy Irish-looking cop on the passenger's side waved Mark to the curb. The cop got out and strolled back to the Volkswagen. "Maybe you can drive like 'at in New York, pal, but aroun' here we got laws against it," he said.

"What did I do?"

"You just went troo 'at red light. Good there wasn't nothin' comin' the other way. A ten-year-old on a bike'd put that tin can ya drivin' outta action. Let's say ya license."

Mark produced his license. "Stapleton," the cop said. "That's a pretty familiar name around here. You one of *the* Stapletons?"

"Judge Stapleton is my father."

"No kiddin'. Hey, Ace," he called to his partner in the cruiser. "Judge Stapleton's his fatha. Ain't that somethin'?" He turned back, smiling nastily. "Now usually we'd let ya go with a warnin'. But because the Judge is so interested in enforcin' the law around here, I feel duty-bound to give a Stapleton a ticket."

Mark started to lose his temper. "I don't like your attitude, Officer," he said. "If you want to keep your badge, just write out the ticket and forget the small talk."

"If I want to keep my badge? Listen to him, Ace. He must think his old man's got influence or somethin'." He peered at Mark's licence. "Let's see, you cleared to drive a car with 'at hook?"

Mark struggled out of the car, fumbling for his reading glasses. "What's your badge number?"

The cop's partner sprang out of the cruiser and barreled around the front fender. He was short and burly, with a swarthy, glowering face. "Get back in the car, Mo," he said.

"I ain't finished writin' the ticket."

"Finish it in the car."

"What's his badge number?" Mark said as Mo retreated.

300

"Now wait a minute, Mr. Stapleton," the partner said. "Before you report him, just lemmy tell ya the story. He got hit by a rock when they was integratin' Buchanan High last winter. He ain't been right since. One more bad report an' he's out of a job."

"Give me his badge number or I'll take yours."

"Seven-eight-two-four-seven."

Mark wrote it down. "Now give me my ticket," he said.

"Forget the ticket. Give him a break. He's got four kids. He was a good cop till he got hit."

"Give me the ticket," Mark said. "I went through a red light. I deserve a ticket."

He pocketed the ticket and drove carefully back to the expressway and resumed his journey to New Grange Township. He had forgotten the gut hatred so many people had for the Stapletons. It reminded him of an incident from his youth, the year before World War II. His brother John had persuaded him to join three of his friends going to a movie in the city. Afterward, John said he knew a bar where they could get a beer, although none of them was twenty-one. The place was downtown on Dock Street and it looked unpromising. In the best of times, their white buckskin shoes and Irish-tweed sports coats and letter sweaters would not have received a warm welcome on Dock Street. In the previous year there had been a series of strikes at Principia Mills that had made the name Stapleton acutely unpopular.

On the way to the men's room, Mark discovered a remarkable dart game being played in the rear. The target was a blowup of his father's face, pasted on a dartboard. He watched, wide-eyed, while Paul Stapleton's cheeks and mouth and forehead were mutilated again and again by those gyrating steel tips. Returning, Mark told John and his friends what he had just seen.

"The sons of bitches," John said. "Let's steal it."

"You'll start a riot. We'll get killed," Mark said.

"Go get the car, Thin Man," John said.

John and his friends, all bruisers like him, marched to the dartboard. They took it off the wall and the three friends crouched to form a football line. John stood

301

behind them calling signals. The bar's regulars watched them, mesmerized. One of the linemen centered the dartboard to John and they charged down the bar, knocking drinkers in all directions. Outside, Mark had backed the car to the door. John emerged with two or three smaller men clinging to him. He threw them off, scaled the dartboard to a friend who had reached the car, and turned to flatten a man coming out the door with a whiskey bottle in his hand. "That's my father," John bellowed. "I'm taking him home where he belongs." He leaped on the running board of the car and they roared away in a shower of bottles and glasses.

The ride home had been hilarious for everyone but Mark. He thought it had been a stupid caper. They could have wound up in the hospital—or worse, the newspapers. He took his responsibility as a Stapleton seriously. He was sure his father would agree with him.

He should have known better. John swaggered into Paul Stapleton's bedroom-study, interrupting the usually sacrosanct four hours of night work, to tell the story and display the trophy. Anyone else in the family would have gotten an angry lecture about law and order, setting an example, befriending the workers. John got that smile which only appeared on the few occasions when Paul Stapleton was genuinely pleased or amused. Mark could not remember a single time when he was the beneficiary of that smile. It was reserved for Randy and John. Mark and George, the lesser breed, never rated more than a cursory or sarcastic grin.

Even now, almost forty years later, with John's heroic muscle and bone so much decay in his grave, the injustice of Paul Stapleton's favoritism still rankled Mark. It was all the more outrageous that an adopted son, someone who did not even belong in the family, should get such treatment. Somehow it made the favoritism a slur, an implication that Mark was deficient, unworthy.

The Volkswagen bounced like a basketball going up the rutted gravel road to the familiar farmhouse. Mark took mild pleasure in parking behind the two Mercedes' in the circular driveway. Two new Mexican houseboys started to lead him through the living room to the patio.

He ignored them and went down the hall to the kitchen. His mother was at the stove sampling a pot of paella. The air was tangy with spices.

"Hello," he said, hesitating in the doorway.

Her face came aglow with that remarkably youthful smile. She limped to him and kissed him on the lips. "I'm so glad you have come."

"Why are you cooking when you can barely walk?"

"I've turned into a Stapleton," she said. "I don't know when to quit." She limped back to the stove and tasted the paella again. She held out the spoon and let him try it. "Remember when you were my taster?" she said. "You always wanted to know in advance."

"Just wary," he said. "I still don't like Mexican cooking very much. Except this dish and a few others."

"How's Dawn?"

"I told you in my last letter. We've separated."

"I thought you might hear from her. Can two people who lived together for over twenty years walk away and never speak again?"

"Apparently."

Maria shoved the paella back in the oven and slammed the door. "You are so much like your great-grandfather, the old general. You forget nothing and forgive nothing."

Mark felt embarrassed and irritated. His mother barely knew Dawn. He disliked Maria's fondness for aphoristic profundities, which usually proved meaningless when analyzed. "I didn't come here to discuss my marital problems," he said.

"I know. Your father's on the patio with Ned and your Aunt Agatha. I'll join you in a moment."

Mark opened the door and stepped into the bright October sunlight. After blinking for a moment, he found them sitting at the glass-topped wrought-iron table beside the reflecting pool. His father stood up, an uncertain smile on his face. Mark was shocked by how wasted, shrunken, he had become. But his handshake still had sinew in it. "Hello Mark," he said. "Good to see you."

Ned said the same thing. He had an animal vitality about him that reminded Mark of John. His handshake was a crusher.

"You look more and more professorial, Mark," Agatha said. She had aged well. There was dignity and serenity in her sharp mannish face.

"You get like the people you work with," he said.

"We were just discussing Ned's sons," his father said. "Who looks like whom. Agatha maintains the youngest boy, Kemble, looks a lot like you."

"How old is he?"

"Ten."

"I weighed about forty pounds when I was ten. A high wind would almost blow me away. I remember how it drove me to despair."

"Kemble's the same way," Ned said. "Always exercising, eating double portions, trying to put on muscle and weight. The middle boy, Rawdon, is built like me and the oldest guy is a hulk, like George."

"Fascinating," Mark said. "Heredity is tough to escape. Kemble has my sympathy."

"He's handling it pretty well," Ned said. "He's twice as smart as the two older guys put together."

"No doubt they beat hell out of him every chance they get, to maintain their superiority."

"Sure," Ned said complacently.

Mark saw that psychologically Ned was an only child. He had no inkling of the wounds brothers could inflict on each other.

Sam Fry emerged from the house to say hello. They shook hands warmly. Sam asked Mark if he still did his exercises. "A hundred push-ups a day," Mark said.

"I still do two hundred," Sam said.

"How about you?" Mark said, turning to his father.

"None, for the past six months," he said glumly. "The doctor told me to cut out everything but riding horseback. Too much of a strain on the ancient ticker. I think this Apache keeps on doing them just to show up old White Eyes. He's malicious that way."

"I prefer squash," Ned said. "Exercises are too boring for me."

"You have to do them in a group when you start, to appreciate them," Mark said. He suddenly felt like an aging tribesman telling an outsider how they had lived in the old days.

Maria and the houseboys appeared with the paella and pitchers of sangría. The conversation grew sketchy. They praised the delicious food, the fine fall weather. Mark told about his run-in with the cop over the ticket.

"Are you going to turn him in?" Paul Stapleton asked.

"I don't know. It probably isn't worth the trouble."

"I think you should give him a break," Paul Stapleton said. "I always tried to make allowances for a guy with a combat record. Those cops were in combat last year, when we started this thing. You should have seen the mob at Buchanan High School. They damn near killed the mayor."

There he was, casually coopting his decision, Mark thought. He could not avoid thinking of the Stapletons as a body with himself as the head.

"Reminds you of the thirties, doesn't it, Mark?" Paul Stapleton said. "They really hated us then, when the union was trying to organize the mills."

"Yes," Mark said. "Remember the night John stole the dartboard?"

Ned had never heard the story before. Mark told it wryly, offhandedly. Ned loved it.

"He was a wild man," Paul Stapleton said. "I'm afraid it was mostly my fault. I should have sat on him a lot harder."

"It was his nature, Paul," Maria said.

The houseboys cleared the table and served coffee. Maria returned to the kitchen to supervise the cleanup. Agatha also excused herself. "I must get down to the hospice. One of our Saturday regulars is ill and I'm filling in."

Speaking more directly to her brother, Agatha added, "I've said my say. It's up to you legal eagles now. Just remember that old adage about vinegar and honey. I don't suppose they teach it in law school. But—"

"It's good advice," Paul Stapleton said. "We'll consider it, don't worry."

"Well," he said as Agatha disappeared into the house. He stirred his coffee. "Ned told you about our problem."

"Yes," Mark said. "I told him I didn't see what I could do about it."

"If the situation turns nasty, I'd like to know where you stand, Mark. This thing could wind up in a courtroom. Or get into the newspapers."

"I wouldn't make a public statement, under any circumstances," Mark said.

Paul Stapleton smiled frostily. "Does that mean you've changed your mind about some of those rotten things you said to me once?"

"Not really. I'm more concerned that some people would try to trace my philosophical ideas to a personal difference with you."

Paul Stapleton nodded curtly. "Fair enough."

Ned was frowning. Was it disapproval of that icy reply? "The last thing we want to do is land in court with this thing."

"What's Kilpatrick found out—that merits this much distress?" Mark asked.

Paul Stapleton hesitated for a moment. He sat back in his chair and gripped the arms. He looked straight at Mark and said, "He has evidence that proves—that would prove in a courtroom—that your brother John was my son by another woman."

Ned's face was somber but unsurprised. He had obviously heard it already. Mark wondered how he had reacted when he first heard it. Probably with not much more emotion than his response to the story of the stolen dartboard. John was a semi-stranger who died when Ned was fifteen. He had never lived in his muscular arrogant shadow.

It was easier to look at Ned than at his father. Mark forced himself to turn his eyes back to Paul Stapleton's face. His father was staring steadily at him, ready to accept whatever response he made. Disbelief, angry scorn, cold contempt. Mark had a sudden sense that he would even welcome anger. But it would be childish. Besides, he did not feel angry.

"Is the other woman still alive?"

Paul Stapleton's graven composure started to crumble. "Yes," he said, lowering his eyes. "I haven't seen her for—decades. I gather she still more or less hates me." He looked past Mark, at the tree-lined hill that marked

306

the western boundary of the farm. "I knew her before I met your mother. She comes from the city. I met her again in Paris in 1917. I was a wild man in those days . . ."

His voice dwindled with each sentence. It was painful to watch him. Mark found himself thinking of his own proud, sullen chastity in the Marines during the war. Listening contemptuously to the make-out artists, telling himself a Stapleton, a true Stapleton, was above such greasy rutting.

His father was struggling through the rest of the story. How he and this woman had separated after his wound in the Argonne, and he did not know John even existed until she dumped him on their doorstep in 1928. Then came words that jerked Mark back into the present and simultaneously evoked another past. "Maybe now you can see why I tended to spoil him. I felt so damn guilty, never being able to tell John that I was his real father. I planned to tell him someday—after Ned grew up. I sort of half planned to tell everyone—someday."

"But Mother knew?" Mark said.

"Yes. That's the main reason I want to stop this thing. For her sake. It was bad enough the first time around, when it was just between the two of us."

Mark nodded mechanically. He felt detached, floating, like a man who had fallen off a building or been blown into the sky by an explosion. Part of him, his mind or memory, roved like a satellite over the past, discovering a new landscape. While his body confronted his father and spoke.

"What does Kilpatrick think about this?"

"It's hard to say. He's been pretty reticent. He's let us do the talking. Especially me. But we know he got mad as hell when he discovered that George was trying to manipulate him. He said some things that gave the impression he was disillusioned with the Stapletons in general and was ready to take us apart. I'm afraid he started with some idealistic, unrealistic notions about us."

"These are the options, as I see it," Ned said. "We can get a court order and try to scare him into surrendering his material, citing various clauses in the contract he

307

signed with us. Or we can forget the contract and pay him whatever he wants, within reason."

"Or appeal to his idealistic side, his feelings for Randy," Paul Stapleton said. "That's what Agatha thinks we should do. She's offered to go see him. She thinks it would be better to approach him in an entirely non-legal, non-threatening way."

"What were his feelings for Randy?" Mark asked.

Paul Stapleton sent Ned into his bedroom to get a letter Kilpatrick had written when Randy died. Reading the effulgent prose, Mark felt his body grow hot, his face flush. First John, now Randy, his other heroically dead, imperishably undefeatable rival. Was this conference a ruse to rub the past into his face? Here was one more proof, in a stranger's words, of his brother's extraordinary capacity for winning admiration, even love. Leaving him with the cold triumphs of the mind.

With which he was content. Thoroughly content.

Suddenly Mark heard Maria's voice: *You forget nothing and forgive nothing.*

This visit was a mistake. He should never have come here. It was absurd, futile, fighting wars with dead men, ghosts.

With a terrific effort, Mark willed himself to concentrate on the problem before him. "That's an impressive letter," he said. "But it's four years old. How does he feel now?"

"Once you feel something that strongly, you never forget it," Paul Stapleton said.

Was that a platitude, or the product of bitter wisdom? Mark wondered. Did it have anything to do with the unnamed woman he had loved in Paris?

"If that's true," Mark said, "I'd forget the first two options for the time being. Court orders seldom solve anything and trying to buy up an idealist is tantamount to insulting him. I think Agatha is right. She—or someone else with nothing personal at stake—should approach him."

"I'm inclined to agree," Paul Stapleton said. "Ned was for getting tough. I didn't want to decide without a third opinion."

"What else can a working-stiff lawyer do but surrender

308

when he's overruled by a judge and a professor?" Ned said with a rueful smile.

"Can you stay for dinner, Mark?" Paul Stapleton asked.

"Sorry," he said, standing up. "I've got a paper to finish. Let me know how this turns out. Now that you've got me—"

He hesitated, but there was no other word: "—involved."

They shook hands. Mark limped to the kitchen and found the houseboys clanking pots in the sink. Maria was in the living room, reading. "Who's your favorite poet these days?" he asked.

"Pablo Neruda," she said, putting the book aside. "A great poet, in spite of his parlor Communism."

"I haven't read a poem in years," Mark said.

"You should," Maria said. "What have you decided?"

"To send Agatha."

"Yes. That is the best thing to do. No question."

She limped beside him to the front door. Mark put his hands on the brass latch. "It was—a shock. About John."

"Yes."

"It changes—a lot."

"It changed a lot then. I had no love to give you—to give anyone—when you needed it most."

"Why did I need it most?" He almost snarled the words.

"Because of your nature."

He shook his head savagely, barely repressing a curse. "When are you going to stop trying to make a saint out of me?"

"I gave that up forty years ago."

"What are you praying for now?"

"That you will become a loving man."

"It isn't part of my heritage."

"You're wrong."

"You can say that, in spite of—?"

"Yes."

For a cruel moment he was tempted to tell her what Paul Stapleton had said to him twenty-five years ago. *It's better to marry one of your own kind.* He suddenly realized the statement was not a denial of love but only a warning about its difficulty.

He thanked Maria for a delicious lunch and kissed her goodbye. He drove home slowly, letting various sentences and phrases ferment in his mind, summoning the way his father had spoken to him, ignoring Ned. *Now you can see why I tended to spoil him.* But the real answer to the spoiling probably lay in those other startling words. *I was a wild man in those days.*

Paul Stapleton wild? That grimly methodical, ruthlessly logical, totally organized man? Impossible. But the evidence was there, in the smile of loving recognition, of secret approval of John's constant recklessness. Above all in John's very existence. Which was also irrefutable proof that there had been passion, and then a choice that left Maria somehow capable of affirming love, in spite of the admission that there had been a terrible wound.

You forget nothing and forgive nothing.

In New York, Mark drove swiftly through the light Saturday traffic to his apartment house. He left the Volkswagen with the black garageman in the basement and rode the elevator to his apartment. For a half hour he walked from empty room to empty room. He ran his finger through the dust on a living-room end table. Jesus, he thought, the place was like a tomb.

Not thinking, teetering down a wire of pure feeling, he grabbed the telephone and dialed. Dawn answered. "This is Mark," he said. "Could we have dinner tonight? We ought to try talking this over. I'm not sure what will come of it. But—it can't do any harm—to talk."

She said yes.

He hung up wondering if he had just made a fool of himself.

XXIV

On the great American road Kilpatrick found temporary peace. The humming tires, the throbbing engine, were anodynes more effective than whiskey. But a man could not keep driving forever. He would have to find something more soothing than the whispered promises of the midnight highway, reaching ahead to sleeping towns and cities, full of supposedly remarkable new experiences. He had tried it before, the dramatic flight from the impossible situation, the escape from responsibility, boredom, disgust. Now he knew how circular such flights inevitably became.

But this was not a flight. It was a search for the truth. Oh yes, the Truth. Put a capital on it, why not? As the miles unraveled Paul Stapleton's story in Kilpatrick's brain, he slowly realized that he had been pursuing the wrong Truth. The bits and pieces of acts that he had assembled all belonged to the man's façade. All were ultimately opaque. Kilpatrick tested this theory against his knowledge of his own father. What did it matter if he assembled every corrupt decision, crooked deal, stolen

election in which James Kilpatrick, Sr., had ever participated? Would he be any closer to discovering the inner
secrets of his arrogant yet ultimately vulnerable soul?

The farther Kilpatrick drove into the American night,
the more he began to discard his original motive for
writing Paul Stapleton's life. To assemble a façade and
pass judgment on it. So many evil pieces, so many good
pieces. Idiocy! Kilpatrick saw it was part of his adolescent view of America. Placed alongside Paul Stapleton,
Kilpatrick was in the Fourth of July stage of American-
ism. It was like comparing the philosphy of a Vatican
cardinal to the faith of a Calabrian peasant.

It was your father. Alone in the dark car, sheltered by
its metal skin, Kilpatrick found those words of Paul
Stapleton no longer painful. He had not sneered them.
Kilpatrick had sensed a certain regret in his voice. Dimly,
just beyond the reach of his headlights, a perception rode.
A sense of—what? Sharing, understanding. *You and I are
in this together, Jim.* In what together? America? No, too
obvious. In the story together, facing the same reality, the
same experience? The wish for the ideal and the brutal
knowledge that it was so often beyond reach, impossible
to uphold, maintain. So often ignored, dismissed by arrogant, careless, hurried Americans.

Kilpatrick flicked his headlights and passed a rumbling
ten-wheel trailer truck. *In it together.* But what he did not
know was where Paul Stapleton had found the strength to
endure this American world, to live out his days with his
will to work, his determination to prevail, his faith in
himself apparently undiminished. That secret lay behind
the façade of his life. It was the truth Kilpatrick wanted
to learn, perhaps needed to learn. He sensed it was
something that had very little to do with America, except
for the accidental fact that Paul Stapleton was American.
Perhaps not even he was completely aware of it. Perhaps
it was the kind of truth that literally lived, flowed, per-
vaded a man's life yet remained as insubstantial as breath.

Would he find it where he was going? Kilpatrick began
to doubt it in Trenton, where he stopped in the State
Library on the banks of the Delaware not far from where
George Washington crossed the river in 1776 to rescue
the sinking American Revolution. That passionate young

rebel, Kemble Stapleton, had been with the ragged freezing men in the big boats.

With the help of a pretty brunette librarian, Kilpatrick found the records of the New Jersey Supreme Court for 1946 and asked her to Xerox the case entitled: *Principia Mills, Inc. v. Smith, Ryan et al.* Kilpatrick sat in the comfortable library, looking out at the green lawn running down to the Delaware, and read the terse legalese summary of the suit of Smith and Ryan, who maintained that the Stapleton-controlled board of directors had defrauded the small stockholders of Principia Mills by selling the company to National Products, Inc., at a bargain price. Writing for a six-man majority of the court, Chief Justice James Kilptarick had dismissed the suit, citing, among other things, the famous English case, *Foss v. Harbottle,* in which the principle was clearly enunciated that "when a fraud on the company or a breach of duty is complained of by a minority only of its shareholders and is approved by the majority, the court cannot interfere."

No inner truth here, just another façade, behind which $100,000 had changed hands, and Smith, Ryan et al. were left to nurse their financial wounds. Kilpatrick spent the rest of the day in the library, reading about the textile industry in New Jersey. It was another façade, and not a very pretty one. In the 1870s, '80s and '90s, the industry made huge profits. It was the era of primitive capitalism. Mill hands worked an average of thirteen and a half hours a day. One writer described their routine: "They rise ere dawn of day, consume their morning meal by candlelight and trudge to the mill to commence their labor ere the rising of the sun; at noon a very short time is allowed them for dinner, and their labor terminates at what is called eight o'clock at night, but which is really (by the time they have their frames cleaned) much nearer nine o'clock. They then take supper and immediately retire to bed in order that they may arise early in the next morning."

No wonder labor troubles were endemic. "Between 1881 and 1900," wrote one historian, "there were 137 strikes in the city. All failed, but the record testifies to a virtual state of war between the employers and the workers."

Around the turn of the century, things started to go sour. Competition multiplied both within the city and outside it, from mills in New England, Pennsylvania, Europe, Japan. Textiles became the "sick man of American industry." The 1912 strike led by the Wobblies had a catastrophic impact, costing the owners tens of millions in cash reserves. From a historical perspective, it was a mortal wound, but neither the victims nor their assailants knew it. The struggle between workers and owners, and the harsh realities of aging plants, low prices, tough competition, continued, with strikes and lockouts, riots and arrests, Communist agitators replacing Wobblies, until the Great Depression of the 1930s snuffed out the whole industry in New Jersey.

Kilpatrick emerged from the library feeling like a witness to blind, ignorant armies clashing by night. He stood outside a bar thinking about scotch, telling himself he was through with booze. He suddenly realized that he had not slept in twenty-four hours. He found a motel, ate a steak in the restaurant and checked into a room. After two hours of staring at television he was sure that he would collapse. Instead, he was even more wide awake. At midnight, he checked out and drove to Washington, D.C. He arrived about 4 A.M., found a medium-priced hotel on Thomas Circle off Connecticut Avenue and tried another hour of television. Still no sleep.

At 9 A.M., fortified by breakfast and several cups of coffee, Kilpatrick called the Senator. He was the first name on the list of Paul Stapleton's purportedly purchased adherents in Congress. Kilpatrick thought of him as the Senator. That was all Randy Stapleton had ever called him. He was National Products, Inc.'s best friend in Washington, a power on the Armed Services Committee. Like a good politician, the Senator remembered Kilpatrick and the name Stapleton still had enough magic to produce an instant appointment.

The Senator had aged in the four years since Kilpatrick had seen him. He had always been a heavy drinker. But he had carried it well. Now it was beginning to show. There were unhealthy pouches beneath his eyes and his cheeks had a flushed scaly sheen. He was a short bulky man with wavy gray hair and a face that sloped to a small combative chin. There was shrewdness and a little sadness in his knowing mouth. The Senator had been in Washington for twenty-four years.

Kilpatrick told him that he was hoping to get his recollections for a biography of Paul Stapleton. The Senator leaned back in his big swivel chair and began taking his own trip into the past.

"I was a captain in his tank battalion. We didn't like him very much when we first got together down in Georgia in the summer of 1941. Most of us were pretty damn pleased with ourselves just to be in the Tank Corps. He shook us up. He told us we were going up against the Germans, the best tankers in the world. He blasted us out of that complacent attitude, that Americans are naturally the best, in peace and war, without hardly trying. He told us the Germans had forgotten more about tank tactics than we'd ever learn, which meant we had to get very tough and very smart in a big hurry, if we wanted to win anything."

The Senator shook his head, smiling to himself. "Pretty soon we plain hated that man. He kept us inside those iron coffins in the Georgia heat for hours at a time, repeating drills, rehearsing tactics. Boys passed out from heat exhaustion, you'd be soakin' sweat into your boots. He didn't give a damn. We'd come back from one of those sessions so beat we could hardly see and he'd get us out of the tanks for an hour of calisthenics. He didn't think much of the Army's exercises. He had his own set. What terrified us was, he didn't just stand there and give orders. He did every exercise right along with us. And he'd been in his tank in the heat right along with us. We couldn't let a World War I veteran get away with that. We gritted our gums and matched him, somehow.

"He was a ferocious disciplinarian. He broke a couple of lieutenants for getting drunk and any enlisted man who didn't salute him got his head taken off. When he inspected our tanks, everything inside them had to be as polished and antiseptic as an operating room.

"But it paid off in combat. That's where we found out why he was so tough with us. In combat you found out the importance of discipline. You don't have time to persuade somebody to go head to head with forty or fifty

Mark IVs and five or six German Tiger tanks, all with guns that outshoot you by five hundred yards. You found out it was worth your life, literally, to know how to handle your tank and your weapons as well as the Germans. They were fantastically good. All I can say is, thank God we outnumbered them."

The Senator talked about battles in North Africa, Sidi-bou-Zid, Sbeitla, Kasserine Pass. His throat grew husky, thinking about friends he had lost. He praised Paul Stapleton's courage, his insistence on taking the same risks as his men. His voice on the tank radio was invariably calm, steady even when the battle was going against them, when there were frantic cries that the Germans were hitting their flanks or rear.

The Senator's most vivid memory was a small battle without a name, after the American defeat at Sidi-bou-Zid. Their battalion, reduced to about eight tanks, had been assigned to guard brigade headquarters. Suddenly they were ordered to retreat. The Germans had broken through at Faïd Pass, far in their rear. Cars, half-tracks and jeeps started west across the desert. They had gone about eight miles when German Mark IV tanks came roaring at them. Paul Stapleton ranged his tanks on both sides of the column and took on the low-slung Nazi monsters, giving the thin-skinned vehicles time to escape.

Toward twilight, Stapleton's tank was hit. He and his crew abandoned it unscathed. He rounded up survivors from other tanks. "I was one of them," the Senator said. "I'd gotten burned pretty bad on my chest and hands and a couple of flying rivets had gone through my leg. I was lyin' in a gully wonderin' if the Germans shot prisoners when the Colonel shows up with ten or twelve others, a lot of them walkin' wounded like me.

"Our column was gone. Nothin' but a dust cloud on the horizon. The Kraut tanks were gone too, probably because they needed gas. But the Colonel said we couldn't just sit there. Brigade was pulling back a good thirty miles and by this time tomorrow the area would be crawling with German patrols. There was only one thing to do, the Colonel decided: start walking.

"We walked all night. Twenty-nine miles. Around dawn I was sure I couldn't go another yard. The Colonel said he'd stay with me. Then I remembered those calisthenics back in the States, how much it hurt to do the last ten push-ups or squats. I said I'd keep going. We made it without losing a man. But we sure as hell collapsed when we got there. The Colonel went straight to brigade headquarters and started wrestling with the red-tape specialists to get new tanks.

"The next day, Ernie Pyle visited our area. The flacks at Brigade told him this guy Stapleton would make good copy. World War I veteran with the endurance of a twenty-year-old. Pyle tried to interview the Colonel. He couldn't get a word out of him about anything he'd done. Pyle finally asked him if he had any message for his family back home.

" 'Just tell them you've seen the old fool,' the Colonel said."

Kilpatrick asked the Senator if Paul Stapleton had helped him get into Congress.

"He put up every damn cent I spent in my first campaign," the Senator said. "About a hundred thousand dollars. Elections were cheaper in 1952."

The Senator assumed he was talking to a friend. He told Kilpatrick he did not think that information was the sort of thing that ought to go into the book. "With Randy's connection to National Products, all sorts of conflict-of-interest shit might hit the fan."

Pretending to be casual, Kilpatrick said he couldn't believe there was anything illegal about it. The Senator emphatically agreed. He had never done anything for Randy or National Products that he wouldn't have done for any other supporter. Sure, he had pushed a few generals around at the Pentagon, to help Randy land a defense contract or two. The generals were getting pushed by a half dozen other senators fighting for *their* boys. That was the way American politics worked. But there were a lot of people these days who wanted to see a dirty deal in every dollar made from or spent by the government.

Kilpatrick could practically hear Peregrine sneering: *Good for the country—and good for the Stapletons.* "Did you ever hear from Judge Stapleton?" he asked.

"He wrote me letters. That was our understanding.

317

He'd write me without any expectation that he could change my mind, that I'd vote a certain way. But I valued those letters. They influenced my attitude. His main point was always caution, care, to avoid doing a thing if we can't do it right. He was appalled by half-ass operations like the Bay of Pigs, by the way we barged into Vietnam, armed people and encouraged them to fight, and got ourselves into a war that violated every military principle in the book."

The Senator talked about the letters Paul Stapleton had written to him during the Vietnam years. "There wasn't any asinine uplift in them. He'd seen us fuck up before. He wasn't surprised and he didn't waste any time wailin' over the latest Niagara of spilt milk."

The Senator sighed. "I just wish I could have done somethin' for him."

Kilpatrick trudged back to his hotel room. Hopeless. The Senator was another façade. Kilpatrick watched television for a while and tried to sleep. Hopeless. He called other congressmen on the list Dwight Slocum had given him and made appointments to see them. He called Lieutenant General Mark Stratton in Alexandria, Virginia, and arranged to see him at his apartment. He watched television and tried to sleep again. Hopeless.

He went out and bought a quart of scotch.

Several days later, Kilpatrick sat on the edge of a bed in a motel reading a paragraph of curious prose.

Perhaps the history of Principia Mills is the best answer to Peregrine's denunciation of Stapleton males. It explains why Bowood was an ice factory for Anne Randolph Stapleton, it might even satisfy Muriel Bennett's bitter curiosity about the Stapleton fascination for tanks. For the Stapletons, peace was only another version of war. They were embattled every moment of their lives. From their first moments of self-consciousness, waves of hatred beat upon them. Inevitably this meant that they steeled their minds, nerves, souls, to resist this psychic destruction. They were warrior knights on the marches of capitalism. Contrary to romance, warriors seldom make good lovers. They find it impossible to shed their armor, to relax nerves contorted against inner fear and outer threat,

318

to escape the ruined faces of the defeated, even in their dreams.

Kilpatrick peered at these fervent words. They were neatly typed. He did not understand them. He did not know where he was or where he had been recently.

The motel room was hot. It had sea-green walls. A painting of the Revolutionary War battle of Gilford Courthouse was on one wall. Charging redcoats were being slaughtered by point-blank cannon fire.

An empty bottle of Ballantine's scotch was on the maple dresser.

The Irish-American's final solution.

Kilpatrick tried to remember what had happened. He slowly reconstructed the trip to Washington, D.C., the interview with the Senator. He recalled not being able to sleep. After that, only fragments. He remembered calling Allyn. He had told her very seriously that even though he was a drunk, she must not become one. A drunk was a waste. The waist went to waste. Or vice versa. He had wanted to make her laugh one more time, the way they had laughed the first time he had visited her. Instead, she had started to cry.

Thereafter he found it hard to separate the real from the possible. He might have called Muriel Bennett and told her she was perfect casting for the shark in *Jaws II*. He might have called Dwight Slocum and told him that he was going to write the book in blood and would he care to contribute a quart? He might have called Agatha Stapleton and told her that he missed Peregrine's cooking on the great American road. He might have called Mark Stapleton and urged him to send his father a birthday card. He might have called Paul Stapeleton and told him how much he was enjoying this trip down the River of Doubt.

The tape recorder sat on the dresser beside the empty scotch bottle. Maybe the machine had a better memory. Kilpatrick rummaged in his briefcase for tapes. He stuck one in the machine.

An old man's ragged voice started roaring recollections of World War I and II. Lieutenant General Mark Stratton had spent too much time talking inside tanks. He was

319

incapable of speaking below a bellow. Kilpatrick remembered meeting him in his apartment. Stratton was built like a tank, wide and low-slung, with a crest of glistening gray hair, a nose like the snout of a cannon, a jaw borrowed from Mount Rushmore.

"PAUL STAPLETON WAS THE IDEAL CITIZEN SOLDIER. HE WAS—HE IS—WHAT'S MADE THE AMERICAN SOLDIER THE BEST IN THE WORLD. IT ISN'T PROFESSIONAL ASSHOLES LIKE ME. WE'RE A TINY GODDAMN MINORITY. WITHOUT MEN LIKE HIM TO PROVIDE THE LEADERSHIP AT THE REGIMENTAL AND COMPANY LEVEL YOU CAN'T BUILD A WINNING ARMY.

"HE WAS THE COOLEST BASTARD I'VE EVER SEEN IN BATTLE. I'VE ONLY MET A HALF DOZEN LIKE HIM. NO FEAR, THE SON OF A BITCH HAD NO FEAR GLANDS. THEY SAY WASHINGTON WAS THAT WAY. PATTON TRIED TO BE. HE WAS ALWAYS TAKING HIS GODDAMN PULSE UNDER FIRE. BUT GEORGO WAS NORMAL. HE JUMPED WHEN A BIG ONE CAME IN. I DON'T THINK STAPLETON HAD A PULSE—

"—DOWN ON THE MEXICAN BORDER IN '16 WE GOT A COUPLE DAYS' LEAVE AND HEADED FOR GALVESTON. STAPLETON BOUGHT UP ONE OF THE BEST WHOREHOUSES IN TOWN. OLD GALVESTON TRADITION. THE BUYER CLOSES THE DOORS AND ANNOUNCES THAT EVERYONE'S HIS GUEST FOR THE NEXT TWENTY-FOUR HOURS. IT'S AN INSULT IF YOU TRY TO GET OUT. GUYS HAVE BEEN SHOT FOR TRYING IT. THAT GODDAMN WEEKEND MUST HAVE COST STAPLETON TWO THOUSAND—"

He spun the tape.

"STAPLETON WAS A BORN TANKER. YOU KNOW WHAT THAT MEANS? HE WENT RIGHT IN, HE BUTTONED UP AND WENT RIGHT IN. THERE WEREN'T MANY LIKE HIM. MOST OF THEM WANTED TO KNOW WHAT THE ARTILLERY WAS DOING, WHY THERE WAS NO AIR SUPPORT. STAPLETON DIDN'T ASK QUESTIONS. HE DIDN'T GIVE SPEECHES. HE JUST SAID 'FOLLOW ME.' "

He spun the tape.

"I'LL NEVER FORGET MOROCCO. IF HE HADN'T STOPPED THOSE GODDAMN VICHY FROG TANKS THEY'D HAVE

KNOCKED US INTO THE ATLANTIC. CAN YOU IMAGINE WHAT THAT WOULD'VE MEANT? KICKED INTO THE SEA BY THE FROGS, IN THE FIRST FIGHT OF THE WAR, BEFORE THE KRAUTS EVEN GOT THERE? IT WOULD'VE TAKEN A YEAR TO PUT MORALE BACK TOGETHER.

"I CAME ASHORE JUST AS THE FIGHT ENDED. STAPLE-TON WAS IN THE TURRET OF HIS TANK LOOKING LIKE A GUY WHO'D JUST RUN NINETY-SIX YARDS FOR A TOUCHDOWN. THERE WERE BURNING TANKS AND DEAD FROGS ALL OVER THE PLACE. I SAID, 'HOW THE FUCK DID YOU DO IT, PAUL, WITH NO RADIOS?' I KNEW HIS TANK RADIOS WEREN'T WORKING. THERE WASN'T A GODDAMN RADIO IN THE WHOLE TASK FORCE THAT WORKED. THE SALT AIR RUINED THE BATTERIES. WE WOULD HAVE DONE BETTER WITH A COUPLE DOZEN FUCKING PIGEONS. HE SAID, 'I GAVE MY ORDERS THE WAY WE DID IN FRANCE THE LAST TIME AROUND.'

"THAT'S WHEN I FOUND OUT HE WALKED FROM TANK TO TANK, WALKED FOR CHRIST'S SAKE, WITH SEVENTEEN FROG MACHINE GUNS AND SEVENTEEN CANNON SHOOTING EVERYTHING THEY COULD LOAD AT HIM. THEN HE STARTED TELLING ME HOW A KID CAPTAIN FROM THE MIDWEST—THE GUY'S A SENATOR NOW—DESERVED THE DSC FOR KNOCKING OUT FOUR OR FIVE FROG TANKS. HE'S TRYING TO GIVE HIS GODDAMN MEDAL AWAY BEFORE HE EVEN GETS IT. TYPICAL. HE DIDN'T WIN THE WAR THAT DAY BUT HE SURE AS HELL STOPPED US FROM LOSING IT. AND SAVED MY THREE-STAR ASS IN THE BARGAIN."

He spun the tape.

"—SON JOHNNY. NEVER THOUGHT THAT KID BELONGED TO HIM. MURIEL BENNETT MUST HAVE SLEPT WITH EVERYONE ON THE GODDAMN GENERAL STAFF BEFORE THE WAR ENDED."

Spin.

"—ANYBODY ELSE FOR A FATHER THAT KID WOULD HAVE BEEN A CRIMINAL. HE WOULD HAVE BEEN ROBBING BANKS BY THE AGE OF SIXTEEN. HE WAS BORN TO RAISE HELL. JOHNNY WAS IN MY DIVISION DURING MOST OF WORLD WAR II. I GOT PATTON TO PIN THOSE LIEUTENANT'S BARS

ON HIM. IF IT WASN'T FOR ME HE WOULD HAVE LOST THEM WITHIN A WEEK. HE WAS ALWAYS GETTING CAUGHT IN BED WITH THE MAYOR'S DAUGHTER OR THE PRIEST'S FAVORITE NIECE. AFTER THE WAR WE WERE STATIONED IN CZECHOSLOVAKIA AND HE STARTED FOOLING AROUND WITH A DAME WHO WAS GOING STEADY WITH A RUSSKY CAPTAIN. THE RUSSKY SHOWS UP ONE NIGHT WHILE JOHNNY'S IN THE MIDDLE OF THINGS. THE RUSSKY GOES FOR HIS PISTOL AND JOHNNY SHOOTS HIM BETWEEN THE EYES. HE WAS LIKE HIS FATHER, A DEAD SHOT WITH A HANDGUN. WE HAD A HELL OF A TIME STRAIGHTENING THAT ONE OUT—"

Spin.

"—SON GEORGE WAS ANOTHER STORY. WHAT A GODDAMN MESS THAT WAS. IN ITALY, YOU KNOW. THE BASTARD JUST TURNED TAIL AND RAN. PAUL WOULDN'T DO A THING FOR HIM. INSISTED ON A REGULAR COURT-MARTIAL. BY THAT TIME THE GUY WAS BABBLING. THEY GAVE HIM A PSYCHIATRIC DISCHARGE—"

Spin.

"—GOT ME TO STICK OUT MY NECK ON DESEGREGATING THE ARMY IN '46 AND '47. I GOT HIM IN TO SEE EISENHOWER, BRADLEY, ALL THE FOUR- AND FIVE-STARS IN THE PENTAGON. HE TALKED A LOT OF THEM INTO RECOMMENDING IT TO TRUMAN. I USED TO TELL HIM HE RUINED MY GODDAMN CAREER. HE SAID ANYBODY AS INSUBORDINATE AS I WAS DIDN'T NEED ANY HELP IN THAT DEPARTMENT—"

The general talked about Korea and Vietnam. He grew murderous. He practically recited the list of names on the honor roll of the dead at West Point. He talked about John Stapleton's death in Korea. The general had been Deputy Chief of Staff at the Pentagon. He had gotten Paul Stapleton the whole sad story. As Stratton drained his fifth martini, he mentioned, as if it was a matter of no importance, that his only son, a major, had been killed in Vietnam.

Kilpatrick played a half dozen tapes of interviews with senators and congressmen. They had all been in World

War II with Paul Stapleton. They all told Kilpatrick, off the record, how he had put up the money for them to run for public office the first time. In return, all he asked was their respectful attention when he wrote to them. Never, they insisted, never, had he asked for a direct political favor, or their vote on a specific question. In the end they coughed and sighed and finally apologized because they couldn't take his advice on national affairs. He was politically unrealistic. He recommended drastic, daring solutions to problems—like a national school integration program passed by Congress, the invasion of North Vietnam or the immediate withdrawal of the American Army from South Vietnam.

Kilpatrick peered into his briefcase. One more tape. On it, a non-political name: Ray Campbell. Who was he? "The Campbells Are Coming." Dwight Slocum's growl. Oh, yes. Now Kilpatrick remembered where he was. In North Carolina, not far from the famous battleground of Guilford Courthouse. In Barnstable, North Carolina, the southern refuge of Principia Mills. He remembered driving past the gray high-windowed mills beside a modest river. A company sign read: *Principia Mills. A Division of National Products. Inc.*

He had driven past the mills to park on a tree-shaded street before a freshly painted two-story tan house. A broad-shouldered black man wearing an undershirt and overalls was sitting on the porch looking at a football game on a portable television set. Yes, he said. He was Ray Campbell. He had been very reluctant to talk about the trouble they had had with union organizers when the mills first moved to Barnstable. Only after Kilpatrick showed him the contract he had signed with the Stapletons to write the book did Campbell reluctantly begin.

The story he told was far from edifying. Why bother to play it? Why bother, period? Ray Campbell was just another façade, like the senators, the congressmen, the general. Paul Stapleton peered at him through their windows, sometimes smiling, sometimes frowning, sometimes good, sometimes evil. But the man himself, the inward man Kilpatrick was now seeking, never emerged.

A knock on the door. He opened it. Agatha Stapleton stood there, a tentative smile on her earnest angular face.

She was wearing a mannish blue suit. Her gray hair peered from beneath a narrow-brimmed blue hat. With her was Allyn, wearing a dark green knit dress. She looked haggard, as if she too had trouble sleeping.

Kilpatrick was sure he was having a hallucination. At any moment they would turn into the Furies. Allyn's russet red hair would go crinkly gray. Agatha's mouth would corrode to a wrinkled sneer. Kilpatrick stood there blinking into the sunlight, waiting for the horror to begin. Beyond them he saw the inner court of the motel, his Corvette, a highway, fields and woods.

"We're real, Mr. Kilpatrick," Agatha said, practically reading his mind.

"Come in," he said.

Agatha sat down on the unmade bed. Kilpatrick chose a chair. He was afraid of getting the shakes. He pressed his shoulders against the back of the chair and gripped the bottom of it to steady himself.

"When is the last time you had anything to eat?" Allyn said.

"I don't know," Kilpatrick said.

"I'll go get something. There's a fast-food place down the road."

Kilpatrick shook his head. "I'll only get sick. Just get coffee. A lot of coffee."

Allyn departed. Agatha put her handbag down on the bed beside her and took off her gloves. "I don't know how to begin, Mr. Kilpatrick," she said. "Perhaps I should explain how we got here. You called Allyn and said some very alarming things. You were drunk. By this time we already knew about George's plan to sabotage the book, and Allyn's—cooperation. When she saw its impact on you, she regretted it, extremely. She told me about your call. We chartered a private plane and flew down here."

"To talk me into quietly withdrawing?"

"That is what Paul and Ned suggested. Allyn is here for the precise opposite reason. To tell you to do what you please. She will supply the money—she has an independent income—to back you. She thinks you deserve the right to scourge the Stapletons. Perhaps you do. But I have a third alternative. I have persuaded Paul to agree to pay you your full fee to complete your research—with the understanding that nothing will be done with it—no book will be published. When you complete your work you will hand over all your material to me, to be placed in my vault."

Kilpatrick shook his head. He did not mean no. He was admiring the subtlety of this smooth, serene old woman. Agatha thought he was disagreeing. She politely pressed her argument.

"It is done all the time, Mr. Kilpatrick. Visit the Oral History Room of the Columbia Library or the presidential libraries at Hyde Park and Independence. You will find all sorts of files containing diaries, recollections, private papers, closed for the next fifty or even a hundred years. When I die, the Stapleton papers will be given to the state historical society with appropriate provisions for when they can be used."

"What do you mean by complete my research?" Kilpatrick asked.

"Interview anyone else you feel is needed to get to—"

"The inner truth?"

"I don't remember saying that to you."

"Your brother told me you said it to him."

"Yes," Agatha said, obviously overcoming some interior reluctance. "Whatever you need to get to—that."

"I need to interview you. And Mrs. Stapleton."

"Yes," Agatha murmured, suddenly almost timid. "Especially Maria."

"Can you arrange it?"

"I'll try."

"Then I agree."

Agatha blinked in disbelief. She had not expected to win so easily. She studied Kilpatrick for a moment. "You know this is a serious matter with us," she said.

"It's serious with me too. You must know that, if Allyn's told you anything about me—and her."

"She's told me very little. But I've been able to guess— a few things," Agatha said.

She fished in her purse for a moment. "I am perfectly willing to take your word. But Ned felt an agreement ought to be signed."

She handed Kilpatrick a letter on Stapleton, Talbot

stationery which repeated the proposition in legal language. Kilpatrick asked Agatha for a pen. He signed it as Allyn returned with a large container of coffee in either hand.

"Mr. Kilpatrick has accepted my suggestion. Isn't that wonderful, Allyn?" Agatha said.

Allyn looked angrily past Agatha at Kilpatrick. "Is that what you really want to do, Jim?" she asked.

"Yes," he said.

Allyn poured the coffee into plastic cups and gave one to Agatha and one to Kilpatrick. They sipped it in silence for several minutes.

"Can you—stop drinking, Mr. Kilpatrick?" Agatha said.

"I'm going to start trying," Kilpatrick said. "I stopped for ten years. I'm pretty sure I can do it again."

"Why did you come down here to North Carolina? Isn't most of the history of Principia Mills in the files of Stapleton, Talbot?"

"I came down here to see a man named Ray Campbell," Kilpatrick said. "Would you like to hear my interview with him?"

Agatha looked dubious. She murmured something about the plane. But that look Allyn had given him made Kilpatrick want to show this charming old lady a sample of what he was giving up. The Stapletons had made him writhe. He was entitled to make them squirm a little.

He dropped the tape into the machine. In a moment Ray Campbell's dark, husky Negro voice filled the room.

"Ah was a sergeant in the 366th Infantry. Colonel Stapleton come up and put me in command of the company after his son George had that—nervous trouble. You know about that? The next night we went back across the Cinquale Canal on a raid and we done pretty good. We killed a couple dozen Germans. He got me a Silver Star. After the war I come home here and started farmin' on shares like my daddy before me.

"One day I get this telegram from Colonel Stapleton to call him long-distance collect. I went down to the village and put through the call. He asked me if I wanted to get my ass off the farm for good. I told him I'd do just about anything for that. He said, 'Good. I want you to round up

326

thirty or forty of the toughest boys you can find. Be sure they know how to shoot a gun. Combat experience preferred.'

"There was a lot of us from the division in my neighborhood. I didn't have no trouble roundin' up forty good boys. The Colonel telegraphed me the cash and we come down here by bus. They were just finishin' Number One mill. Colonel Stapleton took us through it that night. He explained how it was goin' to be the most modern mill in the world. It was going to be a good place to work.

"He said they was comin' down here to get away from the unions. He said the union bosses ruined the business up North, they were always grabbin' money under the table. But the union was comin' after them. They were bringin' in a bunch of bimbos with guns and clubs and they was gonna try to organize the mill.

"That meant a black man was never gonna get a job there. Up North, the union wouldn't let a black man into the mill, except to push a broom and clean the shithouses. If the union won down here, they'd go right in with the rednecks and keep us on the farms for the next hundred years.

"Colonel Stapleton's idea was to stop them before they come to town. He had a spy in their organization. They were comin' down in a week's time in about six or seven cars. They'd have rifles and maybe a few machine guns. He wanted to know if we'd fight them. He offered a hundred dollars cash to every man who said he'd fight. All but five signed up. The Colonel spent the next week trainin' us up in the hills. He got us the best weapons, Garand rifles, Browning automatics.

"We waited for them where the road bent into a big curve in the hills about ten miles north of here. It was deserted country then. We set up a phony accident. Turned over a truck full of watermelons and scattered them all over the highway. People had to come to a dead stop and crawl around it on the shoulder of the road. The union boys had to slow down the same way. We opened up on them and blew out almost every damn tire in the first volley. But those guys were tough. They piled out of the cars with guns in their hands and tried to make a fight of it. We started shootin' to kill, like the colonel told us.

327

They took cover in the woods and we went after them. It was a real hot little war for about a half hour.

"At first they thought they had nothin' to worry about. 'They're just niggers, nothin' but niggers,' one of them yelled. That was the last thing that son of a bitch ever said. I took care of him personally. That was when they found out the niggers had outflanked them. I took about fifteen guys and worked around their right, while the Colonel and the rest of the boys pinned them down from the front. The flank attack broke their backs. They threw down their guns and ran like Satan himself was on their tails. They left behind about ten dead and a dozen wounded. We took the wounded down to a doctor here in town in the truck. Then we come back, picked up our melons, set their cars on fire and went home. Nobody from the sheriff's office ever said a word about it, far as I know. I guess the Colonel took care of them.

"We all got jobs in the mill. I moved right up to foreman as soon as I got the hang of the business. . . ."

Kilpatrick turned off the tape recorder. Agatha was looking dismayed. "How terrible," she said. "It makes me feel—childish. To think that all the money we've made since 1945 depended on—that. And I never knew it. Never even heard of it."

"I'm glad I heard it," Allyn said.

Long before the tape ended, Kilpatrick felt ashamed of himself. Paul Stapleton would never have exposed any woman—above all his sister—to this humiliation. He was going to apologize—until he saw how differently Allyn reacted. He swung between them, not sure which generation he preferred, the man in the middle, ambivalent as usual.

"It's part of what I told you in our first talk," Agatha said. "Grandfather and Father—the influence—the difference, if you will—between them. I'll try to explain it on the flight home. We'll have two uninterrupted hours. Peregrine won't be there to bully me out of telling it my way."

Agatha went looking for a telephone to call the airport. Allyn sat down on the bed and studied Kilpatrick. "You look awful," she said.

"You're looking pretty down yourself."

328

"I'm trying to get off pills, cocaine and booz simultaneously. It isn't easy. They may cart me away."

"Makes my problem seem trivial."

"I didn't mean to sound that way. I came down here to back you up, if necessary. To put up the money you needed if you wanted to tell Aunt Aggie to go to hell. You've got a right to do and say what you please about the Stapletons. I'm not sure I like her third alternative."

"It's a good idea," Kilpatrick said.

"The day after you split I went out to see George. I told him I wanted to drop the whole business. He went berserk. I saw just how crazy he was. How much hate there was. It scared me. Especially after—you."

She smiled sadly. "I guess I really came down here to say I'm sorry. And to tell you—I did care. As usual, I found out too late. It was like my father. All that crazy love I had for him was—is—sort of retrospective. I really kind of disliked or resented him when he was alive, for leaving me at the mercy of the old folks."

Kilpatrick gazed at Allyn's lowered head, her mournful mouth. He felt desire, love, stir in his body. But he forbade it. He said goodbye to facile febrile dreams of second youth. He said goodbye to the ghost of his son Kevin. He would try to repay the debt of gratitude he owed that other ghost, Randy Stapleton, and then say goodbye to him.

"I wanted to tell you something too," he said. "Something that stuff about ghosts left out. I was there too, loving you."

Allyn nodded. "I'm glad. I'm ready to try—again. If you are. Try it for real, this time."

"First I think we ought to finish this trip we've taken together," Kilpatrick said. "That's why I accepted Agatha's offer. It's a chance to go deeper, to ask serious questions."

Allyn looked skeptical. But the idea intrigued her. "There are things I'd like to ask Maria. Do you think I could go with you when you see her?"

"That's something you'll have to ask her."

"I'll call her," Allyn said. "But I'll be very surprised if she or Agatha has much to say."

There was more than skepticism in those words. Kilpatrick also heard echoes of the sullen resentment that had entangled Allyn's life. He looked at the empty scotch bottle and wondered whether he too was in danger if no one else had anything to say. It meant that he would be left outside, still confronting the façade of Paul Stapleton's life, playing with theories when what he needed in his trembling flesh was the hard muscle of personal truth.

XXV

Agatha Stapleton studied Jim Kilpatrick as he called Ray Campbell and asked him to find someone who could drive his car home. Did she really have this wounded, surly man under control? She wished she could ask Allyn, who obviously knew him better—very much better, Agatha feared. But she was not at all certain that Allyn had herself under control.

On the flight down, Agatha had recognized depression on Allyn's frowning forehead and tense, troubled mouth. She had avoided Agatha's attempts at conversation, preferring her own gloomy, silent cocoon. Agatha had felt helpless and sad. In the early sixties, when Allyn had been in her teens, they had been friends. They had gone to plays, shopped together in New York. Agatha had tried to be a helpful listener, an alternative parent, who understood why Allyn resented her grandparents' intense supervision of her life. But this modest hope—and the friendship—had lapsed when Allyn went to Bryn Mawr. The youth culture of the sixties was at its height. Agatha had been relegated to the role of irrelevant aging aunt.

On the ride to the airport Agatha found herself hesitat-

ing to talk to Jim Kilpatrick with Allyn listening. She
shook off this final inhibition. This was history, the truth
as truth, that she was serving now. She would speak in
the same frank spirit in which her long-dead ancestor
Hugh Stapleton had written his shocking diary of his life
as a Continental Congressman. No matter that Allyn
might be disillusioned. It was time for her to learn to live
with disillusion. No matter that Jim Kilpatrick might be
looking forward to asking questions that would make
Agatha Stapleton squirm, as she had in fact squirmed
while she listened to Ray Campbell tell the brutal story of
how Principia Mills went South.

Aboard their rented Lear jet, Kilpatrick unpacked his
compact black tape recorder as soon as they were air-
borne. He placed it on the seat between him and Agatha.
Allyn sat next to him, looking like she was prepared to
disapprove of everything she heard. The first question
made it clear that Kilpatrick was not going to waste any
time getting down to essentials.

"When did you stop hating your brother, and why?
According to Peregrine, he destroyed your chance to have
a happy marriage and Peregrine's chance to live a normal
—that is, straight—life."

"I did hate him for what he did to me and Peregrine,"
Agatha said. "I married Dwight Slocum to spite him. I
thought Paul had become Grandfather and Maria was
some kind of Spanish witch who had masterminded the
transportation. I was through with being a Stapleton. I
wanted Dwight to vulgarize all traces of breeding from
my bones and flesh. I saw him as a prototype of all that
was gross and greasy in the American spirit.

"I was startled to discover that Dwight was not a
walking generalization. He was a very specific human being. He had aspirations to be someone dramatically different from the person he was born—another very common
human failing. He saw me as a magical person, who
carried somewhere within my unremarkable physique the
power to transform him from a boor into a gentleman. I
did not seem to occur to him that headmasters and
college professors had tried and failed. Why he thought
Agatha Stapleton would have the power is a testimony to
human nature's capacity for self-delusion.

"I was amazed when Dwight bought a Park Avenue duplex and began talking about raising a family. He already had a son, Dwight, Jr., by his first marriage. I told him I had no interest in children. All I wanted was a good cook, a decent butler and a reliable bootlegger. I also had no interest in domesticating Dwight Jr., who was already displaying most of his father's worst tendencies. I rounded up artists and writers and other people whom Dwight considered subversive and Paul would gladly have exiled. I tried to outdo Muriel Bennett, who was playing the same lost generation game in Europe. My motto was, why go to Paris to degenerate? It was more fun to do it in New York, where there were more Americans to shock.

"Dwight put up with it for a while because he was sure I would get over it. He was sure my Stapleton genes would triumph. But after a year or so, he tried to exert his authority as a husband. That was when things started going really sour. We had a wild exchange of insults. He told me I was no good in bed—which I'm afraid was true.

"I told him he was boring in bed and everywhere else. I set out to become—shall we say more proficient?—in bed with the help of a psychiatrist and several male friends. Dwight sought the standard consolation of the outraged husband. We were a marvelous pair.

"Then came 1929, and an abrupt end to our private adventures. The great world intruded its dismal distresses on our disordered spirits. Dwight had been one of the big bulls of the Twenties market. He was dreadfully battered by the crash. He emerged from the wreckage with little more than his father's old patent medicine company, which went on selling its junk as if the Depression did not exist. In fact, I believe sales went up as people sought escape from the awful realities of the 1930s. Slocum's Remedy is mostly alcohol."

Agatha looked out the window. They were passing over Washington, D.C. The monuments to the past and the buildings in which the future was being constructed were white toys in the late October sun. From ten thousand feet, both were unreal. Perhaps the only important thing was authenticity, in the past or the present. The truth as

333

felt, experienced, without fear. Agatha was enjoying herself.

"Where did Dwight get the ten million to rescue Principia Mills?" Kilpatrick asked.

"He borrowed it, putting up Slocum's Remedy for collateral. I persuaded him to do it, by promising to be a faithful wife."

"Why did you do that?"

"My mother died in 1935. It was a slow, painful death, from cancer. At first I tried to ignore her. She had spent the previous decade in Europe. My brother Malcolm begged me to go to her. He couldn't spare the time from the mills. Then Peregrine wrote me a long, very moving letter which stirred some of the love I once felt for her. Children take sides in an unhappy marriage, you know. I had sided rather passionately with my father. So had Paul.

"I went over, and was with her for the last month. It was devastating. She was bitter and empty and ultimately pathetic. She had a suite at the Scribe, not the worst but far from the best hotel in Paris. She was short of cash. Paul refused to give her any money although her income from the mills had declined drastically. I had to get money from Dwight to pay her back bills. Peregrine tried to help her. But he had as little money sense as she had. He was inclined to gestures like filling her room with roses.

"But it was Mother's poverty of spirit that distressed me most. I saw how sterile the raw assertion of the ego, the will, came to be at the end. How hollow idealism could become, when the deed seldom matched the word. I tried to comfort her. But she needed something I couldn't give her. Perhaps a chance to live her life again. Or comfort from someone with faith, spiritual resources, which I singularly lacked.

"Her death alone would have sent me home from Europe a troubled woman. I also re-established contact with Peregrine. He was a very contented homosexual, making a rather good living as a fabric designer. It was hard to tell myself that Paul had been totally wrong about preventing our marriage. I brought Mother's body home on the boat with me and we had a funeral service in the city. She had specifically requested it before she died. I think she saw it as a gesture of revenge against Paul. I wasn't averse to one myself, in spite of my second thoughts about Peregrine. Mother's awful death had stirred my sympathy for her, my sense of solidarity with her as a woman. I knew Paul had practically driven her abroad after an ugly scene when she tried to intervene on behalf of me and Peregrine.

"I stayed at Bowood with my brother Malcolm and his wife. Malcolm poured out his anguish over what was happening at the mills. I felt so sorry for him. I could see that he took it as a personal defeat and it was ruining his health and wrecking his marriage. It also dawned on me that if the mills collapsed, I would be penniless, and pretty much at Dwight's mercy. My behavior as his wife would have made it difficult for me to win a decent divorce settlement.

"I will never forget the day of the burial. It was December. The sky was dirty gray, full of low scudding clouds. An absolutely harrrowing wind was blowing off the river. The grave was in our family plot in Woodlawn Cemetery, on the hill just above the mills. Father's tombstone was just to the left, and beside him, Grandfather's. I found myself standing next to Paul. He stared straight ahead, his face rigid, refusing even to look at me. As the minister finished his prayers, we turned away in opposite directions.

"I felt a hand on my arm. It was Maria. 'It must have been a hard death to watch,' she said.

" 'Yes,' I said in a voice as cold as the wind.

" 'It was good that you were with her,' Maria said. 'My mother died last year in Mexico City. I used the children as an excuse—not to go.'

"I was a little staggered by this revelation. It made me realize how little I knew about this woman. But I told myself it was too late to change our relationship now.

"Maria glanced away from me, at Paul and Malcolm, standing side by side, their backs to us. They were talking quietly, looking down at the mills.

" 'Paul is afraid to ask your help to save the company,' Maria said. 'He thinks you will only abuse him.'

"The idea of Paul being afraid of me sounded absurd. I

was about to say something snide about how little she
knew her husband, when Maria said, 'I know it won't be
easy to forgive him. He did a terrible thing to you. I
begged him not to interfere. But he was sure the politicians would use Peregrine to blackmail the family.'

" 'Has he told you to say this?' I asked.

"Maria shook her head. 'I've learned to regret certain
things he has done. To see myself as—independent of
him in some ways.' "

Agatha sat back in her seat, her eyes half closed, no
longer looking at the tape recorder. She was there in the
freezing cemetery, before the open grave, staring down at
the bronze coffin. Below them, the red-brick mills emitted
the muffled clatter of whirling looms and spindles. Beyond their roofs the gray December river flowed like a
sullen, unwilling witness.

"Maria found it terribly difficult to keep talking into
my hostile stare. Remember, too, that I'd been horrible to
her ever since she came into the family. I thought Paul
had made a dreadful mistake, marrying her.

"She said she wanted me to forgive Paul. 'I know
forgiveness is not easy, I know from experience it takes
prayer. Years of prayer. I am not talking about our
foolish quarrels. I am talking about me and Paul.'

"Stupid little Catholic peasant, I thought. I couldn't
decide which offended me most, her assumption that
Agatha Stapleton prayed or the attempt to share her
marital problems.

" 'Love depends on forgiveness,' Maria said. 'I have
learned that much. And without love they wither, these
American men. They grow as cold as your winters. Like
your grandfather.'

"A most incredible thing happened to me," Agatha
continued. "I answered her, answered Maria, from my
heart. It was the first time I had let my heart speak in ten
years. Perhaps only the second time in my whole life. The
first was when I told Peregrine I loved him.

" 'But they don't love us,' I said to Maria. I remember
my voice hissed like a snake. 'They don't love us.'

" 'They don't know how,' she said. 'That is why love
depends on us—forgiving them.'

336

"Those words struck me with stunning force. This woman, this foreigner, talked about loving while I was turning my back on my family, all but gloating over their misfortunes. I remembered my brother Malcolm's haggard face at the dinner table the night before. I walked over to Malcolm and Paul and said, 'Is it possible I could do something to help?'

"That was the beginning of the beginning. The wall of ice between Paul and me did not thaw immediately. I went to Dwight with the news of Principia's woes. He was interested but he simply did not have the money, unless he borrowed heavily on the patent medicine company—his last substantial holding. He asked, with his usual bluntness, why should he risk that for me when all I'd done was make him miserable?

"I detected a note of genuine regret in those last words. I offered to reform, to make a genuine effort to be a loving wife, if he rescued the mills. Dwight accepted the exchange—sincerely, I thought at the time. He borrowed ten million on Slocum's Remedy and loaned it to Principia. I am inclined to think now that it was more like giving Dwight a chance to eat his cake and keep it. He saw even then how useful it would be for him to own a prestigious company like Principia. It would tremendously enhance his somewhat questionable reputation.

"I was trying to rediscover my ability to love. It was not easy. I failed miserably with Dwight. It was partly his fault. He was frightened, really quite frightened by my attempts to be intimate with him, to love him as a friend, an equal as well as a wife. For Dwight, life is all externals. Having had a father who ignored him and a mother who repelled him, he only wanted the props, the furniture of a normal life. He'd lost interest in me sexually. He thought our agreement only meant that I'd behave. It placed no restraints on him. This led to violent quarrels, more serious than our early battles. Around 1940, I asked Paul to arrange a divorce. I accepted a very modest settlement, because Paul was anxious to remain on good terms with Dwight in his role as Principia's major lender.

"I came home because I had no place else to go. For a while I stayed at Bowood with Malcolm, whose wife had recently died. When World War II began, Paul asked me to move out to the farm with Maria and little Ned.

"In those years Maria and I became friends, sisters. I came to appreciate her personality—her directness, her simplicity, so different from our oblique style. For the first time I understood her extraordinary friendship with Grandfather. She had an instinctive respect for our tradition. It came from her Spanish blood—and perhaps from a need for stability after the chaos of Mexico. I—and for a time, Paul—were typical Americans. We were willing to allow tradition to tell us we were superior to everyone else, but we had no patience with being told that it also required some responsibility from us, adherence to a style of life, a code of conduct.

"I shared Paul with Maria during those war years, from 1940 to 1945. We both wrote to him regularly. I could see that the war was a tremendous spiritual experience for him. It exploded many of his presumptions about class and race—and intensified his feeling of responsibility, commitment to the whole American idea.

"In those same years I began collecting Stapleton memorabilia. Reading the old letters and diaries, thinking about Grandfather and Father and Paul, I glimpsed for the first time a dim outline of what I call the Enterprise. I saw us as part of a spiritual drama, Mr. Kilpatrick. The early Stapletons were not religious, as you no doubt know. Not many of the best people were, at the time of the American Revolution. But they were still Protestants. They still had a commitment to a Protestant society where freedom and personal responsibility for the state of your soul were the watchwords. The world was presumed to be manageable on purely secular terms, while one's dialogue with God—if there was one—went on in private.

"But this world turned out to be much more complicated, more corrupt, than anyone suspected. At first, the old aristocrats managed the corruption quite well. Witness the way we ran the state in our railroad days. But after the Civil War, the world grew ugly. Industrialism on a mass scale created staggering evils. Slums, city mobs, a criminal class, and an upper class of new rich with no

338

social responsibility and no interest in anything but their appetites for pleasure and wealth.

"That was when some of the sons of the old aristocrats, men like my father, discovered the ideal. They began the Enterprise. But they were pathetic amateurs at coping with what had evolved, the immense impersonal system of the modern corporation, the modern city and state, with their bureaucracies, their internal and external struggles for power.

"It wasn't enough—the ideal. Most men measured it against the cruel strength of the modern world and found it wanting. They sneered at it, even more cruelly than the old aristocrats like Grandfather had sneered at it. The world seemed to prove them right. The incredible barbarity of the First World War made us all mock it.

"But the Enterprise had begun, and it acquired a spiritual power, a life of its own within the lives of men who more or less rejected it, like Paul. He was uniquely exposed to both sides of it, you see. He had heard his grandfather ridicule it, sneer at it—and at his father. For a while, he rebelled against Grandfather and sided with his father, believed fervently in him and his mission. Then something happened to break that faith. I don't know what it was. Have you found out, Mr. Kilpatrick?"

"No," Kilpatrick said, looking morose.

"For a long time I thought it was something that happened on the River of Doubt. It may have been the First World War, his terrible wound. But Paul never completely abandoned the ideal. He urged it on his sons. At the same time, as you have found out in North Carolina and elsewhere, Mr. Kilpatrick, he was prepared to act with his grandfather's brutal realism, his view of the world as an amoral battleground.

"In the end, I think it is clear that neither Grandfather nor Father prevailed. But I doubt if Paul or his sons could have sustained any connection to the life of the spirit—without Maria. I know that is true in my case. She brought us new spiritual energy when we were in danger of faltering into cynicism—the ultimate disorder."

The frown on Allyn's forehead revealed a strong disagreement with this claim. But Agatha was not going to

339

debate with her. She was witnessing, testifying to the past as she had seen it. Let Allyn, Maria, tell their own pasts. This was Agatha Stapleton's story.

"Do you share Maria's faith?" Kilpatrick asked with barely concealed hostility.

"I don't share Maria's faith in a Holy Spirit, an intensely present God. She taught me to pray to a Guiding Spirit. It helped me to forgive Paul, slowly, painfully. I was able to greet him as a brother again when he came home from the war in 1945. Then I began casting about for a way to play some small part in the Enterprise. This led to founding the hospice in the mid-sixties. I got the idea from an order of Catholic nuns founded by the daughter of Nathaniel Hawthorne, who had set up a similar institution for terminal cancer patients. I've persuaded a great many skeptics to pray at the hospice. I am now convinced that without prayer it is impossible to forgive oneself—or others. Forgiveness, the deep final letting go of hatred and regret, is the crucial step in the acceptance of life—as well as death."

Kilpatrick was looking more and more dubious. So was Allyn. Remembering Peregrine's sneers, Agatha almost gave up. But she reminded herself that she was not just telling this to them, she was stating one Stapleton's experience for future generations of Stapletons. It would be up to them to decide what, if anything, to do about it.

"For a few years after World War II, I had difficulty believing in the Enterprise. I saw nothing but disaster. George's awful breakdowns, Mark's mutilations, which left him hard and bitter, John's death in Korea, Randy's role at National Products as Dwight Slocum's lieutenant. But lately I have begun to see the Enterprise in a new way, as emerging from spiritual and physical suffering. In a way it is a new ideal, more tempered, more modest. There was something egotistic, class-oriented, about Father's approach to it.

"Mark's philosophical work in the law, Paul's judgeship, both of these came out of the war. And something else, I just discovered. You may think me incredibly naïve, but I had no idea that Randy was the real ruler of National Products, that Dwight Slocum was little more

340

than a figurehead. That was a secret that remained closely held between Randy and his father."

"We knew it at the company," Kilpatrick said. "But we didn't think of it as part of any larger—spiritual idea."

He said the word "spiritual" with considerable distaste.

"I don't even know what you're talking about," Allyn said ruefully.

"Please don't think I am trying to convert you, Mr. Kilpatrick," Agatha said. "The Enterprise is not a gospel. It is an explanation. I suppose you think it sounds vague and romantic, something out of the previous century."

"No," Kilpatrick said. "But I do think it's primarily for those who majored in philosophy at Radcliffe." He gestured out the plane window at some distant cumulus clouds. "It's pretty high-flying stuff."

"It's true," Agatha admitted, wondering where he had found out about her education. "But I think it has a very practical application. The goal of the Enterprise, you see, is the Beloved Community. Did you ever get a chance to read that book I recommended, *The Problem of Christianity?*"

Kilpatrick nodded. "Some of it. Until this young lady distracted me."

The pilot told them to fasten their seat belts. They would be landing in a few minutes. They buckled up and Kilpatrick turned off the tape recorder. Soon they began to descend.

Kilpatrick looked down at the city on its hill, shrouded in the usual gray smog. "Is that your beloved community?" Kilpatrick asked sourly.

"Yes," Agatha said. "I hated it once. I was like Muriel Bennett. I couldn't wait to escape its ugliness, its mediocrity, its supposedly second-rate people. But now I see it quite differently."

"Through the rose-colored glasses of the idealist?" Kilpatrick said.

"Not really. I still see the city as it was in my day and is today and probably will remain forever. Ugly and mediocre in many ways. But I see its people as individuals, each making his or her own spiritual journey, which I do my small best for some of them to complete at the hospice. That is my little contribution. God knows, it isn't enough. There is so much more that needs to be done— and so few willing to serve."

Bump bump bump they were on the ground. Agatha felt tired. Her exhilaration faded. She could hear Peregrine sneering. She could see that she had failed to convince Kilpatrick. But Allyn was now looking more puzzled than sullen. Perhaps that was progress. Again Agatha reminded herself that she had been speaking to future generations, hopefully unbrutalized by wars and depressions.

They taxied to a stop near the plane's hangar. As Agatha started to unbuckle her seat belt, Allyn, already free, leaned over and kissed her.

"What's that for?" Agatha said.

"Bravery," Allyn said.

XXVI

Maria Stapleton awoke to pain. The arthritis in her left hip sent lances of agony down her leg. The house was silent. Paul was not up yet. Maria struggled out of bed, dressed and knelt before the small statue of the Blessed Virgin which she had taken from her dresser drawer. She prayed with her eyes closed, her arms outstretched. For days now, there had been no words, no breath of spiritual life.

For Maria, prayer was as essential as oxygen. It was not a rote recitation of words. It was communion with a presence, an energy that flowed into her soul, at times creating unimaginable sweetness. She had known all the subtleties described by her favorite poet, Juan de la Cruz, in his sensuous description of the life of the spirit. She had felt the southern wind for lovers, tasted exquisite pomegranate wine, glimpsed vistas of shining water, embraced flame without pain. Above all, she had learned to love the dark night, "sweeter than anything sunrise can discover," in which, her house at rest, she mounted the secret ladder to spiritual communication. She had also known the rigors of that night, the days and weeks and

343

even years when God had turned away from her, or she from Him.

Maria waited, patiently, stubbornly. There were only random thoughts, mental trivia.

Today she was seeing the writer, Jim Kilpatrick. Agatha had talked to him. He had promised her that he would abandon the book and hand over all his research to be sealed from prying eyes for the next fifty years. But Agatha had not been satisfied with this solution. She added the condition that Kilpatrick should continue to interview family and friends to complete the history of the Stapletons in this century. She had persuaded Maria to agree to a full, frank interview. Maria had consented only out of her love and respect for Agatha. She did not share Agatha's passion for history, her determination to see meaning, progress, in the past. For Maria, history was largely tragic examples of spiritual blindness, deafness, or worse, deliberate refusal to open minds and hearts to God's presence.

George. That was part of her spiritual deadness. Every outbreak of his sickness filled her with resentful grief. For a moment she felt herself slipping back into the morass of meaninglessness in which she had spent two years after Randy's death. She paid for that blasphemy with the revelation of a sin she had committed against love, one of many that burdened her heart.

Perhaps George was another sin, another weakness. A refusal to admit the part she had played in his tragic flaw. She evaded the thought, she pushed it and George away from her. Mechanically, she gave him to the Virgin of Guadalupe, to the Mexico she hated and he loved. The gesture fluttered to her aching knees on the hardwood floor. It was a wish, not a prayer. It had no faith in it.

"Help him find the mystery, the power of forgiveness," she prayed.

That was a prayer. It reached the Virgin's feet. That was the only hope of a new beginning for George. As it had been a new beginning for herself, for Agatha. Maria said the same prayer for Mark.

She heard footsteps in the next room. Taking her cane, she limped down the hall to the kitchen. Sam Fry was already there, pouring the buttermilk for Paul. "How does he look this morning?" she said.

"Bad," Sam said. They spoke with the tough objectivity of two old nurses.

"He's staying up too late. It was one-thirty last night," Maria said.

"You should tell Ned to stay home," Sam said. "He wants to help. But the Colonel just tries to do twice as much."

"I know. But it's good to see Ned—"

There was no need to complete the sentence. For the past week, Ned had been coming over to the farm after supper to help his father with the endless paper work of the school integration case.

"He says he might take a few days off next week, if he gets ahead of the bandits," Sam said. He did not believe it. Neither did Maria.

A half hour later, Paul appeared in the dining room for breakfast. Maria served him his usual toast and coffee, silently deploring his refusal to eat a more robust meal.

"I'll be seeing Mr. Kilpatrick today," she said.

Paul frowned at his plate. They had not talked about Jim Kilpatrick. But Paul had been embarrassed to discover how much this stranger had probably learned about him. At the same time, he had been curiously uncertain about what to do. Ned had urged him to drop the entire project. Paul kept saying he thought he could handle Kilpatrick. He thought they understood each other. Only when she and Ned had sided with Agatha's suggestion to finish the book and put all the research away in the vault had he yielded.

"There's nothing to worry about now," Paul said.

"I'm almost afraid to go back. I'm afraid of what I'll feel."

"I'm not worried," Paul said, smiling.

Perhaps you should be, she thought, with a flash of her old temper. But she only smiled and nodded her agreement. He had enough to worry about.

An hour after Paul departed, Maria was preparing burritos and enchiladas for dinner when Allyn walked into the kitchen. She had called yesterday and asked if

Maria minded her joining Jim Kilpatrick for the interview. Maria had been dubious. But her pleasure at hearing from Allyn had overcome her reluctance. She had agreed.

Maria thought Allyn looked terrible. She had lost weight—something a Stapleton could rarely afford to do without looking like a starvation case. She was wearing the usual sweater and jeans, a costume Maria found extremely unfeminine. She was convinced that Allyn's entire generation of women were determined to look like men.

Maria abandoned her impulse to lecture when Allyn sat down on the stool beside the kitchen counter and asked for some coffee *con leche*. In memory, Maria went back to the sixth-grader who used to plop herself on the same stool and pour out her day's woes and pleasures.

She quickly prepared the coffee and hot milk and handed her the cup, continuing to work on the burritos. Allyn said she had been to see her cousin Paula, the mayor's wife, to plan a benefit for the gallery. She spoke fondly of Paul's two children, especially the little girl, Dolores.

Maria agreed that Dolores was a delightful little girl. "But I'm afraid her father spoils her, just as Paul spoiled you."

"I don't remember being spoiled," Allyn said.

"People never do. You were only five when you came here. He had just lost John. You were a great consolation to him. But you could do nothing wrong. In his opinion."

"All I can remember are the rules. And the lectures."

"That was much later. When he started treating you like a son. Before that, he spoiled you as I spoiled Ned. You were both raised like only children."

Allyn shook her head in that fierce Stapleton way. "I liked growing up here. The trouble started when I got to be seventeen or eighteen and you kept treating me like a child."

"You may be right. I never raised a daughter. I was terribly uncertain. I wasn't a good daughter myself."

"That's hard for me to believe," Allyn said. "I was so sure you were always perfect."

Maria caught an edge of hostility in her voice. She also sensed Allyn was trying to control it.

"Did you really see me that way?" Maria said. The notion was so absurd, it was difficult for her to conceal her irritation.

"I saw you both that way," Allyn said. "You tried to make me perfect morally, spiritually. He tried to make me perfect every other way, athletically, scholastically. Perfect. And perfectly obedient."

Maria felt her temper rising. She handed Allyn a plate of tortillas, a gesture from the time when Allyn was thirteen or fourteen and had been determined to become a good cook. Frowning, Allyn stuffed them with beef and scrambled eggs. Maria turned to the stove and tasted the chili con queso, Paul's favorite soup. She pointed to some enchiladas beside mounds of Chihuahua cheese and raw onion. Allyn began filling them too, meanwhile reminding Maria of the rigid rules she had enforced on her when she was in her teens.

"I had to be in by midnight, no matter how far away the party was. Which meant I had to leave a lot of parties at eleven o'clock. I used to practically die when you asked boys point-blank if they drank or smoked marijuana. When I came home you'd cross-examine me for a half hour about who did what."

"I don't know why you thought I was so perfect when I was clearly such a terrible mother," Maria said.

Jim Kilpatrick's arrival rescued them from a quarrel. One of the houseboys escorted him into the kitchen, Maria asked if he would like some coffee. He accepted, while giving Allyn a warm smile.

"I didn't know you spent any time in the kitchen," he said.

"Once upon a time I was very domestic," Allyn said.

"She is an excellent cook," Maria said.

Maria poured coffee for herself and Kilpatrick and they carried it out onto the patio. It was a warm, sunny day. Kilpatrick took out his tape recorder and set it up on the table near the chaise on which Maria sat. Allyn sat in a straight-backed chair a few feet away, looking intense. Maria had an uneasy feeling that she was submitting to a serious examination. She did not like it.

"I don't know where to begin," she said. "My childhood was uninteresting. I grew up on a big ranch which

Paul has probably mentioned, the Hacienda Gloriosa. I was sent to school in Texas because the Mexican Revolution of 1910 threw the country into chaos. My father was strong enough to keep the war at a distance for a while. But eventually it consumed him. Has Paul told you how Pancho Villa killed my father?"

"Yes."

"He probably omitted some details. For me, they are all important. Villa killed my father with barbaric cruelty. He hanged him like a thief from the hacienda roof. Then, just as he was about to expire, he cut him down and revived him and said he would spare him if he would help him ambush the Americans who were coming to protect him. My father refused. Villa shot him with his own pistol.

"I saw all this. It had a terrible effect on me."

For a moment Maria had to struggle for breath. She lived it again as she had lived it in a thousand nightmares. The big mustached man dangling from the rope, feet flailing against the white adobe wall, then crashing to the cobblestones to be dragged to the carriage in which Villa, his leg broken by a bullet, was traveling like a mad dust-covered prince. Her father's defiant refusal, the roar of Villa's pistol, Carlos O'Reilly sinking to his knees, then toppling back to sprawl in bloody anguish on the cobblestones as more bullets slammed into him.

"We were not the only ones who suffered," Maria said. "On the next ranch, Villa killed the Polancos, the father and three sons, the same way, first pretending to hang them, then shooting them."

She waited for a moment to calm herself.

"I am sure Paul did not tell you what happened when he and his detachment reached the hacienda. The gunfight?"

Jim Kilpatrick shook his head.

"Our peons had told the Villastas that the Americans were coming. Villa left a dozen men behind to ambush them. Their captain was Portínez, who had once been one of our foremen. He was a thin, vicious man with a snake's mouth. He decided to let the Americans ride into the courtyard and kill them there.

I wanted to see Portínez and his murderers die. All that

348

ight I prayed to the Virgin for revenge. I think that was my first sin. Around ten the next morning the Americans came, about twenty of them, led by Paul. Portínez had given guns to our peons. They were on the roof of the house. He and his men hid behind windows in the house. They had locked my mother and me in my father's bedroom, and told us we would die if we made a sound. While my mother sobbed in a corner, I took one of my father's pistols from the secret drawer in the chest beside the bed. I fired the gun out the window as the Americans came in the gate.

"All the Americans except Paul leaped from their horses and took shelter as the peons and Villastas began shooting. Paul stayed in the saddle, utterly indifferent to the bullets, firing back at them with a pistol until a bullet struck his horse between the eyes. The animal crashed to the ground, trapping Paul beneath him. One of the American regulars, a big muscular sergeant, ran out through the bullets, lifted the horse as if it were made of paper and enabled Paul to escape.

"The Americans were deadly shots. They picked off one peon after another. Paul ordered six soldiers to enter the house and gain the rooftop. The Americans quickly drove the peons off the roof. Those who were still alive ran away. That left only Portínez and his men. The Americans picked off one or two of them. Portínez and another tried to escape. They jumped on their horses and galloped across the courtyard toward the gate. Paul raised his pistol and killed them with two shots.

"I will never forget the terrible joy I felt. It was another sin, of course. It is a sin to rejoice in the killing of any human being, even scum like Portínez. I ran down the stairs and flung open the door to the courtyard. I wanted to spit in his face before he died.

"Paul was standing by the door reloading his gun. He caught me by the arm as I came out the door. 'You can't go out there, señorita,' he said. 'They're still shooting.'

"A bullet struck the wall above our heads. 'They killed my father,' I screamed.

"A murderous grief, matching my own, appeared on Paul's face. In that moment of blood and death, I knew everything. I knew I would marry him and he would take

349

me away from the Gloriosa, from everything I knew and loved. I saw Paul would give me great joy and great sorrow. I saw I would do the same thing to him. I saw it and accepted it as my fate. I tore my arm loose and ran out there through the bullets to spit in Portínez's face.

"You see the kind of woman I am?"

Maria looked at Allyn as she said these last words. Allyn had heard the story of the gunfight with the Villastas. But the emphasis had been on her grandfather's heroism. The inner story, the hatred and blasphemy, the sudden overwhelming sense of fate, had been omitted. It was the first time Maria had ever told it to anyone.

"Over the next few weeks, Paul fell in love with me. I did not try to stop him. My mind was numb with grief for my father, my sense of fate crushing us with irresistible events. My mother increased this feeling of inevitability by scheming to bring Paul and me together constantly. She invited him to dinner, she gave little parties for the American officers at which Paul was always treated like a guest of honor. She urged me to do everything in my power to seduce him. I ignored her. I knew it was only a question of time before Paul proposed. But I was totally unprepared for the way he did it. He told me that he loved me. But he was afraid he could do nothing but hurt me. He said he was a man who had lost his sense of direction, a man who did not care whether he lived or died.

"He not only stirred my sympathy, he gave me a sense of purpose, meaning, for the first time in weeks. I could see that he had suffered some bitter blow, some loss that had destroyed his sense of his place in the world. Every man and woman must have that sense above all things. That was what I saw as my first purpose with him. I would help to heal the wound he had received. But I badly misjudged my power to penetrate Paul's soul. Wounds can only be healed by opening our hearts to other hearts or to God. There was a seal on Paul's heart, a seal that I have never really broken.

"We were also very strange to each other. I can see now that we each married out of a terrible need of the moment, a need that a stranger fulfilled. For the rest, I was not ugly and Paul was very handsome.

350

"I don't suppose Paul told you about our honeymoon? We only had a week. We rode into the Sierras, to the Cascada de Basaséachic. It is my favorite place in Mexico. The falls drops a thousand feet, a pure-white spume into the river that runs to the Sea of Cortés. We descended the gorge and swam in the river . . . ."

Naked, she could not tell them that, they swam naked and Paul was ashamed, he did not want to do it, he preferred to make love in the dark but she wanted to see that slim strong body, its fine proportions, from its hard thighs and solid chest to the flat rump and curving calves, with their bunches of muscle. She had run her fingers down the proud neck and along the flat, deceptively powerful biceps and kissed him passionately there in the middle of the foaming river. She saw now that it was Eden she was trying to create. For a few hours they almost succeeded. Never again had Paul loved her in that utterly free, abandoned way.

When it was over, they splashed in the river again like children. "The last time I swam in a river like this," he said, "was in Brazil, in the River of Doubt."

"Let this be the River of Faith," she said. She pointed to the falls. "That is grace, the grace to find your way again. It is falling down from heaven, from the Virgin Mother's hands."

She saw on his face that he did not believe her. No, worse, she saw disappointment, even revulsion at her Catholic way of seeing and speaking.

"All I see is a beautiful falls," he said. "And a beautiful woman I'll always love."

"Always?" she had said, facing once more what she had sensed a dozen times already, their strangeness to each other.

"Always," he said.

Kilpatrick brought her back to the present. "Judge Stapleton told me that he wanted to stay in Mexico," he said.

Maria shook her head. "It was impossible for me. When I saw my father's blood run across the cobblestones of our courtyard, Mexico became a place I could never trust again. A place in which I could never raise a child. My mother wanted Paul to stay and help her run

351

the ranch. My brother was not yet of age. But I fough
the idea. It was cruel of me. I can be very cruel, very
Spanish.

"I had grudges against my mother. She made my father
unhappy. She was one of those women who never stopped
finding fault, who always expected the worst and practically welcomed it when it happened. She was old before
her time. My father was the opposite, always smiling,
singing, full of generosity and vitality. He loved life; he
loved the hacienda. His mother, my grandmother, was
just like him. It was she who taught me to pray to the
Virgin with the faith of a peasant, taught me to love
music and poetry. My mother hated all these things.
Society, status, were what she worshipped.

"She thought we should live in Mexico City and let
someone else run the hacienda. That is why she wanted
Paul to stay. She wanted to take my brother and go to
Mexico City. I took pleasure in inflicting the hacienda on
her for a few more years. Eventually, she persuaded my
brother to sell it and join her ridiculous pursuit of the
famous and the infamous in Mexico City, the Riviera, the
usual places.

"But the decisive event was the arrival of numerous
letters from Paul's grandfather. When I read them
sensed a kindred spirit. I liked the direct way he said
things. Here is a man you can trust, I said to myself, a
man like my father, who knows his place in the world and
fills it with all his strength. That was the first great breach
between Paul and me, when I sided with his grandfather
and told him he had to go home and accept the place that
was prepared for him.

"Paul withdrew from me. I was in agony. But the war
rescued us. It forced him to take me home. When I met
his grandfather, I was sure I was right. We loved each
other on sight. I never once saw that harsh temper, that
cutting sarcasm which Paul had described to me in such
bitter detail. I think the old man yearned for a chance to
talk to a woman who was truly interested in him, who
appreciated him. My heart pitied him when I thought of
his life. His wife dying while he was at the battlefront, his
two sons marrying women he disliked. No wonder he had

352

grown cold and hard. He had been disappointed in so many ways. The political party to which he had given his faith had become corrupt and disgusting to him. But he despised the other party, the Democrats, even more because it was full of men who regarded him as an enemy.

"The Civil War had made a soldier of him forever. He thought always in terms of attack and defense. He had lived an embattled life. You could not blame him. But he dreamt of peace. He dreamt of a time when there would be order in all our lives.

"That summer, 1917, in the evenings we sat on the porch of the house at Paradise Beach and talked. I learned more about American history, American life, in those months than any student at a university. But the pleasure we took in each other's company was nothing compared to the joy he felt when Randy was born. I named him after the General and I would have called him Jonathan. But Paul insisted on Randy.

"I loved the General for another reason. He protected me from Paul's mother, who was a woman very much like my own mother, superficial and willful in small, empty ways. I suspect she made her husband unhappy. I never met Paul's father. He died, as Paul probably told you some years before I came.

"The General spoke of him as a good son. But I wondered if there was some weakness in his character which had inclined him to spoil his wife so horrendously. Mrs. Stapleton was a fifty-year-old child. She had to have her own way in everything. She had a clothes allowance of a thousand dollars a month. Frequently she would spend twice that and dare the General to do something about it. He preferred to pay it rather than quarrel with her. She insisted on two personal maids, her own private chauffeur. When she went home to Virginia for a visit, it was like a royal procession.

"It made me glad the South had not won the Civil War. I once said this to the General. He laughed and said they may have lost the war but they were certainly winning the peace. He despised the way America had freed the Negro and then abandoned him, much as the Spanish

353

treated the Indians in Mexico for a long time. He hired Negroes at the mills, even though it caused dissension among his workers. He was a hard, cynical man, who saw little hope of improving the world, but he could not abide a broken promise. He had many prejudices—against the Irish—the Jews—which he did not have the least hesitation in expressing. He said they were all based on experience, which was his only guide."

"Didn't that include a violent prejudice against Catholicism?" Jim Kilpatrick asked. "I was told that the General and everyone else insisted on you giving up your religion."

"Yes," Maria said. "It was very difficult at first. Mrs. Stapleton and Agatha used religion as a weapon to persecute me. But I sensed neither of them really cared about it. This made it easier to bear their attacks. At first I insisted on going to the Catholic church. I was prepared to be very heroic, a martyr. But then I saw how much it saddened the General. I sensed his spiritual revulsion for Catholicism. My respect for him was so great I had to respect that too. I had to find out why it so offended his Protestant soul.

"He didn't insist on my abandoning my faith. He was indifferent to all religions. But he wanted me to understand that my children would be raised as Protestants, until they reached the age when they would—he hoped—decide that religion was nonsense.

"It was the beginning of a difficult education for me. I had to face the greatness, the inner greatness of the Protestant spirit, which cried out with Luther: 'Here I stand, I can do no other.' Those words: 'I can do no other,' the voice of the personal conscience, of private faith, had modeled men like the General, like Paul, not just religiously but spiritually, psychologically. Gradually I saw—that is, I felt in my heart—that there was something in Catholicism that *offended* men like the General. It went beyond the feeling that it was the religion of the lower classes. It was Catholicism's insistence on invading that private I, the self that said: 'I can do no other.' That was the ultimate offense, to Paul, his grandfather.

354

"Eventually I even saw that they were right, it was an offense. But I also saw how fragile, how frail that private self was, how easily it could be wounded by fate, the brutality of the world. Then, obsessed by its wounds, or crippled by them, it cannot make the assent of faith, it relapses into the human, into belief in nothing but human strength, human will. That can be noble, heroic. It can also be painful to watch with the eyes of love. I saw it in the General. I have lived it with Paul.

"I do not want to portray Paul as a man without faith of any kind, like the General. In the end the old man had neither faith nor hope, in this world or the next one. Paul is capable of acts of faith and hope. But they do not rise from a vision that embodies these ideas. On the contrary, they often struggle from his soul, almost in spite of himself. They spring from his experience. Like his grandfather, he trusts little else—except his own strength, his own perseverance.

"When you interview people at the law firm, Mr. Kilpatrick, you will hear stories of his legendary endurance, of working for twenty-four and thirty-six hours at a time. They are all true—all part of his determination to fill his place in the world with all his strength. It is why, at eighty, he goes on toiling fourteen hours a day.

"I see you looking puzzled, or is it sad? I am using my own words against myself. I still believe in that idea of filling your place in the world. But I wish—how I wish that Paul—and others I loved—had understood how to do it with faith to guide them. Faith makes room for love, for pleasure, for rest. There has never been much room in Paul's life for these things. There has only been work, duty, responsibility, devouring so many of his nights and days."

Maria sighed. "I am turning into a complaining wife. But I understand, I accept the necessity of what Paul has done, what he is. You cannot expect a man to change his inner self. Especially a Stapleton."

Was that all there was to say? Maria wondered. Her mind strayed across the years. The critical tone that had emerged as she answered Kilpatrick's questions unnerved her. This was like exploring an abandoned mine and

355

finding vipers in the watery pit. She remembered how bitter the struggle had been, the hours she had spent weeping before the statue of the Virgin, asking her help.

"I want to hear what you felt about John," Allyn said. "I read Jim's interview with Muriel Bennett."

Maria felt the name like a branding iron on her flesh. "No," she said. "That's too private. Too personal."

"I realize how difficult it is for you to discuss," Kilpatrick said.

"I am used to difficulties," Maria said. For an angry moment she remembered Allyn's remark about her supposed perfection. Perhaps it needed a final refutation. "What do you wish to know?" she said.

"How did you feel when you first heard about John?" Allyn asked.

"I simply refused to believe it. I was like one of the patients at Agatha's hospice when he tries to face his death. After refusal came terrible anger. I raged at Paul and at her. Muriel Bennett. I swore I would go to France and shoot her down in the street. Paul bowed his head and took my abuse without a word of reproach.

"I wish now that he had fought me. I wish he had accused me of betraying him first by siding with his grandfather. But he chose to be stoic. I felt—"

She could not say it at first. After fifty years, the words, the idea, still sickened her.

"I felt that only a random bullet had prevented me from being betrayed. I was sure that he would have left me if he had come out of the Argonne unwounded. I felt I was living a lie with a man who could give me nothing but gratitude for my ability as a nurse."

She was back in the bedroom with Paul the night that he had told her, spitting out the words. "What woman wants gratitude? Jailers get that from their prisoners."

He had answered her with that cold, demoralizing Protestant honesty. "I don't know what I would have done. I might have left you. I don't know."

"You're free to go to her now," she had shouted. "I free you from your obligations, from your gratitude. I would be happy if I never saw your face again on this earth."

"After my anger came cold, consuming hatred. A gray

356

fog enveloped my life. I loved no one, nothing. I did not pray once, in five years. I was barely civil to Paul. I was no longer a woman. I was an automaton, a machine in the kitchen—and in the bedroom, when he wanted me—which was seldom.

"It was John who made me see that I had to forgive Paul. Just before he left for prep school in 1933, I was sitting here on this patio. John came out to say goodbye to me.

" 'Why are you looking so sad?' he asked. 'I thought you'd be happier than anyone to see me go.'

"I asked him what he meant. He said Mark had told him that since he came into the family I had lost my good humor, I never laughed or joked with them. John said he knew it was his fault. He knew he caused trouble with his poor school work and his bad temper. He was always fighting with Mark, who resented terribly the attention John got from his father.

"I put my arms around him and told him none of that mattered. I loved him for his good heart. He was a very lovable boy, innocent in a strange, sad way.

"Paul came out on the patio to tell us that the car was ready. When he saw me with my arms around John, Paul recoiled. I saw such emotion on his face, sadness mixed with hope and a subtle anger to see John receiving the love I was denying him—I realized what I was doing.

"That was when I discovered the agony of forgiveness. How hard it was. How necessary. How complicated. I rediscovered prayer, not the old simple joyous prayer of my girlhood. But penitential prayer, the prayer of the adult. For a year I had to wait in silence, while the Virgin withheld the grace I needed, a punishment far more mild than I deserved. In 1935, Ned was born, the child of our reconciliation.

"Then came World War II and new, more terrible turmoil. There was Mark, with his awful wounds, which destroyed his capacity for love, I think, and intensified that severity in his character that he inherited from his great-grandfather. He most resembles the General, you know. Worse was George's failure. You know what happened."

"Yes," Kilpatrick said.

357

"For a few years he seemed all right. I did not know the true story. His father told me it was nervous exhaustion that brought him to the psychiatric hospital at the end of the war. But the wound, the terrible wound, was bleeding all the time beneath the surface of normality. He did poorly in his studies at Harvard. He was frequently rebellious and insolent to his father. I finally found out the whole truth when we went to his graduation from Harvard. We found him in his room, too drunk to walk, almost to talk."

Maria shuddered inwardly at the memory of the rage that had convulsed her husband's face. It had reminded her of the murderous grief she had seen in Mexico.

"Paul grabbed George by the shirt and dragged him into the shower and ran cold water on him. He pulled him out and ordered him to change his clothes and join his class for the graduation ceremony.

" 'Why don't you have me court-martialed and shot?' George said.

"Paul told him to keep quiet and get dressed. George ignored him. 'You've never told Mother, have you?' he said. 'The hero doesn't have the courage to tell his wife the truth.'

" 'What is the truth, George?' I asked.

"He told me his clever lie, the truth distorted just enough to make him seem a hero who had sacrificed his reputation for his men. Paul denied it, of course, with all his suppressed rage, a terrible merciless condemnation in his voice. He told George it would have been better for all of us if he had died in Italy. I have regretted those awful words, but I never blamed Paul for them. I had become —too much a Stapleton not to be horrified by what George had done.

"But if Paul had told me the truth when he came home from the war, I think something might have been salvaged. I could have dealt with George in my own way. I had always been close to him. He shared my love of poetry and music. Instead, for five years George had been permitted to concoct his fantasy of a skillful lie that would detach me from Paul, and launch us into a destructive war. For five years George wound this lie deep into his soul. My prayers, the skill of psychiatrists, the passage

358

of time, have failed to extract it. His fascination with Mexico, building the hacienda, even his poetry, are part of this forlorn wish."

Maria sighed. "Children know so little of their parents' spiritual lives, their inner marriage. In some ways George is my greatest sorrow, heavier than Randy. I think he might have been the happiest of the boys, if it were not for the war.

"Six months after this confrontation with George, we were in another war, in Korea. Soon we had the terrible news of John's death. Paul was devastated by it. I think it aroused several kinds of guilt in his soul. He wondered why he had not been taken, in all the battles he had fought, the millions of bullets and thousands of shells he had survived. He dreaded the possibility that his heroism in battle had inspired John to become a professional soldier, and an attempt to imitate that heroism had led to his death. He asked himself, the man who had given him life, why John had lived. Without faith such questions are impossible to answer. Even with faith they are agonizing, as I discovered when Randy died.

"For weeks Paul barely slept. He would exercise—skip rope, run, do push-ups until he fell to the ground exhausted. Still sleep eluded him. I tried to help. I opened my heart, my body to him. His suffering scoured the last iota of resentment from my heart. But it was Randy who rescued him."

"How?" Kilpatrick asked.

"By coming back to him. That was part of Paul's agony. He thought he had lost Randy too. Randy was the most sensitive of our sons. He was a child of love. Among my many superstitions is my belief that a child reflects the spirit of his conception. Randy was love. Mark was a child of war, struggle. He was conceived as Paul was recovering from his head wound. George was a child of peace and contentment.

"Even when he was a schoolboy, Randy was questioning our class, our way of life. He was troubled by the gap between the real and the ideal. The older he grew, the more it troubled him. But he never reproached his father. His love was too strong. He had also inherited my habit of prayer. So he chose the life of secret prayer that I had been forced to accept. It suited his private, Protestant spirit.

"But the Second World War caused a terrible crisis in his soul. He emerged from it full of doubts about the meaning, the possibility of any ideal. In that spirit he went to work for Dwight Slocum, and for a while there was a transfer of sonship. Randy was fascinated by Slocum's brutal energy, his frank hunger for power and profits. Paul sensed he had lost him. When John was killed, I did with Randy what the old General had done with Paul—in my own poor way. I wrote Randy letter after letter, describing his father's anguish. It opened his heart to him again. Paul does not know this. I would prefer that he never learned it."

Maria found it easier to tell this part of the story to Jim Kilpatrick. She did not want to see its impact on Allyn. A sneer or a scornful exclamation was all too probable.

"Several months later Randy's wife—Allyn's mother—died. He brought Allyn to us to raise. She was a kind of statement, a reaffirmation of his love. Of course it was unspoken, like almost everything in the Stapleton family. But she was a very special child to Paul.

"Like so many things in life, the gift returned to the giver. Coming home restored Randy's spiritual balance. He began to measure Dwight Slocum against his father and soon Randy was Paul's son again. Together they conceived the plan to slowly, steadily take control of the National Products company, to rescue it from Dwight Slocum's irrational, impulsive, destructive ways.

"Randy became Paul's link with Mark. Failures of love, especially in the family, troubled Randy deeply. He saw Mark frequently in New York and persuaded him to visit us occasionally, on my birthday for instance. He brought many of Mark's ideas to Paul's attention. I think they had some influence on his decision to take the federal judgeship. He knew the school integration case was coming before the court.

"Mark continued these very sporadic visits after Randy died. That was a terrible time for me. For some reason, Paul was not so wounded by Randy's death. Perhaps John's death had prepared him for the death of another son. Perhaps he felt that he had had Randy as a friend, a spiritual companion, longer than most fathers have their sons. I don't know. I do not have a philosophic mind. I only know I felt betrayed, enraged, by Randy's death. I had used John's death to forgive Paul in a total, consuming way. I had helped to restore his favorite son to him. A son who was also in many ways my favorite, who had shared with me thoughts, feelings, about the life of the spirit that he had never been able to express to his father. Night after night on my knees I hurled insults at God. I spent my days in listless wishing for death. I refused to weep. I would not give God the satisfaction of a tear.

"Then Mark came to visit on my birthday. At the supper table, he reached out with his aluminum claw to take a piece of bread. The light flashed from the metal and seemed to fall on his face. I saw his starved, bitter spirit. I saw the failure of love—my love, Paul's love. We had loved Randy and John too much because it was so easy. We had not loved Mark enough because it was so difficult.

"I understood why Randy had been taken. That night my tears flowed until dawn. The next day I began trying to persuade Paul to write letters to Mark, in the style of the General, involving him in the family again. I don't know what good they have done. I expect no miracles. But refusing to reach out to each other, refusing even to try to love—that is the ultimate failure.

"Looking back on our life together, it is clear to me that many of our failures of love were my fault. Our love was my responsibility and at crucial moments I failed Paul. A man cannot be expected to love as intensely, as meaningfully as a woman. He has his work, a consuming passion, he has the world and its harsh demands. Especially a man like Paul, whose spirit was almost crushed by these demands, long ago, when the General thrust them upon him too young.

"I can almost smile now at my girlish dreams of transforming Paul with my love, of changing him into a happy, carefree man like my father. Paul had too many cares ever to be carefree. But I have learned to respect his care as well as his caring. My father was carefree. He was

361

also careless. He thought he could defy a ruthless killer like Villa without worrying about the consequences. Paul would never have made such a mistake.

"Most of all, I have come to respect—or better, to acknowledge—the darkness in my own heart, the primary source of our failures in love. Because I am a woman, I thought there was no violence in my soul—in spite of abundant evidence to the contrary. Because so much of the time we stand aside from the world of men, we get false ideas about ourselves—almost as false as the ideas they have about us."

Maria hesitated, amazed at her own candor. She was telling more than she had thought possible. Agatha had been right, when she predicted that Maria would find the experience irresistible. There was something unique, something liberating about talking to the future that existed in the shining dark beyond the boundaries of one's own time. It was a little like talking to God.

"What else can I say? Perhaps only this: Through all these years, in spite of times when I denounced him in my heart, I never ceased to love Paul. I am not sure if that is true for him. I would not blame him if, looking back, he concluded that his love was closer to duty, to a promise given and kept. I have not been an easy woman to love."

Maria looked at Allyn now. There was anger on her face, she was shaking her head. Maria felt regret, confusion. She had failed Allyn again in some new way. When most of what she had said was an attempt to tell her the difficulty but not the impossibility of love.

XXVII

Allyn Stapleton was shaking her head, saying no, no, simultaneously angry and awed and frightened by what she had just heard from this woman whom she had called Mother in her mind for most of her life. She would not, she would never accept those last words, the guilt trip of the loving woman, committed to superhuman overcoming of male deficiencies, in a shadow world she never made.

"It's ridiculous—outrageous to hear you blame yourself that way," she said. "Why don't you blame him? Isn't he at fault?"

Maria looked strange. She seemed frightened, sad. "I have blamed him, Allyn. Think for a moment of everything I told you. Not just the last words, I blamed him, I saw everything he did as evil, once. Then I saw where that led, the blind blank wall against which you smashed yourself, and eventually hated yourself. I saw the necessity of forgiveness. Not just for his sake. But for my own sake, for the health, the sanity of my own soul."

Allyn shook her head, refusing to surrender. But other questions became more important. "What did you mean,

that Randy—Father—followed your way—of secre
prayer?"

"He was a Christian. But he believed that it was bes
expressed in ordinary ways, ordinary gestures. To preach
it, to make sweeping declarations, to erect articles o
faith, seemed wrong, immodest, arrogant to him. H
believed instead that in each area of his life, in business
with family, friends, all the compartments into which
modern life divides, the Christian must remain invisible
but ready to respond with love to each situation he meets
It is not an easy life to sustain. It requires intense spiritua
effort, which can only be achieved by prayer."

There was a dazed look on Jim Kilpatrick's face. I
grew incredulous as Allyn told the memory that had
tormented her for a long time. "That explains—what
saw just before I got married. I was staying at the New
York apartment. I got up about six A.M. To go to
the bathroom. He was in the living room, praying—hi
arms stretched out like a cross."

Maria nodded. "I remember, when he was fifteen, he
asked me the best way to pray. That was the way I had
learned, from my grandmother. It was the way St. Teresa
and St. John of the Cross prayed."

"Is that—the prayer—being a secret Christian—why
he never married again?"

"In part," Maria said. "He used to joke about being
married to National Products. It was a consuming task he
set himself, in that company. He did not feel he had any
part of his life left over to give a woman. I told him it was
the right decision—although I knew it hurt his father. He
wanted a grandson from Randy. Perhaps if Paul had had
one, he would not have pushed you so hard in sports, in
school, Allyn. On the other hand, knowing you, I doubt if
you would have liked sharing your father with anyone
You were a glutton for his love, Allyn."

For a moment Allyn almost wept. She was appalled by
the volatility of her emotions. For the past two weeks
ever since she had gone off drugs, she could zoom from
hysterical laughter to hysterical tears in a moment. She
told herself insistently that it had to be withdrawal. It had
nothing to do with her feelings for Jim Kilpatrick or
anyone else. In fact, her instability confused her feelings

364

about him and everyone else. One moment she felt guilty and full of pity for him. The next moment she was angry, muttering imaginary insults at him. She was now having similar mood swings toward Maria.

Kilpatrick had turned off the tape recorder before Allyn began questioning Maria. He put the machine in his briefcase and thanked Maria for her candor. He said she had given him a new perspective on Randy. Maria smiled and nodded. But her eyes were on Allyn.

"Would you come to my room with me, Allyn?" she asked. "There's something I'd like to give you."

Kilpatrick led the way to the house. Maria, on her cane, fell some distance behind them. Kilpatrick asked Allyn if she would like to have dinner that night. "Call me," she said with a forced smile.

Kilpatrick said goodbye and went out the front door to his car. Allyn followed Maria down the hall past her husband's bedroom to her much smaller room.

Allyn was startled by the bare gray walls. The bed was a rectangle of wood on low legs, with no mattress, only a thin pallet. The room was totally different from the one Allyn had known as a child. That had been decorated with vivid wallpaper depicting a religious procession in a Mexican village. The bed, a big four-poster, always had a bright Mexican quilt on it.

"What happened to the wallpaper, the quilts?" Allyn asked.

"As we get older, we try to do without things," Maria said, avoiding her eyes.

From a bureau drawer, Maria took a small wooden chest about the size of a jewelry box. "I have hesitated a long time to give you these,' she said. "Your father's letters to me. They were not to be given to a child nor to a young wife whose life I hoped would be simple and joyous. After you read them, give them to Agatha. It is self-indulgence for me to keep them here any longer. I had a sense just now, talking to Mr. Kilpatrick, that I was saying goodbye to Randy, finally and forever."

All the way home in the car, Allyn felt the letters pulsing on the seat beside her, like a bomb. She drove carefully. She no longer needed to flirt with disaster at ninety miles an hour. At the gallery, she barely nodded to

Jacky Chasen, whom she had been avoiding for the pas
two weeks. There was trouble coming on that front. Jacky
was growing sullen.

Upstairs she turned off the telephone and opened the
chest. On top of the letters was a small book bound in
faded red leather. The title was in gold on the spine:

> *Juan*
> *de la*
> *Cruz*
>
> The
> Dark Night
> of the
> Soul

The letters began in 1950. The early ones were full of
anguished references to Allyn's mother, angry questions,
demands, challenges to Maria to tell him why a woman
who had never harmed anyone, who was all love and
gentleness, should die such an agonizing death from cancer. Maria's answers were not included, but it was easy to
see what she was saying. She was urging Randy to accept
his loss, to return to the habit of prayer he had had as a
boy, daily prayer, and he was telling her that he was no
longer a boy, he had stopped praying a long time ago.

Then Maria began writing to Randy about his father's
grief over John's death. At first Randy showed only mild
concern. But soon his sympathy grew more and more
intense. He returned to the family and asked his mother if
she would take Allyn while he sorted out his life. "If you
give her even part of the love you gave me," Randy
wrote, "I know I will never have to worry about her."

Next came a series of letters that hinted at serious
unhappiness. There were references to the struggle with
Dwight Slocum, its consuming, nerve-shredding intensity,
to dissatisfaction or reluctance with women whom he had
been seeing, to bouts of insomnia. "Last night I was
reduced to trying your old remedy," he wrote. "I got
down on my knees and prayed for release, rest. But
nothing happened. It was like speaking into the void. I'm
afraid I've lost the art, if I ever had it."

Then Maria sent him *The Dark Night of the Soul*. "I

ave read your favorite book," Randy wrote in reply. "I
m deeply impressed. You were right, it might have been
 mistake to show it to me when I was a boy or even a
ounger man. I would either have been overwhelmed by it
r ignored it. This makes sense only when you have lived
r a while, won and lost, laughed and wept. You say
ou're not sure if it belongs in my American life. Neither
m I. But it intrigues me enormously."

Allyn put aside the letters and opened the book. It had
een translated from the Spanish by an English priest,
ho had also written an introduction. Allyn skipped
rough it.

"*The number of souls called to the contemplative life is
reater than is commonly supposed. They are not con-
ned to Religious Orders, but are to be found in every
ation of life and in every country, for 'the spirit breath-
h where it will.'* . . .

"*Let us suppose that a soul has been unexpectedly
ruck by a ray of divine grace. Such a soul finds
elight, hitherto unknown, in a world transfigured.* . . .

"*It is a very great thing to be able to do without all
lace, both human and divine, and to be willing to bear
is exile of the heart for the honor of God, and in
othing seek self and not to have regard to one's own
erit.* . . ."

The text began with a poem.

I

*In a dark night
With anxious love inflamed
Oh, happy lot!
Forth unobserved I went
My house being now at rest.*

II

*In darkness and in safety
By the secret ladder, disguised,
Oh, happy lot!
In darkness and concealment
My house being now at rest.*

III

In that happy night,
In secret, seen of no one
Seeing nought myself
Without other light or guide
Save that which in my heart was burning.

IV

That light guided me
More surely than the noonday sun
To the place where He was waiting for me.
Whom I knew well.
And where none appeared.

Juan de la Cruz devoted the rest of his book to a
analysis of this poem as a map to spiritual union wi
God. The pilgrim proceeded through two purgations, on
of the sense and one of the spirit, a process that wa
lifelong.

"The night of sense is common and the lot of many
Juan wrote. "These are the beginners. The spiritual nig
is the portion of very few, those who have made som
progress. The first night is bitter and terrible. The secon
is not to be compared with it, for it is much more awfu
to the spirit."

This was the path Randy had begun to walk in secre
while he smiled and frowned, ordered and congratulate
in offices and boardrooms, dueled with Dwight Slocur
and struggled to be a secret Christian in his dealings wi
everyone. Letter after letter discussed the subtleties, th
paradoxes, of prayer and the relationship between the lov
of God and the love of men and women. At times mothe
and son almost vanished. They were like two athletes o
two artists discussing the finer points of their discipline.

Prayer did not make Randy a happy man overnight. O
the contrary, he repeatedly described near despair, anxiet
in the early years of the night of the senses. Without Ma
ria he might never have survived it. She was at his side o
a path she had obviously walked before him.

"The second test, losing all sense of God, is worse tha
the first, I agree," Randy wrote. "Although I find myse
rebelling, daring God to give me more pain than H

inflicted in the first test, when I thought I had lost my ability to love Allyn. There I felt simply stymied. But this weariness of the spirit, as you call it, this feeling that I'm slipping back, is agonizing. I don't know what I would do if I didn't have your assurance that God is transferring to the spirit the goods and energies of the senses . . . ."

On Allyn read, watching Randy struggle with a love that turned on him, excoriating his saviorism, his presumption to be of special service to God, withering that satisfaction too. His failures, even his compromise victories with Slocum, intensified his sense of worthlessness. Again Maria was there, pointing to where Juan de la Cruz assures the troubled soul that a loss of self-satisfaction is another step in the journey.

Then came letters of profound happiness, describing to Maria the joy that emerged from the passage through the night of the senses. "My house is now at rest," Randy wrote to his mother. The house of sensuality, of passion, had been put in order. He was now able to enjoy the liberty of spirit, patience, gentleness with himself and others that St. John had promised to the doubting soul.

Many stopped at this point. But Randy, being a Stapleton, could not resist the next challenge—to conquer the night of the spirit. He began to struggle up the secret ladder of the second stanza, into the deepest darkness in search of ultimate light, union with God in which all trace of the everyday self vanishes. In this "more awful night," as Juan de la Cruz described it, love and all other pleasures of the spirit, even the pleasure of prayer, are inexorably withdrawn. The soul is stripped to its trembling core.

Very soon, the attempt began to falter. Randy carried too many burdens for such an ascent. He was tormented by his inability to heal the family's wounds. He tried. His letters told of lunches with Mark, of patient listening to his diatribes against Paul Stapleton. Another letter agonized over a drunken outburst by George at a Christmas dinner. Letter after letter fretted over Allyn's rebelliousness, her bad temper.

But Randy's heaviest burden was his love for his father. He was tormented by a dread that somewhere in the darkness he would confront the need to repudiate Paul

Stapleton's commitment to the gritty reality of twentieth-century America. Maria repeatedly assured him that it was a false fear. Randy hinted, but could not bear to explain, that a son's love was different from a wife's love.

The last letter, written the day before he died, had echoes of these things in it, along with a gallant refusal to quit.

I can't preach to Dad or anyone else, you know that, Mother. But try to make him see that there may be some good in our Vietnam trauma. Remind him of what Isaiah said, "Vexation alone shall give understanding in the hearing." St. John has made that truth come home to me so often I can't believe the same thing won't eventually be true for America. Only when you experience the need for atonement in the world of the spirit can you grasp it.

Like America, all I really want now is peace. But there is no point in crying peace peace when there is no peace in this world or in our souls. So we must go on searching for it, using some of Dad's hard wisdom and some of your lovely belief that the only true meaning of the word lies within us. How I long to tell this to Allyn. She is troubled by the state of our American world, like so many people her age. I don't think her marriage is very happy.

If there is anything wrong with the path you and I have chosen to follow, it is its solitary nature. We know it isn't really solitary, our prayers surround each of those we love. But there remains the dread of failed communication, the possibility that those we love most have refused or are unable to respond to His presence. I hope to see you soon. I want to talk to you about Allyn. . . .

Slowly, carefully, Allyn put the letters back in the little chest and put *The Dark Night of the Soul* on top of them. She got up and walked around the apartment touching things. Her bed, her dresser, her hairbrush, her dresses, nightgowns, kitchen cabinets, can openers, faucets, doors, curtains, the framed samples of her abandoned weaving in the bedroom. She turned on the television set and watched a housewife pop some over-the-counter pill and go from gloomy to gay. She turned on the radio and heard the all-news-all-the-time station promise to give her the world in twenty-two minutes if she would only sit down and listen. The telephone sat snugly in its cradle, ready to link her to old friends a hundred or a thousand miles away. Nothing had changed. The world was all still there.

Bing-bong went the bell. It was Jacky. "What's new?" she said.

"Nothing much," Allyn said.

"Big party tonight, at the university drama department."

"I'm too old for university parties."

"There'll be ancient professors, drooling on canes. Horny associates, lecherous assistants, graduate students with satyriasis."

Allyn shook her head. "I'm tired."

"What the hell is going on?" Jacky said. "You've barely said hello to me for two weeks. I thought we were friends. More than friends, after—"

"It's hard to explain."

"Grandpa has said no more games with that little kike slut? And suddenly you're listening because he mentioned some magic words like 'will,' 'inheritance'?"

"Don't be silly."

"I'm not being silly. I'm being mad as hell. I don't like people who fuck around with my feelings this way."

Jacky was almost crying. She looked about seventeen. Allyn suddenly felt thirty years old. She felt embarrassed by the game she had been playing, trying to convince herself that she was a late adolescent. She tried to explain to Jacky that she still liked her but something had happened, something very personal that had made her stop and think about her life. The attempt was a failure. Jacky only got more and more furious at the lack of genuine explanation and finally slammed out of the apartment screaming that their partnership was dissolved.

The telephone rang. It was Jim Kilpatrick, asking her to dinner. Allyn suggested he come to the apartment. She would do the cooking. He sounded surprised but he accepted. She spent the rest of the afternoon in the kitchen making a quiche, baking a chicken in tarragon sauce, preparing crepes for dessert. It was the first serious meal she had cooked since her divorce two years ago. It was another way of making the world seem real.

Jim arrived looking haggard. He said he was not sleeping very well. The last time he had stopped drinking he had not slept well for a year. "Is it just the booze?" Allyn said as she served tomato juice and sat down on the couch beside him.

"It might have something to do with this crazy redhead I met recently," he said. "My brain tells me I'm too old for her but the rest of me disagrees."

"What does the redhead think?"

"I don't know. We don't communicate very well. We've never gotten beyond half-truths."

"Better than no truths."

"The problem is really a generation gap. I'm fifty and she's thirty. Which means that when I'm ninety she'll be seventy. I'm afraid she'll start swinging."

"She has a tendency in that direction?"

"Let's say she's been known to misbehave. But I'm the real problem. I'm a part-time intellectual, which means I'm boring for about three hours every day. I'm also straight, middle-class."

"And she's a Wasp snob?"

"How did you guess?"

"Straight middle-class part-time intellectuals have been known to change."

"Mostly for the worse."

"How about crazy Wasp snob redheads?"

"I've been doing research on that. There was one who supposedly changed for the better in 1851. But several historians refer to it as the Great Henna Hoax."

"I understand that if crazy Wasp snob redheads marry redheaded straight middle-class part-time intellectuals, remarkable changes can occur."

"In what?"

"The temperature of the earth's crust."

"No," he said. "It wouldn't work. You're feeling sorry for me. And a little guilty. But you'll get over it."

"Don't tell me what I'm feeling," Allyn said. "I love you. I love you for those ghosts you talked about. I love you in spite of them. I love you because you make me laugh. I love you because you made me cry. I love you because you've tried to face some of the rotten things you've done, like walking out on your wife and kids. I love you because you love me in spite of the rotten thing I did to you and the things you know I did to other people. If you're willing to take a chance on loving me, I'll try to love you."

Allyn sat on the edge of the couch, clutching her drink. Who had said those amazing words? Allyn the diver who soared from the springboard high above the pool, mocking the lumpy faces of the watchers, the swimmer in the green water bleaching hatred into her flesh, the ecstatic, light-dispensing sniffer of cocaine? None of these people, she was shedding those skins, she was returning to another Allyn, who had been patiently waiting in the dark background of the stage while these actors performed. A new Allyn who walked quietly off the stage, who abandoned performances, who let her heart speak.

Jim was reaching out to her. She saw need and joy on his face. For a moment she wondered if someone else, a separate spirit, had spoken those words. Across the room she saw the small mahogany chest with Randy's letters in it. No, she thought, there is no one here except you and the man you love. But why was she suddenly afraid?

After dinner, they walked arm in arm to the bedroom. In the moment of orgasm, Allyn felt more than flesh, semen, burning deep in her body. There was also the spirit, the power of love, no longer refused, denied, evaded. It was not mere submission, crude surrender, it was a union, a confluence, a sense of meeting behind her closed eyes a shadowed face, without the need or wish to dispel the shadow, to bare an identity. Then she knew that she was embracing in this man not only a beloved individual but the selves of other men whom she had loved but also feared. In his need their power became benevolent, in his knowledge of her life and their lives their presence became not merely bearable, but welcomed. She could say "I love you" to this man and accept within the words the loss, the failure of its meaning when she said it to the others. He was both part of them and separate from them in a profound and reassuring way.

"It's spooky," she said as he cradled her in his arms. "Being able to say that to you. I never thought I could

373

say it to anyone. I almost felt someone else was saying it for me."

"I know what you mean," Jim said. He told her about a dream of flying in a plane with Randy as the pilot. He had smiled and said, "Everything's under control."

"But I don't believe it," he said. "There's no one else here. There's no one anywhere but us. Holding each other this way. Making this promise. The other way cheats us of the—the honor, the risk."

"Why?" she said. "I can accept the idea of an influence. A presence in your life. Not controlling you, but—"

"I used to be that way. When I was a good little obedient Catholic."

"What about Maria? Don't you believe what she told us? What she's done with her prayers?"

"I accept the psychology. It works for her. But I can't do more than—admire it ruefully, from a distance."

She sensed a hard, cold refusal deep in his body. Veering away from it, Allyn decided not to tell him about Randy's letters. She saw that he was more like Paul Stapleton than like Randy. Jim too had been wounded by some early failure of trust or faith.

They talked about possible futures. She might run the gallery, take weaving seriously again. He might try to finish his novel. But he was more inclined to face up to his lack of talent as a novelist and tackle a contemporary topic like busing or abortion. He also had some thoughts about public service. Perhaps there was a job for him somewhere in the city or state. They decided to leave the future indefinite and fell asleep in each other's arms.

Toward dawn, Allyn awoke. Beside her, Jim was still sleeping deeply. She studied his face in the gray light. He was lying on his side, his head bent toward his chest. The downward slant gave his face a sad, solemn cast. She remembered what he had said last night about his inability to be more than a spectator of Maria's faith. A rueful spectator.

Allyn walked into the living room. The chest with Randy's letters still lay on the end table. Allyn studied it for a moment, then turned away. "Oh, Father," she whispered. She dropped to her knees and slowly raised her arms. Closing her eyes, she waited in the cool darkness.

A breath of wind from an open window passed through her nightgown. *Help me to give Jim peace,* she prayed. *Help me to fill his life with love. Help us both begin again.*

She waited in the darkness for another moment. Then it began, curling up through her body, a surging roiling warmth, a sweetness beyond anything she had ever known from pills or cocaine, a soaring within herself higher than any diver had ever sprung. Tears streamed down her cheeks. *Fool fool fool,* she thought. Why were you ever afraid of it? Afraid of your fate, your gift.

XXVIII

For the second consecutive night, Paul Stapleton was dreaming about the River of Doubt. He was in the jungle, thrashing through the green darkness toward the river glinting in the distance. He had to get to the point of land before the boats passed.

Suddenly he was there, the boats were in the rapids and Teddy Roosevelt's voice boomed: *The effort, the effort's still worth it.* They were racing past him, ignoring his shouts. Especially his father. He was in the last boat, crouched low, paddling desperately. Suddenly he turned his head and glared at his son on the point of land. "I hope—" he began.

"No," Paul Stapleton said, and put his hands over his ears. He refused to hear the unbearable words. He turned and plunged back into the jungle.

He awoke wrestling with the sheet. Sam Fry was standing beside him. "Are you O.K., Colonel?" he said. "I heard you call."

"Just a dream, Sam. What time is it?"

"About four."

He told Sam to get some sleep and lay in bed thinking

about the day ahead. It was going to be a tough one. RIP, the citywide coalition that opposed busing, was planning a demonstration in front of the courthouse. Judge Stapleton had the power to ban it. The mayor and the head of the FBI task force that was working with the court had urged him to issue the order. They were afraid of a riot. But he had decided to let them demonstrate. In court, the city's Puerto Ricans were protesting their inclusion with the white majority. They were demanding minority status, and were submitting an integration plan of their own, which carefully avoided schools in black neighborhoods.

Roman Pignatowski, the Judge's clerk, had shaken his head and called the city a crazy quilt. Paul Stapleton had calmed him down with a little history. He told Roman it was no worse than it had been seventy years ago. The Irish and the Germans had hated each other just like the blacks and Puerto Ricans today. The city had coped with it. They would cope with this problem the same way, living with it day by day.

He had decided to dismiss the Puerto Rican plan on the grounds that they were not numerous enough in the city to merit the attention of the court. He knew it would cause screams and might even be reversed in the Court of Appeals. But he wanted the black busing plan to proceed without interruptions.

Who was he lunching with? Agatha. She wanted advice on raising funds to expand her hospice. He should be lunching with Jim Kilpatrick. He had not seen him for well over a week. Maybe he had been using the pressure in court as an excuse to avoid him. It had been embarrassing to discover that he had been talking to Dwight Slocum and Muriel Bennett and Peregrine Stapleton. But he had begun to wonder whether he had been too quick to agree to Agatha's plan, putting the research in her cold-storage vault for the next fifty years. Maybe it would be better to sit down with Kilpatrick and talk it out man to man. They had faced up to a few difficult pieces of the past together—like the $100,000 he had paid to Judge James Kilpatrick, Sr.

Why was he changing his mind? More and more he saw the book as Randy's story. His own story was only the preface to that astonishing multiplication of wealth in National Products. The secret saga of how they took the corporation away from Dwight Slocum's reckless blundering hands step by steady step deserved to be told. Randy's idea of using the money to create the Principia Foundation was the perfect climax. The announcement of plans for the foundation could be timed to coincide with the publication of the book. Perhaps that inner truth would make up for the ones propriety and privacy required him to omit. How much could any man be expected to tell? Even Grandfather had had secrets. When he died in 1918, a woman had come uninvited to the graveside service. She stood apart from the family. She was tall, handsome, straight-backed. Maria thought she had looked Irish. She had walked to a waiting cab and driven away without speaking to anyone.

He would tell Kilpatrick about the foundation in their next talk. He would give him the letters Randy and he had exchanged.

His mind drifted back over his memories of Randy. The pride he had felt when he heard about his Distinguished Service Cross at St.-Lô. His unfailing good humor, so different from Mark's surly temperament, John's roller-coaster disposition. He remembered the pain he had felt during those first postwar years when all he heard from Randy was praise of Dwight Slocum. Then came that mysterious change, after the death of Randy's wife. It was crystallized on that fall day in 1953 when Randy had spent the weekend with them. He had gone for a final horseback ride with him on Sunday afternoon.

They rounded a curve in the road and New Grange Farm lay below them, the sunshine gleaming on the white house, the reflecting pool in the patio, the red barn.

"God, I love this place," Randy said.

Paul Stapleton's eyes had filled with tears. He had said these same words to his own father on a ride they had taken together along this road, the summer before they went down the River of Doubt. He knew what Randy was saying, as his father had known what he had been saying. *I love you.* It was as close as a male Stapleton could come to those dangerous, embarrassing words.

Paul Stapleton went back to sleep until the alarm clock

burst around him like an exploding shell. He struggled out of bed, drank his buttermilk, took his cold shower and began the day. As he was finishing breakfast, he got a call from Ned. "Hey, Judge," he said, "I've got car trouble. Can I bum a ride to the office from you?"

He suspected Ned was lying. He was worried about that demonstration at the courthouse. He thought the old man needed a bodyguard. Paul Stapleton decided to let him get away with it. Maybe he would need one.

Ned's wife, Tracy, drove him over to the farm. Paul Stapleton could not resist needling her. He did not want to let either of them think he knew what was going on. "I guess you've got this fellow so intimidated he's afraid to borrow your car," he said to Tracy. "You southern girls are in a class by yourselves. My mother had the same kind of half nelson on my father."

Tracy began describing the hectic day she faced. Their oldest boy, Paul, was coming home from Pennsgrove for a long weekend and had to be met at the bus terminal in the city. There was a Junior Legaue meeting. She was playing tennis at the country club. Paul Stapleton said he was only teasing. Tracy always took him too seriously.

In the car, Ned asked if he should have brought his National Guard helmet along. Did the FBI predict a big crowd? "Only about a hundred," Paul Stapleton said. "That's why I decided to let them yell. I'm hoping it will make them look silly."

The FBI turned out to be wrong. There were at least three hundred demonstrators in front of the courthouse. There were almost as many city police and FBI agents. As the Stapleton Mercedes came down the street, the protesters unleashed a roar of rage. Sam Fry turned into the parking lot, about a hundred yards before the courthouse steps. The crowd surged into the lot after them. A wall of white-helmeted cops stopped them just inside the gate. Paul Stapleton and Ned got out of the car.

"Hey, Judge, seen any niggers out at Snob Acres?" yelled one man.

"Why don't you buy them cars like you got and let them drive their kids out to your schools?" a woman screamed.

"Goddamn Wasp Hitler!" roared a man.

"He's got Hitler, Jr., with him. What kind of a juicy legal deal are you handing him this morning?"

"Millionaire snob, go fuck yourself."

"Yeah. Screw the Stapletons. Screw all of them."

Ned insisted on going up in the creaking private elevator to escort his father to the door of his chambers. "Reminds me of the 1926 strike," Paul Stapleton said as they strolled down the corridor. "They used to yell things like that all the time. But it was in various foreign languages, so it didn't bother you."

Ned was glowering. "They're such slobs," he said.

"They don't know any better, Ned."

In the chambers, Ned kidded Roman Pignatowski about Kitty Kosciusko, the leader of the demonstration. Were they cousins by any chance? Roman strenuously denied it. Ned asked Paul Stapleton about a ride home. Ned had a date to play squash at the City Club at five. Should he cancel it?

"Why don't you come over and watch the game?" Ned said. "I'm playing the guy I beat for the club championship last year. He's damn good. You may have to take me home on my racquet."

Why not? Paul Stapleton thought, nodding. He had not watched Ned play any sport for a long time, at least four or five years. When Ned was younger, Paul Stapleton had been proud of his athletic ability. The pride had been eroded by his irritation at Ned's seeming refusal to grow up. Now Paul Stapleton wondered if he had lost touch with his youngest son. Ned's coolness under the muzzle of George's gun had been remarkable. That night, on the way back from the sanitarium, he had listened calmly, soberly, as his father told him what Kilpatrick had probably heard from Muriel Bennett, Dwight Slocum, Peregrine. It had been startling, in the middle of it, to realize that Ned was functioning as his attorney. He asked tough, intelligent questions about evidence, documents, proof. He showed that he could think under emotional pressure as well as physical danger. The revelations must have been upsetting—but he kept his feelings to himself like a man—especially a Stapleton—should. The next day he had taken charge of the situation, consulting with Agatha and Allyn, planning and executing the strategy and tactics of getting Mark on their side.

Obviously, he had been letting an opinion formed five or even ten years ago warp his view of Ned. He had never been as close to Ned as he had been to the older boys. For four crucial years, during World War II, he had been away, and the next five years had been so full of turmoil, selling the mills, moving them South, regaining his role in the law firm, fretting over Randy and Dwight Slocum, Ned had been pushed aside again. He had substituted lectures and exhortations for companionship and this may have had something to do with Ned's slowness to mature. Once started, the tendency was hard to stop. As Ned probably saw it, he was still getting orders and reprimands from a father who should be in a rocking chair or dead. It was a little like his father's problem with his grandfather.

Maybe there was some point to all this thinking and talking about the past. It gave a man a few insights into the present.

The morning went smoothly in the courtroom. He listened to the Puerto Rican lawyers argue for a separate busing program. Agatha arrived about 11:45 and sat in the back, seemingly quite interested in the show. Just before he adjourned, Paul Stapleton made a decision that had nothing to do with the arguments before him. He decided to change his will, and make Ned the executor of his estate. At the moment, it was Walter Ackroyd.

Agatha joined her brother in his chambers for lunch. Roman had ordered chef salads from a nearby restaurant. Agatha discoursed on the hospice. She wanted to double its size before she died. Or, as she put it, "became a candidate for one of the beds."

Paul Stapleton had never had much enthusiasm for the hospice. Aside from the fact that it was named after his mother, he did not think dying was such a complicated business as Agatha and her psychiatrist friends were determined to make it. It was something a man had to do, like fight wars or win difficult cases for demanding clients. But Maria had browbeaten him into pretending some enthusiasm, and giving a lot of money to the hospice.

Maria said the place was Agatha's child. He could no fight that kind of feminine logic.

Agatha wanted a large donation from him to start th fund raising for the new wing. He offered twenty-five thousand dollars. She said she was thinking of a hundred thousand. "You can consider fifty thousand of it a dona tion and fifty thousand my fee for rescuing the bool project from disaster," she said.

"O.K.," he said, signifying his agreement on botl counts.

Agatha asked him if he had seen Jim Kilpatrick since he had returned from the South. Paul Stapleton said he had not had time. He wanted to spend a few more hours with him, describing Randy's achievements at Nationa Products.

"He's given me all the tapes and notes from his inter views with you and—the others. I've read and listened to them. It's convinced me all over again about the Enter prise."

"Really?" Paul Stapleton said. He pretended to be interested in this theory of Agatha's. Privately, he consid ered it Cloud Nine stuff.

"I was only disappointed about one thing," Agatha said. "I didn't find what I expected—or hoped to find— about your trip down the River of Doubt."

"You can't expect an eighty-year-old man to remem ber everything that ever happened to him," he said wari ly.

"Maybe it's rather unpleasant and you've just put it out of your mind," Agatha said. "When I was talking to Mr. Kilpatrick at my house, we were looking through a book of snapshots taken at Bowood before the first war. There was a picture of Mother and Father in the garden. I suddenly recalled coming down the path and standing there, behind the hedges, listening to them discuss getting a divorce. I'd forgotten it completely."

"When was that?" Paul Stapleton said.

"It was only a month or two before you went down the River of Doubt. Father warned Mother to stop seeing a certain man. She refused. He threatened a divorce and she dared him to go ahead."

Paul Stapleton felt his body grow hot, whether from

shame or shock or anger, he was not sure at first. "You're not making this up?"

"Of course not. They were terribly unhappy, Paul. You know that."

"Why," he said, struggling not merely for words but for breath, "why are we raising money for a—a monument to her?"

Agatha looked sad. "I wish somehow you could forgive her, Paul. If you could only see it from her side. Tyrannized by Grandfather. Her husband a weak man who couldn't protect her or her children."

"Weak?" Paul Stapleton said with a fierce shake of his head. "I don't accept that."

"He was a dabbler, Paul. A charming, gifted dilettante in architecture, politics. But no one took him seriously. Least of all Grandfather."

"He had—he had his own strength," Paul Stapleton said. "When the time came. When it was necessary. But knowing his state of mind, for the first time I see—"

He was on the River of Doubt again. He saw his father's sad sensitive face confronting Teddy Roosevelt with the possibility that it was all futile, America was a gigantic hoax. Paul Stapleton saw—what he had not told Jim Kilpatrick—what he had not even told himself for a long time—Roosevelt's anger. His charming, cheerful friend Stapleton was challenging him in a way the Great Man did not like.

"What do you see for the first time?" Agatha said.

"It was on the River of Doubt. When things went sour. We were on half rations. This big *camarado,* Júlio, stole food from Roosevelt's pack. Another fellow saw him and reported him. Júlio grabbed a rifle and killed him. Júlio ran into the jungle. The next day, he appeared on a point of land and pleaded with us to take him back. He was afraid of what the Indians in the jungle would do to him. Father talked to TR for a moment, then got in the dugout with me and we went back up the river, hugging the bank to avoid the current.

"When we got to the point of land, Júlio was standing there crying. He was saying something in Portuguese about being sorry, he would go to jail, anything to get away from the Indians. We stopped paddling and Father

383

—Father stood up in the boat and he had his army .45 in his hand. He shot Júlio between the eyes. Júlio fell back into the jungle. The other *camaradas* turned the boat around and we drifted back downstream with the current. Father put his gun away and said to me, 'I hope you haver have to do anything like that.' "

Paul Stapleton sat in his high-backed judicial chair in the room with the inlaid walnut panels and the carved figure of Justice above the black marble fireplace, the room that his father had designed. Tears streamed down his cheeks.

"So that was it," Agatha said.

"He became Grandfather for me. I saw—or thought I saw—that there was no difference between them. All his talk about ideals, what did it mean? Eventually, I explained to myself why he did it. We couldn't take Júlio back with us. We would have had to guard him night and day. We didn't have the manpower, the strength. But they were my explanations. Beneath, behind them, I still felt it was a kind of betrayal, a—sin."

"Perhaps it was an act of mercy. The Indians."

"No. The motive was our safety. They didn't want him following us. They were afraid he might attack us in the night."

Paul Stapleton refused to lie, excuse the crime. For the first time it was not necessary. For the first time he knew why his father talked to his dead brother Rawdon in his last delirium. His father's world had been coming apart. The 1912 strike led by the Wobblies with their dynamite bombs, his wife's defiance, were forcing him to face both the failure of love and the brutal reality of American life. He had been challenging Teddy Roosevelt, daring him to face up to the cruel facts. With the blast of that .45, he was telling his son that he was abandoning his facile hopes for the improvement of mankind. He was trying to grasp his own manhood. But simultaneously, as Paul had done with his own sons, he tried to pass on at least the yearning for the ideal. That was the meaning of those sad words: *I hope you never have to do anything like that.*

Agatha was talking about their mother again. "The saddest part of it, Paul, was her relative innocence. I'm sure there was nothing in the least immoral about her relationship with the man she was seeing. I remember asking her about it once, years later. He was an English professor. They read poetry together."

Agatha coughed violently and drank some tea. "Mother—didn't like sex. Once she warned me about 'the dirty thing men had between their legs.' "

Paul Stapleton did not know what to say. Agatha was blushing. "We should have talked about these things a long time ago," she said.

"I'm glad we talked now," he said.

"Yes. Thank you for the money."

Agatha left her chef salad unfinished. So did he.

Paul Stapleton spent the afternoon listening to the Board of Education's lawyers arguing against the Puerto Ricans. He felt guilty because he did not pay much attention to the legal logic. Most of the time he was thinking about his conversation with Agatha. *So that was it,* she said. He remembered how often, with her usual tact, Agatha had tried to find out what had happened to him on the River of Doubt.

Paul Stapleton sighed. After eighty years it was still a mystery to him, the persistence with which some women cared about a man. Once it had annoyed him, it had seemed prying, intrusive, to probe a man's feelings, his motives, to fret over whether he believed in God or the ideal. But now he understood it was part of their caring, their way of expressing love. They were better at it than men. A man just did his job.

He cut the lawyers short at four o'clock and dismissed the Puerto Ricans' motion. They were predictably furious and demanded an immediate appeal. He granted it. In his chambers, Roman Pignatowski worried about what they would say on television that night. Paul Stapleton ignored him. He was tired of reassuring Roman out of his Polish glooms. He called Walter Ackroyd and told him he wanted to change his will and make Ned executor of his estate. Walter said he would have a codicil ready, if he drove over to the office before he went home. He drove over at four-thirty, signed the codicil and sat in Walter's office enjoying the panoramic view of the city, the river and the countryside beyond it. Walter asked for George and again expressed regret about forcing him to resign.

385

"Don't be ridiculous, Walter," Paul Stapleton said "You should have written six months ago."

Walter talked about how well Ned was heading up the new-business committee. His briefs had improved remarkably in the past year. It was hardly necessary fo him to read them any more.

"Then don't," Paul Stapleton said.

Walter started discussing his retirement. He would b sixty-five in January. He thought he should step down a managing partner. Paul Stapleton had waited until he wa seventy, but Walter confessed to a mild unhappiness with the job. If Paul Stapleton had not chosen him as hi successor, Walter would have gladly let someone els tackle the assignment. He was happier practicing law without worrying about budgets, new clients, quarrelin partners, hiring quotas for women and blacks, the thou sand and one details of running a big office.

Paul Stapleton was sympathetic. He understood ho Walter felt. He had coped with those maddening detail for decades. Walter had been his right-hand man, and very good one, for his last ten years as managing partner He had asked him to accept the job as an act of responsi bility. He had known Walter was not a natural leade But he had guessed—it would seem rightly—that the firn was organized well enough to run itself for about decade. Now it was time to find a new leader. He wishe them luck. Leaders were not easy to find.

After reminiscing with Walter Ackroyd for a few mor minutes, Paul Stapleton rode back uptown to the Cit Club. By the time he sat down in the fifth-floor squas court gallery, Ned and his opponent, a younger, talle man named Pierce, were on the court warming up. Ne looked very solid and trim in his white gym shorts an shirt. He was built like his grandfather, Paul Stapleto thought. Not as tall, but the same meaty thighs, chunk shoulders. It occurred to him that they had similar tem peraments too. What was it Agatha had called thei father? A charming dilettante. He had been charming, n question about it. Paul Stapleton remembered how deftl he handled crowds at political rallies. Always a quic remark, a personal greeting. While his son Paul stoo there tongue-tied. Even today he would be the same way. Something about the very idea of a crowd offended him.

The match began. Pierce had speed and energy, Ned had experience and guile. Nicks and corner shots that dropped off the front wall and died, a serve that drooled down the side wall and forced Pierce to make a half dozen errors in the first game, which Ned won, 15-5. Pierce solved the serve and came slamming back to take the second game, 15-8. Ned coasted for the last five points, gathering his strength for the tie breaker.

Pierce had the serve. He reeled off five quick points before Ned broke through with a drop shot. Ned suddenly unveiled a smash serve that threw off Pierce's timing. Ned grabbed four more points and went ahead on another drop shot. Pierce got the serve back with a scorching alley shot and the score seesawed to 14-14. It was no set—the equivalent of match point in tennis—and Ned looked tired.

Instead of trying for a quick kill, Ned chose to volley. For two full minutes he and Pierce went up and down, back and forth across the small court, smashing the hard black ball at terrific speed. Both players were calling on their last reserves of strength and wind. Finally a Pierce forehand came off the back wall with a high fat bounce. Ned aced it backhand down the left wall into the corner inches off the floor. It was a putaway. Pierce could not touch it.

Paul Stapleton went down to the locker room and shook Pierce's hand. "I've always maintained this fellow was born lucky," he said, smiling at Ned.

"Tough," Pierce gasped. "Born tough."

"He felt sorry for me," Ned said. "It's be-kind-to-the-middle-aged week."

On the way home in the car, Paul Stapleton slapped Ned on the knee. "I liked the way you played that last point. Beat him at his own game."

Ned nodded. "I knew I had to psyche him. That game is fifty percent psychology."

"So is almost everything," Paul Stapleton said. "I've been doing a little thinking about the future. I decided to change my will and make you executor."

"Who was the previous one?"

"Walter Ackroyd. I've decided I want to keep the estate in the family. Besides, Walter tells me he's thinking of retiring next year."

"Really?" Ned said. "Who's going to be the next managing partner?"

"If you keep pushing on this new-business committee, I think it could be you."

He let it go at that, for the time being.

They were on the Parkway, rolling past Bowood. Paul Stapleton paused to take a good look at the old house. He could see his grandfather's picture glaring across the ballroom. He thought of his father and mother in the garden discussing a divorce. *I hope you'll never have to do anything like that.* It was a father's wish. He could bestow it on Ned, now, for whatever it was worth.

"I've never told you—or anyone—the size of my estate, Ned. Frankly, I was a little afraid of the impact on you and George and Allyn. I've always had a dread of giving any of my children the feeling that we were superrich and could start ignoring the everyday realities of life. I think a lot of Allyn's trouble has come from the money she inherited from Randy."

"I understand, Dad," Ned said.

"The estate will be about a hundred and fifty million dollars, most of it in National Products stock. You'll all be well provided for. But most of the money will go into a foundation. That was Randy's idea. He made most of that money by multiplying ten or twenty times the value of the Principia Mills stock that I exchanged for National Products stock. He sold me on the idea of creating a foundation that will devote itself exclusively to improving the life of this city in all areas, business, politics, education. He felt that we took a lot of money out of this city over the past hundred years. It was time to put it back with interest."

Ned nodded. "I'll buy that."

"I was going to wait until I died to have it set up. That way no one could claim it was an ego trip for me. But now I wonder if we ought to wait. I seem to be living forever. A thought that may have occurred to you more than once."

Ned earnestly denied ever having such a thought. He said he would convene a round table of experts at the firm and discuss the best way to organize the foundation. Then they could get down to discussing the board of trustees, the staff.

"That's where I think we can bring Mark into the game. I think he'd have something to contribute to the foundation. He ought to be a trustee, maybe the chairman of the board. I'd like to make him president, but nobody from the family can be an officer."

"Do you have anyone in mind for president?" Ned asked.

"It ought to be someone who knows this city pretty well. Someone born here, preferably. It would also help if he had a business background. He'll be voting the stock on the National Products board. Under the law, the foundation won't have to divest itself of the stock for twenty years."

"How about Jim Kilpatrick?" Ned said. "He fits both sides. He was born and grew up in the city. He knows National Products. He can't stand Slocum."

"I like it," Paul Stapleton said. "Let's sleep on it for a night or two."

"Another thing," Ned added, after a minute of thought. "It would practically guarantee that Kilpatrick would never write anything unpleasant about the Stapletons."

Paul Stapleton avoided his son's eyes. "That occurred to me too," he said.

Arriving home after dropping Ned off, Paul Stapleton found Maria on the telephone in her bedroom. She had the small statute of the Virgin in her free hand. For a moment he felt a flicker of irritation. But the anger, the arguments about that statue, were too far back now. It took him a moment to realize she was talking to George. "I am so glad you called," she said. "So glad you are feeling so well. I'll talk to your father about Mexico."

Maria hung up and smiled up at him as he kissed her. "That was George," she said. "He's off the tranquilizers already. Dr. Kane says he'll be ready to leave in two weeks, if all goes well. He wants to go to Mexico, if you're still willing to provide the money."

"Of course I'm willing."

"He told me—about the gun." Her lips trembled. Paul Stapleton thought she was going to weep. "It's too horrible to think about. You—and Ned."

In his mind Paul Stapleton damned George for a fool. He took Maria's hand and held it for a moment. "It was nothing," he lied. "He took it out and waved it around to make a point. It wasn't even loaded. He obviously had no intention of using it."

"It made me feel responsible. He wanted to go to Mexico many years ago. But I opposed it. I talked him out of it. You know why."

He nodded, feeling sadness tinge his good mood. To him, Mexico was not a land stained by paternal blood. It was freedom, love in the mountains, the stunning sensual power of this woman's glowing body, all lost when he returned to his own cold climate. Not completely lost, he corrected himself. But never as pure, as intense.

He helped her up from her chair to go down the hall to dinner. It had become a daily ritual, this little meeting in her room. Sometimes he would sit down opposite her and chat. He did not enjoy the visits as much since she had removed the wallpaper. The glowing red and yellow and blue peasants parading around the room had made it like a visit to Mexico. She said she had gotten tired of the peasants and planned to replace the paper with another pattern. Instead, she had had the walls painted gray and left them bare.

He inhaled the tangy odors of paella drifting through the house. It was his favorite dish. "That smells as good as ever," he said. A memory from the Twenties came into his head as they went slowly down the hall, Maria leaning on his arm. He had come home to that rich odor and she had met him in the hall, her black hair glowing in the lamplight. He had said something about loving paella. "You have peasant tastes in food," she said, teasing him. "Paella is a peasant dish." He had kissed her hard and said, "I have peasant tastes in women too." He had picked her up, still kissing her, and carried her into her room and made violent love to her while she murmured "Paul, no, the children, the servants will—"

Then came that terrible night in 1928 when he told her

390

about John. The night that had changed so much in their lives. They stopped being lovers. For a long time they were barely husband and wife. Even after she forgave him, it was never the same. Something hard and cold inside him found reasons to refuse to forgive her for the insults she had screamed at him that night. Not until John died in 1950 did he lose the last of those feelings. Only when he saw how her grief matched his mourning was he able to believe completely in her forgiveness.

"I've been thinking about Mexico," Maria said as the houseboys served the paella. "Talking about it to Mr. Kilpatrick made me realize that all these years I have let the bad memories overshadow the good ones—like our honeymoon in the Sierras."

"You didn't tell him all of that, I hope," he said, smiling at the memory of making love after swimming naked in the river below the falls of the Basaseáchic.

"No, of course not," Maria said. "But I remembered it."

"That's why I tried to get you to go back to Mexico for a second honeymoon after" (he was going to say "John died" but changed it to) "the second war. I thought it was the place where we could begin again."

"I'm sorry. I couldn't go back," she said with a sigh.

He nodded. "I've been thinking about John," he said. "What he cost us."

"Yes," she said.

Even now, he could see it was hard for her to think about it. Suddenly he wanted to say or do something to banish the last of the pain.

"That night when we quarreled, I told you I wasn't sure if I would have come back to you—except for the bullet in the Argonne. I think I was trying to hurt you because you were hurting me so much—not that I didn't deserve it."

Maria put down her fork. She was listening with total, alarming attention. For a moment he thought he could not finish what he wanted to say.

"I would have come back, bullet or no bullet. After the Argonne, all my wildness, craziness, would have been over, one way or the other. Just standing there in the middle of that battle, I was defying more odds, taking more chances than I could have found in two lifetimes. I would have come back—for Mexico—and for Randy."

"I have always wanted to believe that," Maria said.

Was it really true? asked a mocking voice as he watched Maria's lined face glow. He remembered that totally different woman in the flat above the Seine, the woman with the long lean legs and small breasts and fragile shoulder bones whispering, "Love me, love me, that's all I want, you loving me." He struggled to be ruthlessly honest and realized it no longer mattered. The woman facing him was part of Randy turning to say: *I love this place.* She was part of watching Ned swing a baseball bat or a squash racquet, she was part of Allyn running to greet him, pigtails flying, somehow curing the exhaustion of a long legal day. Even the anguished memories, John's death and George's cowardice and Mark's bitter withdrawal, could he have endured them without Maria's love? Perhaps. But he would have aged like his grandfather, into a cold, dry husk.

There were tears on Maria's cheeks. Paul Stapleton felt embarrassed by all this emotion. He stood up and kissed her on the forehead. "We're becoming a couple of ancient sentimentalists," he said.

He spent the evening reading legal journals. In the *Journal of Public Law,* he saw an article by Mark, "Busing: Does It Produce Equal Education?" He read it carefully. It was a good performance, well written, with clean, well-organized paragraphs. It argued that the net effect of busing was reverse discrimination against whites and the creation of a "stigma of inferiority" on the public schools in cities where busing had been attempted. Paul Stapleton picked up the microphone of the Stenorette he kept on his desk and dictated a note to his son.

"Dear Mark:

I read your article on busing. It is very well done. You write better and better. Your conclusions are well taken. But I have this one fault to find with your argument. Judges like myself, manning the front-line trenches, have to fight the battle with the weapons that are available. It doesn't do us much good to criticize the weapons. Give us better ones and we'll use them. I would also caution you against a certain Cloud Nine tendency in your approach. Attacking an evil like segregation is a kind of war, and you can't fight a war without some people getting hurt."

In bed, Paul Stapleton had trouble getting to sleep. The conversations of the day seemed to be recorded in his mind. He played them back, one by one. He saw the faces: Agatha saying: *So that was it*. Maria: *I have always wanted to believe that*. Maybe there was, in the confusion, a kind of thread. He suddenly remembered that the word was part of something his father had told him. "You have to keep looking for the golden thread," he said. "It keeps getting trampled underfoot, covered with mud, lost in the undergrowth. But it's there, if you look for it."

He was asleep, dreaming. He was on the River of Doubt again. But this time there was no fear. He and his father were partners, paddling straight down the center of the river, smiles on their faces. Even when the river grew ugly with rapids, when his father became a ragged beaten man lying in the bottom of the dugout, Paul felt no shame, no dread. He told the *camaradas* to stop the boat and held his father in his arms. "It's all right," he said. "Everything is going to be all right now."

With no warning, the river vanished. He was surrounded by whiteness. He was at the beach. He was a little boy. Someone was calling his name. He looked up and saw a woman standing on the crest of the dunes holding out her hand to him. She wore a long white dress, in the style of 1903 or 1904. Around her neck was a light blue scarf that spread onto her shoulders. Everything was so bright he could not see her face. But he was sure it was his mother, looking as beautiful, as happy as he remembered her from those distant days.

"Come, Paul," she said. "Let us look at the sea."

He laughed and ran toward her outstretched hand. Beyond her the sea was a blaze of light.

XXIX

The ringing telephone dragged Agatha Stapleton Slocum up from deep dreamless sleep. It was still dark. There was only the faintest hint of dawn on the windowpane. The belling sound said death. No one would call in the early dawn for any other reason. She reached for the receiver on the night table. "Agatha?" Maria said. "Paul died in his sleep about an hour ago."

"I'll be right over," Agatha said.

"No, no, there is no hurry. Ned and Tracy are coming."

Agatha lay back on the pillows and said a brief prayer of gratitude. If anyone deserved an easy death, it was Paul. He could never have coped with weeks or months of bedridden waiting, the humiliations of helplessness.

She shrugged on a robe and went down the hall to Peregrine's room. She knocked and told him the sad news. She heard the thump of his feet on the floor, the stumbling steps to the door. He stood there blinking in the light, his hair rumpled, his hands shaking. "You're sure?" he said.

"Didn't you hear the phone? It was Maria."

He shook his head. "I'll be next," he said.

Agatha kissed him on the forehead. "Don't be silly. You'll last another decade. You'll turn into a withered old pumpkin."

Back in the bedroom, Agatha began to dress. She went into the bathroom to comb her hair. She looked into the mirror and saw her wrinkled neck, the sagging skin on her cheeks. From 1915 came faint echoes of sensuous music. She saw Paul's face, the one in the Pennsgrove yearbook. Her own grief struck her like an explosion. She clutched the sink and sobbed and sobbed, pressing her forehead against the cool cruel mirror. It lasted for about ten minutes. Then she washed her face, powdered her nose and came downstairs to have coffee with Peregrine.

"To die in the midst of things," Peregrine said. "I wish I could do it."

"You're in the midst of the things you love—your paintings, your furniture, your clothes."

"I mean with power still in your hands. With the sense of your own importance undiminished."

"I don't think Paul thought he was very important."

Peregrine smiled wanly. "You can't even find that much fault with him."

They taxied to the farm through the dusky dawn. In the house a sort of orderly confusion prevailed. Ned was calling relatives. Jim Kilpatrick was on another telephone calling newspapers and a long list of senators, congressmen, lawyers, generals. Maria kissed Agatha and Peregrine and led them into Paul's bedroom. "I thought you would want to say goodbye to him," Maria said.

Paul's face was extraordinarily peaceful. A trace of a smile had relaxed the stoic mouth. It reminded Agatha of the hospice, of the faces of those who had struggled through refusal and anger to acceptance of their deaths. She leaned down and kissed Paul's cold lips. The sensation returned her to the mirror in the bathroom and she wept violently, briefly again.

"Sam awoke me about four," Maria said. "He felt something pass through his room, like a desert wind. He knew Paul had gone."

Maria was remarkably calm. Too calm, Agatha

thought. Her grief would come later. The reactions of other members of the family varied. Maria called George at the sanitarium and he wept for a half hour. Mark, who arrived with his pretty black wife, Dawn, was stoic. But he spontaneously leaned down and kissed his father. Allyn was mournful and teary. Ned was the most surprising —calm, quietly prepared to make the numerous small decisions that every funeral involved. He was obviously the new leader of the family.

Ned decided there would be no wake and the funeral would be in the Episcopal church in New Grange Township. He preferred it to a church in the city because he was afraid anti-busing fanatics might attempt some tasteless disruption of the service.

The small red-brick Episcopal church was jammed for the funeral. A half dozen senators, a dozen congressman, two judges from the Court of Appeals (alumni of Stapleton, Talbot), three or four retired generals led by Mark Stratton, Mayor O'Connor and his wife, and members of the City Council filled the pews behind the family. Members of the Hamilton County Hunt, the entire staff of Stapleton, Talbot, and numerous other friends or sons and daughters of departed friends added to the crush.

Allyn insisted on Jim Kilpatrick's joining the family in the front pews. She sat beside Agatha, waiting for the service to begin. "Jim and I are going to be married," she said in a careful whisper that did not carry beyond Agatha's ear.

"I'm not terribly surprised," Agatha said.

"Do you think Maria will be upset?"

"I doubt it. But give her time, before you tell her."

There was no eulogy. At Agatha's suggestion, Ned had the young minister read "The Portrait of a Good Man."

"Lord, who's the happy man that may to Thy blest courts repair;
Not stranger-like to visit them, but to inhabit there?

'Tis he whose every thought and deed by rules of virtue moves;
Whose generous tongue disdains to speak the thing his heart disproves.

396

Who never did a slander forge his neighbor's name to
*   wound;*
Nor harken to the false report by malice whispered round.

Who vice, in all its pomp and power, can treat with just
*   neglect;*
And piety, though clothed in rags, religiously respect.

Who to his plighted vows and trust has ever firmly stood;
And though he promised to his loss, he makes his promise
*   good.*

Whose soul in usury disdains his treasure to employ;
Whom no rewards can ever bribe the guiltless to destroy.

The man who, by this steady course, has happiness
*   insured.*
When Earth's foundations shake, shall stand by Provi-
*   dence secured."*

In those rolling rhythms, Agatha heard the inescapable
beat of the ideal. Paul had heard it too and had responded in spite of himself, with a crippled, at times
tormented assent. Now that she knew the inner truth of
his ordeal, she could forgive him finally and forever in the
deepest level of her heart, she could love him without a
shadow of regret or doubt. No matter now if Earth's
foundations shook, she too had happiness secured.

The burial was at Woodlawn Cemetery, on the hillside
overlooking the wrecked hulks of Principia Mills. Agatha
stood beside Maria, thinking of the cold day when they
met at this place for Anne Randolph Stapleton's burial.
She took some roses from Paul's coffin and placed them
on her mother's grave. Peregrine was gazing past her at
his father's headstone. It was the only one with sculpture
on it. A warrior figure, sword in hand, charged forever up
San Juan Hill.

The weather was exquisite. Indian-summer sunshine
gleamed on the river and glittered on the distant red and
gold and yellow hills beyond it. Six soldiers wearing shiny
brown helmets and white gloves approached the grave.
Three on each side, they raised their rifles above it and
fired a salute. Inescapable, the sounds of war. But they

belonged here too, those murderous rifles, those blank military faces. What else had had a more pervasive influence on the Stapletons?

The minister folded the American flag on Paul's coffin and handed it to Maria. He asked the mourners to join him in saying the "Our Father." Then a bugler played taps. The sweet sadness of war's end for the warrior. Agatha saw the somber face of Sam Fry on the other side of the grave. Life, history, had made a warrior of Paul as it had made a general of Jonathan Rawdon Stapleton. It had obliterated that smiling carefree boy who danced the Innovation at Paradise Beach in 1915. What was it some survivor had said of World War I? *The war was our youth.* For Paul war had been both his youth and his middle age. He had been a warrior son and a warrior father.

As they walked back toward the waiting limousines, Jim Kilpatrick fell in step with Agatha. "Ned wants me to be president of the Principia Foundation," he said. "I told him he didn't have to make any extravagant offers. I'll just go away quietly."

"I don't understand what you mean," Agatha said.

"I'm not going to write anything. I made a promise. I'm not going to break it."

"Maybe the offer has nothing to do with that," Agatha said.

"That's what Ned claims. He says the Judge was planning to ask me himself. Did he say anything to you about it?"

Jim's head was down, his voice was casual. But Agatha sensed that this was a crucial question. "Yes," she lied. "Only a day or two ago."

Jim looked hard at her for a moment. "Thanks," he said.

You are a deceitful, outrageous woman, Agatha thought as she got into the limousine after Peregrine. A believer in the ideal who can look a man in the eye and tell him a blatant lie. But it was for a good cause. She was certain she had done something Paul would have approved. Nevertheless, she decided not to mention it to Peregrine. He was sure to point out that Stapletons liked to choose good causes that were also good for the Stapletons.

Agatha went home and took a nap. She thought, even hoped, she might dream of Paul. But she sank into two hours of blank absolute sleep. She rose, called a taxi and rode to New Grange Farm. Ned and his wife, Tracy, and their three sons were leaving as she arrived. The boys were solemn and subdued, especially the oldest, Paul. He did not look like his grandfather. Physically he resembled George—a sleeker, more self-assured version of that unfortunate son. Agatha's favorite was the youngest, Kemble. That ascetic mouth, those cool gray eyes, were pure Stapleton. But they all shared the blood and the tradition. The sight of them softened the burr of grief in Agatha's throat. Here was the future that might justify the pain and losses of the past. Would they mock the American enterprise? Or help to guide it? She did not know. But she could, she would, hope in them.

Tracy said Maria was on the patio. Agatha found her sitting in a straight-backed chair beside the reflecting pool, her back to the house. The sun was dropping behind the nearest hill, leaving only hints of russet in the darkening water. Most of the trees on the hill had surrendered their fall foliage. They stood gray and gaunt in the fading light. Agatha shivered in the chill air. She was glad she was wearing a coat. Maria was wearing only a dark blue sweater over her black dress.

"Are you warm enough?" Agatha asked.

"Yes," Maria said, drawing the sweater around her.

Agatha dragged over a chair and sat down beside Maria. They watched the sunset's last streaks of red and gold fade from the sky. Agatha felt no need to speak. Conventional expressions of sympathy, loss, were superfluous.

"I feel close to him here," Maria said. "He built the pool, planted the catcus himself."

"I didn't know that."

"It was in the early thirties. When you were away." Maria sighed. "He was trying to regain a memory we shared from Mexico. I'm afraid I failed him."

"You didn't fail him," Agatha said. "You didn't fail

any of us. I hate to think what would have become o
him—or me—without your love."

"My poor love," Maria said with a deprecating shake
of her head.

"It made the difference," Agatha said.

Maria held out her hand to Agatha in the twilight.
"Both our loves," she said.